Bridge Ices Before Road

The year is 1970. In a blue-collar suburb of Boston, two eleven year-old Catholic girls struggle to come of age in a culture still very much dominated by men. They watch in dismay as their fathers and priests determine the lives of the women around them. Loyalty to family and church is paramount; women and children suffer in silence rather than expose the men who do them harm. Frances Orillio is an adopted, only child; she is self-critical, anxious, and vulnerable. Maddy Malone is one of six children, and grew up in a rough housing project scrapping with the boys. Although they are strikingly different in temperament, they forge an enduring friendship on the path to becoming strong, independent women. Together they battle the tangled jungle of ignorance, racism, and homophobia that goes hand in hand with the culturally entrenched discrimination against women. Like the treacherous roads in a New England winter, the way is fraught with hidden dangers. Family secrets and lies are like the invisible black ice on a bridge: if you don't watch out for the signs, it can be deadly.

Sienna Rose is a Massachusetts native, residing in Florida since 2002. In 1996, she earned a BA in psychology from UMASS Boston, and in 2001, an M.Ed. in school counseling from Cambridge College, Cambridge, MA. Because she has always been concerned for those who are different and vulnerable to bullying or abuse, Ms. Rose wrote her master's thesis on the needs of gay/lesbian/bi/trans youth in school. She currently works as an independent educational consultant and advocate for children with disabilities. *Bridge Ices Before Road* is her first novel.

286

S. Rose

Nut House
Publishing

Nut House Publishing © 2012
The name and logo is a trademark of Sienna Rose.

You may purchase additional copies at Amazon.com or directly from the author at:
Create Space eStore www.createspace.com/3965374

To the children who suffer, and the ones who help them.

Part One

1

At my grandmother's wake I went looking for the bathroom, and happened upon something I was not supposed to see. I got lost and wound up down a service hallway, and couldn't help but notice a door that led outside to the alley was left open-just a crack. In the city that's where they put the ash bins, and I was warned never to play, because it's dirty and there might be broken glass. Besides, Nana always said that's where bad kids hang out, up to God-knows-what. I lived in a suburb with no alleys and we played in the backyard, so I had little opportunity to find out.

McDermott's Funeral Home was in an old part of Charlestown, not far from the harbor. There were endless blocks of red bricks: shops, places of business, and row-houses that had no yards at all. You stepped right off the front stoop and onto the sidewalk. It was all built up at the turn of the century, when no one had cars. People walked everywhere then, so the buildings were jammed close together, some on cobblestone streets just wide enough for a horse and carriage to pass. The long row-houses were separated only by a narrow alley, so even if you had an end house with side windows, all you could see was another wall of bricks, so close you could practically stick your arm out and touch it. Unless the sun happened to be directly overhead, or setting at just the right angle from the street-side, the scant space between the brick walls was kept in shadow.

Inside the funeral home reminded me of Nana's old house. The rooms had very high ceilings and looked squashed from side to side, because they were disproportionately long from front to back. There were lots of small parlors connected by a maze of corridors-it was easy to get lost if you didn't know your way around. I left the room where Nana was laid out and took a left, but missed the staircase that led down to the bathroom, which turned out to be located in the basement. At the end of the long hall I could only go left again, and absently wandered down a corridor so narrow and poorly lit it was like being in a tunnel. It brought to mind how my dad had to turn sideways to squeeze through the back hall that led to Nana's kitchen.

A sharp winter air blew in from outside. It felt good. Back in the funeral parlor I'd suddenly gone kind of wobbly and almost couldn't breathe in the stale, stuffy heat of the forced hot-air furnace. It was the third week in January, and they really cranked that thing high against the New England winter. I suppose it was because of all the old people-they particularly mind the cold. It was nearly the end of the visitation, and more people had turned up. Their bodies made the temperature rise, but no one had thought to adjust the thermostat down. Still, most of the guests wore their thick winter coats that were only unbuttoned, even though it must have made them uncomfortably warm. It was a strange custom: whenever you left your coat on inside, it signaled you didn't intend to stay long enough to need to take it off. I wasn't wearing a coat, but still felt like I was in a dry sauna.

The lilies heaped about the casket had begun to wilt. As I knelt at the rail, a smell like overly ripe fruit about to turn, and something like the air-freshener you spray in the bathroom made my nose wrinkle. I breathed through my mouth to avoid it then wished I hadn't; even with the half-gone flowers against a chemical backdrop, I could still taste the faintest scent of death. I never smelled it before, but I knew death by the way it caught at the back of my throat and made my esophagus snap shut to keep it out.

It was my first wake. Last year when I was ten, my Auntie Helen died of lung-cancer. She was my Godmother, but Mom said I wasn't old enough yet to attend a wake. She said it was especially sad because Auntie Helen left two small boys, but I think it was because my mother had been brought to a wake when she was far too young, and not even properly prepared. At the sight of the body in an open casket she froze in fear, dug her heels into the carpet and refused to go on. When her step-father picked her up to carry her over, she was afraid he was going to stick her straight into the casket. The poor little girl screamed and kicked and got her step-father in the...'ahem', my mother would say, so hard he let go and dropped her on the floor as he bent over double with his hand over his...she always paused at this point in the story and said with an embarrassed look, "You-know-what." I wasn't entirely sure what, but knew I wasn't supposed to ask. Mom would finish by explaining that she hadn't meant to kick him, but got hauled out and spanked anyway, which seemed very unfair, but much better than being put in a casket.

Now I was eleven, almost eleven and a half. Mom said I was nearly a young lady and it was time for me to act like one, time for me to learn how to behave at a wake and besides, everyone would expect me to attend since it was for my own grandmother. My mother fitted me out in a suitable navy-blue wool dress with a perky white collar. Just yesterday she'd explained how everything would look so I wouldn't be shocked, and I remembered exactly what to do. I knelt at the rail and bowed my head over carefully folded hands, and muttered my *Hail Marys* and *Our Fathers* just audible enough to ensure anyone taking notice would approve. I scrunched my eyes tight as if absorbed in prayer, but it was really because I couldn't bear to look at Nana up so close. I wasn't surprised to see her stiff body in the open casket, practically under my nose; but nothing could have prepared me for the sudden storm death whipped up inside me. Fear and anger and a shameful tinge of repugnance blew in my face, mixed with an irreverent sense of the absurd and whirled around until I couldn't tell one from the other. It was like being caught in a tornado, watching helplessly as everyday objects like cars and cows fly past, the ordinary turned bizarre and unfathomable as they're hurtled through space. I guess no matter how much they try to prepare you, there's really nothing like the first time one sees death.

I finally dared to unscrunch my eyes and take a last close-up look at her face. With her eyes closed and her hands folded angelically over the rosary beads at her bosom, Nana looked as if she'd fallen asleep in prayer. I'd seen her asleep many times, and she didn't look much different from when she was alive- except that she usually held a lit cigarette in those stiff bony hands. I didn't know she owned a rosary. Most afternoons she'd conk out on our living room couch, still clutching a smoldering butt. I used to pry them off her and stub them out in the ashtray before she burned the house down. Sometimes I wasn't quick enough, and she managed to sear a few holes in my mother's end table, and one in the marble coffee table too. More than once I'd rearranged the porcelain figurines, fancy ladies with china-white faces and little bug-eyed dogs with gold collars, to cover Nana's sins. I strategically shifted the magazines on the white-marble coffee table, all to stave off the inevitable squall when my mother discovered it.

That coffee table was already a sore spot with Mom, ever since the Christmas when I got the pogo stick. I don't remember what made me want it so badly, but I'd written Santa expressly asking for a pogo stick. On Christmas morning there it was under the tree, a large metal contraption with a heavy black spring. It had an elf tag that said, *Merry Christmas from Santa.* Of course I know now it was my father who'd put it there. I dashed outside to try it out in the driveway, already having been warned not to bounce in the house. It turned out to be disappointing. I didn't weigh enough to compress the tight spring, and I couldn't bounce it at all. "It doesn't work," I said sadly as I dragged it back inside.

Nana had been in an unusually jovial mood, and her face fairly glowed with the Christmas spirit. "Whada ya mean it don't work? Gi'me that thing!" she said. Nana snatched the pogo stick from my hands, hopped on and sprung wildly around the living room for one glorious spree. My eyes nearly popped out of my head as she barely missed the Christmas tree, then careened into the coffee

3

table and crashed to the floor in a laughing heap. I laughed so hard I thought I'd wet myself for sure, but then I noticed my mother did not look happy at all. I thought it was because Nana had broken the rule about playing with the pogo stick in the house, but then I saw that the thing had taken a chunk out of the marble table when she crashed, which underscored the purpose of the rule-no bouncing in the house.

After Nana died, I revealed the black marks on the furniture. I'd begun to wonder how Mom had missed the telltale signs of careless smoking when she did the dusting, but she acted surprised, and lamented that I might have died in a house-fire while she was out. Dad looked about as angry as I'd ever seen, but said nothing. He didn't want to make it worse. We both avoided upsetting my mother, which is why I'd hidden the mess in the first place.

Only last Monday I found Nana asleep on our couch with her fingers clamped tight on a Camel. It was mostly gone to a fragile cylinder of ash that disintegrated when I touched it. She had a stroke and died in her bed on Tuesday night, and I was lucky to be at school when Mom discovered her. Now it was almost over. I was new to the business of being a young lady, and it wasn't turning out to be all that I'd imagined. As I crossed myself and rose to leave her for good, a thought that must have been hiding somewhere in the back of my brain escaped like a chicken flown the coop. I vividly imagined that Nana's black eyes popped open. She looked straight at me and sat bolt upright in her casket, so fast she dropped the rosary. Then she pointed her shaky finger in a nicotine fit and snapped: "Frances! Go get my cigarettes! They're in my purse."

The image of Nana squawking for one last smoke before they laid her to rest went flapping around in my head. I was afraid to turn around, afraid I might actually giggle out loud, like when you're in school assembly or really bored at mass and you think of something funny. I pressed my lips together and squashed it down and tried to think of something else, something sad or serious, but the more I tried not to think of it, the worse it got. Fortunately, I became distracted by the need to pee. It had been a while, and besides, I usually had to go when I felt nervous. I noticed a group of elderly ladies sitting together, and thought I'd better go find the toilets before they all decided to get up and go at once-there'd be no getting in after that. Soon the priest would say the final prayers, and they'd shut the lid. Then we'd head out to the cemetery, and I'd be stuck until we got home.

The ladies were Nana's old friends from Charlestown, where she had lived up until the last few years-it must have been about three years now, come to think of it. She was sixty-three when she died, and had come to live with us for good when I was eight. It had been so long since I'd seen them that I didn't recognize them anymore, not as separate people anyway. Age had worn them away at the edges, melted them into a lumpy bunch of faded winter coats with gray curly heads and wrinkled faces sticking out, like those little hand-made dolls with the heads carved out of peeled, dried apples. I'd forgotten all their names. In her last years, Nana had grown to look just like them, her features shriveled and shrunken until she scarcely resembled the face in old photographs of who she used to be.

I ought to have made an effort to greet them. They had taken the trouble to come out in the bitter cold, most likely on the trolley since none of them had cars. Instead I drew back, as if old age and decrepitude were somehow contagious. Now that I'd seen it up close, I desperately wanted to avoid it-not only death, but the loss of who you were, the things you did, the very features that once distinguished your face from everyone else's.

I decided to try and slip past unnoticed, but couldn't go down either side aisle. They were clogged with people, chatting and catching up on news. You could hear sprinklings of muted laughter, as if they were at a regular party, only with a dead body in the room. On the right was a group of our neighbors who had all come in together at the last minute. They were about the same age as my parents, had bought into the same new sub-development as young couples and raised families there. Now they dutifully attended the wakes of one another's parents, who were drifting away each year like autumn leaves. On the left there was a small crowd of Dad's family-three aunts and two uncles, and my older girl-cousins who were already married. One brought her baby boy, wrapped up in a hand-knit blue bunting that had been made by his grandmother. My mother was with them, making a fuss over the baby and the lovely knitting; if I went out that way I'd have been waylaid for sure. There were no other children, not because they'd been left at home, but because I had no cousins near my age. I was an only child like Mom. My parents had tried so long to have a baby of their own that they'd gone to near middle age before giving up and adopting me.

I reluctantly started down the middle aisle, but only a few rows in I suddenly felt sea-sick. The long squashed parlor with the absurdly high ceiling began to sway, as if I were in one of those crazy houses they set up at carnivals where the floors are warped and everything is out of whack, or distorted by trick mirrors. I gripped the back of an empty folding chair and steadied myself. No one noticed me. Everyone went on chatting while I tried not to throw up. Then I blinked and squinted towards the back of the room and thought I must be seeing things.

There were two strange people, an old woman and a man. It was as if they'd appeared out of nowhere, but they must have come in when my back was turned. Something about them made me even queasier. Though the woman was old, she didn't look like all the other ladies. Her features were still sharply defined with a rather severe, square jaw, and lips pressed so tightly together they all but disappeared into her face, a face that looked as if it were chiseled from a single block of white granite. She sat ramrod straight in a well-fitting dark wool coat, buttoned up to the chin, military style. Her silver gray hair was drawn back in a tight bun, and she wore a pillbox hat that was anchored to her head by a hatpin so large it might be used as a lethal weapon. But the most disconcerting thing about the hat was the bit of net covering her eyes; it made it hard to tell exactly which way she was looking. I had the uneasy feeling she was particularly watching me.

It was old Mrs. Malone! I knew it first by the squirmy feeling in my stomach before I recognized her face. I'd never seen her up this close, even though she was our neighbor. For as long as I could remember she lived just over the hill beyond our backyard, all alone in a monstrous two and a half-story Victorian home with a tall round tower. A long high wooden fence divided her side from ours, but you could just see the tower from our kitchen window; the pointy black roof looked like a witch's hat. Mrs. Malone never visited us or any other neighbors, and her solitude left her vulnerable to gossip and abuse. Some bad kids from the projects broke her front porch windows so many times she stopped having them fixed.

A large man wearing a great black overcoat stood behind Mrs. Malone, with his back up against the wall and his eyes fixed on her head. He had the scariest face I'd ever seen, with a lumpy red nose and a deep scar that dented his chin. But it was his eyes that made my insides curdle. They were small and narrow, and it was hard to judge his intentions, hard to tell if he was watching protectively over the old lady, or was about to lunge from behind and wring her neck. He was more bulky than tall, and so ghastly grim I thought at first he was an undertaker. Then I noticed the awkward way he gripped his Sunday hat, with a fist the size of a small pot-roast; it was a sign of a working man unaccustomed to formal dress. I wondered if they were related. They wore the same stern expression, with a jaw set like cast iron and lips sealed as tight as a clam. The thought of crossing their path brought me up short. I felt trapped with my back to the casket and the only way out past old Mrs. Malone and that dreadful looking man-not to mention the gaggle of old ladies who would have so liked to fuss over me.

I went with the impulse to bow my head as if consumed by the solemnity of the occasion, and made a dash for it. Mrs. Malone's unwavering gaze seemed to devour me as I approached, and nip at my heels like a terrier as I fled past. I don't think my performance fooled her one bit. I couldn't imagine what she was doing at my grandmother's wake, but something told me she hadn't turned up out of sudden burst of neighborliness. I got a peculiar feeling about it, but I figured it would fall under the broad general category of things that were 'none of my business.' I was taught young how to mind my own business. It was more than good manners; it was a way of living together peaceably if not altogether honestly, and began with the premise that every family had secrets they were entitled to keep. Mrs. Malone's sudden appearance at my grandmother's wake set my mind to working. I got that feeling you get when you open up the box of a 3000 piece jigsaw puzzle and dump it onto the card table. At first it makes no sense at all, but little by little you fit the pieces together and the picture begins to take shape.

It's no wonder I got distracted and lost while looking for the toilet. It wasn't just the overheated parlor and bad smells that made me sick. I might as well admit it: I was truly glad to be done with Nana. Even though I had my reasons, I felt guilty as all get-out. I really must be the awful-selfish-ungrateful girl that Nana said I was. I was sure I'd go to hell.

We were never close, but the real trouble with Nana began with the tootsie roll incident of 1966. I knew then for sure that I had got stuck with one unreasonable, disagreeable and downright mean-spirited grandmother. Prior to that she was just Nana, and I'd never thought to hold her up for comparison. Children are naturally trusting, and accept whatever craziness they're dealt with innocent complacency. It's just part of their family, their life; it just is.

It happened one afternoon in late January, that dreadful time of year when the holidays are long over, but spring is still so far off it hurts to think of it. Nana had just come to live with us for good, and she was supposed to be looking after me while Mom was doing errands. Instead, she sent me to the corner store to buy her cigarettes and some milk for her tea. Back then a child could ask the storekeeper-who knew whose child you were- for cigarettes, so long as you explained they were for your dad or grandmother. Some kids would lie and buy cigarettes for themselves, and they knew a shop where the man at the register didn't ask questions.

I'd only just come home from school, and didn't really feel like walking two blocks to the store, which seems a long way when you're small. There was wet slushy snow too, the kind that sticks and bogs you down; but refusing was out of the question. I pulled back on my red rubber boots that I'd just kicked off. They went over your shoes and kept your feet dry, but frozen, because they had no insulation. I slogged to the store. I chose a quart of milk-she hadn't been specific, remembered to ask for the Camels-the kind with no filters, and gave the shopkeeper the money. I didn't count it, just emptied the contents of my fist onto the counter. When the man handed back seventeen cents, I was delighted. I hungrily grabbed a tootsie roll from that tempting shelf right in front of the register-I think it was seven cents including the tax-and began to eat it on the way home.

The journey took a while longer than expected; I hadn't fastened my boots and they slipped up and down with each step. I clutched the candy in my right fist and tore the wrapper back with my teeth, because the bag with the milk and cigarettes was carefully tucked under my left arm. I pressed it close to my body so as not to drop it. When I was nearly home, I looked up to see Nana standing at the backdoor, watching for me-I could make out her skinny face peering through the windowpane. As I climbed the back stairs, she flung the door open and stood wringing her hands in a nicotine tizzy. I proffered the bag and the change to Nana, and announced proudly through the mouth full of tootsie roll sticking to my teeth that I'd taken only seven cents for my trouble. I hoped that was alright.

Apparently, it wasn't. I'd barely stepped into the kitchen when she snatched the brown paper bag. She pulled out the Camels and glowered at me, speechless with horror; I'd squashed the pack. Then she scowled indignantly at the quart of milk. I could see she was very angry. Nana's small black eyes shifted like a caged animal when she was angry. Her eyes made me want to turn and run away.

"You knowed you was supposed to get a half-gallon," Nana declared, employing her own interpretation of English grammar. "I gave you enough money for a half-gallon of milk. You stole from me! How selfish! You're a very bad girl, Frances. I'll never trust you again."

I felt sick inside for having committed such an egregious sin. I choked up and began to cry piteously with my mouth open so wide that a chunk of half-chewed tootsie-roll landed at my feet. "I didn't know," I protested through my tears. And I hadn't. I wasn't at all sure if the money was enough for a half-gallon, but trying to reason with her was a big mistake.

"Don't lie!" She was furious now. "You just made it worse on yourself! You'd better tell the priest in confession; if you die with a sin on your soul, you'll go straight to purgatory!"

The candy I'd managed to swallow sat in my gut like a lump of lead. Then Nana tore into her pack of Camels like a vulture, stuck one in her face and struggled to light it with a trembling hand. Before the nicotine kicked in enough to quell her, she took the opportunity to complain about the dirty snow my boots had tracked onto the doormat, and finished by reiterating that on account of my criminal tendency, she could never trust me to go to the store for her again.

After that I began to notice that other kids had grandmothers that were plump and hugged you and smelled of cookies; I don't think Nana baked a cookie in her life. The worst part was that I had waited a lifetime for her to love me, to light within my child's heart some warmth so I could love her back, and have something good inside to remember her by. I tried to dig down and grasp it, but came up empty handed. It was like trying to lay hold of the wisp of smoke curling from her omnipresent cigarette. I stood by and watched as it carried her away bit by bit with each breath until she was gone, and left me with nothing inside but a pile of ash.

It was going onto four o'clock. The brief winter sun was about to duck behind a row of flat roof-tops for the night, but one last sliver of light snuck through the door and crept into the hallway like a stray cat. The draft of cold air interrupted my runaway train of thought. I breathed deeply; even the whiff of auto exhaust was better than the smells in the parlor. The single bulb hanging from the ceiling was out, so the light cut across the carpet like a tiny lighthouse beacon on a dark night. It almost seemed to point a disdainful finger at the torn wallpaper, turned yellow-brown with age like an old man's teeth. There was nothing else but a broom closet-I peeked in to make sure. Seeing as there were no facilities in sight, I was about to turn around and leave, but figured I should go close the door first. If something is left open in the winter, you usually ought to close it. I went nearer and listened, but heard only the whoosh of cars in the late afternoon traffic. Suddenly I felt a rare surge of defiance: I decided to take a look into that alley, perhaps even poke my head outside, just because Nana always told me not to. I didn't expect to find anything but the ashbins, and maybe some broken glass.

I pressed my eye to the crack and pushed on the door just a bit. It didn't go as planned. As soon as my hand gripped the cold brass knob, the door was jerked open from the other side with such force it pulled me off balance. I hung on tight for a moment as my body leaned precariously into the alley at a ninety degree angle, with my feet still planted on the threshold. I would have fallen flat on my face if it weren't for the thick fist that grabbed me right by the perky white collar of my navy blue dress, and yanked me through the doorway. I was nearly lifted off my feet and in one deft motion shoved up against the frigid brick wall. I blinked in the last horizontal rays of a winter sun and gulped the freezing air. The breath was knocked out of me, more by fear than the impact. On the other end of the fist was a great, dull-eyed brute with a fat mug the color of pie dough. He towered over me, effortlessly pinned me with one hand while his boss looked me right in the face, barely six inches from my nose. Now I was looking into the business end of trouble, into a pair of eyes that were hard and gray as the mortar between the thousands of bricks around us. I heard an ominous click as the door closed behind me. There was no going back. I was trapped in an alley with Mad-Dog Malone.

Mad-Dog Malone was a fierce and fearless fighter-something of a local legend. The big one was Tommy two-steps, a name nobody said to his face if they wanted to live long. He was called that because he always seemed to follow about two-steps behind Mad-Dog. They said he was dumb as a post. The two came from Middlefield, from the crumbling old housing projects on the other side of a polluted river that divided it from the nicer town of Mapleton, the town where I lived. They called themselves river-rats. They were meaner and tougher than the East Mapleton project kids, and had a proud Irish tradition of settling everything with their fists. If a gang of them crossed the bridge and came to town, most Mapleton kids had the sense to stay out of their way. I couldn't imagine what in God's name were they doing in Charlestown, out in the alley by McDermott's Funeral Home.

Mad-Dog sucked hard on a little stub of cigarette, handed it wordlessly to dough-face and exhaled so sharply the smoke went straight into my open mouth. All the while those gray eyes were fixed on me, boring down like iron nails. I began to cough and choke, not only from the smoke but because of the fat fist that gripped and twisted the collar of my dress, just about strangling me.

"Jesus Tommy, let up. You'll kill 'er," Mad-Dog said with a touch of exasperation. He immediately dropped me like an undersized fish. "What the hell do ya think you're doin', spying on us?" Mad-Dog growled.

"Yeah, spying on us," Tommy parroted.

"Lemme do the talkin'," Mad-Dog directed at Tommy.

"I wasn't spying," I interjected, disrupting their squabble. "I didn't know anyone was out here. I...I was just..." I was trying to catch my breath and come up with an acceptable explanation. Then I recalled why I had wandered down that hallway in the first place. The nausea had passed, but I really had to pee bad now. Holding it the cold made it even worse, and I squeezed my muscles together so I wouldn't wet myself. "I was only trying to find the bathroom," I blustered; my words frosted in the air between our faces. "I saw the door open and went to look before I closed it, in case someone was outside emptying the ashbins...so I didn't lock them out," I gestured with one hand towards the rusty metal cans lined against the brick wall. "I didn't see anything, honest!" Now I knew why Nana warned me to stay out of the alleys; I imagined she must be laughing at me from somewhere. I began to sniffle, and was about to break down and cry when I noticed those eyes that were locked like steel bulkheads seemed to give a crack, and let just a bit of light slip through.

Mad-Dog was at least half a head taller than me, and had to bend down to be at my eye-level. It wasn't so much her height, but rather her angular jaw and pinched cheeks that made her look much older than me, much older than eleven years, though I thought we were about the same age. One corner of her mouth twisted up in a sort grimace, almost a half-grin, as if it wrestled with itself to avoid smiling outright. Then she stood up to full height, relaxed a bit and snorted smoke from both nostrils like a dragon while emitting a deep phlegmy chortle that I took for a laugh. "Just so long as ya don't go blabbin'. Mind ya business," she warned. There was the slightest inflection of Irish laid over her thick, East Boston accent. Her voice was low and rumbling, already harshened from smoking, but it wasn't unpleasant. It reminded me of that soft crunching sound from under your feet when you walk alone down a gravel road.

"Mind ya business," snarled Tommy, trying to imitate her tone and manners. Though he was large, his voice hadn't broken. It had a grating, metallic edge, like when a man plunges a shovel deep into gritty, hard-packed dirt. Something about it made me shudder inside.

Mad-Dog glowered at him, clearly annoyed with having an echo. He shut his pie-hole. I glanced up and down the alley, anxious and wondering what terrible thing I wasn't supposed to see or tell. "The cigarettes," she said, patting the pocket of her jacket. "Dad will crucify us if he finds out; he wore his Sunday coat and left 'em in his work jacket. I lifted the whole pack so he'd think he dropped 'em somewhere, or got mixed up about where he put 'em when he changed his coat." As she related the logic behind the heist, Tommy looked on in admiration; he was the muscle, and she was clearly the mastermind.

"I won't tell anyone," I gushed. I wasn't a tattletale; I knew how to mind my business. Anyway, who would be dumb enough to make an enemy of the Malone kids? I thought it was kind of funny that it wasn't the smoking, but the stealing of their father's pack of cigarettes that would bring down the sentence of crucifixion. How could he not know that she smoked like a fiend, with her nicotine stained hands and stinky clothes. I sniffed- just like Nana.

11

Mad-Dog continued to make a study of me while she held her hand out to Tommy, who wordlessly passed her another lit cigarette-he'd finished off the first. She inhaled deeply and smoothly, not like other kids I'd seen who snuck an occasional cigarette to act grown up-which I had never done, not even once. This kid smoked like she meant business, and looked as though she'd been doing it since she was three. She cocked her head quizzically and held it out as an offering to me. I shook my head no and she shrugged like it made no difference to her either way. "You're Frances," she declared before exhaling. "Evelyn's kid," she added, as if informing me of who I was.

"How do you know me?" I was surprised. Of course I knew who she was, not that I'd ever actually met them; but everyone knew of the Malones. I'd always kept a wide latitude between me and anything resembling trouble, so it was unlikely that Mad-Dog or her compadres had ever directly crossed paths with me. Besides, I was too pathetic to be of any interest to them.

"I know just about everybody," she boasted. "My Gramma Malone knowed your Gramma and your Ma from way back. I know all about you." She squinted one eye and twisted one corner of her mouth again, something between a scowl and a satisfied smirk. "Your father's *I*talian." The local Irish population usually pronounced 'Italian' with a strong emphasis on the first syllable and a long 'I' that made it sound very foreign. "And you're adapted, ain't ya?" she added with obvious satisfaction.

"Uh, adopted." I instantly regretted it; she shot me a look that let me know she was unaccustomed to correction, but would let it go this once.

"And your Gramma...you called her Nana, right?" she added with an air of mystery.

"What about her?" I was getting really interested.

"Well... we won't talk about it now," she said, as if changing her mind about something, the same way that grownups did when they evaded your questions. "Anyways, me and Tommy come over with Dad in his cab-he's a cabdriver and owns his own cab-to drive Gramma Malone to your Nana's wake. My Ma's at home with Annie and baby Michael. She's not feeling well," she added. "So my big sister Joanie and my older brother Eddie Murphy had to stay home to help her."

I knew the Irish viewed funeral attendance as a serious obligation, no matter how tenuous the connection had been to the living. She wanted to emphasize that her other family members had a good excuse for their absence. But that wasn't all of it, and she continued with hardly a pause.

"'Cause they're still in the middle of packin' up, 'cause we're all of us movin' to that big house behind you, to live with my Gramma Malone."

"Mrs. Malone is your grandmother?" I was astonished. I'd assumed Mrs. Malone was a childless old widow. She always went out alone, and no one ever seemed to visit.

"Yup, she's our Gramma; and now me and Tommy and my little sister Annie are gonna go to school at Edmunds. Me and Tommy," she jerked her chin towards her brother for emphasis, "are in sixth grade too, so I'll need you to tell me all about it." She pointed her sharp finger at my chest like a pistol, and there was no doubt that I was expected to oblige. "Annie's in kindergarten," she added. Her strenuous avoidance of the 'R' in the middle of words made kindergarten particularly difficult to pronounce; it sounded like *Kindagaht'n*.

The local accent always struck me as comical and just plain wrong, even though I'd been brought up to it. I'd always formed my words with care, used the letter 'R' where it belonged and refused to drag one syllable words into two, such as 'dowah' and 'flowah' instead of door and floor. It was as if I'd grown up someplace else altogether, an odd trait that brought down mockery and ridicule from other children, and even some adults. I couldn't help it. My fascination with letters and sounds and the words they made began early. I learned to read by age three just from being read to, as naturally as other children learn to speak; but I was very aware that not everyone had such an easy time of it. I furtively sized-up Tommy, who seemed far too big to be in the sixth grade. I expected he'd been kept back in school-maybe twice, but I knew enough to keep my mouth shut.

"You're not going to St. Clément's anymore?" I asked. I had heard about Mad-Dog and Tommy from the kids in our neighborhood that went to St. Clément's Parish School, across the Middlefield River. Many of them had relatives who'd gone to school with the older generation of Malones. There was a rumor that an uncle was in prison, and that's probably where their bad reputation began. I wondered if the wild stories the Catholic school kids told about them were exaggerated.

"Nah...Tommy got kicked outa St. Clément's," she said with a casual air, as if it were hardly worth mentioning.

Tommy enjoyed the attention and broke out in a wide toothy grin, like a carved Halloween pumpkin. "I got kicked out," he repeated with a nasal chuckle.

"How?" I felt my eyes widen with awe. I'd never met anyone who got expelled from school, and I was dying to know what it took to pull it off.

Mad-Dog leaned in with her face close to mine. Her flinty eyes sparked like a devil as she spoke in a lowered voice. "He tossed a lit firecracker into the hall, and when Sister Ignatius went to stomp it out..." she paused for dramatic effect, "...it blew a piece off the hem of her habit!" She broke out in a fit of raucous laughter that ended in a smoker's cough. Regaining composure, she continued, "It about scared the crap outa old Iggy-she screamed bloody murder and jumped around slappin' her habit to make sure it wasn't on fire. Our classes was all lined up at the lavatories, the girls on one side and the boys on the other. The girls were all shrieking and covering their ears...some started crying. I didn't even know Tommy was in there 'cause he ain't in my class-and he picks that time to open the door to the boy's room and chuck it out, without even lookin' first to see if anyone's gonna catch him-you dumb ass," she directed at Tommy. "I didn't mean to laugh at Iggy-it just come out. And she didn't get hurt or nothin'."

I wondered if that was the end of the story, but she was just getting warmed up.

"Then Father O'Donnell-he's assistant principal-O'Donnell heard the racket and come runnin' down the hall, mad as hell. He's a big man with a fat belly-I didn't know he could run that fast, and he was all red in the face. He was swearin' under his breath, but we all heard it: 'This time I'll murder that damned kid!' Then he marched us both to his office. I told him I didn't know nothin' about it-it was the truth, but he didn't believe me; and I was in trouble anyway for laughing. Then he sent me to stand out in the hall while he whaled on Tommy with a paddle, so hard I thought he might really kill him this time. Tommy didn't even holler or nothin'." She glanced up at him with admiration. "We had to wait the rest of the day in O'Donnell's office, even after the bell rang. Dad finally came in to find us when we didn't turn up at home."

"My God," I muttered. I could see she was all fired up now, in the time honored tradition of Irish story-telling.

"Jesus! Was Dad ever mad! Not only at us-he had some words with Father O'Donnell, on account of he's Tommy's father and would decide how to punish him, and 'cause my mother was worried sick when we didn't show up. So Father yells back at Dad, 'Don't you understand that Tommy threw a firecracker at a group of children, and almost set one of the Sisters on fire?'" She puffed up her face and scowled in imitation of the irate priest. "Then he tells Dad that someone better set Tommy right soon, 'cause he was headed straight to hell, or to prison. That made Dad even madder and he swore to send Father straight to hell if he ever touched his boy again. You could hear them clear down the hallway! I was standin' outside the door the whole time, and I could see all of the nuns poking their heads outa the classrooms to listen. So Father O'Donnell shouts back that Dad could take Tommy home and try teaching him hisself if he didn't like how he done it. When Dad hauled us both out to the cab, I could see it was gonna be bad 'cause he didn't say nothin', nothin' on the way home neither. Back home he took off his belt and beat the crap outa Tommy his own self, all over again. He threw a couple of belts my way before he was finished..." she paused, choking back laughter, "'cause he didn't like the smart-ass look on my face! So that's why we're not going back to St. Clément's," she finished, in case I needed clarification. "By next week," she announced triumphantly, "we'll be neighbors." With that, Mad-Dog drew the last cigarette down to her fingernails and flicked it into the alley for emphasis.

I was so lost in the story that I didn't notice it had suddenly grown dark and even colder-the sun was gone down all the way behind the buildings now. I wore a lined winter dress, and my legs were covered in heavy knit, ribbed tights, but I was still shivering. My bladder must have been frozen by now. Mad-Dog wore a boy's navy pea jacket with only one button left to close it. It was a bit too short and her skinny wrists stuck out of the sleeves. I could see she wasn't wearing a slip under her thin cotton dress. The washed-out plaid fabric clung to her bare knees, red with cold because she wore only knee socks in the middle of winter. But if she felt cold, she didn't show it. I knew I should hurry back inside, but I had to know more.

"But I don't understand...I mean...if Mrs. Malone is your grandmother, how is it that she had a whole family just over in Middlefield...and I never saw any of you visit? What made your parents decide to move in with her now? And why did you all come to my grandmother's wake?"

She cocked her head, scrunched her face in thought and considered my bold inquiries. "You're a funny kid, Frances," she said evasively; it was another one of those things adults said when they wanted to change the subject. "Let's get out of this damned cold!" She'd decided the conversation was over. Without a word, Tommy rattled the doorknob, but it had locked. Mad-Dog turned on her heel abruptly and yanked me along by the arm to underscore that we were going inside together. "I gotta take a wicked piss too," she added.

I stifled a giggle; she talked just like a boy. Tommy ambled behind like a Labrador retriever as we left the alley and walked around to the big double-doors by the street. That's where they would soon carry out the casket, I thought with a bit of dread. Some of the gold painted letters on the glass doors were missing, so it read, "McDermott's Funeral Ho ". Mad-Dog noticed it and sniggered as we went in. I didn't get it. Then I saw the lit sign for the ladies' room that pointed towards the stairs. It was obvious as you came in the front, but not as you left the parlor. When we got to the basement level, Mad-Dog gave Tommy a hard shove towards the men's room; he looked as though he would have followed her inside, blindly and without question.

15

We entered adjacent stalls. I could see her feet, and I noticed she wore scuffed penny loafers that were a little too big and slipped off at the heels. The pennies were gone.

"Hey Frances?" She spoke over the sound of her vigorous stream. I had been self-conscious and tinkling modestly.

"Yeah?"

"Sorry about your Nana."

I felt my previous pang of guilt return; I wasn't sorry about Nana. "Thanks... uh, what's your name?" I didn't know her real name.

"It's Mad'lin," she said. "As in Madeline Dorothy Malone, but everyone calls me Mad-Dog. Maddy for short...only my mother and Gramma call me Mad'lin, my little sister too, but no one else can...aw, shit," she hissed in the middle of her introduction. "Hey-you got toilet paper over there Frances?"

"Yeah," I answered, pulling on the roll. "Why do they call you Mad-Dog?"

"I'm named after my uncle, Daniel Maddox Malone. He was a boxer, and they called him Mad-Dog Malone, but the neighbor kids all called 'im Uncle Danny. My older brother Eddie Murphy says he was the best uncle ever, and my Ma loved him too. I didn't know 'im myself, 'cause he went to jail just after I was born."

"Oh," I said, wadding up the toilet paper.

Having finished her explanation and her business, Mad-Dog stuck her boney white hand under the stall so I could pass it over to her, just like we always had to do at school when it ran out. At the sight of her hand I was momentarily taken aback, struck by how much smaller it seemed all by itself, cut off from the rest of her. It was bigger than mine, but despite the dirty fingernails and rough red knuckles, it was still the hand of a young girl. The hand wasn't cocked like a pistol or brandishing a cigarette; it was open, waiting expectantly like a little animal looking to be fed. I pressed in a generous bunch of toilet paper, and the hand disappeared. I realized then that she was just like me. Despite the fearsome reputation, she was only a girl. I would never let on what I knew. We flushed.

We stood at the sinks in front of a large, rather grimy mirror with a giant crack that looked like a lightning bolt heading straight for her head. The fluorescents flickered and made me squint my eyes and the unflattering light made us both look rather washed out and sickly, but the contrast between our appearances was striking. My face was chubby, still baby-like. I was shorter, broader across the chest-and through the middle. Not really fat, but amply padded all over. With her bulky coat opened, I could see that Mad-Dog was built like a beanpole, all hard and wiry like a boy. Everything about her was bony and sharp, and the hollows in her cheeks were more pronounced in the awful light. I knew I should mind my own business, but I couldn't contain my curiosity. "Um...Why did your uncle go to jail?"

"For killin' a guy in a fight at some bar...but it wasn't on purpose. Gramma said they was drunk and just havin' a regular fight and it went bad," she answered casually, as if she'd been explaining what he did to earn a living. "So i' twasn't like a murder exactly; he'll be comin' home in a few years now...maybe."

"Why are you named after your uncle?" I asked in a small voice.

"Cause I grew up in the projects playin' with my older brother-that's Tommy. I didn't like dolls or girl-stuff. I was always scrappin' with the boys and I could beat them all, even Tommy when we were little, but now he's got so much bigger; I bet he could take me, but he never would. He's always lookin' out for me. If ya ask me, Tommy's really the Mad-Dog of the family. Doesn't growl, just bites when you least expect it. He doesn't say much, and I'm the only one who can talk any sense into him; but once he's fired up, he don't listen to me neither. No one in the projects bothers either of us on account of him," she finished.

"I wish I had a big brother to watch out for me," I lamented. "The kids all pick on me. Mostly they just call me names, like Franny bannany with the big fat fanny-I wish they'd grow up! They always tease me about being too fat-and I'm not even the fattest girl. And if somebody farts they all blame it on me. I never fart in class. They make fun of the way I talk too, and the way I read library books outside at recess; but when I play games I make all the outs and they just get mad. It doesn't really matter what I say or do; they find a reason. And I hate being called Franny; it's Frances, or Fran," I asserted. She studied me closely in the mirror as I spoke and grunted in acknowledgement. Then she surprised me by casually lifting the back of my dress to complete her inspection.

"You don't have a fat ass, Frances. Who calls you that?"

It took me a moment to put it together. "Oh, just some mean girls from the projects-not that there's anything wrong with being from the projects," I added, worried that I had offended her. "They're tougher than me. They push me around just because they can; they always make me get off the playground swings if they want them-even if they don't want them, just to make me get off. They tell me they're gonna 'get me' after school, and if I tattle to the teacher about any of it, I'm 'dead.' Then I feel worried sick all day. Usually nothing happens after school, but onetime in fourth grade they chased me and pushed me down and a big girl sat on me. I cried and they all laughed and I never forgot it. They like making me scared. I mostly hate school," I declared, surprising myself. I don't think I'd realized how bad I felt about it all until I'd said it out loud to someone my own age; Mom never paid much attention when I complained.

Mad-Dog curled that same corner of her upper lip and scrunched one eye, but there was more of an edge to it than before. "Which girls?" she asked deliberately.

"Hmm, Kathy Kelly is the worst…she's the one who sat on me." Kathy was a tall, stout, barrel shaped Irish girl with frizzy red hair and a fat freckled face. Her legs were like tree trunks that just sort of ended in two large feet without stopping for ankles. "Dotty Day is just about as bad," I complained. "They're always together, and they egg the others on. "I never know if they might start in on me, for no reason at all. Kathy Kelly's made school hell since third grade," I declared, feeling a bit proud of my expletive. "There's JoEllen too-from the neighborhood. She's really tall, even though she's younger than us. She's blond and pretty and popular with her group of snobby friends. Her mom had her in some fancy private Kindergarten, so she skipped first grade. Now everyone thinks she's the smartest girl in school. I don't know why she has in for me, but she runs by me real fast and likes to jab me on the way by- and she's so fast, I can't ever catch her to get her back. It doesn't really hurt, but the other kids all laugh at me; she just loves to make the other kids laugh at me."

Her eyes narrowed and her face grew a bit more pinched as she thoughtfully considered my pathetic tale. "They do, huh? Well, I know who Kathy is-Smelly Kelly, we call 'er," she said with a sneer. I laughed out loud, and wished I had the nerve to call her that to her face. "And Dirty Dotty…one thing I can't stand is a dirty fighter. She still scratchin' and flingin' dirt?"

I nodded; I'd seen that trick. In those days, there was still a code of honor on both sides of the river. When kids got in a fight, they were supposed to fight fair-no two against one, no biting, scratching, or throwing dirt, no kicking someone if they were down. And boys weren't supposed to hit girls.

"Those two girls ain't nothin' to be afraid of," Maddy said. "They just pick on you 'cause they know you scare easy. You'll have to point-out this JoEllen to me," she added.

"Smelly Kelly?" I giggled again. It was just too good. "She's the one with the fat ass," I blurted out, suddenly feeling liberated from the lifetime of good manners my mother insisted upon. "Why doesn't she pick on someone her own size?"

"She can't," Maddy said with a sly look, "'cause all the other elephants live in the zoo!"

I laughed so hard I doubled over, and each time I tried to stop, one look at her gleaming eyes and half-cocked grin got me going again. It wasn't just the allusion to Kathy Kelley's girth; I laughed because I suddenly felt happier than I had in a very long time. While I was cackling like a hen, she took her final reckoning of me, seemed to look straight through my insides and back again. I wasn't used to anything like it. Usually no one was that interested in me unless they were trying to find fault, but I sensed that her scrutiny came from a different place...from a desire to know me.

"You're alright Frances," she affirmed, informing me of her final determination. "Wait 'til I get to school. Don't say nothin', just wait. I'll take care of them girls for ya," she said with assurance.

We left together to join the adults. By the clock in the main hall I'd been gone a half hour, but it might as well have been a half year. When Mom saw me walk in, the look on her face spoke louder than words: 'Where in God's name have you been?' I knew I'd hear about it when I got home, but I didn't care. I had better things to think about. No one had ever taken my side at school before, and I had a feeling that this girl didn't make empty promises. I had a real friend to stick up for me now, and nothing would ever be the same.

From across the long squashed parlor I watched as Mrs. Malone steered her granddaughter out the door, with a talon-like grip on her shoulder. At the last moment she managed to look back around at me with that half-smirk on her face, and slip me a 'we have a secret wink'. I smiled back. Nana had been all wrong about who you might find in an alley. Maybe she was all wrong about me too, because I was alright by Mad-Dog Malone.

2

I was born in 1958, at St. Mary's charity hospital in Dorchester, a poor section of Boston. It would be many years, half a lifetime, before I learned that or any other detail of my birth or parentage. For a long time I only knew I was adopted at five months of age, and lived from then on with my new parents in a modest home, in a small working class neighborhood of East Mapleton.

My parents liked to tell the story of how Father Doherty called to say that their long awaited baby had arrived, but they left out what was to me the most important part: where had I arrived from? I wasn't supposed to ask, or even want to know. To be curious of my origins and of my brief life before becoming an Orillio was ingratitude tantamount to treason. When I finally dared to ask, they briskly swatted aside my questions, flatly stating that they knew nothing at all about *that*, as if even to acknowledge there was *that*, which came before, was distasteful to them. Then they clammed up for a while in indignant silence. I wasn't supposed to care about that. I was only supposed to feel gratitude for my good fortune, and be satisfied with the image that I sprang into being at aged five months, custom-ordered, and handed over all dressed up like a beautiful doll in ruffles and lace. I learned from experience to keep my mouth shut and let them recollect the story on their terms if I wanted to hear it at all, and listened acutely for any additional details or variations in the retelling.

I knew that I was adopted long before I could possibly understand what it meant. My parents had to swear to the priest that they would tell me, just as they had to swear to bring me up Catholic; otherwise, they explained, they would have kept it a secret. Mom had advised me not to discuss it outside of the house, while reassuring me in the same breath that it was nothing to be ashamed of, a blatant contradiction even to a child.

My earliest notion was that to be adopted meant your parents went to collect you from a priest, and to be a regular kid meant your parents went to collect you from the hospital. That was before I became aware enough of the world around me to notice the swollen tummies on some of the ladies. Then there was no avoiding the explanation that they were growing a baby inside. Naturally, I wanted to know how that happened. We all did. We were only told that when mommies and daddies loved each other very, very much, God planted a seed in the mommy's tummy, which grew into a baby. I remember asking

Mom, "Why didn't God plant a seed in your tummy? Didn't you and daddy love each other enough?" I was so small that I was looking way up at her chin, which puckered and quivered.

Then she began to weep as she said, "Yes, we did, but God chose this way for me to have a baby." She looked so sad that I never asked again.

Like all curious children, I wanted to know how the baby came out of the mommy. I'd already learned not to ask Mom such questions; she clearly didn't want to talk about it, so it must have been bad manners. A little girl from a large Catholic family finally informed me: "Mommy goes to the hospital, and the doctor cuts the baby out with a big knife!" I decided that when I grew up, I would adopt all my babies.

By the time I entered their lives, my mother was already thirty-seven. Like other working class Catholic girls, she'd been married at age twenty-one, and assumed the babies would follow. Most of her friends already had a houseful of children. By the time I entered their lives, my mother had waited out her youth for this moment-for me. The extra-long wait was attributed to holding out for a Catholic baby, who would be perfectly matched for nationality-half Irish, half Italian-as well as size, shape, and eye color. This was so I would look just like their own child would have looked, and turn out just as their own child would have; or so they were convinced at the time by the Catholic Charitable Association.

Our relationship began with a serious misunderstanding. They were very excited to finally become my parents. "I just couldn't wait to get you home and make you mine," my mother had said. I had my own opinion on the matter. When my new parents carried me out to the sidewalk, I began to cry loudly, but when they tried to load me into their car, I drew back at the sight of the open passenger door and began to scream. I got so worked up they became worried that people on the street would think they were kidnapping a baby. Several times they backed away from the car, and tried again. Each time I would pause in my howling and catch my breath, only to resume at their next attempt to get me into the car. I was a strong, healthy baby, and screamed myself all red in the face, kicking and struggling. My father came to the brilliant conclusion that the baby must not like that particular car. To solve the problem, he left my mother standing on the sidewalk, trying unsuccessfully to quiet a terrified baby, while he frantically drove home for their other car. We were a rare, two-car family. "You just cried and cried, and I was afraid someone was going to come out of that building and snatch you away and take you back," Mom had said piteously during several narrations. It took over twenty minutes for Dad to return. "The whole time I was pacing up and down the sidewalk, trying to get you to shut-up," she said at a later date, sounding decidedly less sympathetic. I had gone placidly into the alternate vehicle, and slept all the way home. Over ten years later, they were still confident that I preferred the newer car. It never seemed to dawn on them that I had most likely cried myself to exhaustion.

So they drove me home at last, and tucked me into the crib in the little back nursery, lovingly furnished and decorated long ago for someone else who never arrived. I wondered if my parents were truly oblivious to the feelings of an infant, who must have been taken from someone's arms forever, to be driven away by strangers. In the yellowed, black and white pictures of the first days with my new family, I looked shell-shocked. I sat stiffly with a faraway gaze, swathed in frilly layers of chiffon and petticoats with matching bonnets. In one, my new mother held me forth at arm's length, as if not yet comfortable with my foreign flesh touching her bare arms. She displayed me proudly and beamed straight into the camera, and Dad must have been on the other side of it. Our new family pictures were framed with the belief that my earlier objection had been to the car.

We lived on 15 Mulligan Street. Our house was one in a row of identical, small houses that were built on a tract of land across from the Veteran's Housing Projects. They were cape-style starter-homes, with an unfinished upstairs and four little rooms down: an eat-in kitchen, a living room, a bedroom just big enough for a married couple to squeeze in the double bed and dressers, and a little back bedroom for the first baby. Working folks who were the first generation to own homes bought them for a price they could afford, and finished them off upstairs later when they could manage. They often did the work themselves, but no matter how many rooms they squeezed inside, the homes were still small. Some of the families had eight or more children, with three or four crammed in a tiny bedroom under the sloping roofline upstairs, the boys in one and the girls in the other.

Before the projects and new neighborhood went up, the surrounding area had been farmland. The only house in sight was Mrs. Malone's 'old monster of a house,' as my mother called it. It was built by the Harahans, the first generation to come over from Ireland, and had stayed in the family ever since. They'd been unusually wealthy immigrants, and the house was once very grand. Now it was over eighty years old and badly in need of repair. Most of the yellow paint had peeled away, except for some that hung in large curls on the weathered gray clapboard. Part of the roof visibly sagged, and the front porch had nearly fallen in. Nobody used it. My mother said it was an eyesore, and wished out loud it would burn to the ground-when Mrs. Malone was out, of course! "Jeez, it looks like the house in the Adams Family," Dad once said. I liked the old house with the tower like a witch's hat; us kids would've given anything to see what was in that tower.

When I was small, there were still a few acres of vegetable farms beyond the first new suburban blocks. I was barely past a toddler, but I remember an Italian lady who lived close by. She grew a field of tomatoes, and raised poultry on her lot. My mother took me over to feed her ducks. Her name was Camellia, and she was different from my mother, or Nana or anyone else I knew. She wore a full skirt down to her ankles with a long apron. Her hair was wrapped in a scarf, and she had gold hoop earrings. She smelled like good food. Camellia was very fond of me, and one summer day she waltzed up our front walk carrying an enormous white Peking duck. It was meant as pet for me. There's a picture of me, sitting on the grass with my legs spread to accommodate the duck, holding it close with both arms wrapped round tight. The duck didn't seem to mind. My mother took the picture before declining the gift, and I was told that Camellia was offended. She walked away in a dignified manner, with her head held high and her fine duck tucked under one arm. It was the most marvelous gift anyone had ever given me, and it was taken as quickly as it had been given. Mom felt bad to have hurt her feelings, but insisted that she couldn't help it. "Ducks are loud," she explained. "What would the neighbors think if I kept a duck?"

By the time I began to walk the block to Kindergarten at Edmunds Elementary School, Camellia and her ducks were gone forever. Across from the schoolyard, there remained one last small field where pansies for landscaping were grown. They were deep purple with little yellow faces, and I loved to look at them in the springtime. But by first grade, the field was a new street with rows of four-room ranches, and there were no farms left at all.

When my father came home from serving in WWII, he used the GI bill to train as a driver and mechanic for the big diesel trucks. He drove a truck for a large freight line and kept working until he was sixty-two, already old and worn-out from a life of labor. The terminal was located on the outskirts of the city, close to the freight trains. He commuted longer than most of the other fathers, and always worked overtime. When I was little, he was gone before I got up and came home after I was asleep.

We were a blue-collar, working class family, but compared to the rest of the neighborhood, we were noticeably better off, and sometimes the project kids referred to me as the 'rich kid.' The houses on our block looked nearly alike, but we always kept two cars in the driveway, and they tended to be a bit showy for our neighborhood. Every five years my father bought a brand new car for my mother, and took the older one to work. For a long time, she was the only mom in the neighborhood with her own car. I was constantly reminded of how much more we had, because my father worked so hard-for me. I was also reminded of how I was adopted, and therefore extra lucky, as if somehow I'd gotten away with something. It was a prominent theme in our house. Every night my dad came home exhausted and bleary-eyed, sometimes after working fourteen to sixteen hour shifts, hauling and unloading freight. It was grueling and sometimes dangerous work. He drove in bad weather, on icy roads, and my mom always worried out loud that he'd be hurt or even killed in an accident. When she felt particularly distraught, she'd invariably circle round to how he worked so hard and came home so late, all for me. The other fathers on our street worked in factories or grocery stores or some unskilled labor, and came home on a regular schedule after five. The women all stayed home with their children.

As I grew up, I began to understand the bigger financial picture, and just where we fit. It began to sink in one Christmas Season as we drove through the neighborhoods to see the lights and decorations. We always drove up to Mapleton Heights, and into an entirely different world. It wasn't just that the big houses in *The Heights* boasted the best Christmas lights, from the front-walkway and the shrubbery to the roofline. Under the pretext of admiring the decorations, you could gawk into the windows, which was at least half the entertainment. My parents were always in awe of the things those people had, and they were greener than a Christmas tree with envy.

The houses in Mapleton Heights were huge-two or more stories, and not all the same like ours. There were Tudor style homes, spacious colonials and even Victorian houses with towers, all painted and nicely kept up. There were no projects anywhere in sight. Tall, stately Maple trees lined the streets, and the front and back yards were three or more times the size of our yards. These houses had wrap around porches, front entry-halls, formal dining rooms, and big garages for the cars.

"Look at the size of that home!" Mom would exclaim. "Look at that dining room furniture, and oh, the chandelier...they must have at least ten rooms!" She spied on the rich folks as we drove by. "Our house is no bigger than their garage," she added like a sulking child. "What do they all do to make such money?"

"Must all be doctors...maybe lawyers," Dad grumbled. "I'd hate to have to mow that yard!" He consoled himself, not understanding that the people who lived in those great houses didn't mow their own lawns. It was the same conversation every year. No matter how hard he worked, I understood we would never live in a place like that. I could almost taste the bitter resentment from the back seat of the car. I didn't mind that our house was small, but I did wonder how you got to be a doctor instead of a truck driver. I didn't know what a lawyer was, and I didn't dare ask.

There were certainly no doctors living in our neighborhood, but I was still part of the elite at Edmunds Elementary School. Most of the kids came from the projects. Living in the projects was a mark of poverty, and you always knew who was a project kid and who was a neighborhood kid. Most of them were dressed decently, had enough to eat, and owned at least a few toys, though usually not a bicycle. Everyone said that if you had a bicycle, you never left it out because a project kid would come steal it. That only happened once in our neighborhood, but that was enough to give them a bad reputation. Some of the families were very poor. The children had no toys at all, lacked proper clothes for the four seasons, and wore sneakers all winter long. A few came to school grimy on a regular basis. Our teachers started the morning by inspecting everyone's hands and faces; dirty kids were sent to the art sink to wash.

Every family on our street had two parents, and every dad had a job. I didn't know it could be any other way until second grade, when I met a girl from the projects who didn't have a father. I thought he must have died. Then I came to understand that many of the project kids had no fathers because they just left. Some of their mothers worked as waitresses, or in department stores, while the children were cared for by extended family that also lived in the projects. Most of the single mothers didn't work, and were on welfare. Quite a few of the neighborhood kids were warned to avoid playing with the project kids, and told never to invite them home. My mother disagreed, and taught me to take each person as I found them; I should never judge someone because they were poor. When I was very little I noticed that she was polite to any project kids that I brought home, but never asked them to stay to supper-only the neighborhood kids.

The adults around me carefully demarcated their own group, not only by socioeconomics, but by nationality and religion. They were wary of outsiders to the degree of paranoia, and their prejudice was evident in their children. The first encounter between kids began with a standard interrogation. 'What's your name? How old are you? Where do you live-projects or neighborhood? What's your nationality? Are you Catholic?' Since most of the project kids were Irish, I usually had to explain that our name was not O'Rillio. When they learnt I was Italian, they made Italian jokes, like, 'How do you get a dozen WOPS into a Volkswagen?' By throwing a penny in, of course; you got them out by throwing in a bar of soap. The consensus among the Irish was that Italians were dirty and stupid, while most Italians held the belief that Irishmen were of an inferior race, drank too much, didn't work hard enough and could never be trusted to give you a square deal. I heard it from my father's own lips, which seemed odd because Mom was of Irish decent. Each group swore the other would cheat you if you didn't watch out. There were Italian owned businesses and Irish owned businesses, from small grocers to funeral parlors and gas stations, each frequented mostly by their own kind. Not that my parents didn't have plenty of Irish friends, but if my father didn't like someone who was Irish, he might privately label them a 'slick mick' or a 'thick mick.' Dad never called Italian people names, even if he didn't like them, but I heard Mom refer to one of his cousins as a real grease-ball. She didn't like it when he spoke Italian with his brothers and sisters, and remarked that they sounded like they just stepped off the boat. I don't think the Orillios appreciated it.

It's not surprising that for my first cognizant years I thought everyone was either Irish or Italian, and assumed all of them were Catholic. Then I learned there was a *Five and Dime* in Mapleton Heights owned by a Jewish family, who also owned the adjacent delicatessen. I didn't know what Jewish meant; I only knew it wasn't Catholic, and therefore not good. Sometimes my father brought me to the delicatessen to buy meat, which he admitted was of high quality, but he always remarked, "You have to watch those people-they're crafty and they'll swindle you if you're not careful." My father paid close attention to the scale as the cold cuts were weighed, and made a point of checking the package carefully against the bill, but it was never wrong, not even once.

I heard kids say some really mean things about those Jewish people, but had no idea why. I also heard both children and adults make jokes about Polish people, who were reputed to be exceptionally dumb. I don't know where they got that impression; there weren't any Polish people in East Mapleton.

I grew up amidst tensions and petty rivalry between Irish and Italians, and jealously amongst the working class towards those more privileged, but we had no trouble at all with people of different races. There simply weren't any. There were no people of color working at the town library, or in local grocery stores-none at the bank either. The teachers and nurses and our family doctor were all white. I never saw any colored people waiting on tables, and the school janitors and garbage men, as our sanitation workers were called, were all white too. No one we knew had domestic servants of any color.

Since our immediate world was as white as homogenized milk, I was about four years old before I leaned that not everyone on the planet looked like us; like my mom and dad, all the neighbors-everyone I had ever known or seen. We were at a department store in town, as everyone referred to Boston, and I was barely eye level to a bin heaped high with discounted items. Mom was holding her own in a thick mob of ladies, each guarding her turf. She was up to her elbows, sifting through clothes, selecting some and tossing others back. I was to stay right by her skirt and not stray. I'd done this before; thinking back, it was probably a sale at Filene's basement.

I was watching it all from the vantage point of three feet from the floor, when I suddenly noticed some people that didn't look like anyone I'd ever seen before. I was genuinely shocked at the sight of four human beings with dark brown skin, and strikingly different faces. By that age, you start to think you have at least a basic understanding of the way certain things are, the way certain things ought to be. People just didn't look like that; my weltanschauung was suddenly turned on its small head. Since they looked alike, I knew they must be some kind of family. One was a heavy-set matriarch with a prominent jaw, and broad features. She had three, almost grown children with her. The big kids had black fuzzy hair that stuck straight up, and their dark skin made the whites of their eyes look bigger and whiter. I stared in disbelief, trying to reconcile the visage with everything and anything in my limited knowledge bank. Then I recalled that my mother would often exclaim when I came inside from playing in the dirt, "Look at you! You're covered with dirt!" Holding up my earth-stained hands, she would lament that I was, "Black with dirt!" But it had nothing to do with race. So with no other experience to go on, I employed the logic of cause and effect, and reasoned that these folks must have been playing in the mud all day to get like that.

I tugged at my mother's dress and signaled her to bend down so I could ask my question in private. I'd already learned that you weren't supposed to talk about people in front of them, but I couldn't wait. I cupped my hand around my mouth, and in a child's whisper that could be heard over traffic, asked, "How did those people get all dirty?"

Mom looked suitably embarrassed and shushed me as she pulled me by the hand, dropping some of her prizes as we left. I still couldn't believe my eyes, and turned to gawk over my shoulder as I was dragged off. The woman held her head high and glowered down at me with unmistakable distain. I can imagine now what she must have thought of that ill-mannered white child, but I had no idea what I had done wrong.

"They're not dirty, they're colored," my mother whispered when we were out of sight and hearing. "I'll explain when we get home."

Later that afternoon, my formal training about the different races began. "They're called Negros. They aren't black because they're dirty. They just have dark skin."

"Why?"

"Because that's the way God made them. Now you must never," she lectured on, "say the word 'nigger' if you talk about them. You may hear other children say that word, but you are never to say it. If you have to say anything at all, you say Negroes, or colored people."

That's when I realized there were more people like the family I had seen at the store. Up until that point in the explanation, I had thought they were the only ones, a family singled out by God to have darker skin, just because He made them that way. Since you were never supposed to ask why God did anything the way He did it, that always signified the final answer on any given subject. Now I was very curious as to where all the others were. Where did these people live and why hadn't I ever seen them? But I couldn't ask, because Mom continued in her best school-teacher manner to hammer home the point about not saying that word.

"If you happen to hear a grownup say 'nigger', you mustn't correct them; just don't say anything about it," she continued.

OK, I thought. Got it. I had already been trained that there were words grownups said that I mustn't repeat.

"And you don't need to tell other kids what to say; that's up to their mothers. Just mind your business and make sure you don't say it." I nodded solemnly, already well versed in the virtues of minding my business, but she still wasn't finished with the word. "Now, if you're playing 'eaney, meany, miny, moe'... be sure to say, 'catch a nickel by the toe', or 'catch a tiger'. That's what I said," she added. "And you mustn't ever make fun of colored people. They can't help the way they look; that's just the way God made them," she concluded at last.

I guessed that was that, but I wondered why God would be so mean as to make some people with black skin, if everybody was just going to call them names and make fun of them. I didn't like it when kids did that to me. It made me feel sorry for those people. At the time, my mother's explanation sounded rational, moral, and even considerate. I learned much later that compared to some, it was elevated thinking.

As I grew up, I became naturally more curious about the world around me, and took notice of things outside my own neighborhood. When we drove over the Middlefield River Bridge, I saw that there was a separate playground on the far side where every child was black, but the playground on the Mapleton side of the bridge was full of white children. I only played at the park by Edmunds Elementary, so I usually didn't see any black children, not even from a distance. Since I had no opportunity to speak to a colored child, or even see one up close, I assumed they were all like Buckwheat in the *Little Rascals*. I liked Buckwheat, and thought it might be nice to go and play with them.

"Why can't I play over in that park?" I asked from the back seat of the car.

"Because the Negro children play there...that's *their* section of town," Mom said.

I wanted to understand this thing once and for all, so I bluntly asked my parents, "Why do the Negro children all play over in that park?"

"Because they need their own playground," Mom explained.

"But *why*?"

"Because, that's-where-they-live," Mom enunciated slowly, as if I were a pathetically stupid child not get it the first time.

"But why do they all have to live-over-there?" I asked in the same slow, deliberate tone, trying to get my point across. "Why can't some live over here?"

Without turning around, Dad took one hand off the wheel and swung his palm backwards, answering my query with a swift Dago backhand that brushed me off the side of the head. "Don't be so ignorant," he grunted.

3

"You know the Malones? You knew they were moving back with their grandmother? How? Why didn't you tell me?" Out of respect, I'd waited until a couple of days after my grandmother's wake before telling my mother the news-or what I thought was news.

"I only just learned they were all coming back to live with her, right after your Nana died," Mom answered. "Your father went around back to tell Mrs. Malone, old hard-headed Hannah, your Nana used to call her. She had to know, had to know your Nana died so she could do the right thing."

I looked at her expectantly, waiting for an explanation, but none seemed to be forthcoming. "How did Mrs. Malone know Nana?"

"They were related," she answered with obvious discomfort.

"What? How were they related?"

"I suppose you have to know before one of those kids tells you anyway."

Even after conceding the fact that she finally had to tell me something, Mom held back. I could see that if there were any way around it, she would have kept the secret to herself for good.

"They were sisters," she said flatly.

It was like getting kicked in the stomach. I was more insulted than shocked. This was serious. Whatever was going on, it was a family matter; I was plenty old enough to know, and I should have been told. Once again, my mother had kept me in the dark, and treated me as if I'd been an outsider rather than a daughter, as if it had been none of my business.

"Nana grew up in that house," she went on. "Her sister Hannah raised her; she was sixteen when their parents died, and your nana was about two, I think. They went one right after the other-first the mother, then the father within months. Nana didn't remember, of course. There was a brother too, but he'd gone off to World War One and died. Afterwards, an uncle came over from Ireland and stayed a while. Then he sent back for an Irishman-he knew their family-for her to marry. She'd never met him before; she was barely seventeen! His name was Michael Malone, and he was quite a bit older, and very wealthy-until the depression hit. They had everything, and lost almost all of it, all but that old house. The two of them had five children together too, but most of them died, from diphtheria I think it was. Aunt Hannah had only two boys left.

Nana didn't really talk about her time growing-up. Aunt Hannah may have raised your Nana, but I don't think they ever got along. Even when they were speaking, something wasn't quite right. I never asked, of course; your Nana didn't want to talk about it, and I didn't want to upset her."

I plopped down onto the kitchen chair. Bitter indignation curdled in my stomach and crept upwards until my eyes burned with dry tears. I sensed that there was a whole volume behind each detail my mother had reluctantly told me, but I wasn't going to get it out of her easily. She never did tell me who her own father was, or where he'd gone; she claimed not to know, but I was never sure if that was true. Even though the answer was predictable, I just had to ask, "But why didn't you tell me?"

"Because you didn't need to know," she answered smartly.

My face went hot as if I'd been slapped. I had a few things I wanted to say to her, but held back. Starting a fight now wouldn't get me the information I wanted. I sniffed back the anger and looked away from her.

"What's the matter with you?" she asked unsympathetically.

"Oh, it's a sad story," I fibbed. If I complained about being left out, she'd just turn it around and find some reason to be mad at me. Then I'd have to wait even longer before I'd learn more about it. I blinked back tears of indignation and composed myself. "So the sisters weren't speaking," I said, stating the obvious. The fact that they had fallen out, as grownups said, was not shocking. I knew that families feuded. My father's two brothers didn't speak for a month after their father died, because they'd quarreled about who would pay for how much of their own father's funeral. Not that anyone had explained it to me; I had to overhear the whole thing, eaves-dropping from the staircase when I was supposed to be in bed. I learned a lot that way. They were soon reconciled, weeping in one another's arms and each taking the blame for the misunderstanding. I was very young, but I remembered how strange it was to see grown men cry. "Italians!" my mother had said, in a way that indicated her superiority.

Then there was the time Dad's sister, my Auntie Angela, quarreled with her sister over a sweater. It was a Christmas gift from Filenes, but she told Auntie Nellie that it was from the upstairs store when it was really from Filenes' basement. Auntie Nellie found out when she returned the gift-and that's what set-off Auntie Angela. They didn't say a word to one another until Easter. I tried to imagine what sort of controversy kept a mother apart from her son and grandchildren for over ten years.

"What did they fight about?"

"I really don't know, Frances."

31

"Mrs. Malone is your aunt, but you don't know why you couldn't speak to her all those years?" It was still hard to believe no one had told me. She shrugged and nodded with a sigh. "And Mr. Malone, Madeline's dad, is your...*cousin*? He's not much younger than Nana was, is he?" I went on, putting the pieces together aloud.

"No, only about two years younger." Suddenly she spat out, "That drunken Irishman... that rotten son-of-a-bitch is my cousin. But I didn't really think of him as a cousin when I was growing up. I didn't have anything to do with him, and I didn't miss him one bit all these years. The only reason I saw Tom at all is because I used to be good friends with his wife; her name is Joan," she added.

"Really?" Yet another surprise.

"But I always found Tom Malone a scary sort of man. Even when Nana was on speaking terms with her sister, she never had two words for him. Something was very, very wrong there. I don't know what he did, what it was all about, but..."

"I know," I interrupted. "You didn't ask about it. It would be bad manners."

"Well, it's true!" she said in exasperation. "There are just some things you don't talk about."

I had been told this so many times that I stopped asking why. My parents' generation considered it far more of an offence to air the family's dirty laundry than to commit whatever transgressions warranted secrecy in the first place. In that regard, my mother was no different from anyone else, and people suffered more for it. The expenditure of energy required to keep the truth out of sight and mind, warped your spiritual spine and twisted your guts, until the true source of your anguish took the more acceptable form of a physical malady. One alternative was to replace the original problem with alcoholism, which wasn't openly called alcoholism if the sufferer were a woman, or a man who managed to hide it and function well enough to get by. Men who drank too much and didn't work might be called drunks and bums behind their backs, even scorned or pitied. But drunks or not, they were still part of the family. On the other hand, people with mental disorders were feared and reviled, and sufferers might be shunned, sometimes forever. Ordinarily nice people would turn cruel and make remarks about how they knew some individual always 'had a screw loose' or claim they knew so and so had been wrong in the head all along. Even a rumor that some poor woman had 'gone to McClain's' severed connections, and the whole family was avoided as if it might be contagious, as if she'd contracted an unmentionable disease due to a scandalous moral failing.

The antidote to living mired in the shame born of deep ignorance was to keep secrets. The only way to bury the truth was to cover it with lies-not just every day lies, but elaborate, meticulous revisionism that required collusion between some family members to the exclusion of others. The all-consuming challenge of rewriting one's family history with such craft that it became a sort of virtual truth left people exhausted, disconnected, and always a little lost. It was like driving down a highway, trying to find your way in the dark while sitting on a bucket of shit. To avoid a spill, you have to take absurdly long detours, go so far out of your way to dodge every bump and pothole, and miss the sharp turns that you end up somewhere else entirely, and late at that.

"How am I related to the Malones?" I asked, even though I didn't feel as if I were related to my adoptive parents by anything but documents and good intentions. Only one step removed and the illusion became harder to maintain. My paternal aunts and uncles and their grown children always felt like my father's family, not mine, while Nana was Mom's family. But there was something about Maddy that made me feel connected, like a real relative even before I knew she was supposed to be one. It was the way she looked right into me and liked what she saw. It was acceptance. "You're a funny kid, Frances," that's how she put it; but I was still alright. Even with only eleven years of experience to go on, I knew that to truly see another and claim them as your own, just as they are with no regrets, was a tie thicker than blood, and a rare quality in an individual.

"Oh...hmm," Mom mused aloud. "I guess you're some sort of second cousin, and I think something like second cousins twice-removed to all those kids; and Aunt Hannah is your great aunt," she added. She suddenly changed her tone, and forced a smile, as if delivering some pleasant news. "Won't it be...*nice* to have family close by?" she asked rhetorically. I guess she figured that since family reunification was inevitable, she might as well make the best of it.

Whenever my mother had to tell me something out of absolute necessity, something she didn't want to talk about but couldn't avoid, she affected that particular smile. It never fooled me. It was the same smile she'd worn when delivering her speeches about adoption, about how 'special' I was because I was adopted-how my parents had loved me so much that they gave me away. I didn't buy it, but I had been told so early and often that I couldn't remember not knowing. It had never been a shock. This time was different; this

33

sudden revelation changed the way I thought of my mother, of Nana, and especially myself. I wasn't alone anymore. I had a cousin my own age!

I hadn't been this blindsided since Mom first told me about menstruation. The facts of life had been just as carefully hidden from me; I'd turned eleven years old before having any idea of the monthly cycles I might soon experience. Mom just popped into my room one day carrying a lovely gift box, bound with a pink ribbon and inscribed in gold script, *A Kotex Gift from Mother to Daughter*. She put on a brave face and smiled her special smile as I opened the box, stunned and confused. Inside was an assortment of fat, cotton sanitary napkins, in various thicknesses to accommodate your flow. They had long pieces of gauze hanging from each end that made them look like surgical dressings for a serious wound. It was terrifying. There was a huge pair of panties with a moisture resistant coating and two metal clasps at either end of the crotch to secure the pad. They reminded me of the plastic pants that babies wore over their diapers. The kit included a little booklet explaining the menstrual cycle, complete with diagrams of the internal female reproductive organs. Mom began to read in her most pleasant voice about the wonders of impending womanhood. She was clearly uncomfortable, but I've got to hand it to her: she went all out and tried to do it justice. Neither she nor the book explained how the sperm actually got in there to meet up with that little egg. I asked, but she told me that would have wait until I was older...much older.

Now my mother's tone gave her away; she was about as comfortable talking about her relatives as she was talking about sex.

***

"It will be good to see Joan Murphy again," Mom said, next morning over breakfast. "She was such a good friend."

"Who's Joan Murphy?" I asked.

"I mean Joan Malone; she's Joan Malone now. I haven't seen or heard from Joan since you were a baby. She was always a, ah...special sort of woman. I knew her back when we were girls, living over in Charlestown on the same block; all the neighbors knew each other. I was older, so we didn't go to class together. But I got to know her over the years while walking to and from school. Joan was the sweetest, prettiest little thing-she's French. I think the French are such beautiful people. Her mother was a bit...well...different. She'd been widowed very young, and dressed in black for the rest of her life, just like an old lady! And she always seemed so sad, that's what I remember. They were very devout Catholics-went to mass every day. It was just Joan and her mother. They were together all the time, and they spoke French at home. Joan was a lovely girl, small boned, delicate...I always felt like a big Irish washer woman next to her. But you couldn't be jealous; she wasn't the least bit conceited. And she was so religious! We all assumed she would become a nun-that's what her mother wanted. Then she met Ed Murphy. Her mother died shortly after they married, and we were all glad she'd found a good man to take care of her. They were so in love, but she only got to keep him a few years. We reconnected when she married Tommy Malone-not so much because of him, but because my Aunt Hannah became Joan's new mother-in-law. She already had her oldest boy, little Eddie. He must be almost grown-up now." I looked questioningly at my mother. "Eddie's father was her first husband." She sighed. "Now Ed Murphy was a wonderful man-a saint of a man! He was a fireman, and always loved to help people. He fixed toys for poor children, and took them around at Christmas. I remember Joan telling me how he went out of his way to do things, like spend his one day off mending the back stoop of some old widow's house. Joan would glow with pride when she spoke of him. He was just so good-the neighborhood children all called him Uncle Ed. He'd give you the shirt off his back! He and Joan were meant for each other, truly a match made in heaven."

"What happened?"

"He got hurt in a terrible accident, a fire. He didn't die right away, but lay home with horrible burns that never healed right. The day he died a little bird flew in the window; she never cared for birds after that."

"Why?"

"She thought it was a bad omen. I don't believe in that nonsense, but I never contradicted her. Now, she told me about this a long time ago-you mustn't bring it up," she warned. "That would be inconsiderate of their feelings." I nodded solemnly. "Joan was with him when he died, and a piece of her died with him. When she married that s... Tommy Malone, we became related by marriage. They moved in with his mother-the house is so big, I never understood why she rattled around alone in there for so long. Anyway, that was as close as I ever got to having a sister. We'd both grown up as only children, and we both wanted a big family. Joan got hers right away. I remember how in springtime it seemed like when everyone took off their big winter coats, they were all pregnant, all except me. I'd see some young woman pushing a stroller while pregnant with the next one, and I'd feel so jealous; but I never could feel jealous of Joan. She was just so kind and so good, you couldn't envy her. She lit a candle in church every week for me, and prayed for the Virgin to intercede. Joan is a rare woman, a truly devout Catholic, not just for show. She was always concerned about someone else-never herself. You never heard Joan complain

the way most of us do. Sometimes I babysat for her when she went to..." Here
her story stalled out, and I could tell she was looking for something to say in
place of what she'd almost let slip. I was used to this, and learned to hold on to
each word almost spoken, and weave the bits together patiently over time. "Uh,
visit someone," she finished awkwardly.

"You really don't know what happened between Nana and her sister...the
reason they didn't speak for all those years?" I was still incredulous.

"No; I really, truly don't know. Nana never told me, and I didn't feel I
should ask if she didn't want to tell me. I wouldn't upset my mother that way,"
she added with emphasis. "All I know is that my mother had some sort of
disagreement with her sister. Just think- I built a house right behind my aunt,
and they quit speaking. I assumed it would blow over, but the years just slipped
by and that was that!" She spread her hands out in a gesture of helpless
acceptance. "Not long afterwards, Tom Malone had some blowout with his
mother...it probably had to do with his drinking, but Joan never told me the
details. She was always one of those rare people who never said a bad thing
about anyone, never gossiped at all. Tom just up and moved the family out of
their home."

As I listened, I began to realize that the fight between Nana and her sister
had really hurt my mother, but it was Mr. Malone that took her best friend away.
I wondered how two grown women could let that happen. Mom had lots of
friends, and now that Nana was gone, my parents met to play cards with the
aunts and uncles, and had more people over to dinner. But I'd never heard her
speak of any of them the way she spoke about Joan Malone.

"Tom Malone hardly earned a living at all," she went on. "He drove a
cab-when he bothered to work. They ended up in those awful projects over in
Middlefield. I drove over to visit once after Joan had Madeline Dorothy-I wish
you wouldn't refer to her as 'Mad-Dog'" she added, making a face. "It's so
unlady-like."

"I call her Maddy."

"That's almost as bad. It sounds like a boy's name...like short for
Mathew. Madeline is such a nice Catholic name. You should call her Madeline."
Not a chance, I thought. Mom continued, "I brought her a little baby outfit, and I
brought you along-you were just a baby, but you sort of met your...cousin. Joan
cried. She was really sorry we didn't get together anymore, and you could tell it
was hard on her to live in those awful projects, not that she complained. There
are some rough people over there-of course, not all poor people who live in the
projects are bad people. Tom Malone fit right in. He told her they would save
money and buy their own house, but it never did happen. The babies kept

36

coming; I've never even seen little Annie or Michael. Tom barely made enough to support them all, and he drank most of what he earned. He's supposed to be out driving the cab, but he stops during the day at every bar in Middlefield. I'm not really gossiping because it's common knowledge, but..."

"I know. Don't talk about it-bad manners. I wouldn't be that dumb. Do you think I'd say, 'Hey, I hear your dad's a drunk'?"

She laughed. "No, I know you'd know better than that at your age. Just don't ever let it slip in conversation."

"Do you know anything about the uncle in prison?" I asked innocently. I never would reveal what Maddy told me in the bathroom, and besides, I wanted gauge how much Mom knew about it.

She looked annoyed, but answered, "You've heard that old gossip, have you? Well, it's true; but don't ask me about the details. I really don't know. It was a long time ago, and I know one thing: none of them talk about that, so..."

"I know; don't mention it, and mind my own business."

Mom sighed and shook her head, then informed me in all seriousness. "Men! A good one will make your life wonderful, and a bad one will ruin it. You have to be so careful, Frances. When you're a child, your life is in the hands of your parents; really, it's in the hands of our fathers," she said, looking off somewhere. "Everything depends upon whether a man is good and takes care of his wife and children. Then when you grow up, it's a man's world; they're in charge. Boys get to become men and do what they like, but a woman's life is only as good as her husband makes it. And there're only a few good ones like your father and Ed Murphy-God bless his soul," she added earnestly.

4

Monday came, and I went off to school feeling as if I'd just joined the human race. I would no longer be that odd kid with no real friends, no siblings or even cousins. Now I could talk about my new relatives the way other kids talked about their families. I wondered if Maddy would come around to call on me for school, but she didn't. When I didn't see her on the playground before school, my heart sank. The bell rang, and she wasn't inside either. It was too good to be true, I thought. Other than that, it wasn't a bad day. The teacher came up to me and offered her condolences on my grandmother's passing in front of the whole class. I felt special and grown-up. The kids left me alone, with none of the usual teasing. Dotty Day didn't push past me in the lunch line. Even 'Smelly Kelly' was decent, almost deferential. Tuesday and Wednesday were the same, and by Thursday I gave up. The Malones must have changed their minds. The elation I'd felt in the ladies' room when I suddenly had a new friend and confidant began to fade.

Friday morning she was there. I was finishing breakfast, and looked up to see my cousin standing on our back steps. My heart jumped as Mom let her in.

"Good Mornin', Mrs. Orillio," I heard her say.

"Good Morning, Madeline," mother answered. "Please come in... Frances is almost ready. And Madeline...I want you to call me Aunt Evelyn, because...we're family. OK dear?"

"OK by me, Aunt Evelyn."

"Hey Maddy!" I was so happy and relieved that I wanted to rush over and hug her, but somehow I knew you just didn't do that with this girl. I looked at her eyes, and thought the fortress seemed a bit less guarded for the moment. One corner of her mouth kind of turned up when she saw me, like she was secretly glad too. Mom looked her up and down, and I knew she'd have plenty to say later about her clothes, shoes, hair, and stale cigarette odor. Maddy only pretended she wasn't aware of the scrutiny.

"Aren't you going to be awfully cold this time of year in knee socks?" Mom asked, glaring down at Maddy's bare knees-apparently she wasn't going to wait until later to make comments.

"No, I'm fine thanks." Maddy wasn't fazed.

"I see...well, isn't Annie going to school?" my mother questioned as if she worked for social services.

"She's in afta'noon *Kindagaht'n*," Maddy explained patiently. "I have to come home for lunch and walk her to school for Ma."

"That's a good girl," my mother said approvingly. "How is your mother?" she added earnestly.

"She's fine, thank you."

"C'mon, we'll be late." I was glad to interrupt the interrogation. Maddy held the door for me, and I gave my mother the expected peck on the cheek before bolting outside.

I noticed that she still carried the shabby, navy blue schoolbag with the tattered gold St. Clément's logo. It was a simple sack with a draw-string top, and she slung it over her shoulder like a boy as we left. We walked fast in the chilly morning air-at least it was dry, with no snow on the ground.

"Hey, Maddy," I began.

"Hey," she answered absently.

"Ah, where were you all week? I was beginning to think you weren't coming, weren't moving after all," I explained.

"I said it'd be next week. It's next week."

I was a bit stung by the curt answer. I changed the subject. "Where's Tommy?" I'd almost forgotten about him.

"He's around."

Edmunds Elementary was only a block away, but you had to go around the corner of my street and walk on the sidewalk opposite the projects. That's the place where I sometimes ran into trouble. I stayed on the neighborhood side, and the project kids stayed on their side, except when they deliberately crossed over to start something. As we rounded the corner of Mulligan Street, I wondered where Maddy would feel she belonged. River-rat kids usually stayed in the old-projects, and they fought with new-project kids. Now she wasn't even a project kid anymore, but she wasn't one of the neighborhood kids either. I guess living in 'Old Lady Malone's' house was different altogether. It was uncharted territory. She seemed anxious about something, and suddenly pushed her school-bag into my hands, whipped a cigarette out of her pocket and lit it fast without breaking her stride. That's when I heard the quickening footsteps behind us.

A couple of boys were following, keeping pace. They seemed to come out of nowhere, as if they'd been waiting all along. They must have been behind the tall hedges that bordered the last yard we'd passed. Maddy didn't look back or change her pace, and I knew she'd already seen them. I kept quiet. They were walking faster, closing the gap. I wanted to run, not that it ever did me any good. They were right behind us now, and she just kept walking at the same pace, puffing away. I glanced back and recognized them: Billy Smith and Kevin Day, one of Dotty's cousins. They were pure meanness.

"Hey, *girly*," came a taunting voice that was, ironically, still high-pitched like a girl. Said in that provocative tone, it was a simple but effective insult, as if it were somehow distasteful, even shameful just to be a girl. We hated it, and there was no gender-equivalent insult to hurl back at them-not that we knew of anyway. It sent shivers of fear through me. Maddy acted as if she hadn't noticed.

"What's a matter, *girly*?"

She stopped, slowly turned towards them and shrugged nonchalantly. "Nothin'. Somthin' the matter with you?"

"Yeah, your face!" Kevin sneered, then he and his side-kick laughed.

This was the kind of encounter that made me sick, that made me hate school, and hate being a kid. She just calmly shrugged as if it made no difference, and turned her back to them as we walked on.

"Hey girly!" Billy wanted to get in on the action. "Where do ya think you're goin'? Don't ya hear me? I'm talkin' to ya!" The words were drawn out in a sickening sing-song that struck a raw nerve; it was the denigration that frightened me. I'd witnessed that to devalue another is the first requirement of violence. Whatever this boy had in mind wasn't good, and he was clearly savoring the process.

Maddy came to a full stop and took a resolute drag on her cigarette before handing it to me. She turned around and faced them, then exhaled slowly, like she was mildly annoyed and only a bit bothered. I was already scared to death. Although she tried to act as if she weren't particularly concerned with the boys, her eyes gave her away. They kind of smoldered, like molten lead; it should have been enough to warn even an animal to stay back. It transformed her face until she looked just like her father, all mean and hateful. The boys didn't seem to notice. They sauntered over until Billy stood directly in front of her, less than an arm's length away, signaling that he wouldn't let her go on until he got an answer. I inched backwards reflexively, but his eyes were fixed on Maddy as if I weren't even there.

"Yeah," she answered slowly, "but see, I just don't want to talk to *you*!" As she finished the last word, her right fist shot from her side like a bullet. I didn't see it coming, and neither did Billy. The undercut smashed him up the nose, and he stumbled back with his eyes closed and his hand over his face. When he took his hand away, blood spurted out all over. I'd never seen that

40

much blood from one punch. Kevin was smaller, but quick and wiry. He rushed forward and grabbed her right arm, twisting it behind in a furious mission to rescue manhood, for Billy, for himself, for all of the boys gathering round to watch. I screeched so loud that they both paused involuntarily and looked over in surprise. That gave Maddy a moment to twist around and free her arm. She clocked him hard on the ear with her left fist. Then he punched her full force in the stomach, so fast she hadn't time to get out of the way. I could see that it hurt, but she didn't make a sound. A few of the boys crossed the road chanting, "fight, fight..."

"Stop, please stop!" I pleaded.

Maddy's fists were up as she danced from foot to foot like a boxer, sizing up her opponent. Then she let fly at Kevin's head and landed a few solid punches as she ducked and dodged his every attempt. She seemed to be enjoying the sport of it, calm and in her element, and it looked as though she was easily going to win. But this time something different happened, something terrible that changed everything; I still don't know exactly what, because I could never bring myself to ask.

Kevin bent down as if he were going to tackle her, but suddenly grabbed the skirt of her dress with both fists and yanked her in close. This was out of bounds. They were having a fistfight and he should have respected that. Maddy was pulled off balance and almost fell over his back. Then he reached around and thrust his hand under her dress from behind. I was standing at just the right angle to see, and I wasn't sure if anyone else noticed.

A deep groan escaped her lips, and for a moment her face was transformed from a fighter to a terrified child. Then she shoved Kevin away with all her might. He leered up at her with a sickeningly smug smile of triumph, even though he'd landed hard on his ass. Maddy stumbled a few steps backwards from the effort of knocking him down, but she stayed on her feet. She breathed hard, collected herself, and the look on her face passed from shocked disbelief to rage, and settled upon a chilling calm.

"You little *muthah fuckah*," she hissed like a snake through clenched teeth. "I'm gonna kill you." Mad-Dog stated her intentions with slow deliberation.

Kevin tried to smirk, tried to laugh as if he weren't scared, but couldn't quite pull it off. He had some welts on his face and one eye was puffing up. Still, he stood up with a swagger, cocked his head back and stuck out his small pelvis. "I'm not afraid of you, ya little *cunt*."

The project kids collectively sucked in their breath and chorused, "Oooh" with overtones of awe and a fair degree of disapproval, while Kevin clenched his fists and stood defiant, ready for another round. That dirty word was usually only taken out after dark, bandied about the projects amongst wretched little boys when no adult was in earshot. It was the ultimate denunciation of anything female, and somehow affirmed their status as males. Kevin had crossed a line, and most of his supporters pulled back. They still had some sense of shame. But Billy Smith had been standing on the sideline, holding his bloody nose and watching the fight with interest. The C word seemed to buoy him, fill him with a renewed determination. He stepped closer to Kevin, poised like a bantam rooster and crowed, "Come on, Kev!" Now that he had back-up, Kevin grinned in perverse delight and pranced a few steps to the other side, trying to get around Maddy and attack from behind, two against one.

I was about to run to school and get help, when a huge boy flew out of nowhere and hurled Kevin to the ground like a stone. He began kicking him hard in the ribs and in the buttocks. You could hear a dull thud when he kicked his ribs, and each blow drew a cry of anguished pain. Tommy had been watching out for his sister all along. He had a wild look in his eyes, and his usually dough-white face was blood red. Then he grabbed Kevin by the collar and hauled him back to his feet, demanding and explanation.

"What the fuck's a matter with ya, pussy?!" He punched Kevin in the face, sending him back to the ground. Tommy began to strut slowly around the prostrate boy as he listed the charges. "Punchin' a girl in the stomach?! You guys think ya gonna to go two against one cause she was kickin' your ass?" he scoffed. Then he leaned down close to Kevin's face and said in a low menacing voice, "I seen what you did, ya filthy little bastahd!"

Kevin couldn't stand up, so he tried to crawl away on all fours. Tommy took the opportunity to underscore his displeasure by sending the toe of his shoe right between Kevin's buttocks. The blow shot up his spine and came out his mouth in a howl of pain-it sounded like a dog who'd been hit by a car, a sound you never forget once you hear it. Kevin collapsed flat on his face, and began to sob loudly with his arms shielding his head. I thought that was the end of it, but Tommy was just getting warmed up.

"I said, what the fuck's a matter with ya?" Tommy reiterated.

"I'm s, s, sorry," Kevin whimpered into the ground. He didn't dare look up.

"I can't hear ya," Tommy sang out as he bent down and hauled him to his feet for the last time. With one fat hand he gripped the back of Kevin's neck and pulled him close to his face.

"I'm s..." Kevin began, but he didn't get a chance to finish. Tommy slapped him hard in the mouth a few times. Kevin put his hands over his face and cried.

Tommy shook him by the neck like a dog killing a rodent. "Take 'em down," he barked, "I didn't hear ya."

I had never witnessed this level of brutality, had never seen someone so thoroughly broken down; not just defeated, but broken down completely. I had a feeling I knew where Tommy learnt it.

"No...please...I...I'm sorry," Kevin sobbed behind his hands.

"I said take 'em down," Tommy shook the kid again.

"Please stop," Billy Smith began to beg. He was crying too. "He won't do it again," he pleaded. Some of the other boys had looked as if they were deciding whether or not to get involved, but Tommy's blazing eyes made up their minds.

"It's alright, Tommy," Maddy interjected softly. "Forget it-they won't bother me anymore."

Tommy wasn't finished. He turned Kevin's head by the back of the neck as if he were a ventriloquist's dummy, until he was facing his sister. "Take your hands down and tell her *sorry*, or I'll break your fuckin' neck," he informed with finality.

Kevin took his shaking hands down from his face. His lips were split and growing fat. "I'm s,s,sorry," he whimpered. Tommy released his grip, dropping Kevin to his knees. He turned and walked away quickly without looking back.

Maddy hurried after him. "Here Tommy," she said, offering him what was left of her cigarette. I'd somehow held it the whole time, but was surprised when she took it from my hand. He grasped it between his fat fingers and sucked greedily, quelling the rage. It seemed to calm him, like a big irritated baby with his bottle.

"Let's get the hell outa here or we'll be late the first day," Maddy said, as if nothing much had happened. She shouldered her bag and we resumed our walk to school while Tommy loped along behind us. My legs felt like lead. It was an effort to put one foot in front of the other, and I was unsure of the very ground beneath my feet. I have no clear memory of the rest of that day or the next, only that Kevin and Billy skipped school. Nobody got in trouble-nobody ratted, and the matter just dropped. I'd walked that block to school hundreds of times, but now the way seemed strange and unfamiliar. In the space of ten minutes, I came to understand the new order of things. Now we were growing up and boys always had to win; it was as if their very lives depended on it. One brave girl punched a hole through the wall, but it was quickly rebuilt the moment

Tommy took over. Mad-dog Malone lost the fight because she wasn't allowed to finish it, fair and square like in the old days. And although her brother rescued her, he could never fully restore her dignity.

5

It was the third week of February. We'd been going to school together every day, but Maddy still hadn't brought me home to meet the rest of the family; they hadn't completely unpacked. She said I couldn't come in yet because the house was hell-all-over. Finally they were ready, and I was invited to meet her mother and play indoors the following Saturday. Daylight lasted a little longer, 'til almost five-thirty, but it was still raw and wet outside. You could only play in the snow when it first fell, if it stayed cold long enough. Otherwise it was just dirty slush and half-frozen mud. It was one of those overcast, mushy days. We could stay inside, but we'd have to play quietly, because their grandmother napped in the afternoon.

Maddy came around the corner to get me, and on the way back explained that I was going to meet her mother, baby brother, big sister Joanie, and older brother Eddie Murphy. Tommy wasn't home. On Saturday he spent as much time out of the house as possible, usually turning up in the early evening for supper. Nobody seemed to miss him.

We hung our coats on wooden pegs in the back entryway and kicked off our dirty boots. The little room had a strong odor like tobacco and sweat and stinky feet. I could already hear a commotion from around the corner, and I picked up my head to listen, trying to make out the strange sound. "That's just Baby Michael," Maddy explained.

The Malone's kitchen was a scene of undifferentiated chaos; I couldn't imagine what it looked like before. They still hadn't completely unpacked, and some open boxes with various odds and ends poking out were pushed against the wall, partly obscuring a window. I could see a ball of yarn with only one needle stuffed in an old shoe, and what looked like a plastic turtle tank turned on its side, its occupant probably long gone. The sink was piled with dishes, and a clothesline full of drying diapers stretched across the room. It smelled like poop.

I took one look at Maddy's baby brother and a thought struck me like a bolt of lightning: Baby Michael is crazy. He was running in circles on the cracked linoleum as if chased by demons. Dubbed 'Baby Michael' by the family, he was said to be a holy terror, and they feared he would be the death of his mother. He wore her out day and night. Baby Michael was loud, loud enough to be heard as I came in the door, and I couldn't imagine how their grandmother possibly slept through it. As the toddler ran in circles he made a monotonous, throaty sound, something like, "eeeeeeeh"-until he was out of breath. Then he paused to suck down enough air for another go at it. He didn't look at me when I came in, or seem to notice anyone in the room. One small hand was held in front as if gripping the handle of some object that was invisible to the rest of us, and his gaze seemed permanently fixed on his own hand. Somehow he managed not to trip on his footy pajamas, which swished and flopped wildly as he ran round and round. His diaper visibly sagged with its load. What made me most uncomfortable, besides the unnatural sound, was that he didn't appear to be having any fun at his game. He looked stuck, like a battery operated toy with the switch left on. Baby Michael was already growing hoarse when I arrived, and showed no signs of stopping. The family acted as if it were all perfectly normal. It was one of those moments when you look around and wonder if something is wrong with everyone else in the room, or is it you; it can't be both.

Joan Malone was exactly as my mother described her. She embodied patience and grace, smiling upon her difficult child with calm resignation, unruffled by the noise and mess around her. There was a large crucifix on the kitchen wall, and I soon learned that Joan lived her life in a continual state of working prayer and a rapturous devotion to Christ, asking nothing for herself but the strength to serve God and her family. It was enough to keep even the Blessed Virgin on her toes-at least Mary had asked for the wine at Cana. Joan made me think of the holy pictures of suffering saints. She wore a wretched housedress, a faded sack of nondescript floral frumpiness. It was what most mothers wore at home, since they mightn't leave the house for days at a time and besides, cooking and cleaning ruined good clothes. My mother called them the prison uniform of the blue-collar housewife. She never wore a housedress, but cleaned up in stylish slacks.

"You know my little sister Annie; this is my big sister Joanie, and that's," Maddy announced, shaking her head and rolling her eyes, "Baby Michael. He's gonna be three this spring," she added.

Joanie was a skinny girl of fourteen-she was going on fifteen. She and Tommy were nine months apart. Mom told me that Joanie and Tommy were called 'Irish twins', but warned me not to repeat it. Even though they were nearly the same age, Joanie was two grades ahead, and seemed much older. I had been warned never to call her Joan, always Joanie, because she hated the sound of 'Joan Malone'. She had the same, dull brown hair as her sister, but her small eyes were a metallic, silver-gray. Depending on her state of mind, Maddy's eyes were like a stormy sea, or a steel trapdoor, but Joanie's eyes reminded me of something sharp, like the shiny little blade of a jackknife. She was standing over an ironing board grimly pressing what looked like a big white apron, and barely acknowledged me with a nod. Joanie wore a sullen expression and had prematurely hollowed cheeks, a face that had lost all traces of childhood. She seemed like a grownup to me, a jaded but resolute adult who had given over childish things. Maddy had informed me that her big sister now got to smoke cigarettes without having to sneak them, but not near the baby or in front of Gramma.

Little Annie stood by her mother's knee, and you could see how much she loved her. She was a beautiful child, with a heart-shaped face, and deep blue-gray eyes that were like still pools of water. She was the only one in the family with a creamy white complexion and pink-rose cheeks. We were all pale-none of us spent much time out of doors for more than half the year, but the rest of the Malones seemed to suffer from a diet of Kraft Dinner, cereal, and a few overly boiled vegetables with the weekly ham. Their coloring ranged from paste white to a dull, sallow candle-wax. Annie was small for five years, delicate of build, with little hands and feet, and wispy, baby-fine hair. She was certainly different from the rest of the Malones-her mother all over, with none of the rough edges the others inherited from their father. Seeing her for the first time amidst the noise and mess, I felt the sudden impulse to pick her up and carry her off.

"This is Frances," Maddy introduced me to her mother.

"It's so good to see you, Frances," Mrs. Malone gushed. Although her face was drawn and lined about the mouth, she was clearly once a beauty, like Annie. She couldn't have been much more than forty, but already had fixed, black circles under her eyes and sunken cheeks, as though she were being siphoned away from the inside. She looked as if she hadn't had a decent night's sleep in a long time. Somehow, it made her enormous, dark-blue eyes appear even more radiant, as if nothing could diminish their light.

"I'm very pleased to meet you Mrs. Malone," I answered formally, as I'd been taught. I was always a bit uneasy when meeting anyone for the first time. She smiled at me. It was an amazing smile that made her eyes glow even brighter. It was somehow childlike, given as a gift with no consciousness of its own value. Simply, wordlessly, the smile told me I was good, no matter what I might believe about myself.

"Call me Auntie Joan, darlin'" she said, summoning me with an outstretched arm. Her voice was like gentle water. I moved obediently towards her, and she pulled me close. She lifted my face with her fingertips and looked at me with a kind of wonder, as if I were some rare treasure she'd discovered while strolling by the seaside. I felt my eyes begin to fill, and I swallowed to stop it. Something almost palpable flowed from her insides and washed over me, filled me suddenly to the brim like an empty tide pool. I felt I might drown. "You call me Auntie Joan," she said again, to make certain I understood. I couldn't answer, so I just nodded. "You'll have to excuse me while I change the baby," she sighed after a moment. "Please excuse the mess," she added with deference, as if I were grown-up company.

Auntie Joan rose from her kitchen chair with some effort, supporting her weight on the table with one hand. She held her hands out to Baby Michael. "Come to mummy sweetheart, it's time for a change," she crooned in a sing-song voice, drawing out the word 'change' into two syllables. He kept on running; his 'eeeeeeh' grew louder. When she bent down to catch him in her arms, he shrieked and arched his back rigidly, making it difficult to gather him up, and as she lifted him, he struggled like a wild animal. He fought her, not with kicking legs like I'd seen most toddlers do, but with his torso and head. Michael was a big toddler, and strong. He wouldn't ride on his mother's hip, but squirmed about so that his back was towards her. He was furious, and began to beat his head backwards like a bludgeon. Auntie Joan carried him to the kitchen table, craning her neck to avoid being bashed in the face. He was deliberately trying to get her in the face! I got a sick feeling. I felt so mad at the kid I could've smacked him.

"Holy Mother of God," Joanie hissed, clearly disgusted. "Why in hell does he do this?" Auntie Joan looked at her daughter with such sorrowful disappointment that Joanie went silently back to her ironing. Annie looked pained and frightened. I hadn't noticed, but Maddy had left the kitchen.

"Eddie Murphy, can you please come down here and help our mother!" I heard Maddy call up the service staircase behind the back entry. The fancy staircase was down the hall by the front door.

"Careful," her mother called out as loud as she dared, "don't wake your grandmother."

Maddy always referred to her half-brother as "My older brother Eddie Murphy," with a touch of reserve that conveyed respect. "My older brother Eddie Murphy is gonna be a priest," she'd told me proudly. "Eddie Murphy doesn't smoke. He doesn't fight or swear, or do nothin' wrong. Ma says he's always been like that, 'cause his father told him-when he was dying-to be good and take care of his mother, so they'll meet in heaven. But he's real nice, and not a tattletale at all." At seventeen, Eddie was just over three years older than Joanie, who arrived barely nine months after the marriage. I was curious about

Eddie Murphy, and anxious to meet him. From the way Maddy spoke of him, I half expected him to have a halo.

Eddie Murphy bounded down the stairs and into the kitchen, moving with a light step and unusual grace, like a dancer. He paused, surprised to see a stranger. "This is my son, Eddie," Joan told me. "His father is in heaven," she explained casually, as if he were away on a business trip. "Eddie's father was such a good man that God had to take him home a little early," she divulged God's plan. "But we'll all be together in heaven...that's the promise of Christ our Lord." Joan finished with a sigh, looking up at the crucifix as if talking to a regular person in the room. I wasn't used to this level of daily spiritual involvement, and inadvertently followed her gaze, almost expecting Jesus to answer her. That was some crucifix! The cross alone must have been over two feet long, and the brass sculpture of Christ was big enough to appreciate all the details. I wondered how anyone could eat with Him suffering right over the kitchen table.

Eddie smiled sweetly at me before rushing to help his mother. "There now, little man, there now, your big brother Eddie is here," he crooned to the baby in a soft, resonant tenor. His voice was at once gentle and strong, just right for saying the mass, or absolving sins in the confessional. He lifted the heavy toddler as if he were light as a feather, and began to swing him in a high arc. "Wee, wee," he said. I'd never seen a teenaged boy act that way, so tender and fatherly already. Baby Michael stopped struggling and screeching. Eddie kept it up while his mother laid a towel on the table, and fetched the diaper. He laid him down quickly and held him, trying to distract him while his mother pulled off the pajamas. As soon as he was put down, Baby Michael began to bang the back of his head on the metal kitchen table with such force that I feared he might split his skull. The table rattled. No matter how Eddie tried to hold him and keep him from it, the poor tormented baby battled them both as if he were the victim of torture. The concern on everyone's faces was obvious now, so I took Annie by the hand and quietly asked if she would like to show me her dolls or something. She brightened, and led me out of the kitchen.

"Let's go to our room," she said. I could still hear the screaming and banging, but at least we didn't have to watch. Maddy followed us out, and the look on her face told me I shouldn't ask questions-not now anyway. We filed into the hallway.

The fifteen foot ceilings and large-paned, wood-framed windows made the rambling Victorian house nearly impossible to heat. It probably didn't have insulation. The kitchen had been warm, but I felt the temperature drop as soon as we went into the hallway. The house had been built with a fireplace in most of the rooms, and a central steam-heat furnace had been installed later. By now, most of the fireplaces had been boarded over. A permanent chill set in each fall, and lasted until summer was firmly established.

There seemed to be endless rooms. There was a little parlor by the front door. No one came through that way on account of the front piazza was falling off, but you could also get to it through a narrow side-hall. The floors were a beautiful dark-stained oak, with matching woodwork, although the finish down the middle of the main hallway was long worn away, and the floorboards deeply scuffed from generations of Harahans and Malones. I peeked into doorways as we passed the various rooms. One was filled with a large, overstuffed sofa and matching wing chairs that looked nearly as old as the house. Marble topped tables were covered with framed family portraits and china nick-knacks, while a porcelain statue of the Virgin Mary graced an ornate mantle-piece. There was a very old-looking black and white portrait of a bride and groom in a silver frame. It hung beside the mantel, and a small crucifix hung next to that. I knew by the style of the wedding gown that it must have been the elder Mr. and Mrs. Malone. She had a round face, and seemed so young that she looked more like a child playing dress-up than a bride. I couldn't make out the rest of the pictures from the hallway, and stuck my head in a bit. I was curious, though I would never walk in uninvited. The room smelled musty and unused, like a museum.

"That's Gramma's best parlor," Annie warned in an awed whisper. "We can't never play in there." It opened at the back through glass doors, into a formal dining room. I could make out a glass-front cabinet holding the china. There was even a crystal chandelier over the polished dining room table. I realized that the swinging doors we had first passed must have led from the kitchen straight to the dining-room, for service.

"My mother would love this stuff!" I whispered. Maddy looked as if she were going to say something, but changed her mind.

"Shhh," Annie placed a little finger over her lips, pointing to a closed door beyond the fancy front staircase. She mouthed the words, "Gramma's bedroom." We ascended the old mahogany staircase on tiptoe. A few of the stairs creaked so loudly they seemed almost alive. One squeaked out two distinct high-pitched notes and I froze, placing my hand over my mouth so as not to giggle. Maddy smirked and pointed to the places on the stair treads where it was safe to step without making a sound. I ran my hand over the smooth, curved banister along the way.

"Do you ever slide down it?" I whispered.

"Sometimes," Maddy said softly, and Annie giggled with her hand over her mouth.

Upstairs it was even colder, which was typical. There were five bedrooms on the second floor, not counting the three tiny rooms in the third half-story. Five bedrooms, but only one bathroom in the whole house! It was a huge, old fashioned bathroom, big enough to hold a chair and a small chest of drawers. The window was frosted glass that you couldn't see through, for privacy. It was tiled from the floor to the ceiling, all black and white, with the original white porcelain sink and claw foot tub, both stained dull red with iron. Our modern cape-style house had only two bedrooms, but we had two bathrooms, one tub, and one with a shower stall. I guess I was a bit spoiled, but I had to wonder how they all managed with only one toilet.

In the upstairs hallway there were more recent, framed portraits of the family. There were separate pictures of Maddy, Tommy, and Joanie, each at about age six, wearing their first communion outfits and posing with folded hands. We had all made Holy Communion in the first grade. Joanie looked truly moved, while Maddy looked as though she had her doubts about the whole thing. The striking thing about Tommy's communion picture was that he looked exactly the same, only smaller. The same flat, puffy face and dull eyes showed neither religious devotion nor spiritual doubt. He looked as if he had no idea what he was supposed to be doing in that little white suit.

"Hey, how do you get up to the tower?" I asked excitedly. I'd always wanted to see what was up there; everybody did.

"You don't," she answered.

"Aw, why not?" I was disappointed.

"It's not allowed. Behind there," she pointed to a closed door at the end of the hall, "is another staircase that goes to three small bedrooms on the third half-story. It's locked, but I got to go up there once with Dad and look around. The rooms are full of old stuff! You can only get to the tower from there, and that door's locked; only Gramma has the key. I ain't never been up there, and Dad told us not to ask, or even talk about it around Gramma. So there's that." She shrugged. That's when I noticed that every door in the place had a crystal doorknob in a brass fitting, with a keyhole designed for a skeleton key.

"This is our room!" Annie announced, pulling me into a bedroom that looked like the bottom of a laundry-shoot. Except for the mess, it was beautiful. The walls were papered with patterns of delicate flowery vines, all pink and yellow. It was faded, but still charming. There were two matching four-poster beds-unmade-and two identical chests of drawers. A couple of the handles had come off. The furniture looked as though it must have once been very fine, and I knew this room had been lovingly outfitted for two little girls long ago. I wondered how old they were when they died, and the thought made me sad. I

51

imagined it must feel strange to sleep in their beds...could they have died in that very room? Now that, I thought, is definitely one of those 'not to be asked' questions.

The jumble of clothes and modern toys scattered throughout the old room chased away the ghosts of children long passed. There were half dressed Barbie dolls with their tiny wardrobe strewn about them. Standing next to the indisposed Barbies was a blind Mr. Potato Head, sporting a nose with a mustache and ears, but only two pin-holes where the eyes should have been. The closet door was left open, and lots of spring and summer weight clothes were still hanging out of boxes on the floor, as if the kids had torn into them searching for something to wear. Everything was left-in-the-middle, as though it had been interrupted by a fire drill. I was over the initial shock of 'Malone mess', but one thing caught my attention. There on the floor, in the small space between one of the beds and its matching dresser was a baby's potty seat-and it had pee in it. I tried to act as if I hadn't noticed, but Maddy didn't miss a thing. When Annie went over to the closet and disappeared inside, Maddy collected the little plastic pot and left the room. I heard the toilet flush. When she returned, Annie was still rummaging around in the closet.

"She won't go to the bathroom at night 'cause she's afraid to go out of the room...swears she saw a ghost walking the hall once. I never seen a kid so terrified," Maddy dropped her voice to a low, rumbly whisper. "This place is kind of scary at night. I tell her the house is creaky 'cause it's old, 's all...some nights I hear it too, especially when it storms. I had to do somethin' about the bed-wettin," she said with a smirk, "'cause half the time she gets so scared she ends up in bed with me!" She chuckled softly over the dilemma of waking up to find your little sister had wet your bed. "I figure Annie'll outgrow it soon enough if we just let her have her way for now," she finished with a shrug. I nodded in agreement. I saw a different side of her, emptying that pee-pot. Here she was always praising her 'older brother Eddie Murphy,' and I had to wonder if anyone appreciated her quiet devotion to her young sister.

Annie seemed to have vanished into the recesses of that closet. At first you could hear her bumping around behind the wall, but then it went quiet. She finally reemerged carrying a faded polyester robe that was permanently creased from being folded. It was like the choir robes worn in church, only it was child-sized. "Look what I found in one of Tommy's boxes," she squealed with delight, waving it about. Maddy tried to affect a stern look, but I could see she found her sister's antics charming.

"You know you're not to go into Tommy's stuff; he'll have a holy fit if he finds out!"

"Why did Tommy have a dress?" Annie held the robe up questioningly.

"You silly goose! It's not a dress, it's an altar boy's robe," Maddy sniggered good-naturedly. "Now go put it back like you found it and don't say nothin' about it, OK?"

Annie grinned and disappeared into the closet, then popped her head back out and said, "Come Frances, come inside and see." I looked questioningly at Maddy.

"It's kind of cool," she said. "Go take a look."

The closet was a walk-in that went the length of one side of the house, and the back had storage space under the eaves where the roof-line sloped. It was freezing in the winter, and would be boiling hot in summer. The narrow space was so jammed with stuff it was hard to get through without stumbling over things. I made out an iron Christmas-tree stand, a couple of fancy, old-fashioned party dresses that had hung a long time on the rack, winter hats and assorted mismatched mittens. There were some toys, or what was left of them; board-game pieces scattered on the floor, some legs and antennae for the *Cootie Bugs* game, and a forlorn looking plastic baby doll that'd lost one arm. Annie got down on her hands and knees and moved aside some boxes.

"Look here," she said, pointing to a little square door near the floor at the back, by the short side of the closet. I crawled over; brrr...like crawling into a meat locker. She slid the door aside, and I could see it went into the closet in the next bedroom. "That's Tommy's room. You can't tell him! He doesn't know, and it's a secret for us girls," she confided. "And it goes right through to Eddie's room at the front corner of the house. You can even get through to the linen closet in the bathroom. It's like a fort in here."

"Wow...this is cool. Now you better put that back and close the door so nobody finds out," I whispered. I'd never been part of a sisterly conspiracy before. We turned and crawled until I could stand. When I emerged, I was assaulted by a blast of cold outdoor air and the smell of tobacco. Maddy was at the window seat, holding a cigarette out the window that was open just enough to accommodate her skinny wrist. She ducked her head down and exhaled outside, but the wind was blowing the wrong way.

"You can still smell it," I warned. Wordlessly, she stuck her arm farther out, and held it up higher. I don't think it helped much, but I didn't say anything. Since she was occupied, I turned to Annie and asked, "Would you like me to help you unpack? We could organize your clothes and toys so you can find them better. It'll be like playing house." An elfish smile spread over her face and she popped up and down on her toes with a look of delight that I took for a 'yes'.

"OK?" I asked Maddy

"Sure. Sounds like lots of fun. I'll watch," she said sarcastically.

Annie and I spent the rest of the afternoon sorting, folding, and organizing. She put on one of the dresses and pretended to be a grownup keeping house. She discovered the arm to the baby doll that had been lying naked on the closet floor, and brought it over to me. "Can you fix her Fran?" She was suddenly concerned for the neglected toy. I popped the stiff plastic arm back into its socket. Annie found some doll clothes, and began to dress it on her bed. "Be quiet baby, be quiet or you'll have to go away," she scolded the doll. Just as abruptly, she lost all interest in her imaginative play and crawled back into the closet to see what else she could find.

The short winter day was all but gone. It was past four o'clock, that time just before you realize that you've been straining to see in the dim light for the last half-hour. Suddenly the lights snapped on with a loud click, and Mr. Malone was standing with his bulk filling the doorframe. "Mad'lin! What are you kids doin' in the dark?" he growled. My heart leapt to my throat.

"Nothin'," Maddy answered casually, unconcerned. She had seen him drive up, and finished her last smoke before shutting the window. Annie looked scared again. "This is Frances," she added.

"Evelyn's girl?" He raised one eyebrow, mildly interested.

"Yup. This is my dad," she said to me.

I jumped up from the floor. "Pleased to meet you, Mr. Malone."

"Ah, likewise," he said awkwardly. He scowled at Maddy. "Why can't you learn some manners like that?"

"Who'd I learn 'em from, you?" she shot back.

Mr. Malone smiled in a way that twisted one corner of his mouth and showed his big yellow teeth. It stretched the thin, almost vertical white scar on his chin and made his upper lip all but disappear. You could see the family resemblance, but there was no warmth in the smile; it skated on the edge of menacing. His face made me want to look away, and at the same time watch it vigilantly, like when you meet a large stray dog in the street, and you're not sure if he's going to wag his tail and go along, or suddenly tear your arm off.

"You're a devil," Mr. Malone grumbled, before turning and disappearing down the hallway.

A few seconds after he had gone down the stairs I blurted out, "I need to go home now. I mean, Mom must have dinner ready and I gotta go set the table. Goodbye Annie. I like your room, and your dolls, and your secret closet-fort. We'll play again soon."

"Remember," Annie said seriously, lowering her voice, "don't tell anyone about..." She pointed towards the closet with one finger and placed the other over her lips: "Shhh."

"Don't worry. It's a secret for just us girls." I winked.

"I'll walk you out," Annie said. She took my hand gently and led me down the hall as if I were a small child and might get lost. It was comforting after the surprise encounter with their father. We tiptoed downstairs.

In contrast to baby Michael's screaming earlier in the afternoon, it was eerily quiet. I had to pass by the kitchen to go out the back door. Joanie and her grandmother were preparing for supper, and Joanie was setting the table. Gramma Malone looked larger than I remembered from the funeral parlor. I only saw her from the back, clad in a bleached white apron that wrapped fully around and tied with a crisp bow. She was tending an enormous pot at full boil on the stove. It took up two burners and looked like it must have held about ten gallons. I smelled ham and cabbage that filled the room with thick greasy steam. The diapers were gone. Baby Michael must have been asleep at last, and Auntie Joan must have been resting too. Only Mr. Malone sat at the kitchen table smoking, with a Saturday paper opened in front of him. He wore battered leather slippers and a well-worn flannel shirt. Over the ham and tobacco was the strong smell of a man who had worked hard all day. It was acrid, and somehow different from the way my father smelled after work. Whiskey, I realized. Not just the glass in front of him, but his breath, his clothes, his very skin. I shuddered in disgust, and secretly agreed with my mother. He was a scary man.

At the sight of their grandmother in her apron, I wasn't sure what I should do. She'd only seen me in passing at Nana's wake, but we still hadn't exactly been introduced. Old Mrs. Malone seemed pretty scary too as she labored over the steaming pot like a witch at her cauldron. I nodded politely and said goodnight as I left, and was relieved when no one took notice.

Maddy grabbed the pea coat off one of the pegs in the back entryway and followed me out. "It's gone dark," she said, "I'll see you 'round the corner."

"Thanks," I said. I had so many questions I wanted to ask that they tumbled over one another in my head and got stuck, like a crowd trying to rush out the door all at once. We walked in silence. At the corner, within sight of my back door, she stopped.

"Go on." She jerked her head towards my house. "I'll watch."

"Thank you for a lovely afternoon." As soon as it came out I knew I'd been too formal. It was the first time I'd visited anyone in such long time that my mother's lessons in manners just sort of kicked in. She studied me a moment to see if I was serious, then laughed through her nose a bit, but not unkindly.

"You really are something else, Frances. See ya," she said.

Our outdoor light was on, and I knew my mother was waiting inside. Everything would be clean. It would smell of fresh-cooked food, probably an oven roast, and Jubilee kitchen wax. Dad would come home soon and I'd be glad to see him. After dinner, we would all sit a bit around the TV and talk. Then I'd go to bed in crisp sheets, in a neat, orderly room with all of my clothes washed and ironed and put away; but I would go to bed alone. I thought of Annie taking my hand, and the trusting look on her face when she showed me her secret closet.

That night as I tried to sleep, all the people I'd met and the many scenes of the day played round in my head, but my thoughts kept circling back to Eddie Murphy...ah...what a fine priest he would make! There was a gentleness about his blue-gray eyes that made him look so like his mother. His smile melted your heart, but looking back, it was his voice that made me fall in love. I found myself plunged into a fantasy, on my knees in the darkness making my confession to Father Eddie in religious rapture. I completely missed the significance of my accelerated heartbeat and the flush of warm giddiness that spread throughout my body.

***

On our walk to school the following Wednesday morning, Maddy casually mentioned that her birthday was coming up in two days, on February 28th. I stopped in my tracks.

"You're going to turn twelve in two days? Wow!" My birthday was August third, and I usually started counting the days in July.

"Yeah," Maddy shrugged. "Ma's gonna make a cake and...uh...you could come over Friday night if you want."

"'Course I will! What do you want for your birthday?"

"You don't have to bring nothin'," she said without looking at me.

"Won't the other guests bring birthday presents?" I was confused.

"It's just my family."

For the next forty-eight waking hours I thought about Maddy's birthday party. I just couldn't understand how she could be so nonchalant about turning twelve; twelve was almost thirteen, and thirteen seemed very grown-up. But Mom wasn't surprised that I got such short notice. "Auntie Joan is so exhausted with that baby-she doesn't know if she's on foot or on horseback," Mom explained. "Don't expect...well...your Auntie Joan won't have the time to do things the way you're used to."

When Mom drove me to a department store to pick out a gift, I was completely kerflommoxed. Aside from smoking, I wasn't sure what Maddy enjoyed. I liked books, but she only seemed to read what we had to for school. I secretly loved playing with my Barbies...I even got a new one last Christmas, but that was out of the question; I never even mentioned my Barbies to Maddy. I saw what happened to board games at her house, so I didn't think it would be a good idea to add more pieces to the closet floor. I liked to get new clothes too, but knew she couldn't care less what she wore. So what would make her happy on her birthday? I certainly couldn't buy her a pack of cigarettes. Then I remembered that Maddy admired the radio in my room; she didn't have her own radio, and wasn't allowed to touch the one in their parlor. I saw a battery operated transistor radio that would be just perfect, but Mom said it was much too expensive. In the end I picked out a funny little naked troll with shocking pink hair that stuck straight up. They were all the rage. Mom insisted on a sturdy sweater and a pair of matching tights to go with the troll. Girls always wore dresses to school, and Mom was still concerned about Maddy's bare knees in the cold. I tried to argue about the tights, but she wouldn't listen.

Friday night after supper I put on a dress. I'd been wearing play clothes all afternoon, but this was a birthday party and called for a dress. Mom warned me to pick a plain one so I wouldn't show-up the birthday girl, which was very considerate of her. She put the sweater and the tights in a box with pink tissue paper. I wanted to wrap the troll separately, but Mom said it might seem awkward if I came with two gifts. I suggested that she designate the clothes as a gift from her, and let me have sole ownership of the troll. I really didn't want to be associated with those tights. Mom let me have my way, and I walked around the corner balancing a large, giftwrapped box with a ribbon, and the smaller box with the troll resting on top. The paper was shiny, and he almost slipped off a couple of times, but we made it.

When I knocked at the back door, Maddy came to open it right away; she must have been watching for me. "Happy Birthday!" I said. She stared at the boxes a moment; my mother really went over the top with her giftwrapping.

"Holy crap! You didn't have to..." Maddy began as I came into the dark smelly entryway.

"It's not much," I insisted. "My mother sent the big one. The little one is from me." I proffered the boxes. Maddy took them carefully and I could see she was more excited than she let on. I thought of the dull sweater and cringed at the thought of the tights. I hoped she like the troll, but I really wished that Mom hadn't been such a cheapskate about the little radio.

My mother had tried to warn me that things wouldn't be the way I was used to. I'm not sure what I expected to find in the kitchen, but any signs of celebration were conspicuous by their absence-no balloons, no paper hats, no streamers or party napkins. Someone had cleaned the place up a bit more, and Auntie Joan had baked a Betty Crocker chocolate cake with chocolate frosting, but no one had thought to get ice cream. The cake was kind of flat, and sat in the middle of the big kitchen table-the one where they changed Baby Michael's diapers-looking rather like an oversized mud pie with twelve candles stuck in it. It looked sad; even the Jesus on the kitchen wall seemed to agree as he gazed down upon it. When Maddy laid the lovely giftwrapped boxes on the table by the cake, it somehow looked a little sadder.

After we sang Happy Birthday, Tommy came in with a half-gallon of vanilla ice cream and silently dropped it on the table. He must have slipped out and gone to the corner store on his bike, and no one even noticed he was absent until he came back. Maddy started a round of applause, and he actually blushed. Her dad pulled a grimy five dollar bill from his wallet and unceremoniously handed it to her. She grunted acknowledgement and stuffed it into the pocket of her blue jeans-even in a plain dress, I had inadvertently outshone the birthday girl. Joanie gave her a key-ring with a yellow enamel smiley face on a chain; the smiley face was even trendier than the trolls, but I don't think it could have cost more than seventy-five cents. I don't think Maddy even had any keys-they just left the house unlocked. Annie presented a big card she had made, with a crayon drawing of herself hugging her sister Mad'lin.

Auntie Joan had been especially quiet, and I thought she looked more tired than usual. She pulled a tiny box from her apron pocket and explained the gift was from both herself and Gramma-she was upstairs with the baby. When Maddy unwrapped the little nickel plated cross on a chain, I could tell she wasn't exactly thrilled, even though she tried to pretend otherwise. She held it up carefully for all to see, and then went and gave her mother a hug and a kiss on the cheek in a rare display of public affection. As if that weren't uncomfortable enough for Maddy, Auntie Joan insisted on making her wear it. Maddy patiently allowed her mother to fasten it around her neck, and I made a show of admiring the unremarkable gift with all the smiles and social graces Mom had instilled.

Eddie Murphy was away at a church function. I was secretly very disappointed, as I loved any excuse to be in the same room with him. He'd sent a grown-up card through the mail on purpose so Maddy had a real stamped envelope to open. It had a religious theme, and began, *To my Dear Sister on Her*

Special Day. Inside there was a poem about how God created sisters as a special gift for brothers. Auntie Joan asked her to read it aloud, but Maddy suddenly grew bashful and handed it to me. As I read, I got choked up on the overly sentimental lines, and just managed to finish with tears in my eyes. "I can't help it," I sniffed. Then I laughed at myself.

Since the family was finished giving their gifts, I pointed to the box with the troll. "Open the little one first," I said, "it's from me; my mom sent the big one." As Maddy tore off the giftwrap I suddenly had the most awful thought: was a troll anything like a doll? Kids of all ages were collecting them. You didn't exactly play with them like you would a doll, but what would Maddy think? I could tell from the first look on her face that the gift was a complete surprise. Then she held it aloft by its shock of pink hair and began to laugh.

Annie studied it a moment and asked seriously, "Is it a boy or a girl?" It was funny because the trolls all had the same round plastic eyes and the same innocent smile-the only difference was in the wild-colored hair; but they had no secondary sex characteristics at all, only little bare buttocks. Everyone had a chuckle over it-even Tommy sniggered.

"It's got pink hair, so it must be a girl," Maddy informed her.
"What are you going to name her?" Annie wanted to know. Maddy didn't have to think long. She looked at me with that mischievous half-grin. "I'll call her Frances; she looks just like you!"

6

In the month of March, the New England climate begins its crazy contra dance between winter and spring. Spring rarely just arrives, but rather whirls round from one season to the other and back so many times you lose track. Some years a proper spring never comes at all, and a cool, rainy June might suddenly explode into a sweltering Fourth of July with no time to catch your breath. Throughout March and even into April, one day you might wake up to a blanket of snow, only to have it melt the next day and reveal purple crocuses. It was the time of year when you start to bring out your spring clothes and try them on to see if you'd outgrown them all, so you didn't get caught with nothing to wear if the temperature suddenly shot up to 70 degrees. Still, you didn't put the winter clothes-coats, scarves, and even mittens- in moth balls until after Easter, as it might suddenly drop below freezing.

When my mother told me it was time to sort through the clothes, it signaled that the weather would eventually have to obey the calendar, settle down and stay reasonably warm for at least a few months. Soon we would go Easter shopping, and I would get a whole new outfit-a dress and shoes, complete with a little spring pocketbook and a white straw hat with a ribbon to wear to church. I'd even get a new Sunday dress-coat if I'd outgrown last-years.
We began the yearly ritual by putting aside the winter clothes I had outgrown last season. Next we would take down the boxes marked 'Frances-spring clothes' from the storage closet shelf, and iron whatever still fit so it would be ready for the first warm day. But this time Mom asked me to help with something extra. She opened the pull-down hatch to the attic and ascended the folding steps. "Careful," I said, standing behind her as she maneuvered a large cardboard box through the square opening over her head. She handed it down to me, and I left to put it in my bedroom.

"Comeback, we're not done," she said. She handed down three more in all. I set them out on the floor. They were labeled: Frances, 1960-63; Frances, 1964-65; Frances, 1965-1967; Frances-Special.

"What is all this?" I'm not sure why, but I had an uneasy feeling.

"Well...ah..." She seemed to have the same uneasy feeling. "I saved all your best clothes, ever since you were a baby. You know how much I loved to dress you."

"Who were you saving them for?"

"I thought you might like a few things for your own children someday. Your Christening gown is in that one." She pointed to the 'Special' box. I had a feeling there was more to this.

"I wasn't sure...I thought that maybe...well, I might have had another child," she blurted out. "You never know, after all. It does happen."

I was surprised at first that she'd considered adopting another child-then I realized what she meant. Even after my arrival, for years afterward, she had still hoped. The beautiful clothes had been waiting, tangible evidence that there might still be a miracle.

"After I saw little Annie going to school with only a couple of dresses to wear...and a coat that looked as though it'd been passed down all the way from Joanie, I got to thinking about these clothes. It's just a shame to waste them all. By the time you have children in school, they probably won't be in style anymore."

"No, they probably won't," I agreed.

We opened the boxes from 1964-1967 in reverse chronological order; Frances-1960-1963 would be too small. The dresses were mostly fancy party-type or Sunday best, but some were sturdy school dresses. There were snowsuits, little mittens, and two woolen Sunday dress coats with velvet collars, one clearly already too small. A third had a fake rabbit-fur collar, fur trimmed hat, and a matching muff with fur inside and out. I slipped my fingers into the little muff, pressed the soft fur to my face and sniffed myself back in time.

"Do little girls still use muffs?" I asked.

"I think so," she answered. "You wore this in Kindergarten; it's probably too small."

"Mmm..." I held it up. "She's a lot smaller than I was. It may still fit her by next Christmas."

"We'll put it aside for now," Mom said.

There was a navy-blue, spring-weight coat, and a tam style navy hat with a wide, white band. The coat had bright, brass-tone double-breasted buttons. I remember loving that coat because it looked so grown up. "This is just her size now," I remarked, "in time for Easter next month. And this dress too!" I picked up the dress I'd worn that same year. It was a drop-waist, white up top with a pleated navy skirt. Lying at the bottom of the box was a deep pink-plaid, Macintosh style raincoat, next to a miniature child's umbrella-pink with ruffles. I remembered my pink phase, and wondered what Annie's favorite color was. Everything was a bit crumpled, but it was all clean, almost like new. We opened the box marked *Special* last. It was mostly baby clothes, and the Christening gown was in blue plastic from the drycleaners.

"What do you think?" Mom had taken out a plastic clothing bag and unzipped it. It was my first communion dress. I had been so proud of that dress.

"Ooh, look at the veil," I said, shaking it out gently. I remembered the events surrounding the dress; shopping, trying several on, and finally selecting this special dress with the matching veil. Then I had modeled it for Dad when we got home. When the big day came, no matter how much the nuns had tried to prepare me for the Holy Eucharist, the only thought on my mind had been that dress. I remember feeling like a bride, secretly pretending it was my wedding day. I wondered if any six year old really understood or appreciated the mystery, or if I had just been the most vain, self-centered girl in Sunday school.

"It's up to you," Mom said wistfully. "And Joan, of course; she may want to use one of her older girl's dresses, or buy a new one herself. But first you decide."

I ran my fingers over the embroidered flowers, white on white, awakening my love affair with the dress; I almost wanted to put it on again. I tried to imagine my own little girl wearing it, but all I could see in my mind was Annie in the dress. I was pretty sure that if they wanted it, I would give it to her. Still, she wouldn't be making her first communion until spring of next year. "I'd like to think about it, if that's OK. It's still over a year away. Besides," I paused, thinking of a nice way to put it, "they're still working on organizing the closets; if we decide to give it to Annie, it would be better to save it for her here, for the time being."

Mom gave me a knowing look, and nodded in agreement while carefully zipping the layers of white chiffon and lace into its plastic case. "I'm going to air and iron up everything, and sort it by size and season for Joan," Mom planned out loud. "And I'll have to stop by Woolworth's for little girls' coat hangers-they won't have the right ones and I didn't save any. We'll bring it all over after church on Sunday. I'll call Joan and make sure it's alright to come by for a visit, but I won't say anything about the clothes for Annie. I don't want to embarrass Joan."

I assured her that I wouldn't mention it. At times like this I was amazed at how thoughtful and gracious my mother could be to others. It made me sad. Why did she go off in tirades against me? It wasn't as if she didn't know how to behave, or didn't have any goodness in her. I pushed the thought aside, and enjoyed looking at clothes together. She was always so proud of the way she'd dressed me, and I knew that the care she put into it was her way to show love.

7

"It's time you met your Great Aunt Hannah," Mom announced resolutely that evening, as if it was something that was going to happen sooner or later-might as well get it over with. Even though I had been going to school every day with Maddy and playing afterschool with the girls, I'd never been formally presented to the matriarch of the Malone clan.

"Yeah, Old Ma Malone; can't wait to see her again," Dad said sarcastically.

"Why do you say that, Dad?"

"That old battleax! Know what she said when your Ma introduced me? As soon as she thought I was out of earshot, she said, 'Oh Evelyn! An *Italian* boy?! Why couldn't you bring home a nice *Irish* boy?' He scowled in imitation, and affected a brisk, matronly falsetto with a bit of an Irish inflection. Even my mom giggled.

Although Dad wasn't too keen on his aunt-in-law, he liked the Malone kids. When I related the story of how they got kicked out of St. Clément's, Dad laughed so hard his belly shook. He asked me to repeat the part about Sister Ignatius putting out her habit. "Old Iggy!" he guffawed, with a robust slap to his thigh.

"Joseph!" Mom had reproached, "That's terrible! Think of how poor Joan must have felt."

Dad sat up straight, cleared his throat and assumed a grave expression. "Yes dear, it's very serious," he said, before busting out in another round of laughter, albeit with a sheepish grin. The more he tried, the harder it was to stop. He looked just like a kid trying not to laugh in school.

"Honestly," Mom said, "you're as bad as the kids."

I thought Dad would've about killed me if I behaved like Maddy, but he laughed at her exploits- the fighting, smoking, and even the colorful language. When she happened to be around on a Saturday, he always made a point to engage her. Sometimes he'd say 'put-em up, Mad-Dog!' Then my dad would dance around a bit, pretending to box, or hold her wrist up like a referee: 'And the winner is, Mad-Dog Malone of the Fightin' Irish!' She played along, and the smile in her eyes seemed to last all afternoon.

The morning of our much anticipated Sunday visit to the Malones arrived, and I would be formally presented to my Great Aunt Hannah. I hadn't been inside the house much over the last several weeks, and then it was only to see if Maddy wanted to come out and play. We almost always played outdoors, and if we had to work on a school project, my house was the obvious choice for peace and quiet. The few times I did stop in to see Auntie Joan, their Gramma was always napping. Except for the glimpse of her backside through a curtain of steam, I hadn't seen her at all since my grandmother's wake.

Mom fussed so much you'd think Christmas was coming. I helped make her best carrot cake Saturday morning; I got to grate the carrots. The cake had to set before we frosted it with cream cheese frosting. I also licked the bowl and beaters clean, although Mom said it was a babyish thing for me to do, and thought I should have outgrown the pleasure by now. "Don't make a pig of yourself over there," she warned, "this is for them; just one small piece."

We had done our spring shopping, and I put on a new spring dress for the occasion- not my Easter dress, but new this season, and a new Sunday straw hat with a ribbon. The dress was peach-color, a strait, A-line, very chic and grown-up. Mom said it made me look slimmer. Best of all, I got to wear nylon stockings-they were a matching color peach, not the flesh-tone nylons like Mom wore, but nylons all the same. There would be no more ruffled ankle socks for me. Underneath my slip I wore one of my first training bras, which no one but Mom knew, of course. I felt very proud, and when Mom checked me over she gave a rare smile of approval.

After mass, we stopped home to get the cake; I also suggested that everybody use the bathroom. "They've only got the one," I reminded, "and all those people...and the door locks from the inside with a skeleton key, or else one of the kids is likely to walk in." I recalled the first time I used the Malone's solitary toilet. Annie walked right in, sat on a chair and talked away. I was accustomed to privacy, so I was pretty embarrassed, but I don't think she even noticed. The next time I needed to go, I asked how to lock the door. There was a rusty old skeleton key on a hook in the linen closet. It was a nuisance, and no one in the family used it. Joanie usually announced her intention to use the bathroom, along with the warning that if anyone bothered her they'd live to regret it. Once I managed to lock myself in, and had to jiggle and rattle the key for five minutes to get out.

"Thanks for the warning," Mom said as she ran to the upstairs bathroom. I used the down. Dad waited in the car, where the boxes of clothes for Annie were already loaded into the trunk. In order not to crush the freshly ironed things, Mom had used even more boxes, with layers of white tissue paper in-between.

"I'm a nervous wreck," Mom declared candidly when we pulled up to the front of the house. The drive around the corner had taken scarcely two minutes. "I haven't been in this house for almost twelve years, I think. I wanted to come by not long after-whatever happened, but I didn't dare. I didn't want to upset my mother."

"If we don't get out of the damned car we'll be here for another twelve years," Dad grumbled. "Let's just get this the hell over with. I'll get the trunk," he said, getting out of the car.

"I'll help," I went after him.

"Frances, be careful of your dress," Mom warned. "There might be dirt on the boxes. We'll send the boys out for them."

She was right. Even though the boxes were new, and the trunk vacuumed clean, I couldn't take any chances with a light peach dress. I stood there uselessly. "I'll get the cake," I offered.

"No. I'll carry it. You might drop it," she said briskly. Mom really was a nervous wreck. I shrugged and followed behind her. Dad brought up the rear. He had a box under one arm, and something I hadn't noticed before in the other hand-a small brown paper bag.

"Wait, we can't go the front way; the porch floor is bad," I warned. There were floorboards missing, and a couple of holes where someone's foot went right through before they gave up using it.

"I know," Mom answered. "We're going through the side porch, to the door by the little front parlor." She had to tread cautiously along the narrow, cobblestone walkway by the side of the house. It was uneven because some of the stones were pushed up by weeds, with moss growing in between. She had to balance the cake, and watch the ground so she didn't get her high heels sunk in the earth. I went ahead and knocked on the door of the glassed in porch-I finally had a role in this procession. It was called a three-season porch, because it was partly closed in with big glass windows. Since most of the panes were broken it was kind of a one or two season porch, depending on the weather we got that year. It was another of Maddy and Tommy's winter smoking hangouts-when their dad wasn't home. Otherwise, it was his private smoking hangout. The filthy old sofa and chair, along with a wooden cable spool for a table came from their former residence in the projects. "Well, I see they still decorate in early Morgan Memorial," Mom remarked in an undertone. "Just go into the porch-it'll be open, and knock on the inside door."

I held the first door for both of them, and then went to knock. I was already standing with my knuckles raised to wrap on it when it opened from the inside. Uncle Malone was standing in front of me, looking stiff and uncomfortable in his Sunday suit. He cleared his throat, and spoke over my head. "Ah...Evelyn...ah...you'll be wantin' to see your aunt, then." He stepped back and held the door to let us by. I turned to see Mom nod briskly to her cousin as she passed, holding the cake plate so tightly her knuckles were white. We filed through yet another odd little room with a single tall window topped with stained glass, before accessing the main hallway. Dad took the opportunity to slip the little bag into Uncle Malone's hand with a sly look. I knew it must be some sort of liqueur-it was always that way when he went to another man's house.

"Tommy-boy!" he said in a husky voice, patting him on the shoulder. I had long ago noticed than when men spoke to one another privately, their voices sounded deeper.

"Ah, thanks," said Uncle Malone in a rumbling whisper, "we'll have at that a bit later, eh Joe?" He winked. "What's all this?" He eyed the big box warily.

"Who knows?" Dad affected ignorance. "Somethin' Ev's brought for the kids. I'll put it down in here for now." He seemed glad to be rid of it. Dad hadn't been so sure that my used clothes would be appreciated. "Tom's a proud man," he'd said. "He might take it the wrong way."

"Nonsense," Mom had answered back. "Joan doesn't have the time to go shop for things, even if she did have the money-which she doesn't. She'll appreciate having these lovely clothes for Annie, and that's all I care about. To hell with what he thinks!"

We wound our way through that maze of a house to the front parlor, where the rest of the family was seated-except for Baby Michael, who must have been asleep by some miracle. They were all still dressed for church. Great Aunt Hannah sat in state, strait as a poker in the best wing chair. Even in her own home, she kept her suit jacket buttoned up to her chin. Her gray head was framed by the crocheted doilies draped over the back of the chair. In her crisp blue spring suit with the white lace collar, she reminded me of pictures I'd seen of Queen Elizabeth. Mom had explained why she had that pillar-like posture, even when seated. Ever since she was sixteen, her aunt had always worn an old-fashioned corset with stays-ribs that used to be made of whalebone, but were now plastic. She couldn't slouch even if she wanted to!

Everyone else stood up and came to great us; Tommy needed a discrete poke in the arm from Maddy before he caught on. I had been coached to call her Madeline for the day, at least as long as we were in front of the adults. For a few seconds that seemed to last much longer, we all stood looking at one another. I thought, *Holy crap, now what do we do?* Even Mom looked flustered; she gripped that cake plate so hard I thought it might snap in two.

"Evie, dear," Auntie Joan gushed as she stepped in front. She gently pried the plate from my mother's fingers. "Thank you so much! Joanie, be a good girl and put this on the sideboard in the dining room." As soon as Joanie relieved her of the cake, the hugs began in earnest. I exhaled. Auntie Joan began telling me how lovely I looked, while Mom admired Annie, Madeline and especially Joanie.

"What a lovely young lady you've become!" My mother's best social smile glowed like a beacon as Joanie set the cake out and got plates from the china cabinet.

From across the other side of the room I could hear Dad's voice carry over the chirping of the ladies' voices, even though he was speaking quietly. He had his arm around Tommy's shoulder in a firm clasp, and was speaking close to his ear. "Look at ya," he said with admiration, "you're almost big enough to go to work now. Whada ya wanna do for work when you get out of school?" Dad knew Tommy had stayed back twice, and he was concerned.

"Ah...dunno, really," Tommy shrugged.

"Well, as soon as we get done with the hen party, we'll go out and talk about it, okay?" He looked at Big Tommy, who shrugged like he didn't know what Dad had in mind, but didn't much care, so long as it got them out of the parlor and at the little bottle. Tommy nodded, smiling a bit but avoiding eye-contact.

Hens? I felt indignant; but my eves-dropping was interrupted by Mom's hands propelling me towards Aunt Hannah's 'throne', as Dad whispered humorously when he thought she wasn't listening. In her zeal, Mom herded me so close I almost fell into her aunt's lap, so close my dress brushed her knees, while she stood sheltered behind me. The stern looking matriarch pursed her lips and looked me up and down, as if inspecting the troops. Maddy stood clear of her line of vision and enjoyed my discomfort. It didn't faze me when she rolled her eyes, but when she drew herself up stiffly, pursed her lips in imitation and looked down her nose, I almost lost it. I managed to stick out my hand bravely, and began, "I'm very glad to meet you, ah..." I stopped with my mouth open. Mom said she had called her Auntie Hannah, about twelve years ago. What was I supposed to call her? Was it Great Aunt Hannah, or Aunt Malone, or what? It certainly wasn't hard-headed Hannah or Old Ma Malone, as Dad said in private. How is it we hadn't rehearsed this part?

"I'm your Great Aunt Hannah," she informed me. "Great Aunt Hannah Harahan-Malone!" she added deliberately. "Do you hear that everyone? Thanks to Frances, I get to be a Great Aunt. I like the sound of that!" She looked around the room, commanding attention.

"I'm pleased to meet you, Great Aunt Hannah," I recited hurriedly. Everybody started to snigger awkwardly while I stood there embarrassed, trying yet again to determine what I had said that was so funny. But Dad knew just what to do-he scurried over and leaned down to give her a big Italian smooch on the cheek.

"Aunt Hannah," he declared, "you've always been great in my book! Ha ha ha! How the hell 'av ya been?"

"Don't give me that!" She made a show of wiping the kiss away with the back of her hand. "You're a terrible liar and you know it, Joseph." She looked at him so seriously I thought she meant it. Then the sly old thing screwed up one corner of her mouth and smirked like a mischievous child. Everyone laughed again, this time at their banter instead of at me. Aunt Hannah reached out and squeezed my hand with a surprisingly strong grip and said, "Aunt Hannah is just fine, dear," and gave me a little wink. I decided I liked her. Then Mom bent down and kissed the air near her aunt's powdered cheek, saying something about how good it was to see her, and how big her grandchildren had grown.

They all began chatting at once. I had a moment to relax and think...Harahan? Was that her maiden name? My mother's maiden name had been Harahan. Then I was distracted by a more important concern-Auntie Joan and Joanie had brought in tea and sliced the cake. They were all lining up over at the sideboard, and I wanted at least one big piece. I loved this cake! Good thing Mom had warned me not to make a pig of myself. Eddie Murphy told his mother and mine to sit, and then waited on them, while Joanie served her grandmother. I realized afterwards that he stayed by his mom's elbow the whole time, and never ventured near the corner Dad staked-out for the men.

"How's school?" Mom asked Eddie. "You're in your senior year, I hear, and going on to seminary?" She was smiling in earnest now. Everybody loved Eddie; you just couldn't help it.

Mom had remarked privately that if she'd had a son, she wouldn't have wished for him to go into the priesthood. "I'm too selfish," she'd said. "I'd want to have grandchildren, and I'd want him to make a fuss over me in my old age. Priests don't have much time for their own mothers. They're too busy looking after their flock. But becoming a priest," she'd emphasized, "is just perfect for Eddie Murphy."

"Your mother must be so proud of you," she added, looking at Auntie Joan. "And Joanie, you're going into high school next fall?"

"I'm already a freshman," she corrected.

"Oh, I see. Already?" Mom paid her special attention. "What do you want to do when you graduate? Three years will fly by fast, you know…"

The Queen Mother was sipping her tea audibly. She interrupted my mom pointedly, and her old voice crackled. "She should be going to St. Agnes's School for girls, and prepare for the sacrament of Catholic marriage and motherhood. Unless she's called to a vocation," she added, meaning the convent. I didn't really know Joanie, but the last place I'd imagine her is a convent.

Joanie's lips tightened into two thin, pale lines, and she turned to her mother. "Ma," she hissed, with her sharp eyes flashing.

"Now, Grandma," Auntie Joan said sweetly, you know Joanie doesn't want…"

"Humph," Aunt Hannah interrupted her, "in my day, children respected their elders."

"Well of course we respect you, Grandma; it's just that today the kids have to make up their own minds about some things."

"I can go to college too!" Joanie pouted.

"Oh, that'll be the day," Aunt Hannah scoffed. "College indeed! I watch the news. I know what those girls are up to in college." Joanie was still fuming when Aunt Hannah turned and asked, "Well Frances, I suppose you'll be wanting to go off to college too?"

"Ah…I…yes." I was caught by surprise at first. "I'm interested in animals and science, and…conservation," I explained. Conservation was all the rage in 1970, and a new concept to most ordinary people.

"Oh my…*conservation* is it?" I couldn't tell if she was mocking or interested, but decided to go on.

"Yes," I answered confidently. "I want to do some sort of research out in the field, like Jane Goodall. She studies wild chimpanzees in the jungles of Africa," I explained, hoping Aunt Hannah would take me seriously. Mom always laughed at me first before telling me she wasn't about to pay to send me to college. I had discovered Miss Jane on PBS, and it was love at first sight. She gave a generation of girls like me our first real hope that there might be something we could do besides becoming a teacher, a nurse, a housewife and mother, or a nun. Though I wanted to have a child someday, I still craved something more, and none of the other professions appealed. Besides, Jane

Goodall spoke in the most beautiful English I'd ever heard, and no one laughed at her for it.

"Is that so...research too?!" The old lady raised her bushy gray eyebrows. I wasn't sure if she was impressed, or about to laugh at me. I'd probably increased the party's vocabulary by two words in one conversation. "Humph. Happen you could take Madeline along with you. She'd do well out in the jungles."

"Sounds great to me!" Maddy chimed in heartily.

Dad started to laugh, a deep, belly laugh. "Ha, ha, ha!!! I'd like to see that! You two out in the jungle, swingin' from the trees with the monkeys!"

Everyone chuckled and seemed amused while I stood there hurt and deflated. This was the most important thing in the world to me, and my father had made a big joke out of it. There was a real struggle brewing between Mom and me about college, and all he did was laugh it off as if it were some childish phase. But I had to put off the fight for another day. The good natured laughter was contagious, and the image of us swinging from trees was pretty funny. Aunt Hannah held her teacup and slurped without so much as a tremor. Her face remained impassive, but I saw the telltale sparkle in her eye. That cunning old lady had said those things deliberately to make mischief!

The little party went on for another ten minutes with nothing remarkable. They fell easily into an old pattern, as if there hadn't been a twelve year hiatus since the last family gathering. I doubted Mom would ever know what set the sisters apart. It was one of those things you just weren't supposed to ask; it would have been bad manners.

When the men excused themselves to go smoke a cigar, Mom quietly asked Dad to get the other things out of the trunk. She turned to the ladies and said by way of explanation, as if it were hardly worth mentioning, "Frances brought a few little things she wanted to share with Annie." *Now that's polish,* I thought. Mom could finesse her way through anything.

"Well, that's all for us," Aunt Hannah abruptly interrupted the chatter. "I'll be going for my nap now." Eddie jumped up and went to help her from her chair. She took his arm, but I don't think she needed any help. Just before leaving the room she turned and said, "It's good to see you, Evelyn. And we'll be seeing you again soon, Frances. I want to hear more about those monkeys." She sounded sincerely interested now, and gave me a knowing look. I definitely saw her granddaughter in her.

"I'll look forward to it, Aunt Hannah," I said. I truly did want to get to know her better. I could see there was a lot more to this tough old lady than you might first think. Whatever happened with Nana was long past. I decided that Great Aunt Hannah Harahan Malone was alright by me.

8

In the early spring of that year, our school library acquired Jane Goodall's book, <u>My Friends, the Wild Chimpanzees</u>. The shiny new books were always displayed upright on a center library table. Then our librarian would introduce them by reading the book jacket or a page to pique our interest. Afterwards we'd all line up for a chance to select a new book. They put us in alphabetical order for everything, and with a name like Orillio the good stuff was usually gone before I got there, although it was a lot worse for Suzanne Zeolla. Since no one's last name began with N, Madeline Malone was always in line right in front of me, but she had a way of reaching around other kids and grabbing what she wanted, whether it was the last brownie on the holiday cookie tray or the coveted gold glitter on the art table. She never got caught and nobody told on her. I didn't get the chimpanzee book that day. All the girls wanted it, mostly because of the cute pictures of chimps on the cover. At least I had the good sense to put my name down first on the reserve list. When I finally got my hands on Jane Goodall's wild chimpanzees, I renewed it three times.

Not long afterwards, the school library got another new book unlike any other, one I just had to have. It sat behind more new books about John F. Kennedy; he was as popular as ever, and the books were snapped up fast. But I didn't want a book about Kennedy; I wanted the one with the picture of a black man's face on the shiny book cover. I had no idea who he was, or what the book could be about. For some reason, the librarian hadn't said a thing about that book, which made me want it even more. I felt it might hold the answers to some of my questions, like why all the black kids lived someplace across the river and played in their own parks, and why everyone in our school was white. Maybe I'd even find out why some people used the N word, while others disapproved. I certainly wasn't going to get answers at home.

As each child filed by the round table, the books disappeared, but my luck seemed to be holding out. Finally, I was going to learn why my father called me ignorant and bopped me off the head in the back seat of the car, when he was usually so patient. No one else seemed to share my curiosity, and the others passed it by without so much as picking it up for a closer look. "Hey Maddy, I want that!" I whispered urgently, pointing at the book. She slipped her long arm around and reached in front of two boys-they were at least six inches shorter-and whisked it off the table into my waiting hands.

"It's all yours," she said. One of the boys turned around and flashed an annoyed look, but he didn't tell.

The book turned out to be one of the scholastic series. Looking back, it was a rather dry biography of Martin Luther King, but for me it was a treasure-trove of information. I was introduced to the concept of segregation, and the meaning of the civil rights movement began to take some form in my mind. It had been impossible to grasp the latter without having at least an awareness of the former. The notion that there were actual laws in the southern states forbidding black people from going to school with white people, or drinking from a fountain if it wasn't marked *Colored*, was a complete shock. Why hadn't anyone told us? Our history books had a passing line or two about slavery-a little about rum and cotton fields and a lot of how the North won the civil war and President Lincoln freed the slaves. We got the distinct impression that slavery had been a very bad thing, and wondered how anyone could have thought otherwise. Yet it seemed like ancient history to us. There was no emotional connection, nothing to make it relevant. Now I had at least some understanding of all the marching and protests-things I'd overheard or briefly glimpsed in a Sunday paper left lying about. We'd never met anyone from the south, so I hadn't known that so many black people even lived in one place. I suddenly realized that I'd never even seen a book with pictures of black people. After I'd read and reread that book, I knew just enough about the outside world to taste my own ignorance, and it was bitter. Without any adult guidance, it was difficult to fully understand. It didn't explicitly teach me why anyone hated Dr. King so much that they wanted to kill him, and that's the very thing I wanted most to know.

We were getting ready to go to lunch, and I pretended I couldn't find my lunch money so I could hang back. I approached Miss Callaway's desk. Miss Callaway was a fairly new teacher. She was young and pretty, the first teacher we'd had who wasn't a stern middle-aged matron. Compared to the rest, she had modern ideas. She wore shorter dresses, and had her dark hair in a stylish flip. Somehow she managed to teach all day in attractive pumps with a little heel, not the orthopedic oxfords worn by our other teachers. We all liked Miss Callaway, mostly because she really seemed to like all of us.

"Miss Callaway...ah...do we have racial segregation here in Mapleton?"

"No; not in Mapleton, nor Massachusetts or New England," she answered in a matter of fact tone.

73

"Hmm…" I looked thoughtful and hoped she would elaborate; she didn't. "Why?"

"Well, the southern states had segregation laws because that's where the slavery was most prevalent," she explained it as if it were a rule of English grammar.

I was just dying to ask why there were no black kids in our schools, but something held me back. After my father's reaction, I think I was afraid of making Miss Callaway dislike me. Finally I blurted it out: "If there's no segregation, how come no black children go to our school?"

"Frances, you'd better go before you miss lunch…you'll have to ask your parents when you go home." She gathered her things and got up. I mumbled a thank you and went to lunch.

That same afternoon, I took the book home and left it out on the counter in plain sight. I was hoping to spark a conversation. I did.

"Where did you get that book?" Mom looked vexed and alarmed, as if she'd discovered me with contraband.

"The school library. I'm going to do a book report on Martin Luther King," I chirped bravely, acting as if it were no big deal.

"Did the teacher assign that book?" Her tone was tierce as she prepared to direct anger at the teacher.

"No. I picked it out from the new book collection."

"Oh. Well…why couldn't you do a book report on John F. Kennedy?"

"Everybody was doing a book report on Kennedy. I wanted to learn about Martin Luther King."

Mom was flustered. She was clearly unhappy with my choice, but for once in her life she was unclear as to what exactly she should say. After all, bringing home a school library book couldn't be categorized as misbehavior. I looked quizzically at Mom, without coming out and asking her to explain herself. "Well, ah, well then…" she blustered. "You just put that away somewhere; bring it back to school and read it there if you have to. But don't show it to your father! Honestly, Frances, where do you get these…" she searched for a word, "ideas?"

It sounded like a rhetorical question, and I decided it was time to quit while I was ahead. I'd stood my ground, and made it plain that I would not passively accept their opinions or echo their views without thinking first. I would read books they didn't like, and work out my own understanding of things.

9

When we flipped the calendar to May I could hardly believe it; school would be out the next month. Now that I had a friend the days somehow grew shorter, and our walk to school seemed to have shrunk by half. Not that we had far to go; Maddy complained that there was only a short space beyond the corner of Mulligan Street where she could light up and smoke the first one of the day, without being seen by my mother's prying eyes or the crossing guard in front of Edmunds Elementary. She got as much mileage as possible from it, but had nicotine fits beginning after lunch. By the end of the school day, she was wrecked. In the morning she was sometimes a bit edgy until we got around the corner, but on one particular day she seemed to barely contain her agitation. I knew something was up that went beyond her addiction. If you didn't know her well, you mightn't notice the difference; but I could see that her face was a little more pinched, her eyes a bit more strained from the effort of holding something back. She walked faster than usual, and I had to work to keep up.

"Tommy's really done it this time," she said after the first long drag.

"What did he do?"

"The fire drill yesterday," she spat out the words without slowing down or looking at me. "It wasn't no fire drill."

"He pulled the alarm?" I was concerned, but not shocked. That was a pretty serious offence, but he wouldn't have been the first boy to do it.

"It wasn't a false alarm either," she corrected. "Tommy lit a real fire in the janitor's closet. The janitor had it out before the firemen even got there, but still..."

"How do they know he did it?"

"Wasn't too hard to figure out. Tommy was out of class when it happened, and he managed to singe his pants. What a damned idiot!"

"Was he smoking in there? Did it happen by accident?"

"No, they could tell he lit it on purpose, in the waste can."

"Why did he do that?"

"When they asked him all he said was, 'I dunno'. Same thing at home, same blank stare-you know how Tommy is-he just stands there and says, 'I dunno.' It's the truth. Even he don't know why he pulls this crap most of the time."

"What are they going to do to him?"

"He's been charged with arson-got to appear in juvenile court. He's suspended for...I'm not sure how long. My parents have got to go to a meeting at school. Ma is sick to death over it. She looks like hell. Of course, Dad whaled the crap out of him-as if that's ever solved anything! That just makes 'im worse. Tommy's already mad, mad as hell all the time," she emphasized. She had been walking fast since my driveway, as if to outrun the problem. Now we had to stop or we'd be at school too soon. I wasn't supposed to stop on the way, but I did.

"My older brother Eddie Murphy," she said deliberately, "thinks it's because he has such a hard time with school. Tommy's always had trouble reading. Dad blames St. Clément's. 'All that good money I wasted on tuition for Catholic school, and you can't even read! What the hell's wrong with you? Are you feeble minded?!'" She affected her father's tirade. "It's really my dad's fault," she continued, lowering her voice while some kids walked around us. "When we started at Edmunds, they gave Tommy some tests. They told Ma and Dad he needed some special classes for reading-Tommy's already stayed back twice, in Kindergarten and third grade. Dad said no. Ma said that he needed extra help and he should have it-nothing wrong with that. Jeezes! Dad yelled his head off-said no son of his was goin' to some class for idiots. Tommy just has to buckle down, he says, and make an effort. He's not applying himself. 'I'll make him work harder', he says. No one knows this Frances, but I been doin' most of Tommy's homework-except for the math, since I caught up with him in the fourth grade," she finished in a whisper. "Tommy doesn't talk about his problem with reading, but God help any kid who teases him about it...or about staying back...or anything else."

Though she didn't come out and say it, I knew Maddy loved her brother, and if Tommy could love anybody at all, it was Maddy. He probably wouldn't tell her if they lived to be one hundred. All that day I found my thoughts drifting back to Tommy's problem, not only with reading but with that explosive anger; it seemed to be getting worse. I knew my father was right: Big Tommy was just like his son, and I suspected that the two shared more than a bad temper. An image of Mr. Malone sitting with his newspaper spread out on the table came to mind. Something nagged at me...what was it? I thought about how he seemed to stare at the front page, not like when my dad read the paper. Mr. Malone probably couldn't read any better than his son! How could he be so unfair?

On the way home that same afternoon I asked, "Couldn't Eddie explain it to your dad? He's real smart. Maybe he could convince him that Tommy needs special classes." Eddie Murphy went to St. Thomas's Academy, a Catholic school for boys, on a full scholarship. When he wasn't involved with school and church activities, he studied-unless he was helping his mom. He had definite plans to begin seminary after high school. Mom said Eddie was turning out just like his father-a saint of a man, she said. I assumed his step-father, Uncle Malone, must be very proud of him too. Maybe he'd listen to Eddie.

"Hell no!" Maddy replied in the tone reserved for dumb questions. I was embarrassed, and a bit hurt. I didn't bother to ask why my suggestion was so wrong, and we walked on a few minutes in silence. "Listen," her voice was toned down, "when Dad's made up his mind, there's not much anyone can do to change it. Not my mother, not even Gramma, and especially not Eddie Murphy. It's like this: Dad doesn't really...appreciate Eddie, the way you'd think. And now Eddie's almost a grown man, planning for the priesthood and college," she said with awe. "Well, it don't look like any of his kids," she added with eyebrows raised for emphasis, "will be goin' to college."

"Who says you won't go to college? It's a long way off-Annie's in Kindergarten for gosh sakes. And you get all As and Bs! You're the smartest girl in math I know. Besides, what's that got to do with anything?" I was really confused now.

"Girls don't go to college," she said resolutely. "Dad says it's a waste. He wouldn't have the money, and anyhow he wouldn't spend it on college for girls if he did. Besides, my dad says college is only for men who aren't fit to do real work. That's what he says about Eddie Murphy. The only time Eddie tried to give advice about Tommy-it was last winter, when he got kicked out of St. Clément's-Dad got in one of his tempers. He told Eddie to mind his own damned business if he wanted to live in his house and besides, he said 'It's not like you'll ever have any sons...if it weren't for the priesthood, I don't know what they'd do with a fruit like you!' He said it in front of Ma and made her cry."

"That's terrible," I said, not knowing what the insult actually meant. "Eddie's not a fruit. I think he's wonderful." I sighed as I pictured him again. She looked like she was about to say something, but changed her mind. "Your dad must really be jealous, because Eddie's so much smarter than he is," I said.

Maddy kind of screwed up her face, considering it. "We're all kind of jealous of Eddie Murphy. Ma loves him more than the rest of us kids, except maybe Annie; definitely more than my father." She turned to me with a smirk. "Can you blame her? Just look at us-the Malones are a big step down from the Murphys. And Eddie is protective of her. After all, she belonged to him first. But he's real good to us kids, so you can't get mad at him. He tells us girls he loves us all the time. Tommy won't take that stuff anymore...he's too big. Dad never tells us things like that; the Malone men just aren't made that way."

"Eddie is so lucky to have his real mother and brothers and sisters," I said. "I'll bet his real father would have been proud of him."

"Probably would've," she agreed.

"Whenever my mother hurts my feelings, I imagine my real mother wouldn't say such things-she'd understand me."

"Maybe, but my real dad sure doesn't understand us much. I think your dad's the greatest."

She was right. My adopted dad was a much better father to me than Tom Malone was to them. "Sometimes I think my mother picks on me because I'm not the girl she would have had, if she'd had her own child," I explained. "Mom's prettier than me. She's tall, and still has a nice figure; she always curls her hair. She picks on my hair and says I'm too fat, but mostly she's disappointed that I'm not popular. Mom likes parties and has lots of friends. She laughs at me for wanting to be a scientist and study animals, like Jane Goodall."

"Do you have to go to college for that?"

"I'm pretty sure you do. I think you have to study science or something. And you can tell by the way Jane Goodall talks...well, she sounds really smart. Mom says she's not spending all that money. No one sent her to college, but she still had a good job-before she adopted me. That's what she says all the time; she worked her way up as a secretary, but gave up a good job to stay home with me."

"What'd she adopt you for then?" Maddy sounded annoyed.

"That's what I finally asked her when I was about ten. I was tired of hearing about her perfect life before me. She just went off on one of her screaming sessions about what a selfish, ungrateful girl I was. She threatened to send me back to the orphanage."

"Ha!"

"It sounds funny now, but for a long time I believed her. She'd get mad about something and tell me, 'This is it! This time I'm calling the orphanage to come and get you.' Then she'd go to the phone, pick it up, and even start dialing! I'd put my arms around her and cry and beg her to stop, beg her for one last chance. Sometimes she started walking up the stairs to get my suitcase and pack my things. Usually Nana joined in-they'd kind of gang up on me. I've never told anyone, but I was almost nine years old before I finally realized they were full of crap! It dawned on me one time when Nana really overdid it. She told me how she, 'Knew a little girl who was adopted by a nice family, but she just didn't behave. So they had to send her back to the orphanage. She was just your age too...so sad.' I imitated Nana's melodramatic performance. "All my life, I'd been afraid of getting sent away, and here it was a big joke to them. I'd belonged to someone else once and they gave me away, so I figured it would be just as easy to get given away again." I paused, and then dared to add, "I never felt very attached to her, but I think that's when I really started to hate Nana. I feel so bad about it, but I'm glad she's…" I still couldn't say it.

"Dead?" Maddy asked. "Who wouldn't be! What did your dad say about all that?"

"Nothing. I never told him because I was afraid he might agree with my mother. He always backs her up or makes excuses, like, 'Mom gets the winter blues'…or it's because Nana's been so difficult-or was difficult anyway. Mom's been much better without her around…it's really OK now," I added, trying to wrap up the subject. I felt twinges of guilt I thought I'd buried along with Nana.

"No Frances, it's really not OK; it's fucked up," Maddy summed it up succinctly. "No matter how mad my father gets at us, no matter how much he punishes us, I never felt like I was going to get sent off. If someone had offered, I would've told them I might like it better at the orphanage." I imagined she would have.

We sat down on the curb before turning onto Mulligan Street, and Maddy whipped out a cigarette. I was supposed to go straight home, but we stopped from time to time when we had something very important to talk about. If my mother asked why I was late, I'd just tell her we stayed to wipe down the blackboards for Miss Callaway. So far, I hadn't been caught.

"My Ma," Maddy went on, "well, you know what she's like. I can't imagine us being without her. But my dad drinks too much, yells too much…he's way too…strict. He thinks he's right about everything and doesn't listen to no one. Sometimes I think life would be great if he'd just go away, just drive off in that yellow cab and never come back. Sometimes he's such a bastard I wish he'd drop dead," she said unapologetically. "Then I remember how he used to be more fun. Like…sometimes he'd drive us to Revere Beach and we'd go on the roller coaster. He'd watch me and Tommy ride, and maybe get us some cotton candy. That was before Michael came along. Anyway, if Dad dropped dead, I'd think of those things too. The tricky thing is: when your ma or dad or grandma hurts you, it hurts because you love them. Or tried to love them. Or maybe just wanted them to love you back. But even my dad never made me afraid he'd send me away. He don't even threaten to send Tommy away." She sniggered a bit, then looked at me with something close to sympathy. "There's a difference between being mean and hating someone so much you want them dead, and just wantin' someone to stop makin' you miserable. If the only way your Nana was gonna to stop tormentin' you was to drop dead, then it's her own damned

79

fault if you're glad she's gone. You can't spend the rest of your life feeling bad about it. And another thing: don't even give a thought about why you got adopted out. Listen to me Frances, it didn't have nothin' to do with you! Some poor girl got herself knocked up and couldn't take care of a baby. And if your mother doesn't appreciate…" the words seemed to catch in her throat, and she coughed and spat in the street. "If she don't know how lucky she is, she's an idiot. So don't give it another thought. If you do, it'll be like they can hurt you forever."

I can't say that I never gave it another thought, but Maddy's gritty philosophy loosened me from a stranglehold of guilt. When I rose from the curb I felt a bit taller, and walked home with a lighter step.

10

W^e were washing the Buick Electra. It was an enormous, 1969, four-door sedan, brushed metallic gold with a black vinyl roof and deep, soft, black leather seats. The model came out just last year, and it was the classiest car in the neighborhood. We were the first to have air-conditioning too. When my parents went to pick it out, Mom thought it was a bit too showy, and groaned, "It's as big as an ocean-liner-it's half the size of our house!" But it made Dad happy, so she relented. I felt proud of that car, and in spite of myself, a little smug. Throughout the winter and so long as the weather stayed cold, we drove our cars through the carwash every week. If you didn't, the salt they put on the road for snow and ice would eat holes in the body. In springtime we saved money by washing it ourselves, hosing it down in the driveway every Saturday afternoon so it looked extra good for church on Sunday. Dad had hauled the old canister vacuum out of the basement and attached a long extension cord so I could vacuum the interior. Then it was my job to crawl around, detailing the inside. I went over the seats with leather polish, and rubbed special cleaner on the dashboard and inside the doors. All the glass got Windex.

My cousins had come over with nothing to do, and now Maddy was helping me clean the inside of the car while Annie played with the garden hose instead of rinsing down the suds. Tommy was sort of hanging out, sitting nearby on the sidewalk curb alone, like some distant satellite in orbit. I'd told Dad all about the fire he lit in the janitor's closet, and my theory that Tommy's trouble with reading was behind it all. "That hothead!" he said. "I don't know what's the matter with those people! The Irish are over there now, shooting and bombing each other-they're all hotheads! Big Tommy isn't doing the kid any favor by keeping him from getting help. He ain't gonna learn a thing from his father's belt."

"Hey, Tommy!" Dad called over to him. Tommy looked up with something like mild surprise on his puffy face. The sunshine was beginning to bring out some color, and a peppering of freckles that made him look more like child, a child in an over-sized body. "Why don't ya come over here and help me with the hubcaps and white walls," Dad said. Tommy got up right away and ambled over with downcast eyes. He stood awkwardly beside Dad and studied the tires while my father explained the technique. "This here's the polish for the hubcaps. Ya got to really rub it in and clean all the dirt out of the grooves. And this here's the tire cleaner." He held forth the other jar of goop. "It'll take all the crap off the whitewalls, make 'em like new; but don't get any of this stuff on the rest of the car. Take the paint right off! You got to really rub hard, though. It's too tough for the girls," he said. "It'll spoil their fingernails. Do a good job, and there's two bucks for ya! OK?" Tommy nodded and a look of interest spread across his face. I think he would have done it for free. He got right to it, and was still at it long after we'd cleaned ourselves up and gone around to the backyard picnic table for snacks.

Mom brought out a brightly colored plastic party tray holding four dishes with warm, home-made brownies, each with a large scoop of vanilla ice cream on top. There was a bottle of root beer and four matching plastic glasses with straws.

"Wow!" exclaimed Annie, wide eyed.

"Thanks Aunt Evelyn," Maddy said appreciatively. It was a warm day, and we'd worked up an appetite-not that I need an excuse for desert.

"Where's Tommy?" Mom asked after a moment.

I jerked my head in the direction of the driveway. I had already taken a huge mouthful of ice cream and brownie, making sure the first bite had equal parts. "Mmmm," was all I could say.

Tommy had finished the wheels, and they looked as if the car had just rolled out of the showroom. Now he and Dad had their heads stuck under the hood, doing guy stuff. It never occurred to me that I ought to learn a thing about car maintenance, and I would live to regret it. Dad was pointing to the engine and whatnot, and explaining things to Tommy that made no sense to me. Then I realized Tommy was asking questions, almost like a real conversation. I don't know who was having more fun. Mom brought the extra desert back inside without saying a word.

That afternoon gave my father a great idea to help Tommy. He arranged to bring him to work while he was suspended from school. Uncle Malone gave his consent, but insisted that Tommy shouldn't get paid; he wanted it to be more like a punishment. Dad would leave early each morning and drive around the corner to pick him up. "It'll give him something to do while he's suspended," he said. "The kid can't just hang around by himself all day-that's asking for trouble."

For the next two weeks, my father worked patiently to transform Tommy from a juvenile delinquent into a hard working young man. It was a noble effort, but it would have taken a great deal more to solve his problems. No one could truly understand the source of Tommy's rage, least of all Tommy. It would be a long time, far too long before anyone knew, but he was struggling with a lot more than reading.

"On the first day he was on the sidewalk on time-but he's smokin'. So I tell him 'You're on time-that's good, but throw that butt away-no smokin' in the car,' and he drops it in the gutter without a fuss. He gets in the car, and I let him know right off that this is going to be work: no foolin' around, no smokin' on the job'. So he just nods, and doesn't say nothin' the whole way. The first thing I showed him was how to sweep off the platform at the terminal. Then I showed him how to use the hand-truck to move freight. Next I had him clean the windshields- they're up high, you gotta be careful. Whatever I show him, he does it straight away without complaining and takes right to it. I brought him on a few runs, and he works so fast the boxes are unloaded in no time. He didn't light up once that I saw unless it was after lunch break-I know he's a smoker, and it's hard to go all day. I told him, 'Hey, it's okay to enjoy a couple of cigarettes, but you don't need to chain-smoke. I seen guys that started at your age, and they can't climb into the cab without huffin' and puffin', and they're not even thirty-five yet.' I can't give him pocket money, but I take him over to the diner for a good lunch. Today we had chopped steak and onions; you should see that boy put it away! He's gonna be big one! Afterwards I say, 'Now if ya really gotta smoke, go out and have one.' This week, I had to do some work on an engine-I won't bother with the details, cause I know it don't make no sense to you girls, but he watched my every move, and handed me the tools I asked for. After a while he knew which ones I wanted before I asked. He's got aptitude. It's been almost two weeks, and I'm gonna miss the kid. I think he's gonna be alright now. He finally came out and asked me a question-he don't say two words most of the time, but he says, 'Uncle Joe, how do I get to be a truck driver?' I told him you got to stay in school, and go to vocational training for mechanics, diesel engine maintenance, and earn a c-class license. I talked to Big Tommy about it-says it's fine with him. The kid's comin' 'round." Dad smiled with satisfaction.

11

As school was winding down that June, my mother broached the subject of returning to her old job at the insurance agency next September, after I started seventh grade. Dad flipped, as the new expression went, and the tirade that followed was a rarity in our house.

"What do you need to go to work for? What do you need that I don't give you?"

"It's not that you don't give me enough Joe...I just want a job like I had before...just a little part-time job..."

"Your job is to take care of that kid!"

"But Frances is going into seventh grade...she's a big girl and she's gone all day long..."

"That's fine! So all day long you can do whatever you like, but when I come home from work, I expect you here, not working for minimum wage while some asshole makes money off you!"

"I'd be home on time...I'll make sure supper is ready." I heard my mother plead like a child.

"It's not about always gettin' my supper on time," Dad bellowed. "Ev," he said more calmly. "I wouldn't care if you was out with your girlfriends shopping...or havin' a cup of coffee once in a while. So long as there was some leftovers...but your place is here."

"Joe, you're a wonderful provider. But wouldn't it be nice to have just a little something extra...maybe take a nice vacation sometime..."

"That's what I'm tryin' to tell ya! If you go work, your little paycheck will be just enough to push me right into the next tax bracket. Know what you'll work for then? Nothin'!" Dad finished the last word with force and then fell silent.

I was hiding in the stairwell so I couldn't see their faces, but when my father spoke again he didn't sound angry. He sounded sad.

"I just don't understand it Ev...I give you every penny I make and let you decide how to run things. I don't get myself a thing without askin' ya...I don't even buy a car without askin' your opinion. What more could any woman want?" The words seemed to catch in his throat like a fishbone.

I felt sick inside as I crept to my room. It was the only time I ever heard my father raise his voice to my mother; it made me feel afraid, and somehow ashamed to be a girl. If Mom worked, would she really earn so little that it'd be like working for nothing? I didn't know for sure, but I was certain of two things: Mom was terribly unhappy just staying at home, and Dad would be even more unhappy if she didn't. I guess she hadn't realized that adopting me would sentence her to life under house arrest. Now at least I understood why she was so resentful when I talked about going to college. I couldn't even bring it up without setting her off. My father's insistence on keeping Mom at home just wasn't fair. It wasn't fair to either of us.

***

I'm looking for Jane Goodall. Shafts of light break through the dense forest canopy in mottled patterns, revealing shades of deep green that blur into murky shadows. At my feet, the bush is so dense I can hardly move. Tangles of vine grow everywhere, running seamlessly from forest floor to the treetops and back again. I can't break through; the damned plants seem to trip me up on purpose. One minute I was following along behind her, towards the distant hoots and cries of chimpanzees in the jungle. I couldn't keep up, and she grew smaller and smaller until she disappeared altogether. I stop and listen again.

"Frances!"

The voice is far away, as if calling me from a dream. I charge headlong into the brush, thrashing and tearing it aside with my hands. I stumble and nearly fall into a small open space filled with dense mist. It's like a room made of damp, moss covered tree trunks, impenetrable, curtained on all sides with thick hanks of vine, and lit from above by a harsh white light. There's something hanging overhead, but it's so dark and the mist is so thick I can't tell what. My eyes finally become accustomed to the fog and I can't believe what I see. It's a child! I can't make out the face, but it's a little girl, and she's not moving. I try to reach for her, but my arms hang uselessly. I try to call for help, but my voice is silent. Now I see other shapes...even more children...there must be hundreds! Their bodies hang helplessly, oddly contorted by bonds of ropelike vine, as if they'd become tangled while playing some dangerous game and then couldn't break free. I see boys and girls, but none of them climb or swing or move at all. I hoped it was a game, hoped that they'd suddenly awaken to laugh at the fright they'd given me. But now I can see their eyes are wide open, and still as death.

It is so quiet that the sudden sound of a match strike is as loud as thunder, so dark that the flame is like lighting. I can see her crouching close to

85

the ground in the center of the clearing, like a soldier on recognizance. One bony white hand is strangely illuminated by the lit end of a cigarette, and she blows smoke from both nostrils like a sleepy dragon. Somehow she can see me right through the fog.

"Look!" I am finally able to speak one word aloud as I point upwards.

Maddy just shrugged and gave me that 'we have a secret' wink I know so well. Wordlessly she tells me that yes, she sees them too, and places one finger silently over her lips. "Shhh."

"Frances?" I opened my eyes and looked about my room in the first gray light of predawn. I could still hear the howling.

"Mom?"

"I think you were having a bad dream, Frances." She came in and sat on the bed. "I heard you kind of moaning in your sleep-that kid will give us all nightmares. I couldn't sleep either; the noise woke me up and once I wake up I have to go to the bathroom...and it's so damned humid. I can't seem to get comfortable and go back to sleep. It's like a sauna bath already, and it's not even July," she complained.

The windows were wide open. June had suddenly turned very warm this year when a large humid air mass moved in from the coast and hung like a vast wet blanket. My sheets were pasted to my body with sweat. "What time is it?" I asked sleepily.

"It's almost 5:30."

My head began to clear, and I realized that the wild calls of the chimpanzees were really Baby Michael; his crying and carrying on broke into my dreams. We could still hear it from over the hill out back, and I shuddered to think what it must sound like over there. It wasn't the first time I'd heard the baby cry this season. It depended on which way the wind was blowing, or whether or not I was in a deep sleep. I'd been tossing and turning; my sheet was all twisted around and my summer nighty was bunched up...like tangled vines.

"Last night I watched that program on PBS, about Jane Goodall and the chimps," I explained. "I dreamed I was in the jungle, and I could hear the chimpanzees. When I woke up, it turned out to be the crying from over there." I remembered the dream clearly, and the vivid image of the children would haunt me for a long time. I couldn't tell Mom or anyone else, not even Maddy. It was much too scary; crazy scary. They'd think I was nuts. I was beginning to wonder about that myself.

"That's funny. Well, it's not funny-but you know what I mean." Mom sighed. "I'll shut the window. Try and go back to sleep."

"It'll be too hot," I whined. "I'll never go back to sleep."

"Just try," she said, wrestling with the double-hung wood-framed window, which was swollen and stuck in the humidity.

I rolled over and closed my eyes. Suddenly, there was a blinding bright light shining in my face. I opened my eyes again and saw that the full morning sun was up and beaming through the window by my bed. I looked at the clock; it was just after 8:30. I sat bolt upright. We'd overslept. I jumped up to tell Mom I'd be late for school, and instantly remembered that school ended a couple of days ago. I fell back in bed. What a night! It was summer vacation. I was done with Edmunds Elementary for good, but for the first time in my life I felt kind of sorry that school was out.

The last few months at school were the best ever. No one bothered me again for rest of that year. In fact, most of my former enemies treated me with a friendliness that took a bit of getting used to. All I did was show up with my cousin Maddy. She never said one word about it, but everyone talked about the big fight with the boys on her first day at Edmunds. I thought about all the years of bullying! My attempts to reason with those children had been worse than useless, but fighting was something they could grasp.

It finally made sense in the context of Jane Goodall's wild chimpanzees; they had a similar social order. Ever since first grade, Kathy Kelley had been the dominant female due to her advantage in size and strength, even though she was dumb as a box of rocks. Kathy was what my mother called an 'Irish washer-woman' in the making, and looked as though she were constructed for hard labor and lots of babies. She was followed closely by Dotty, who was smaller but more aggressive, and smarter, though not by much. The two of them used to have me chasing my tail, but when Maddy stepped in, both of them rolled over and greeted her with deference and a warm familiarity that made me kind of jealous. Maddy went right along with it. It turned out that she really wasn't a trouble maker at all, but more of a peacemaker. She had a way of talking with anybody that made them feel at ease, along with the muscle to take care of things if they didn't behave themselves. She was a natural alpha female, with a fair-mindedness that rubbed off. The whole group got along better with her around.

Some things changed and other things stayed the same. We still played jump-rope, and I still stunk at it. But now the girls that used to make fun of me offered tips and encouragement, even slowing down the rope to give me half a chance rather than tripping me on purpose so they could laugh about it. I'm not sure whether it was because of my new status as Maddy's cousin, or perhaps they were just growing up, but I think it was both. Sometimes at recess we'd run to the swings like before, but quickly lose interest. Then we'd look around confused for a bit, wondering why it just wasn't the same exhilarating fun it had been only last autumn. We gradually fell into a pattern of long gossip sessions, still punctuated here and there by outbursts of childhood that sparked impromptu games of tag. But mostly the girls just wanted to talk, and we had a lot more to talk about this year.

We were all excited and a bit scared of going to junior high school next fall. We weren't sure what to wear anymore either; for the first time, a few brave girls wore pants to school. When they did, Maddy jumped on that bandwagon and turned up in dungarees; she was promptly told they were inappropriate. The other girls wore dressy polyester pants with bell-bottoms. Maddy said she was going to save up and buy some appropriate pants and never have to wear a stupid dress again. We planned to take the bus into town and go shopping, which seemed like a very grown-up plan. I think only the promise of avoiding a skirt motivated her to go clothes shopping, something she had never cared about before. My mother said we'd wait and see what the girls wore next year in junior high, but for now I'd stick with dresses for school.

In the last warm weeks of sixth grade, there were far more interesting things to talk about on the playground than new clothing styles. We were all wrapped up our changing bodies, and discussed at length which girls were getting boobs and might be wearing a bra. Most of us fell into two categories: skinny girls like Maddy and Dotty were flat-chested beanpoles, and the chubby girls like me had rounded torsos that were thick in the middle, with fatty lumps on our chests that we covered with a training bra. Training bras didn't count as much as real bras, but girls who needed one felt a bit superior to those who didn't, and at the same time a bit self-conscious. If you wore a training bra, you had to watch out on the playground, because a boy might sneak up behind and snap your bra-strap.

Girls didn't reach puberty so early in life back then, and there was only one Italian girl named Angie who had actually developed. She looked like a little woman with a clearly defined bust-line and a waist, made more noticeable by her wide hips that swayed when she walked, just like a grown lady. She only had one close friend and they spoke together in Italian, so no one dared ask her personal questions. We were all fascinated, and a little envious of Angie.

One afternoon under the big Maple tree, Suzanne Zeolla finally raised the question on all our minds. "Do you think she got her period?" Suzanne was one of the daring wearers of bell-bottomed pants, and had risen in rank because of them. Our eyes went wide and we looked about nervously to make sure no one outside our group had overheard. We were awed and impressed at her ability to speak of menstruation with such confidence. Once she did, the other girls followed her lead.

"Of course she has. I can tell," Kathy Kelly quipped. I'd known Kathy Kelly since Kindergarten, and she readily provided her opinion on any subject whether she knew anything or not. She usually didn't, but this time she might know what she was talking about. After all, she was bigger than the rest of us. I wondered if she got her period, but no one would ever ask to her face. I tended to hang around the edges of these conversations, interested, but not wanting to make a fool of myself by displaying my naivety. I pretended to give the matter thoughtful consideration. Maddy never seemed to join in either, although I suspected that with an older sister like Joanie, she knew much more than the rest of us about the facts of life that we found so interesting. Maddy could probably have enlightened all of us, but she just looked off beyond the gossip as if she couldn't have cared less.

Each time we got together, the talk became more daring, venturing farther into the unknown. Finally Dotty Day dropped the bombshell. "I know how the egg gets with the sperm. My big sister told me." We looked at her with a curious admixture of amazement, incredulity, excited anticipation, and fear.

"Bet ya don't," Kathy shot back, although she seemed to doubt herself.

"Ya huh."

"Then tell us."

"I'm not supposed to tell."

"Ha! Told ya, she don't know!" Kathy and Dotty squabbled like an old married couple. Then Dotty paused, and looked at our faces with drama. Was she really about to spill it? I looked over at Maddy to gauge her opinion. She was within earshot, sitting sideways on one of those rocking playground animals that little kids used, a great hippo on a fat spring, but she seemed to be studying the distant horizon. The girls went silent, with all eyes on Dotty.

"Ya gotta promise not to tell...cross your heart and hope to die." Dotty made a big X across her flat chest and raised two fingers. We all followed in a solemn oath. Then she spoke in a hushed whisper. "Their two..." she paused, cast her eyes furtively downwards and pointed as inconspicuously as possible towards her crotch, "their two 'mm-mms' have to touch." There was an audible gasp.

"No way!" It slipped from my lips and as soon as it did, I felt like an idiot.

"Ya huh," Dotty affirmed, nodding smugly.

The group looked at me in embarrassment, but said nothing. I knew in my heart Dotty was telling the truth. Those forbidden parts down there that we weren't supposed to speak of, touch, or ever even look at, had to be involved. I hadn't the faintest idea what a grown man's mm-mm might look like; I'd never seen a penis, except for on a baby boy being diapered. The little book that came with my Kotex gift didn't even use the word penis; I don't think my mother ever spoke it aloud. Having one touch me down there was a horrible thought. Maybe I could become a nun...

After such a serious discussion shared in the utmost secrecy, our group became more cohesive. I wasn't an outsider anymore, but was firmly embedded in a middle rank. That's probably what set-off JoEllen. She was younger and less mature, and became jealous at being left out of the conversations. She still stuck up her nose and snubbed me, but I thought she was past the silly snipe and run game. Maybe it was jealousy, or maybe the spring air just got to her that day, but suddenly there she was, just like old times. She ran by as fast as a deer and gave me a sharp jab in the arm with her boney fingers as she shouted, "Franny bannany with the big fat fanny!" The only two girls who had remained her friends giggled childishly from a safe distance.

Maddy popped off her hippo perch and tore after her so fast she caught right up. JoEllen looked over her shoulder and shrieked in fear. I guess she wasn't expecting some scruffy kid just out of the projects to go after her-no one ever stuck up for me before. JoEllen ran faster. She was the fastest runner of all the girls, all long arms and legs, slender and exceptionally well-coordinated. Maddy matched her speed, seemingly without effort and began to reach out her hand as she ran, as if to grab her long blond ponytail. The gap between them was closing fast. JoEllen swerved and dodged like a gazelle trying to evade capture, but Maddy managed to jump around and get in front of her. She raised her arms, blocking her way like a basketball player.

"Help!" JoEllen screeched to her silly friends, who just stood there looking like they didn't care to get involved. "Tell the teacher!" she cried out pathetically, trying to twist and dash away once more.

"Tell her what?" Maddy panted in front of JoEllen; her eyes gleamed like a devil.

A grin spread across Kathy Kelly's shiny fat face. Then she laughed so hard her big belly shook, and she folded her arms over it to hold it in. The other girls squealed with laughter, most of it directed at Kathy. Even some of the boys who usually couldn't bother to look our way were watching the show with interest. Now JoEllen was running back towards us again, running fast with tears streaming down her red face. I could see she was scared to death, like she really believed this kid they called Mad-Dog was going to beat her up or something. I started not to like it anymore. I didn't want Maddy to do something dumb and get herself in trouble so close to the end of school, but I should have known she had more sense than that. It ended when JoEllen tripped right over the root of a tree and went down hard on her hands and knees. I'd never seen her fall, but I guess she was exhausted; she was also scared silly. Maddy just stopped short in front of her, grinning and breathing so hard she bent over and rested her hands on her knees. She coughed a bit.

"I'm telling," JoEllen began to sob, "Don't you dare touch me!"

"OK," Maddy said casually. "I won't touch you."

The laughing stopped suddenly, not because the girls felt sorry, but because our teacher had appeared out of nowhere. "What's going on girls? What are you up to Madeline?" she asked suspiciously.

"Nothin' Miss Callaway" Maddy said respectfully while straightening her posture. "We was just playin' tag. I'm IT." The other girls nodded in agreement with a collective expression of innocence. Then they composed their faces into a semblance of sympathy.

"Are you alright, JoEllen?" Kathy walked over and extended her big sweaty hand, offering to help her up.

"Eeeehw! Yuck; don't you touch me!" JoEllen's voice was shrill and she drew back her hand as if from a cockroach.

Miss Callaway cast a disappointed look in her direction. "JoEllen, that's not very nice. I'm a little surprised at you." JoEllen's mouth dropped open in indignation. Then she sprung to her feet unaided and brushed off her knees, where little bits of playground grit were lodged in the flesh. Miss Callaway turned back to Maddy and took the opportunity to correct her grammar. "Were playing, Madeline, it's, 'We were playing tag.'"

"Yes Miss Callaway, we *were*," Maddy pronounced carefully. Having been schooled by nuns, she had developed a studied deference that was second nature. It scored big points with the teachers and even the principal. They trusted her implicitly, so she sometimes got away with little things where others might be questioned. I wasn't sure whether Miss Callaway was on to the whole thing and secretly thought JoEllen had it coming, or if she was swayed by my cousin's charm. I was still marveling at how fast Maddy could run. I knew she was exceptionally strong and athletic. She was always one of the first team picks, but she'd never shown any inclination to be competitive in P.E., or even at games of kickball during recess. She ran fast enough to make it to base and avoid losing points for the team. She won some of the running races, and lost others, and now I suspected that was probably by design. I guess she didn't want to be a big show-off like JoEllen. It was just one more surprise.

The bell rang and recess was over. "Line up class." Miss Callaway strode briskly to the front of the group to lead us back in a double line. JoEllen skedaddled in behind her with her nose in the air. When the teacher's back was turned, the others made faces at JoEllen. I joined in the guilty pleasure; I knew it was childish, but I'd spent years on the receiving end of ridicule.

Back in class I dared to take it a step further. I got JoEllen's attention when the teacher wasn't looking, then I snatched back my hand in mock disgust and dramatically mouthed the words, 'Yuck, don't touch me!' It made Kathy Kelly accidently snort out loud.

With only three days to go until the last day of school, we were all giddy with excitement. Discipline was a little more relaxed, and recess lasted longer and longer, because the teachers wanted to be out in the nice weather as much as we did. It was warm enough to leave the back door open mornings, so the spring air could come through the screen. The lilac bushes on the back hill were in full bloom, and when the wind blew just right, the smell in the kitchen was so sweet you could eat it for breakfast.

On just such a perfect morning, instead of her trademark whistle from the driveway I heard Maddy call, "Hey, you comin' already?" One look at her face and I knew something was wrong. I hoped Tommy hadn't screwed-up again.

"How's Tommy been doing in school," I ventured, hoping my dad's influence hadn't worn off.

"Better; at least he's stayin' outa' trouble mostly...I still gotta do his homework...but he's better," she seemed relieved to talk about him. "He told me all about truck drivin'. It sounds cool," she said. Cool was a new and exciting expression to us, and if something was cool, it must be really good. I'd never thought of Dad's work as cool. "Tommy says he can't wait to be done with school and start drivin' a truck." I was relieved to hear good news about Tommy, but still wondered what was bothering her. "Did you ever go to work with your dad?" Maddy asked in an off-hand manner.

The thought had never occurred to me, but now that she asked I somehow assumed it wouldn't be allowed. "No. He never asked, and I never thought it sounded very interesting."

"Are there any girl truck drivers?"

"Uh, I don't think so...all the guys he works with are, well, guys. All men- the foreman, the dispatcher, the boss, of course. It's hard work; the freight is heavy and they unload it by hand. Dad works on the engines sometimes and comes home filthy!" I wrinkled my nose at the thought of getting that black gunk stuck under my fingernails. "Mom has to soak his uniforms in gasoline to get the grease out," I said, as if that ought to dissuade any sensible person. "I don't think ladies are allowed."

"Figures...men get to do all the cool stuff." I still didn't see it as cool, but didn't argue. "So...ah, what do ya do if ya ain't goin' to college?"

"What do you do for what?" I asked.

"For work!" She looked at me like I was kind of dumb, and then went on. "I sure as hell ain't stayin' home with kids all day. I'm never getting married," she said emphatically.

"I'm getting married," I responded matter-of-factly.

"Thought you were goin' to be a scientist and work in the jungle?"

"I'll be a scientist that gets married. I want a little girl just like Annie, and I'll take her everywhere with me," I added.

"I want to go somewhere...really far away," she said wistfully.

"Maybe an airline stewardess?" As soon as I suggested it, I knew it was somehow absurd-I couldn't see her in a little blue skirt and cap, serving coffee. I could see her flying the airplane...but ladies didn't fly planes either.

As we walked on, I took a hard look at my cousin. I tried to imagine her all grown up. She was nearly as tall as my mom, but showed no sign of growing a bosom or acting more 'lady-like' as my mom put it. "You've got plenty of time to decide what to do when you grow up," I reassured. "And I still think you can go to college if that's what you want to do. You're smart!" I said sincerely.

"I wish I was a boy," she said longingly, "if I was a boy, I'd drive a truck someday...and I wouldn't be a draft dodger either. I'd sign up! I wouldn't be a dirty hippy. I'd wanna fight."

At that point we went into school and our strange conversation was abruptly over. I couldn't imagine what brought it all on, and it was hard to concentrate on spelling words that morning. I'd heard about draft dodgers on the news, and my mother knew somebody who knew somebody whose son had fled to Canada. She said it was a shame. Of course I challenged her, and asked if she would want to fight and get killed.

"I would if I were a man," she'd emphasized. "I feel sorry for those boys' mothers-what a disgrace," she'd insisted with self-righteous indignation.

My father had fought in the Philippines in WWII, but to hear him talk, it sounded like some great adventure. When I thought of war, I envisioned one of those old black and white WWII movies Dad was so fond of. It just wasn't real. Our parents sheltered us so effectively from the war in Vietnam that it wasn't much more than a vague backdrop in our lives. My parents had quietly watched the late news on a TV in their bedroom behind a closed door; I was an adult before I even knew that the theater of war had actually been televised.

We didn't understand hippies either. When I traveled into Boston to go shopping with my mother, the Boston Common was covered with young people sprawled out on blankets. Some played guitars or hand-drums, but mostly they just sat. I had never seen people dressed in such raggedy clothes, with long flowing hair and beads and fringe. Even the boys had long hair. Mom always ushered me past with her nose in the air while I gawked over my shoulder. I had no idea what they were supposed to be doing. We knew just what our parents wanted us to think: they were bad kids, and the boys only went to college because they were draft-dodgers. We kids couldn't have cared less about all that, and on Halloween night in 1969, dressing as a hippy was the most popular trick or treat costume.

I had no idea why Maddy was suddenly so interested in the war and the hippies. I could understand wanting to be a boy, after hearing what Dad said to my mother about having a job. But the war had been going on for some time, and she'd never mentioned it before. Then a thought smacked me in the face like cold rain. Eddie Murphy must be nearly eighteen, and I knew that meant registering for the draft. The idea of him going to war was more than terrifying; it was impossible. How could those gentle hands even hold a gun, let alone shoot someone? Poor Auntie Joan must be so worried, and I could only imagine what Uncle Malone had to say about it. Suddenly the thousands reported dead weren't numbers any longer.

I wanted to ask Maddy about her brother and the draft, but by the end of the day I figured I'd better mind my own business. I decided to let her tell me what was going on over the back hill when she was ready, but I had one thought I just couldn't contain on our short walk home. "I think…at least I hope that by the time we grow up, girls will get to do cool things too. But I'm glad you're a girl. Really glad," I blurted out with emotion. I'd begun to realize how desperately hard it was, just being girl. Thank God Maddy was in it with me. I never would have figured it out up all by myself.

Maddy looked quizzically at me, and then her mouth turned up at one corner, something between a grin and a smirk. She tossed away a spent cigarette and said with a bit of the old spark in her eye. "You're a funny kid, Frances."

12

"You look so tired," I said with concern. It was finally here-the morning of the last day of school. I was looking forward to a fun summer, and I wanted my old Maddy back. She'd been tense and far away ever since confiding in me that she wanted to drive a truck and go off to war.

"The baby wakes us all up," she began to complain for once. "Ma is wrecked from no sleep. Dad sleeps on the sofa in the front parlor 'cause he can't stand the noise. Ma says Baby Michael's just going through a phase, but I think it's more than that. She used to take naps when he did, and now she can't. The kid learned to climb outa his crib. She hasn't been able to use the playpen anymore; he climbs outa that too. If you take your eye offa him, he tears stuff outa the cupboards. We had to put all the cleaning stuff way up because he tore it out and dumped Comet everywhere-even had some on his mouth, but he was OK. Ma can't even go to the bathroom anymore. A few days ago when she was on the toilet, the baby pushed a kitchen chair over to the stove and climbed up. Before she got back he was sitting on top, trying to twist the gas knobs."

"Oh my God. What does your Gramma say?"

"She never complained all this time. We thought she must be sleeping through it, but lately I've been hearing someone walk around at night. There's creaking upstairs, way up the third floor, sounds like. Gramma says it's just the old house breathing. Anyway, she was the one who found Baby Michael on the stove. It's a good thing she woke up from her nap. She told Ma that something had to be done before he got hurt or burned the house down, told her she should be strict with him and make him stay put in the playpen. I don't think it has anything to do with being strict or not; I think somethin's wrong with 'im. He's not toilet training at all, and he doesn't really talk, only says 'da-da' for Eddie, which really pisses off my dad. He screams 'nah nah!' It means 'no'. He says that a lot. It's kind of a mess at my house."

Mess was an understatement. One day Maddy was out sick so I walked Annie home from school. When we stepped into the back entry, it was the smell that hit me first, and I don't mean stinky socks. I entered the kitchen with trepidation, trying not to inhale. Then I saw Auntie Joan and Maddy both on the floor, scrubbing the legs of the tables, the edges of the chairs. It seemed strange, but then I saw what they were doing. Everywhere I looked-the fronts of the cupboards, the fridge-the whole place was covered in shit! I stood there with my hand over my nose and mouth. Annie started towards her mom, but Auntie Joan held up her hand: "Stay back honey, you'll get all dirty." Maddy looked at me, almost too sick with some intestinal virus to be embarrassed, but I saw her face flush. Annie had explained that her Ma and her sister had been throwing up all night.

"I took my eyes off him one minute," she spat out, "and he takes his diaper off and rubs his shit all over the place." Auntie Joan was too exhausted to rebuke her for the language, and just sighed as she wrung out a nasty rag in a bucket of brown water by where she knelt on the floor. I thought that I should probably offer to help too, but couldn't bring myself to do it. Auntie Joan asked me if I could take Annie upstairs to change into her play clothes, and hang up her dress. I was happy to do something other than stand there and watch, or just turn and leave like a shmuck when they were so sick.

I told Mom all about the baby when I got home. "Is that normal?" I asked.

"Well, it happens sometimes, mostly with baby boys, I think. You never did anything like that, thank God," she exclaimed, making a disgusted face. "It can also result from leaving a toddler in a diaper loaded with you-know-what," she arched her eyebrows. "You really can't leave them unattended like that."

"Won't Michael outgrow all this soon?"

I knew he'd turned three some months ago, because Mom had brought over a card and a little gift. It was a toy vacuum that made a whirring noise when you pushed it. She thought he might like it since he seemed to play vacuum a lot-I found out that was what he pretended with his hand extended, running in circles while droning, *eeeeeehhh*. It had started up one day after Joanie had been vacuuming. At first they thought it was cute, but then it seemed to become an obsession. He did it for over an hour at a time, often until his little voice was hoarse from making the vacuum sound. Mom felt he should play with a real toy, instead of running in circles with an invisible machine. She presented the gift and told him, "Now you can help Mommy vacuum, see," she pushed the toy and its plastic motor whirred. For some reason, Baby Michael flew into a rage at the sound of the real toy vacuum.

"His eyes went sort of wild, and then he started screaming, 'Nah-Nah-Nah-Nah!'" Mom looked horrified as she described it. "Then he swung the thing over his head so fast I barely had time to duck! It wacked the wall a couple of times before I jumped up and just yanked it out of his hands-he was like a demolition squad! It took a piece out of the plaster, and cracked the stupid toy that was supposed to be toddler-proof. Poor Joan! She was just so embarrassed, she started to cry. I tried to laugh it off. 'He's just all boy…silly Aunt Evelyn; boys don't want Suzie Homemaker toys!' I told Joan I'd take it away and come by another time with a little truck. Now, I'm no expert on babies, but I get a bad feeling…something is very wrong there, I think. But of course, you can't say anything about it. You can't say, 'I think your kid has a screw loose.' No one wants to hear there's something wrong with their child. You just can't talk about it," she warned, shaking her head for emphasis. "Well, maybe he's just a little behind; maybe he'll catch up and start talking eventually."

"Do you think maybe Michael's just a little behind?" I ventured cautiously to Maddy. "Maybe he'll still outgrow this stuff?"

"I don't know much about babies, but it looks like he's getting worse, not better," Maddy said. "I don't remember Annie acting like that at all. I was just a kid, but she was like a little doll. They say Tommy was a 'tough' baby, active and into things. I wouldn't know…but they tell me I was not as easy as Annie. My dad always said I was 'full of the devil.'"

"That didn't change." I tried to get a smile out of her, but she was too exhausted.

I wasn't surprised when Maddy said she felt kind of sick after lunch. She hadn't looked right all morning, and I hoped she wasn't coming down with another tummy bug. "Why don't you ask Miss Callaway to go to the nurse? Maybe you should just go home. I'll walk Annie." She just shook her head no. Come to think of it, she probably wasn't in a hurry to go home at all, and this was the last day, the day everyone looked forward to. "You can come over after school," I offered. "We could do something. Cheer up; this is it!"

"Yeah, maybe. After I get Annie home and make sure Ma doesn't need me for anything."

We were cleaning out our desks. The textbooks were all wiped clean, and we buffed the edges of the pages with an eraser to whiten them up. I liked this part of the year. Maddy had asked Miss Callaway to go to the girls' room, which was unremarkable. But when she didn't come back over ten minutes later, Miss Callaway asked to see me in the hall for a moment. Being asked out to the hall always gave me the willies. It was what teachers did when you had done something wrong, or got a bad grade. Sometimes it was just that your mother called to have you dismissed for the dentist or something else you'd forgotten. I was pretty sure it wasn't that, and I knew I hadn't done anything that might need to be addressed in the hall. I reassured myself it was nothing. Miss Callaway closed the door behind us. "Madeline's been in the girls' room for over ten minutes." She pointed down the hall towards the bathroom door. "Please go check on her."

"She wasn't feeling well after lunch," I explained, starting on my way.

"Oh-oh," she said, concerned. Miss Callaway opened the door a bit and checked on the class, then watched me go down the hall.

I hoped Maddy was OK. I also hoped she was really in there, and not gone off somewhere else, up to something. Then I would have the unpleasant duty of reporting it to Miss Callaway-there'd be no avoiding it. I went in, and right away saw her trademark penny loafers parked on the floor behind the door of stall number three, the one over by the far wall. They were new this year, and still had shiny pennies in the little slots on the tops.

"Maddy?" I called softly.

"Yeah, what?"

"Ah, are you OK? Miss Callaway sent me down to check on you-she says it's been over ten minutes."

"Great," she said sarcastically.

"Do you have diarrhea?" I asked in a grown-up tone, just the way Mom asked me if I were stuck in the bathroom a while.

"No, I don't got diarrhea," she answered, clearly annoyed. "Go away Frances. Leave me alone."

"What? Why? What am I supposed to tell Miss Callaway? She's standing by the classroom door waiting."

"Shit," she said.

"Maddy, what's wrong? Are you sick?"

"I got my period. I got my fuckin' period and bled all over myself. I can't come out."

If I didn't know better, I'd almost think she was about to cry. "Oh, I'm sorry. I don't have any napkins-I haven't got my period yet. I'll tell Miss Callaway, and she'll send me to the nurse for sanitary napkins. Remember how the nurse told us if it happened in school we could go to her and get a sanitary napkin?"

"No way!"

"Maddy...ah, you can't just stay in the toilet stall all day. Don't worry. It'll be alright."

"Oh, Christ...I just want to die," she said mournfully.

"I'll be right back." I hurried off to have Miss Callaway send me to the nurse. I was a little envious, but not at all envious of how it happened.

We girls had a complex relationship with puberty. On the one hand, it signified growing up, and we all wanted to be grown-up. On the other, you got to look forward to bleeding twelve or more times a year for the next thirty-five years or so. I had asked my mom when I should start carrying my Kotex gifts in the little pink plastic travel case, but she said I didn't need to worry about *that* yet, since I hadn't really developed. I wanted to be prepared, but the very idea obviously made my mother uncomfortable. She explained that in her day, the subject was so taboo that many girls didn't learn about menstruation until it started. There were no health education films. She recalled the time when she was in sixth grade and some poor girl got her period in the middle of class. The worst part was that the girl didn't even know what was happening to her. She kept trying to wipe the blood from her seat with Kleenex.

When I explained the situation to Nurse Rose, she went to straight to her closet and came back with a small plain brown paper bag. She thought it might be best if I went along with her to the girls' room. When we got there poor Maddy was still sitting where I'd left her.

"Adeline, open the door a bit and take this," Nurse Rose directed gently.

"It's *Madeline*," I whispered to the nurse.

The door opened, barely enough to allow her bony hand to grasp the bag; she drew it back quickly and locked the stall, muttering "Thank you."

Then Nurse Rose began to instruct Maddy in the techniques of feminine hygiene. "Now dear, first you step into the elastic belt like you're putting on your *panthies*-the belt goes under your *panthies*." Nurse Rose spoke with a lisp, and I had to be careful not to smirk. "Put the back end of the gauze through the metal clip and wind it around once before you *fasthen* it. Otherwise, your napkin might slip out and fall off." That sounded like a fate worse than death.

"Uh, which end is the back?" Maddy's voice from the other side of the stall door was uncharacteristically meek.

"Oh, the napkin has no front or back, dear, you just hook up the belt starting at the back, and pull it between your legs. Your napkin goes with pink stripe facing down towards your *panthies*, and the plain white side up," she instructed formally. "Then you tighten it at the front; don't forget to wind it through once and make sure it's secure."

I had practiced this maneuver at home to make sure I got it right, to be ready for my big day. It was all diagramed in the booklet that came with my gift-box. Poor Maddy...I guessed she hadn't given it a trial run. I'd assumed her sister or mom had explained the whole routine before now.

When the stall door creaked open, I almost didn't recognize the girl standing in front of the toilet, holding her underwear rolled up in one hand and the crumpled paper bag in the other. She seemed to have shrunk. Now I felt like I was going to cry; getting your period must be a lot worse than Mom or the nurse or the booklet let on. "I can't wear these," Maddy said, looking at the floor.

Nurse Rose placed a motherly arm around her shoulder. "There, there, Adeline" she comforted. "Just put your *thoiled panthies* in the bag. The *twick* is to *thoak* them in cold water as soon as you get home." I didn't think Maddy could look much worse, but she seemed to collapse in on herself a little more. I watched as the nurse ushered her to the office, to have her dismissed before the bell rang so she could go straight home. Maddy shuffled along ahead of Nurse Rose like a prisoner of war.

"I'll get your stuff. I'll carry it home for you, and I'll walk Annie. You go on," I reassured her. Maddy acknowledged with a slight nod of thanks.

It took a little longer to gather up Annie that last day of school. She was carrying some big cardboard framed picture that she'd painted earlier that year. It was pretty good for a little kid-really good, I decided, studying it more carefully. Every member of the family was in it, and a few extras. She explained that they were some of her dead aunties. I didn't know she knew about that. The teacher had chosen her painting as one of the best examples, and it had hung on the wall for over a month. I offered to carry it for her. It was mounted on heavy cardboard, and nearly as big as she was.

When we left the school building, I was surprised and glad to see the big gold Buick parked out in front with Mom sitting at the wheel. It was thoughtful of her. I figured she expected we would all be lugging more stuff home the last day. The engine was idling, and I was anxious to see if Mom had only just showed up or had arrived in time to collect Maddy. The back windows were tinted dark-we had some of the first tinted windows around. When I opened the back door, there she was, sunk down in the black leather seat, looking miserable. I wondered if she had explained her predicament to Mom. I knew she would be really embarrassed; she didn't usually talk much to my mother, not about anything personal if she could help it. The paper bag was on the floor by her feet, and she just stared out the window.

Annie jumped into the back with her sister. "What's the matter Mad'lin?" Her small child's voice was filled with concern. I had explained that her sister had a tummy ache, and had gone home a bit early-not to worry. I decided to put the painting on the back seat beside them, and their school bags on the floor. Maddy looked like she'd rather be alone, so I carefully shut the door, mindful of Annie's hands and the big painting. I climbed into the front beside Mom, who had barely said hello-which seemed strange. I thought the last day of school would be more festive.

"Everybody in OK?" Mom checked before putting the car in gear and heading around the block. I was confused when we pulled up in front of our house.

"Aren't we going to drive them around the corner?" I asked.

"No. Girls, your father asked me to pick you up and bring you home with me today. Come on; let's get all this stuff out of the car."

Maddy looked up, roused from her sulking. "What's going on Aunt Evelyn?" she demanded. "Why aren't we going home?" Maddy didn't mean to be rude, but I knew my mother would be appalled. I sure hoped she didn't correct her, not right now especially.

"Please come inside," Mom said firmly, but not unkindly. I hopped out and opened the back door by Annie. Maddy grabbed the strap to her book sack and jumped out of her door, looking at my mother expectantly; she was clearly alarmed, and had forgotten all about her indisposition.

Annie began gathering up her things, and thoughtfully collected the paper bag from the floor of the car. Like any typical curious child, she opened it and pulled out the bloody underwear before I could stop her. We were all standing in the driveway, and she was waving them in air. I was right beside her, but didn't notice until it was too late. There was nothing left to the imagination. The crotch of the white cotton panties was soaked through with dark, half-dried blood. Annie looked horrified. It even freaked me out. "Oh, Mad'lin, what happened? What is it?" She began to cry. I snatched the panties away with one hand and the bag with the other. Maddy had run around the back of the car and took them from me, stuffing them quickly back into the paper bag, and squirrelling that deep into the drawstring school sack.

Mom had seen the personal hygiene crisis, but tactfully pretended that she hadn't. "Come on in," she said. Maddy gazed across my backyard, towards the tower of her grandmother's house looming over the hill on the horizon. I don't know whether she was looking to see if it was still there, or thinking about bolting home. Mom watched her carefully, and repeated, "Come in. We'll have a little snack and I'll explain."

I felt a sense of dread as we followed Mom inside. Annie was still crying. "Your mom didn't feel well," she began, shutting the door behind us and standing in front of it. "Please sit down." Maddy wasn't sitting. At the mention of her mother the muscles in her face twitched. I think she would have walked out the door if Mom weren't in the way.

101

"I'm goin' home," she said firmly, standing directly in front of Mom. I noticed she was about the same height. If I'd defied my mother that way I'd likely get a slap in the face, and the thought of what either of them might do next scared me.

"No," Mom spoke with studied restraint. There's no one at home, and your father told me to keep you here until they get back. Your father has taken your mom to the doctor, and Joanie and Grandma went too. Besides, Annie needs you here."

Maddy stepped back and looked away. Her paste-white face turned blue-gray around the eyes like a corpse. "Where's my brother Eddie Murphy?" Her voice crackled a little, and I could see she was barely holding together.

"They called over to St. Thomas's, and he got right on the train in Boston, to be with your mother," Mom said. Maddy began to breathe again, but she still had a sickly pallor. We'd all but forgotten Annie. She'd stopped crying and just stared off into space, like she was looking at something. Mom sat on a kitchen chair and gathered her onto her lap. "I know you had a bad day. I'll look after her," she added, "you two go on upstairs."

We picked up our school stuff and trudged upstairs to my room. There was one twin bed, a child's desk and chair set that was getting too small, and an old upholstered chair that had become too shabby for the living room. It was covered up with a soft chenille slipcover that my mother had sewn herself, the same fabric as the bedspread. Not a thing was out of place. I shut the door behind us. I took my special box from the closet and put it on the bed. In my most motherly fashion, I opened it up and began to explain the wonders of modern feminine protection. She help up her hand like a traffic cop and shook her head.

"No thanks, it's OK. I've seen Joanie's stuff lying around for years. I just never had to use it before," she added.

I felt a little disappointed, but so it wouldn't be a total loss, added, "Do you want to look at the booklet that came with my Kotex gift box?"

"No thanks," she said.

"Are you sure? It explains lots of things, like cramps, and why you feel so emotionally sensitive," I insisted.

"Frances," she said evenly, "I don't want to look at your booklet right now."

"I can read it to you," I offered.

"You can take your damned Kotex gift and shove it up your ass!"

I shut the lid and looked away from her. It was the first time she'd snapped at me. I'd heard her get like that with Tommy, and especially Joanie-they fought like cats and dogs-but it had never been directed at me. "Fine!" I said. "I don't care." I sat on the bed and felt my eyes begin to smart. I just wanted her to love me. I wanted everyone to love me and I tried so hard. It seemed that the more I tried, the worse people treated me. I wanted to say something snappy back, but I just didn't have it in me. I broke down into tears. "I'm sorry... it's all my fault," I said, then hid my face in my hands and sobbed.

"Frances," she said softly. I kept my hands over my face. "Frances!" She demanded my attention. "Don't you dare be sorry. I acted like an asshole-which is nothing new...but don't let me get away with it. Don't say you're sorry to me." She sat opposite me and hiked the chair close so our knees almost touched. I was still covering my face but could see through my fingers. "Look at me," she said. I looked up. "I'm sorry. And I really appreciate how you helped me out today. Without you I'd probably still be sittin' on the damned toilet. I just feel so stupid."

"You had an awful day," I said, quick to excuse her outburst. "Mom told me that what happened to you is every girl's worst nightmare."

"Did she? Well, it's not my worst...it was pretty bad, but I'm actually more worried about Ma, and the baby and..." she trailed off, and then almost whispered, "Annie."

I wiped my eyes with the back of my hand and sniffed. "What's wrong with Annie?" I saw an invisible veil pass over her face, like the third eyelid of a reptile. I'd seen it before when she was about to tell me something, but changed her mind.

"I'm upset all the time lately because...it's just that...I don't want it! That's it. I don't want any of this!" Maddy exclaimed.

"What don't you want?" I was confused.

"I don't want to get my period, or get married; and I never ever want to be pregnant and have kids. There's somethin' else." She stopped and took a deep breath. "My ma's pregnant again," she spat it out as if it were something shameful.

I knew that this was not good news. No wonder Auntie Joan looked so terrible. "Oh no," I mumbled.

"Oh-no is right. Jesus! What was Dad thinking?"

"How did it happen?" I asked innocently.

She looked incredulous. "Frances, you really are a baby, aren't ya." It was a statement of fact, not meant to be unkind. I shrugged. "It happened the usual way. He did it to her," she said with disgust.

I really was a pathetic baby. All I knew-thanks to Dotty Day-was that their two 'mm-mm's' had to touch, but as for who did what to whom or exactly how...I hadn't a clue. "You're right; I don't really understand. I don't have any brothers, and my father has always been...extremely protective of my modesty." I felt embarrassed as I explained my ignorance.

"Well, you're lucky then," she said. "All I can say is it's the man who actually does it. It takes two, but he's the one who makes it happen or not."

"That's sounds like what my mother told me," I affirmed. "Mom says men are in charge of everything. 'It's in our father's hands,' she says."

Maddy gave me her best wry look, with one eyebrow raised and her mouth twisted in a half-grin, in spite of her recent misery. "Well, you could put it that way," she quipped, "but it's not their hands that you gotta worry about, Frances." I got the gist of the remark, although the details would remain a mystery to me for some time. "I can't believe what Annie got into," Maddy said, changing the subject. "I hope she's not scared to death. Why did I bring those things home in a bag?" She groaned out loud and gave her head a vigorous shake, as if hoping to snap herself awake from a bad dream.

"Because the nurse told you to," I offered. "You were kind of shook up and just did it."

"Jeez," Maddy said, "that nurse is somethin' else! *'Adeline*, take your *panthies* home and *thoak* them in cold water," she imitated Nurse Rose perfectly and it made us both laugh.

"Maybe you could tell Annie you had a nosebleed," I offered, trying to help.

"What? How the hell could I have a nosebleed in my underwear?" She started to chuckle in her low, gravelly way, half coughing, a kind of phlegmy admixture that ended in a snorting sound. I shrugged sheepishly. "Jeezes...a nosebleed?!" She was sniggering. I was glad to have cheered her up at least. "Hey Frances," she said after she stopped laughing at me. "Do ya think you could spare me one of your...uh...Kotex gifts?"

"Sure-take your pick." I opened the cover and displayed the smorgasbord of sanitary products.

"Hmm," she said, as she selected a fat one. "And could ya loan me a pair of clean underpants? As soon as I get a chance I'm throwing those away," she added, alluding to the contents of her school sack on the floor.

"Sure thing." I went to my dresser drawer.

"And I don't suppose there's a chance in hell I could sneak a quick smoke out the window?"

"Not one," I said sympathetically.

"Now that really is a nightmare," she sighed.

I'd never been so close to anyone. I knew it was the same for Maddy, even though she had a sister nearly her own age. We could even get mad, and it would still be alright. She wouldn't leave me. I could tell her anything, and I could wait patiently for her to tell me what was on her mind. And I'd always keep her secrets.

I got a pair of clean underwear from the dresser, and on an impulse stretched the elastic so they flew like a slingshot and hit her in the head. I was able to make her laugh one more time before we had to go back downstairs.

My cousins stayed to supper that night. Afterwards we watched TV in silence. Annie fell asleep. It was getting late when Uncle Malone finally came over. His harsh man-voice rumbled throughout the house, and even though he was trying to speak to my mother in private, we could hear every word. "She just needs rest. The doctor said she probably hadn't slept through the night since the day the poor child was born," he said. "I thought she was getting some sleep during the day, but the older kids, Joanie and Eddie, told me no, not for a long time. And Joan is, ah, expecting again, too. She's about three months along. The kids don't know yet," he added.

"Like hell they don't," Maddy whispered to me.

"They took her to the local hospital first, but they sent her along to…to McClain's. They gave her something to calm her," he said, as we strained to hear every word.

"What exactly happened?" Mom usually spoke as little as possible to Tom Malone, but her concern got the upper hand.

"Michael got the door open and just walked out. Joan was in the bathroom, and my muther was asleep. Muther's awake all night. She sleeps like the dead in the afternoons, so she didn't hear him. When Joan come downstairs, he was gone. She went tearing out the door in 'er nightgown to search for 'im. Then one of the kids from the projects said she saw a little boy walk across the road all alone; he'd wandered off into the projects. Joan went runnin' through the place, half-dressed and half out of her mind calling out for Michael, crying and banging on people's doors. Someone called the police and they tried to talk to her…they told me afterwards that she made no sense at all. Then she started having pain in her, ah, stomach. They took her to the hospital in an ambulance. Some little kids found Michael even before the police did; he was sitting by someone's back stoop, digging in the dirt with a spoon. One of the women carried him home. Eddie's looking after him."

As we eaves-dropped, Maddy went all dark and quiet. It was as if a shadow had fallen over her face, and she was devoid of expression. Then she turned away from me.

13

It was a rough start to our summer vacation, but I figured Auntie Joan would get better and everything would go back to normal. Instead it got worse. During her two-week stay at McClain's, Mr. Malone took the baby to a specialist at a children's hospital. By then it was obvious to everyone that something was seriously wrong with Michael, but when they blamed his odd behavior and slow development on his mother, that didn't seem right at all. On the strength of one doctor's recommendation, it was determined that Joan wasn't fit to care for the baby. His father voluntarily relinquished Michael to an institution.

While Joan was away, my mother saw to it that the girls got a good lunch every day, and they had supper with us every evening. She was becoming like a second mother to Annie, who seemed to relish the attention, and loved having her hair brushed and put into barrettes. She spent more time outdoors, ate more fresh fruit, and looked a lot better for it. I thought she must have grown an inch in those two weeks.

My cousins were supposed to stay with us until their father returned home from work. After supper Maddy and I would climb up the back hill and sit by the fence that divided our small lot from the two acre parcel surrounding the old Victorian home. We sat amidst the lilac bushes that were full of green leaves, but no longer in bloom. She smoked, hidden behind the thick bushes as the summer sun sank low and glowed deep orange in the heat of July. The grass was tall and full of tiny wildflowers, because Dad didn't push the mower up the hill. Giant fuzzy bumblebees buzzed loudly and dove in and amongst the wildflowers, but they didn't bother us. I think the smoke kept them away.

Maddy kept watch on her house through a gap in the fence where one of the rotted boards was missing. When the last horizontal rays of the sun hit the stained glass windows on the circular tower, they seemed to light up, all fiery red and yellow. Just about then we would hear Tommy's shrill whistle from over the fence. It signaled that their dad was back, and they could come home. I don't know how Tommy spent his days; he seemed to be left on his own.

***

"When are we going to visit Auntie Joan?" I asked my mother. It had been over three weeks since she'd come home from the hospital, and we still hadn't gone. I had my cousins with me every day for two weeks, and now I hardly saw them at all. Annie was afraid if she left the house, they'd come take her mother again. I think Maddy was afraid too, though she'd never come out and say it. She just didn't seem to want to play outside very long. For some reason, my mother insisted I stay away for a while; but it was long past a while.

"She needs rest. I don't want you bothering them," Mom answered tersely.

"I miss Maddy! I miss Annie! Don't you care about Auntie Joan?" I asked. "I thought she was your friend!"

The accusation made my mother bristle, but she refused to be drawn into a debate about loyalty. "That's enough," she said unsympathetically. "It's time you made some other friends anyway. In the fall you'll be going to junior high school; there'll be lots of new kids to meet. You'll develop new interests-maybe join a club," she reasoned.

"I don't want other friends," I protested. "I'm not joining any clubs. I want things to be the way they were."

"Too bad," she said. "Everything changes, and..."

I interrupted her, and spoke slowly and evenly. "Mom, don't tell me it's 'too bad'. Maddy's more than my cousin: she's my best friend...and the closest I'll ever have to a sister."

Even if I'd thought through all the possible ramifications before I spoke, I wouldn't have predicted Mom's reaction. Her face blanched, then went red to the roots of her hair. I knew a holy fit was coming, but I didn't know what exactly had set her off.

"Do you think it's *my* fault that you don't have a sister?" she screeched. "Don't you think I wanted more children? I thought I would have a family," she stressed. "I gave up a career to have a family! And this is all I get? One ungrateful kid who doesn't even listen to me! You are so disrespectful young lady...I wouldn't have dared to talk to my mother that way. I get no appreciation from you...you don't give a damn about my feelings. You argue with me about everything...I don't know why I even bother to try and be your mother. You shouldn't have had a mother; you should have been hatched from an egg!"

I'd heard this many times over the course of my life. Mom seemed to think my propensity to form my own opinions reflected badly on her, as if it were a deliberate rejection. She wanted an agreeable kid who looked up to her for guidance. I have to admit, I must've been sorely disappointing.

I knew I should have shut-up then, but I couldn't hold back. "So why didn't you adopt more children if you wanted a whole family of kids? Is that my fault too? Why did you save all those clothes anyway?" I thought I knew the answer, but I wanted to hear it out loud. I couldn't drive down the road sitting on that particular bucket of shit any longer. Better to let it spill, stink up the place and then dry up once and for all.

Mom's pencil-line eyebrows rose in surprise at my backtalk, but she took the bait. "Why didn't I adopt more children?" She placed her hand over her heart, and her voice rose to such a shrill pitch that I expected dogs to start howling. Her eyes were like shining nuggets of coal, about to go into spontaneous combustion. "Because," she paused, "one of *you* was enough!"

I'd thought I was ready for something like this, but actually hearing the words cut like a whip. I felt my face burn and I fought back tears. I was tired of my mother making me cry. All I had to do was stop caring, and no one could ever hurt me again. Or, I could apologize for making her upset and beg forgiveness and promise to try harder and be better. In the middle of the deliberation I was provided with comic relief by our neighbor's Beagle. He lived a couple of doors down the street from us, but must have heard her screeching-the whole neighborhood must have heard. The little hound started baying mournfully: "Ahwoo...Ahwoo, Ahw, Ahw, Ahwoo!" Instead of crying, I found myself smirking; I could feel one corner of my mouth kind of twist up sardonically, as if it were struggling between a smile and a scowl.

Mom was so absorbed in her dramatic performance that she hadn't noticed the dog. She paused and caught her breath to deliver her final line, and it was worthy of an Oscar nomination. "I hoped that maybe, just maybe if I gave one poor unwanted child a good home," she glared at me and continued, "God would reward me with a baby; my own baby! It does happen that way sometimes, for some people...but not for me." She finished quietly, and, I had to admit, with genuine sadness.

Well, it was finally out. She'd said it and the world didn't end. I felt terrible, but at the same time relieved. Now I knew for certain that there was nothing I could ever do to make her happy, so I finally absolved myself from the burden of trying. I'd always known she wanted her own baby, but only got a consolation prize. Now I knew I wasn't even that; I was the booby prize, the 'Zonk' in Mom's life, like the dreaded item from the popular game show, *Let's Make a Deal!* The contestant got to choose between door number one, door number two, or door number three. If she chose the best door, there might be: A sports car! The second best choice might reveal a whole house full of brand new appliances; that wouldn't be so bad. Or she might get a new color TV for the living room-the whole family would enjoy that. Then the audience would groan with sympathy that she didn't get the car, but they'd applaud anyway for second prize. Finally, there was the last door, the one no contestant wanted, but the audience secretly hoped for: the Zonk. Eventually some poor bitch would pick the door with a prize that made everybody laugh, because it was large, awkward, and more trouble than it was worth-like maybe a thousand boxes of cereal. Where would you store all that cereal? How would you even get it home? Sometimes the prize was absurdly useless. On one program they even had a donkey, all harnessed up to a flower cart, complete with flowers. The audience began to roar with laughter, while the contestant covered her face to hide her disappointment. She tried to be a good sport and laugh along through tears of embarrassment, but she really wanted that car, and this was her only chance to get one. The frightened donkey tossed his head and brayed, which made the audience go wild.

Evelyn Orillio tried to make a deal with God, but picked the wrong door and got a donkey. It looked like she'd never forgive either of them.

We barely spoke for the next couple of days. I didn't mind. I decided that since I no longer had to worry about disappointing my mother, I'd do as pleased and damn the torpedoes. Let her try and send me back to the orphanage! I'd bake a carrot cake and go visit Auntie Joan all by myself. After all, I'd been taught that was the thoughtful and appropriate thing to do when a friend or relative got sick or suffered a loss.

I waited until Mom was out and raided her recipe box. I thought if I got it done quickly, I could take it over before she came home. When it came to baking, I'd watched and helped with the frosting, but I'd never gone solo. How hard could it be? After puzzling over the recipe with all that fuss about sifting flour, and separating the wet from the dry ingredients-they all ended up together anyway-I devised a strategy to streamline the process. And since we didn't have a bag of fresh carrots on hand, I just used canned carrots.

About an hour and a half later, I had two pans of burnt orange-brown goo. I'd softened a pound of butter, but I'd forgotten that you needed cream cheese to make the frosting. It didn't look like the cake would hold up to frosting anyway. I was about to dump the whole thing, clean the mess and wash away the evidence when the Buick rolled under the carport, right up by the kitchen door. "Crap," I said aloud. There was no getting it out to the trash, and we didn't have a garbage disposal. I briefly considered flushing it down the toilet, but if it got stopped up the mess would be a lot worse.

"Jesus, Mary and Joseph!" Mom almost dropped a big brown bag of groceries. "What are you doing?"

"Baking a carrot cake."

"Look at this place!"

"I'll clean it up."

"We didn't even have any carrots..."

"I used canned carrots."

Mom put the bag on the kitchen table; the counter was covered with flour and sugar, spilled eggs and drippy batter. I hadn't had time to wash the dishes yet.

"Just go get the groceries out of the trunk," she said resolutely, shaking her head. After the initial shock, she didn't even yell about the mess, or ask why I was trying to bake a cake. Wordlessly, she scraped the whole fiasco into a garbage bag, and had the bake-ware and utensils soaking in a sink full of suds by the time I'd brought in the rest of the bags. "We'll go over Sunday, after Mass. I'll call first." Out of context, it took me a moment to grasp what Mom meant. Before I could speak, she went on, "Frances, I was thinking that maybe we could do something special for your twelfth birthday." She suddenly seemed to change the subject.

My birthday was next month, August, and we hadn't talked about it yet. After the things my mother said, I hadn't expected to celebrate at all. Now I was really confused. "Mom, what are we talking about? Where exactly are we going Sunday?"

"To see your Aunt and cousins," she began, "our relatives...Frances, you were right. I've been self-centered. The family needs help, and I stayed away because...what happened to Joan, well, don't ever repeat this, but it scares the livin' Jesus out of me. I just didn't know how to deal with it."

I was stunned at the apology; it was a first. Since the big blowout, I'd told myself that my mother couldn't hurt me anymore because I didn't care about her. Now I choked with pent-up emotion. I really did care what she thought about me after all.

"I'm just not sure what I should do..." she faltered.

"We'll bring a carrot cake, of course. That's how you brought me up," I smiled genuinely as I confirmed that she certainly did have a good influence on me, and it was appreciated.

"I did, didn't I," she responded with just a hint of a smile. "It's just that I don't know quite what to say...under the circumstances."

I thought a moment. "I don't think you have to say anything special. I think it helps just by being there. It's what I'd want if I had a nervous breakdown and they came and took my baby away."

Mom winced. "It's just so...so...awful. I don't know how else to put it."

"It's pretty awful," I agreed. Then I remembered she'd said something about my birthday. "Ah, what did you mean about doing something special for my birthday?"

Mom brightened a bit. "Your father and I have a surprise: we rented a cottage on the lake in New Hampshire for two whole weeks. We leave next week, and we'll celebrate your birthday. Of course, it's a vacation for everyone, but I know how much you loved the lake. We just couldn't go the last three summers because Nana was here, and she wasn't well."

"Oh Mom, thank you!" I gave her a hug around the middle, something I hadn't done in a while and thought I might never do again. This was clearly a peace offering. I'd take it.

"There's one more thing," she continued. "We can take Madeline and Annie, if you like, and if their parents agree."

I couldn't believe it. "Thank you Mom! That would be great-we'll have so much fun! I'll bet they never went away to a lake before. This will be the best birthday ever!"

Mom decided that carrot cake wouldn't be appropriate. Joan wasn't eating well, and banana nut-bread would be more nourishing. We made it that night and planned to visit the very next day.

When we walked into the Malone's house, I was struck by how quiet it was. Baby Michael was really gone. Aunt Hannah brought us into the parlor just off the kitchen that had been turned into a sick room-it was easier than going up and down the stairs for everything. Auntie Joan was lying on a lumpy worn-out sofa made up with bed sheets. There was a plastic TV tray with a glass of juice, a box of tissues, and a couple of bottles of prescription pills. It smelled like sickness. Joan lay on her side, and I could see her pregnant belly under the thick housecoat. Otherwise she was strikingly thin and her face was drawn, as if she'd aged ten years. Gramma explained that Auntie Joan was four months pregnant, anemic and suffering from exhaustion. The doctor ordered her to lie down and stay that way until she delivered, if she didn't want to lose the baby.

"What can I do, Joan? Just tell me," Mom said with feeling. "Can I make some tea for you? I brought banana nut-bread."

Joan seemed to look past us with glassy eyes, full of unspeakable pain. At last she spoke. "Yes, Evie dear, I'd like some tea and bread-thank you so much.

I've got to build up my strength. As soon as I'm strong again we can bring Michael home," she brightened a little. Aunt Hannah was standing off to the side where Joan couldn't see, and shook her head slightly to let us know Michael wasn't coming home.

We hadn't been there long when someone came to the front door. Soon Aunt Hannah ushered in a priest. "This is Father Mahood," she said. He was an older, white-haired man, but definitely not frail. He still moved with a youthful vigor, and looked to be in his late fifties or so. I was surprised to learn later that he was actually many years older.

Mom vacated the chair. "Good afternoon, Father," she said deferentially. He took the chair with a nod and we left the room. When my mother and aunt retired to the kitchen, I pretended I was going upstairs to find Maddy, but first I just had to linger in the hallway and listen a bit. It was the only way we kids ever found out what was really going on.

I heard the priest ask Auntie Joan, "Well, how are we holding up?" He had a bit of an Irish brogue.

"I'm fine, Father. It's just...if only little Michael could come home..."

"That's in God's hands. He's looking after little Michael," Father said with authority.

"I'm so sorry," she said plaintively. "They said something is...wrong with him, and I don't understand, but I know it's all my fault...and they won't let me visit or even tell me where he is...if only I could have another chance." She began to cry.

"Joan, you've got to be strong for all the children," he admonished. "You have to think of the one on the way. We all have trials. You can't let it defeat you. God will provide strength enough for this and anything else He sends us."

"Yes, I pray every hour for God to give me strength so I can be a better mother. Will you pray with me, Father?"

I was poised in the hallway, about to tiptoe upstairs when I heard Aunt Hannah from the kitchen. "Well, she's bad as can be, that's plain," she said flatly. "Father'll help her if anyone can. He was with me back in the terrible time when...when I lost them all," she said with a touch of bitterness. I knew that she had lost her husband and two or three children. I'd never heard her mention it before, and I was very curious. "They were taken from me one right after the other. Father Mahood came almost every day. He was a young priest back then, of course, and just like a second father to my boys," she said with gratitude. "As long as Father is with us, Joan will come round."

113

After Father Mahood left, we went to say goodbye to Auntie Joan. She seemed more comfortable, and told us about the family's relationship with their priest. "He was so good to Tommy when we lived over in Middlefield," she said. "Tommy was always getting into trouble in school, but he still wanted to be an altar boy. He tried so hard, but just couldn't learn the communion responses, or ring the bell at the right time during the blessing of the sacrament." She smiled, shaking her head at the recollection. "But Father Mahood let him serve anyway. He has a real understanding for Tommy."

"She used to be so lovely," Mom mused when we got home. "It's a shame, a terrible shame; she's completely worn out with all those children, and another on the way! She really should have known better. It just wasn't smart," she asserted.

"Huh? I thought you had to have babies if you were Catholic. I thought you couldn't use birth control," I blurted out, without really understanding how birth control worked.

"What? Where did you hear about that?" she asked indignantly.

"Oh, kids talk about stuff. I've heard the aunts and cousins talk too."

"Well you shouldn't listen in. It's not polite and it's certainly none of your business. As for me, if I could have had children, I would have had four. Maybe three, but no more than four; I wasn't going to end up like one of those poor women with a houseful of kids, looking like some old worn-out rag by the time I was forty. You can bet I would have done something about it! And I wouldn't have let some priest, or even the Pope tell me otherwise," she added with a bit of sass.

"Good for you."

"Oh, uh, Fran..."

"Yeah Mom?"

"You don't need to tell your father about our little talk," she said, somewhat deflated from her previous bravado.

"Of course not," I reassured her.

"You're getting to be a big girl, Frances. You've got to start thinking about these things. You've got to plan ahead for yourself."

I nodded. "I do, Mom. That's why I want to go to college, and have a career. And I love Dad, but I want a husband who'll allow me to work when my kids are big."

"Well, then I guess that's what you'll do. It's your life," she sighed.

I couldn't believe it. I never thought she'd come around and then all of a sudden, it was my life. Then I had an idea. "Mom..."

"Hmm?"

"This fall, when I start junior high, well, it'll only be six years to graduation..."

"Six years is still a while. What are you getting at?"

"You could start to talk to Dad about saving for college. Maybe he'd feel different about you getting a part-time job if was for college. It's expensive," I said, although I had no idea what expensive meant in dollars.

Mom looked interested. "It's true; I don't see where we would find the money in the budget if it were now. He'd have to give up those new cars for a few years." She was catching my drift. "I'll think about it. Meanwhile, we don't need to mention it," she cautioned.

"No, there's nothing to mention," I said conspiratorially.

14

"It's beautiful," Maddy's voice rumbled soft and low. "I've never seen real mountains before." Then she turned her head away sharply towards the window, but not before I saw her eyes, wide open in childlike wonder. She recovered herself and asked, "Think we should wake Annie?"

Annie was knocked out on Dramamine. No one had realized that she got car sick, since the family hardly traveled by car, and it never happened on short rides to school. The three of us were nestled deep in the polished black leather of the back seat; we'd cleaned the Buick before we left, and it was spotless. We'd been on the road for about forty minutes, when Annie suddenly started to drool and heave without warning. Maddy and I were sharing the driver side window, and I was in the middle hanging over her shoulder to sightsee. We'd given Annie the other window, and sat her on a pillow so she could look out. She was so small that the seat kind of swallowed her up. Suddenly I heard that unmistakable gagging sound that you make just before you hurl. "Dad, stop the car, Annie's gonna be sick!"

Mom whipped her head around. "Oh God, Joe, pull over. Girls, do something, cover her mouth!" Dad calmly swerved to the shoulder and we got her out just in time for her to throw up on her little red sneakers. Mom tried to be understanding, but her patient tone was studied. "Honey, why didn't you tell us you got carsick?" Annie's face was pale as a ghost. All she could do was shrug as Mom wiped her mouth with Kleenex. Mom pointed to her sneakers and asked us, "What am I supposed to do? Did she bring other shoes?"

Maddy had her arm protectively around her sister. Her posture was defensive as a mother bear. "No, Aunt Evelyn...she doesn't have any others." She dropped to one knee to help Annie out of the sneakers and socks and got vomit on her hands while undoing the laces. I would've been grossed out, but Maddy didn't even flinch. Mom wrinkled her nose, and handed her a wad of Kleenex so she could finish cleaning up. The sneakers were gritty with layers of dirt, and the rubber heels were worn down. The socks had holes. Other than that, she wore a crisp, poplin summer frock of yellow and white pinstripe. Mom had sent me to make sure they packed appropriate clothes. My hand-me-downs provided plenty of adorable little outfits; there was even a red, white and blue bathing suit with a ruffled skirt and matching sunhat. But I hadn't thought about the shoes. I wore summer sandals, and packed two pairs of sneakers and some flip-flops.

"What a mess." Mom almost looked as though she regretted inviting them.

"Well, at least it's not in the car," I offered, handing Maddy a few more Kleenex to wipe Annie's ankles.

"We'll stop at the next gas station and get some Dramamine. There are all sorts of tourist stops where we can get beach shoes, at least. These have got to go," Mom said with finality.

Annie gasped. I thought she was going to vomit, but she began to cry.

"What's the matter?" I asked.

She sobbed even louder. "I, I, uh," she struggled to explain. "I can't throw away my sneakers. Daddy bought them for me…he'll get maaaahhhd," she wailed. I was puzzled. I didn't have much experience with little kids, but something felt wrong. She seemed more frightened than sick now.

"Aw, no he won't," Maddy reassured her.

"I'll replace them, of course," Mom said. "I'm sorry Madeline, but I hadn't planned on doing laundry until the end of the week," she explained, "and those just aren't worth washing anyway."

We bundled Annie into the car. She was still crying, turning to look one last time at the forlorn footwear left by the side of the road. Dad had opened the trunk and come back with one of the toy sand pails we'd brought for making castles by the lake; he handed it to me, jerking his head towards Annie. "Good thinking," I said, ready with the pail just in case. Annie covered her face with a beach towel and wept softly all the way to the convenience store.

The four of us crowded into the tiny restroom at the gas station. Mom held Annie with her feet in the sink. "Wash her with soap, Frances," she commanded. I lathered the pink liquid hand-soap and rubbed it in between her toes. She was quiet and passive as Mom balanced her on one hip. Maddy grabbed a wad of paper towels and dried.

"There you go, my princess," I said. Then Dad carried her inside so she wouldn't get her feet dirty or cut-I was never allowed to go barefoot. While Mom found the Dramamine, I selected a pair of shiny red plastic beach shoes from a bin. "These OK Mom?"

"Perfect," she said with a bit of an edge, still disgruntled from the messy ordeal. "Stick them on her feet and see if they fit."

I took one little foot in my hand and slid it on. "Oh, Cinderella, they fit!" I tried to cheer her up. She looked at the shoes with wide eyes, and smiled the sweetest smile.

When we were all sitting in the back seat again, she extended her legs and pointed both toes like a ballerina, twisting her feet this way and that, admiring the cheap shoes. Suddenly all was right in her world, and she fell asleep peacefully, drugged on Dramamine. We traveled another hour or so, and the magnificent White Mountain range suddenly rose up before us.

"God no, don't wake her up," Mom whispered emphatically. Then she added, "The poor little thing was so sick back there; she needs to sleep. They'll be mountains enough all week, plenty of mountains all around a nice lake where you can swim."

The afternoon sun was casting a golden light on the mountain tops, and the valleys were already in deep green shadow. "We're almost there," I whispered excitedly. "Wait 'til you see it!"

The little cottage was one of six almost identical dwellings, all white painted shingles with peeked roofs. The only difference was the front doors, which were each done in a different primary color, like a box of crayons. It was so you didn't get mixed up and walk into the wrong one. Ours had a bright yellow door. Inside, they looked just like dollhouses. The walls were knotty pine, and everything was crisp and clean, with white and blue checked curtains and matching bedspreads. It smelled like pine cleaner. "Open the windows," Mom said, sniffing. There were two bedrooms, and we got the biggest, with one double bed and an extra cot.

"I want to sleep with Fran," Annie announced, hugging my arm.

"Ok with me," I said.

"Great, I get my own bed for a change!" Maddy exclaimed.

We brought everything inside and helped Mom unpack while Dad went for a takeout supper. We had planned to stop for lunch, but the incident by the side of the road kind of dulled everyone's appetite. After eating only some saltine crackers we'd bought to calm Annie's nausea, we were all ravenous. When Dad walked in with a bucket full of fried chicken, I'd never smelled anything so good! As soon as it was on the table, we kids dove in with both fists.

Half-way through the meal, Annie was munching away on a drumstick with a far-off, but deeply satisfied expression, and grease smeared across her face. She looked sort of like a contented carnivorous cow. Maddy had put away three pieces and some biscuits, and was furtively eyeing the bucket, wanting

118

more but trying to be polite. "Go on," I said, gesturing towards the bucket with a chicken wing, "have another piece." Maddy looked to my mom for a signal that it was OK to eat more. She really had surprisingly good manners, even if they were wrapped up in rough brown paper.

"You go ahead and eat as much as you like," Mom said sincerely. "You need to fill out those bones. You, on the other hand, have had enough," she informed me.

I had always liked to eat, and ranged from amply padded to slightly chubby my whole life. Now I was filling out all over. I'd begun wearing a real bra, but I had a roll of belly fat that was more prominent than my budding bosom. Mom started telling me to be careful, and watch what I ate. I joked that I watched it just fine, as it passed right under my nose and into my mouth.

"You'll be sorry," she warned.

"I know; I ate like a pig." I looked sheepishly at my protruding belly. Annie had sat beside me all along, so quiet we nearly forgot she was there. She'd finished her drumstick but was still gripping the bone in her little fist, absently staring out the window. Annie always seemed to drift on an invisible cloud between our world and someplace else. Slowly, she looked around, reorienting to our universe; in these transitional moments, you never knew what she might say. This time she came into focus and looked down at my stomach. Her eyes widened, and she patted it gingerly.

"Is it gonna bust?" Her concern was so genuine it was hilarious. Maddy started laughing so hard that she had to put both hands over a mouthful of food.

"Honestly, Frances," Mom started. "You need to learn to eat like a lady, not a truck driver."

"Hey! What's wrong with eatin' like a truck driver?" Dad chimed in.

"Nothing dear, if you're a man who happens to drive a truck," Mom answered wryly.

"Aw, she's fine," Maddy volunteered, after she'd managed to swallow and compose herself. "Frances just has a healthy appetite, 's all."

"Yeah, healthy like a truck driver," Dad retorted, laughing heartily.

"Frances is not like you, Madeline," Mom said. "She has a genetic tendency to get fat; she has to learn to watch what she eats."

Oh God not this again, I thought. Not the 'genetic tendency' as in, 'if you were my own child you'd have a perfect figure like me.' "Jeez, Mom, it's vacation...it's my birthday," I whined.

"Let the girl eat how she likes, Ev." Dad said. "She's not too fat."

"She's not fat," Maddy agreed. "She's just right."

I gave Mom a smug look. "See! Some people like me the way I am."

119

That night we lay down in a cozy room in crisp white sheets. Our double bed was pushed up against one wall, with the extra cot for Maddy against the other and only a few feet in between. Little Annie fell asleep beside me as soon as she hit the pillow. The breeze from the open window lifted the starched curtains gently. It smelled of trees and the lake. You could hear the water as it lapped against the rocks. "I can't wait until tomorrow," I whispered.

"Well, tomorrow'll come sooner if you go to sleep," Maddy answered quietly. "I'm exhausted."

"I'm so tired too-and so full," I whispered. I felt as if I might actually pop. "Maybe Mom's right," I sighed.

"You'd better get some sleep before Annie, uh, wakes up."

"Does she get up at the crack of dawn?" I asked, recalling that little kids sometimes did, especially if they were excited about a big day. "I once tried to get my parents up at 4:00 am for Christmas," I recalled aloud.

"Uh, no, that's not it," she answered in the darkness. "That's not what I mean. It's that she wakes up at night really scared. She gets bad dreams. She gets confused and thinks she sees things, like her dreams are still goin' on. Sometimes she sleepwalks. That's why we share a room-that and because me and Joanie can't stand each other. But Annie does better with me. I can usually calm her before she gets too loud and wakes up Dad. Then he comes bargin' in and yells at her. What an idiot," she added, so quietly I could barely hear, probably so Mom couldn't overhear.

"How long has that been going on? Does it happen every night?" I had a sense of foreboding.

"No, not every single night, or at least not really bad most of the time; but bad enough. She'll wake up everyone if she goes off," Maddy warned. "The trick is to get up and calm her before it's too late."

I inhaled deeply; the mountain air was cool and crisp with no humidity. It was quiet and peaceful. "Maybe she'll be alright here," I offered. I thought a moment and ventured in my softest night voice, "Do you think maybe Michael frightened her with his crying?"

"Who knows," she sighed in the darkness. "He sure scared the crap outa me."

"Oh well...if she wakes up, we'll deal with it. And tomorrow we'll go swimming-I love swimming. It's the only athletic thing I can do without falling down."

"Sounds great," she said sleepily. "I'll watch you swim."

"Huh?"

"I...never learned to swim. None of us did. We didn't get lessons or nothing; I'll have to watch Annie like a hawk."

I propped myself up on one elbow and tried to see her in the darkness. "Really? Gosh, we'll both watch her alright." Then I added on a lighter note, "I'll teach you to swim. I'm so fat you can use me as a flotation device!" I giggled as quietly as I could so as not to disturb my parents. I could hear Maddy chuckle gently in her deep, gravelly way, trying to stifle it.

"You kill me, Frances," she whispered. "You really are one funny kid...a floatation device? Ha ha..."

I was glad to have made her laugh. "See, being fat can come in handy."

"You're not fat."

"Am too. After this vacation I'm going to diet."

"OK...so go on a diet. Now go to sleep."

"OK."

She was drifting off. "You don't really need to go on a diet...you're fine...just...perfect," she said sleepily.

Annie slept pretty well the first night; there was probably residual Dramamine. She sat up and mumbled something a few times, confused and a little frightened, but I was able to settle her down. Once she woke me when the moonlight was shining in so brightly you could see everything in the room. She just popped right up in bed and stared at nothing. I could see her wide eyes gleaming. When I looked over to see if Maddy was asleep, she was gone. Must have gone to the bathroom. She took a while, and I hoped she wasn't sick, or got her period or something. Mine had started that summer. It came on lightly and without any major crisis, but I found becoming a 'young lady' a colossal pain in the ass. Finally, I heard the wooden screen door creek, as if someone were sneaking in quietly. I lay back down and pretended to be asleep. Maddy padded into the room like a cat and settled noiselessly onto the cot without squeaking the springs. The odor of cigarettes collided with the bleachy freshness of the room. I'd wondered how she would manage to quit for two weeks. I was there when Mom had told her there'd be absolutely no smoking. Before she could answer, Dad had chimed in with the warning: "That's right. Don't you let me catch you with a cigarette, OK?" She'd said 'OK' a bit glumly. Then I saw him sneak her a quick wink. I guess he understood that it's pretty hard to go cold-turkey, even for a kid. Dad gave her a way out without breaking her word. She wouldn't get caught, I'd pretend not to know, and everybody'd be happy.

"I can't believe no one mentioned that those kids can't swim," Mom whispered, obviously annoyed. It was early morning and they were in their bedroom, but the pine walls were thin and you could hear everything.

"Don't worry about it. I'll watch out for the little gal. The big one has enough sense not to get into trouble," Dad said. "You can't blame them," he added. "How could they learn? Joan couldn't take those kids anywhere, with no car and no money. She had no time anyway, not with that poor little baby boy... what a shame."

I looked at Maddy and mouthed the word 'sorry'. I was embarrassed, but she shrugged it off like it didn't bother her in the least.

"Your dad's right," Maddy said as we went out to the sandy beach with the pails and towels. "I never realized how much we didn't have until I saw what you got. Not that I care for myself, but I wish Annie got more stuff-like real birthday parties with other kids, and trips to the zoo. I wish she'd learn to swim, and get to see the mountains every summer. She likes those nice clothes too," she added.

I spread a towel on the sand and showed Annie how to fill the pail with the shovel. We had walked her into the water up to her ankles to fill up a pail, and warned her not to go one step further without a lifejacket. Still, we felt someone always had to watch her. As she worked on her castle, Annie chatted away about the house she was making out of sand. "We could build a big house out of sand, and we could all live in it together." She added some water and patted the sand with her little hands.

"I'm going to take a swim now, OK?"

"'Sure. Let's see," Maddy said.

I waded up to my waist and dove in, swimming out to the deep part of the lake before turning parallel to the shoreline for a stretch. About twenty minutes later I swam back to the shore, and didn't stand-up until I was thigh-deep. I always felt so light and graceful in the water. Then gravity weighed me down as I clambered out. It was as if I'd suddenly gained a hundred pounds. I lumbered through the dense sand that had been trucked in to create a beach and flopped down like a big walrus, puffing from exertion. I was out of shape, and hadn't kept up with swimming practice at the public pool.

My floral print bathing suit was two-piece, with an apron top that clung to my ample mid-section when wet. I chose this style because I looked even worse in a form-fitting one-piece, and I sure wasn't going to wear a bikini. I had needed a real bra rather suddenly this summer, after unceremoniously sprouting some pendulant, fat little boobies that jiggled when I walked, like my belly. The wet bathing suit was unforgiving of my figure. I sighed, and decided to forget about how I looked and enjoy myself. But my mother was right; I really ought to start a diet after vacation.

Maddy didn't own a bathing suit, and my spare one wouldn't fit her even if she would wear one-which she declined. Mom offered to take her shopping for a suit, but she said no thanks, she'd wear cut-offs and a t-shirt. She had grown taller, and had the boniest knees and elbows I'd ever seen on a girl. She was broad shouldered, but skinny as a rail and didn't seem to need a bra. Maddy didn't care about clothes at all, and wore boy's dungarees, cast-offs from Tommy, I expect. Her hair had grown longer and she pulled it into a messy pony-tail. She sat with her legs crossed, looking out over the water while absently sifting sand through her fingers. As I waddled across the sand, I thought she kind of smirked in spite of herself, then looked away and pretended she hadn't.

"What?" I asked.

"Nothing." She shrugged. "You're a good swimmer," she added.

"Thanks. I look like a baby whale and swim like one too. I saw that smirk," I said good-naturedly. "You know," I lowered my voice, "I got my period this summer. Before I was a chubby kid, but all of a sudden I'm blowing up like a balloon. I gained eight pounds since school ended."

"Did you grow even one inch taller all year? I feel like a giant next to you."

"Yeah, I grew about an inch and a quarter taller, and about six inches side-ways! How can you eat so much and stay so thin?"

"I have no idea."

"I wonder if my mother, you know, my biological mother, was fat. Or maybe my father was fat. My adopted dad is kind of portly, and people who don't know I was adopted are always saying, 'Oh, she looks just like her father.'"

"Uh huh," she mumbled, drifting into her own thoughts.

"Are you hungry," I asked.

"Yeah, I'm hungry, especially since I've had to give up smoking-for the most part," she said quietly.

"I know. Annie woke me up the other night when you stepped out. Just be careful."

"Oh...sorry," she said.

"Let's get something to eat and then go out in one of the rowboats," I suggested. There were half a dozen wooden rowboats available for summer guests. Someone had made them by hand a long time ago. They were all painted in pine green, with white trim. I loved those boats almost as much as swimming. I could row all day, and this year I had a friend to go with me.

"OK," she said flatly.

"It's really fun," I added. I had hoped she'd be more enthusiastic about it.

"It's just that I never been in a boat before," she explained. "Probably 'cause I can't swim. Hey Frances...could you teach Annie to swim? Even a little, so she wouldn't drown if she fell in?"

"I can if she wants to learn, if she's not afraid. And I can teach you too."

"Nah, I'm probably too old to learn," she said. I wondered if she was afraid of the water, but I didn't want to embarrass her by asking.

We went inside and ate some sandwiches. After lunch we picked a boat, and Dad helped us push-off, making sure there were two floatation cushions on board. I gripped both oars. "This is how you row," I explained, sitting squarely in the middle of the wooden seat with my back to the bow.

"Uh, isn't the pointy part of the boat the front?"

"Yes. That's the bow, and that's the stern," I lectured.

"Then why are you going backwards?"

"I don't know. It's just the way you row a boat." I shrugged, never having questioned it before.

"Ass-backwards? Ha, ha. How do you know where you're going?"

"You can tell me," I suggested. "You be the first-mate."

"Aye-Aye, Captain Ass-backwards!" She saluted. We rowed out into the middle of the big lake. It was round and deep, and the mountains behind us were mirrored in the clear water. The sharp mountain peaks seemed to shimmer as the water rippled. "It's real deep; I can see clear to the bottom and it must be twenty feet or more!" she said looking over the side in awe. "Holy crap!" she exclaimed.

"What is it?" I asked.

"Fish! Big fish! I can see 'em swimming!"

I'd never seen Maddy so unreservedly happy. I looked over the side and acted like I'd never seen fish swimming in the lake before. "Wow, they're huge!" She was still leaning over, mesmerized. "Do you want to get some poles and try fishing? I can ask Dad..."

"You mean kill 'em?" She looked incredulously at me.

"Well, only if you want to eat some, but I used to just fish for fun and then throw them back."

"How is that fun for the fish?"

"I suppose it isn't fun for the fish...I never thought of that." I rowed across to the other side, until the people back on the beach looked far away. Maddy reached into the pocket of her jeans and pulled out a ballpoint pen with a click top; then she took out a matchbook. She unscrewed the pen, and shook out a cigarette, holding it low in the boat between her legs. She'd taken the guts out of the pen.

"Whada ya think...pretty sneaky, huh?"

"I think you could be a spy."

"Which way is the wind blowing?"

"Not sure, but we're too far off anyway."

"Sorry Frances, but I'm dyin'," she said.

I maneuvered the boat around and began to row slowly along the opposite shore. There was no one else on the water. Maddy bent down, ducked her head and lit up, waving her hand to disperse the smoke. "No one's looking this way," I said. "Just don't throw it in the water when you're done," I added. She nodded, and sucked it down to a butt in no time. After dousing it in the water, she stuck it back into the empty shell of a ballpoint pen. Then she took a squashed packet of peppermints from her pocket and popped one into her mouth.

"Ya know, I do kinda feel better, not smokin' so much. Maybe I'll quit someday."

"That'd be great," I encouraged, rowing the boat along. "It's supposed to be really bad for you...splish...much worse than people thought...splash. I had a Godmother...splish...she was only thirty-four...splash...my Mom's good friend...splish...died of lung cancer...splash."

"Now there's a cheerful thought."

"Sorry. It's just that...splish...I worry about you...splash...I don't want anything to...splish...happen to you...splash."

"Don't worry Frances. Nothin's gonna' happen to me," Maddy said, with a devilish gleam in her eye. The sun was getting low, and I could see her face was already sunburnt. "My Gramma says that heaven won't have me, and hell's afraid I'll take over."

"Come on! I can teach you to swim-it'll be fun." It was a perfect morning, with white puffy clouds in a great blue sky.

"I sink like a cement block," Maddy said. "You go on." She sat in the sand and showed no sign of relenting.

"Please," I whined, "what if you fall out of a boat someday?" I playfully grabbed her wrist with both hands and began to tug. She sat in the sand with her heels dug in, smirking at me with that half-grin I'd come to love. I leaned back and used my weight for leverage. With only one muscular arm she could easily pull me forward. It was an all-out tug 'o war and she was winning with one arm! I threw myself back with full force, and finally started to lift her off her butt. She laughed, and drew her arm in tighter. I was determined to win. I held on tight and suddenly flopped back onto the sand like a beached whale, just managing to pull her over on top of me. "I won! I won! Now you have to come swimming!" I crowed.

"You won?!" She laughed into my face. "If you won, how come you're flat on your back and I'm on top?" She sat up, straddling my girth, propped up with her knees in the sand so as not to crush me. "Hey, this is comfy, like a big pillow," she said playfully while pretending to bounce up and down on my middle. "I think I'll sit here a while." She looked happier and more relaxed than I'd ever seen her. I tried to raise myself up but didn't get far with her sitting on me, which got us laughing more.

"You're squashing my belly...I can't breathe," I giggled, trying to wriggle out from under her-but I couldn't. "OK, you win," I surrendered. "Now please come swimming with me," I begged.

"Oh for chrisakes!" She only pretended to be put out. "You're not gonna give me any peace 'til I do." She sprung up on her muscled legs, gripped my hand and pulled me to my feet as if I were light as a feather.

"My God!" I marveled. "How'd you get to be so strong?"

"Dunno." She shrugged.

We walked into the water and I went about waist deep. Maddy hesitated just a moment and then waded in until she came right up to where I was standing. She wasn't used to moving in water, and walked like she was slogging through quicksand.

"OK. The first think you've got to learn is how to float," I began. "Actually, before that you need to put your face in the water and learn how to blow bubbles out your nose, so as not to breathe in water."

"Ah, I think I know not to breathe in the water," she said sarcastically.

"Well, just to be on the safe side, try going under and holding your breath, then exhale through your nose gently, and come back up. You can do that," I added pointedly. "It's just like smoking." She snorted in amusement and then just sort of sat down on the sand beneath our feet. She really did sink like a stone! It went fine at first, and she calmly blew bubbles, sitting there cross-legged with her eyes closed, like an underwater Buddha. Then she tried to stand-up just like you would on land. She had no natural instinct to push off the bottom, and lost her balance. Maddy swayed like a drunken sailor, then fell back under and started to flounder. I grabbed her forearm and hoisted her to her feet. She coughed and sputtered because water went up her nose when she went down again unexpectedly. Her lung capacity couldn't be too good, I thought. "You OK?"

"Just fine." She coughed a bit. "Now what?"

I was relieved that she wasn't going to quit because of a shaky start. "Well, holding your breath needs to become a reflex," I said seriously. "Let me show you how to get off the bottom." In order to sink, I had to hop up and plunge myself under, because I was so buoyant. Then I used my arms in a kind of breast-stroke and pushed up with my legs gently. Being in the water was so natural for me that I had to stop and think about it first in order to explain it. We spent the next ten minutes submerging, falling backwards and standing up without breathing in water. Soon she was pushing off from the lake-bed and shooting up like a torpedo to make a big splash. She learned when to breathe, and could consistently regain her footing. Maddy seemed liberated from her fear of the water.

"Now let's start floating," I said. "Learning how to float properly can save your life; you can do it when you're too tired to swim, like if you fell from a boat far from shore," I added seriously.

She was ready to give it a try, but warned, "You saw how I float."

"Yeah, like a bag of rocks. But even a bag of rocks will float if you put air in it," I said, taking a few steps back until I was in up to my chest. "Come out a bit further," I coaxed, stretching my arm to her. "You'll be more buoyant," I explained. She moved in closer. "Now take a deep breath, hold it, and lay back. I'll hold you up at first 'til you float. I promise I won't let you go under."

She centered herself, and sucked in air before letting herself fall backwards. I put my hand under her spine to arch her back, but she resisted and would have sunk if I'd let go. A body is so light in the water; I held her easily, as if she were a small child. "Spread your arms a bit. Put your shoulders back." She was working against me as I tried to lay her back, so I placed one hand on her opposite shoulder to keep her from folding like a pretzel. This was harder than I expected. "Chin up. Let the water go around your ears…it's OK, I whispered." Maddy was rigid in the water, breathing shallowly. She seemed to be fighting the urge to stand up and quit. "Relax…open your eyes. You've got to arch your back-you're caving in the middle. Breathe in and fill your lungs with air so you'll float."

She sucked in a big breath and willed herself back so her chest lifted. I felt her rise from my hand, floating on her own now. Suddenly an impressive pair of fully formed breasts rose up from the water, covered only by a wet t-shirt. Looked to be about a B cup, round and solid, not wiggly jiggley like mine. How had she kept those hidden, and for that matter, why? I knew she must have her reasons-maybe she was just bashful, or her mother couldn't take her out shopping for a bra. I went on with my swimming instruction and pretended not to notice. "There, feel that? You're floating! I'm going to take my hand away-just let yourself float a while."

Her eyes were closed in concentration. I hovered protectively, ready to hold her up and keep her from sinking. Her breasts rose and fell evenly as she lay on the water; I could feel her breath gently on my face like a lover. All at once she pulled her arms over her chest and folded up quickly, ready to sink. I steadied her until she regained her footing. "Great!" I cheered. She stood back up with ease, and kind of squared her shoulders, hunching forward a bit in her customary stance. Her breasts disappeared, as if they were swallowed up somewhere for safe keeping. Now her distinctive posture and rather stiff, masculine gait made sense. She had to keep them from moving as she walked unfettered by a brassiere.

"We'll work on it every day," I said. "You can float; you just need to take in a big breath of air because you're so...solid," I said.   "Watch me," I added, falling back and spreading my arms gracefully. My belly quickly rose to the surface and my fatty breasts bobbed gently. I could practically sleep on the water. My ears were submerged, but I still heard her chuckling, so I stood up.

"You float like a duck!" she marveled.

"More like a whale," I countered, laughing at myself. We went back to shore. I swam a few strokes to get knee deep before walking out. Maddy maneuvered by propelling herself forcefully, flailing and splashing, actually enjoying the water. I was proud of my success as a water safety instructor. This time, I got to be the confident and protective one. I thought about how Maddy had struggled just to float-the one thing that I did so easily. I suspected there was something she feared more than drowning.

Those two weeks at the lake flew by like the summer clouds, yet remained with me in memory as solid as the surrounding mountains. I was never alone. We ate and slept and did everything together; it was like having sisters at last. Every day we rowed the boat and swam in the lake. I think I loved the old wooden rowboats even more than swimming. I loved the way the oarlocks creaked, the way it bobbed in the current. Maddy had never been in a boat, but she took to it naturally and soon handled the craft with more skill and grace than I. Dad had taken Annie out once, but she clung nervously to the seat and looked over the side into the water with dread. She didn't want to do it again. My dad took her down to the water, but she only wanted to wade in to fill her pail, to make sandcastles and mud pies on the beach. But the thing she loved best was to feed the Mallard ducks that swam in the lake. If you threw bread, they'd come quacking and waddling to shore and eat it. Annie was endlessly fascinated with the ducks, and would have cleaned out a day's supply of bread if Mom hadn't caught on to where it was going, and established a two slice limit.

The simplest things made us happy. We were allowed to walk to the little tourist strip a mile or so down the road. With a few dollars for ice cream and trinkets, we felt like millionaires. The country road leading from the cabins was gravel until it met up with the highway. I ground my feet a bit, enjoying the sound. I'd always liked crunching that gravel; it signified vacation. When we came to the quiet rural highway, one of us always held on to Annie's hand, mindful of her propensity to suddenly flit and prance about like a baby deer. I'd almost learned the hard way how vulnerable she was. It was the only dark cloud in an otherwise perfect vacation, but it could have ended badly.

The first time we went to the shops, she'd nearly turned a cartwheel into a car that was backing slowly from a parking spot. I was busy fishing a piece of candy out of a brown paper bag-those little drops of colored sugar pasted to a strip of paper. Kids just loved sucking those off the paper. One second she was right by my side, and then suddenly she just flung herself onto her hands with her little bare legs lifting in the air. The driver sure didn't expect that! In the time it took me to drop the bag and screech, Maddy had burst into motion, whisked her straight into the air by her little waist and spun around, neatly stepping out of the car's path.   Annie just froze, hanging motionless like a snared rabbit.

"I'm so sorry," I said. I was shaken. I felt horrid, and lost my appetite for candy.

Maddy put her sister down and warned, "You've got to stop and think, Annie. You've got to look around before you go turning cartwheels. Someday you're gonna get hurt. Next time I might not be there to catch you! Then what?!" Annie's chin started to quiver, and she sniffed before crying in earnest.

"Oh, don't cry." I moved in to comfort her.

"She's gotta learn!" Maddy snapped.

We walked back in silence. I was supposed to be watching her and I let everyone down. I imagined what might have happened in the blink of an eye. One minute we were so happy, and the next...Annie would have been seriously hurt or killed if Maddy wasn't lightning quick and agile as an Olympic athlete, while I stood there like a big fat idiot and screeched like a baby. My parents would have assumed responsibility, and both families would have been permanently scarred. That night as she slept, I inhaled the fragrance of Annie's soft hair, and knew I couldn't have loved her more if she had been my sister by birth. I offered sincere prayers of thanks to God, something I hadn't bothered to do in a long time. When daylight came I looked out at the glistening lake as if it were the first morning of creation.

For my twelfth birthday, Mom and Dad gave me a gold ring with my birthstone, a green Peridot cut in the shape of a little heart. It was the first real piece of jewelry I had received, and I was completely surprised, and moved. We were sitting around a festive table; Mom had driven to a nice bakery and got a fancy cake, with pink icing flowers and *Happy Birthday Fran* on top. They remembered the ice cream.

"It's beautiful," I said. "This is the best birthday I ever had." After I'd put on the ring, I hugged Mom and Dad. I felt tears coming, and for the first time in my life cried because I felt so happy. Maddy squirmed a bit, uncomfortable at all the emotional fuss. Then Annie suddenly became aware of what was happening around her again.

"What's the matter, Fran?" Her sweet little voice was full of concern. "Why is Fran crying?" She looked to her sister for an explanation, but only got a shrug.

I wiped my eyes with a party napkin and began to laugh at myself. "Nothing's the matter. I'm crying because I'm happy," I explained to her. Seeing her looking up full of tenderness for me made me think again how special and fragile life was. It made me cry more, this time, with gratitude.

"That's silly. You're only supposed to cry if you're sad," she corrected. We all laughed at her serious explanation.

"I...um, I mean, we got somthin' for ya. Annie decorated the paper." Maddy thrust a package at me. "Here, open it." It was gift-wrapped in a paper bag with the logo from the Mapleton Center Bookstore. Annie had decorated it with a picture of three girls holding hands, surrounded by hearts and flowers. On the right was a chubby form, with a tall thin figure on the left and a little girl with long hair in the middle. The faces were smiling, and there was a yellow sun.

"That's us," Annie announced proudly.

I marveled at the artwork, and pretended not to know it was a book until I opened it. It wasn't just any book, but a hard-cover copy of <u>My Friends the Wild Chimpanzees</u>, the second edition published just this year by the National Geographic Society. I'd admired it at the library many times, and Maddy knew it. I'd wanted that book, but didn't expect to get it. Mom certainly wouldn't have picked it out. Even though she'd softened in her attitude towards college, she still wasn't ready to encourage my interest in science.

"Thank you," I began, "it's one of the best gifts ever...and I love you both so much!" I threw my arms around my cousins and started to cry again. I'd taken the liberty many times with Annie-she was naturally affectionate, but had always held back with Maddy. My tears were streaming like rain.

She patted me roughly on the back and said sarcastically, "Watch out, you'll soak the pages and make the ink run."

It was our last night on the lake, and I wasn't ready for it to end. Maddy had worked hard and learned the beginners backstroke with the frog-kick, well enough to swim thirty yards or so along the shoreline. We took our last trip out in the rowboat and just drifted.

"I ran out of cigs the day before yesterday," she mentioned absently with a shrug. "Hey, watch this." She stood up deliberately with a mischievous grin. The boat rocked gently, but she counter-balanced to stop it.

"What are you doing?" I asked, confused. Her gray eyes gleamed with the light that danced on the surface of the water in the setting sun. Then she turned and plunged over the side, carefully, so as not to tip the boat. I was propelled back, and pulled once with the oars to steady it. She hit hard and sank down, down deep. When I looked over the side, she hadn't even started back up. We hadn't practiced any deep water swimming, no diving or jumping at all. I grabbed the floatation square she'd been sitting on and held it ready. The water was clear, and I watched her kick and pull her way up. It seemed like slow motion. Finally her head emerged and she was treading water with great effort, trying to catch her breath. She spouted water from her mouth like a dolphin and shook her lank hair out of her eyes with a thwack. "What the hell are you doing?" I asked, a bit less alarmed now.

"Swimming!" She rolled onto her back and started frog-kicking to shore. We were pretty far out. I rowed along so that I was never more than a few yards away and kept watch. I knew how fast someone could get tired and drown, especially a new swimmer who hadn't learned her limits. A couple of times she picked up her head and looked to shore to see how much further, or glanced back to check and see if I was still there. A couple of times she stopped kicking and floated for a rest, arching her back just like I taught her, but she never quit. She made it back, so exhausted she staggered onto the sand and fell face forward, playing out the drama of a shipwrecked sailor. We laughed over her antics all evening, and couldn't stop talking long after dark.

"I wish we could stay here longer," I said, "maybe forever. I wish it would always be just like this…I don't want summer to end."

"Mmmm…that'd be the best. And we'd have never ending buckets of fried chicken."

15

We drove home before Labor Day weekend. School would begin on September sixth, and we scrambled to do last minute shopping. Back in July, Mom saw how fast I was growing and changing; she thought it best to wait until the end of the summer to buy fall clothing. Now I suddenly had a brand new body to dress, and I had decidedly mixed feelings about it. To complicate things, the clothing styles had changed more drastically in the last year than they had in previous years. It was nearing the end of 1970. Mom tried to tell me nicely that I didn't have the figure for it, but I picked out the latest fashion, and went decked out in a pair of purple hot-pants with a long matching vest, all made of woven polyester. It's embarrassing to look back at the pictures of my chubby thighs in those shorts, set off by the white vinyl boots that came to my kneecaps. At the time I thought I looked gorgeous. Good thing Maddy didn't accidently flick some hot ashes my way; I would've probably blown up.

On the first morning of school, we met up with Kathy Kelly and Dotty Day, and a girl named Pamela who'd recently moved into the projects. She was going into the eighth grade. We'd already decided to walk together for safety. The junior high school had a reputation for being a rough place.

When we got there, they herded us all to an assembly in the huge auditorium. The school was packed. The kids were so wild it was like a zoo with all the cage doors left open. The principal was a tiny bald man with a squeaky voice, and the microphone kept making a high pitched feed-back noise. They roared with harsh laughter, imitating and mocking him. Some of them stood on the wooden folding seats and hooted like a troupe of chimpanzees. I'd never seen kids defy a teacher, let alone the principal. They'd had us under control back at Edmunds Elementary. Then a big male gym teacher grabbed a couple of boys off the chairs by their arms, spun them around and slammed them up against the wall hard. "You!" He bellowed pointing his finger at another. "Sit down and shut up!" A boy sniggered, and was promptly hauled out of his seat and thrown over with the other miscreants. "Detention!" he yelled. "Anybody else?" He glowered at the boys and they went quiet. I'd never seen a teacher handle students that way, not physically, not in public school. I was afraid, even though I knew I'd never do anything to get treated like that.

It was a mean place. In the corridors, they didn't care who you were, they just pushed and shoved and called names. The favorites were homosexual slurs like 'faggot' and 'queer', which competed for popularity with the old standby, 'retard'; the insults were usually predicated with the F word. By now I'd heard something about gay men and lesbians, but since I didn't know exactly what went on when people had sex, I was fuzzy about what those terms actually meant.

With thirty-five to forty students to a room, my classes were crowded and noisy. Most of the teachers couldn't control the students. It wasn't just that they didn't care about learning; these kids seemed to think that the whole purpose of school was to see how disruptive they could be. It was a source of amusement, and a way to gain popularity. The worst offenders were looked up to by the rest.

Hooliganism was rampant. They threw everything out the windows-books, pencils, and the stapler from the teacher's desk. One girl came to school on crutches, and while she was sitting in her seat someone took them and got the screws out. Then a bunch of them just threw the pieces out the window one by one, the screws and handles and rubber cushions. I sat rigid in my seat, afraid to move lest I draw the attention of the pack. The teacher was clearly afraid of them too. She turned to the girl with the cast on her leg and told her hold on to her things next time.

Like jackals, they preyed upon the weak and vulnerable. The seventh grade English teacher was an older man with snow white hair, who always dressed formally in a suit and tie. He was soft spoken and genteel, and I'm sure he could have taught us much if anyone had let him. The poor man was rumored to have shell-shock from WWII. I can't say for sure if that was true, but he was very timid. The boys would wait until his back was turned and then dump over one of the heavy metal desks-the kind with the chairs attached. The loud noise made me jump even though I saw it coming. It made the teacher run out of the room; he must have really needed that job to put up with them.

I couldn't bear it. Clearly, Jr. High East was run-down, over-crowded and staffed by teachers who were either young and inexperienced, or too old to care and just hanging on until retirement. All the kids from the poorer section of Mapleton were funneled there, kids with less educated parents and no clue as to how important school was. Some of them were already counting the years until they could legally drop out. Mapleton Heights kids all went to Jr. High West. It was up the other end of town, but it might as well have been on another planet. They had the best of everything. I tried to explain the situation to my parents, but they didn't seem to understand how bad it was, or else they didn't want to. I brought up the subject of Catholic school. Mom got annoyed and told me public school was good enough: they already paid high taxes and they weren't going to pay for private tuition. She insisted that it couldn't be *that* bad, and told me I'd just have to make the best of it.

As the weeks wore on, I noticed that Maddy was disappearing for more and more of the day. The classes were so big and chaotic that you could slip off without being missed. I don't think anyone really cared. The less kids, the easier it was for them. I'd look for her after school, but she was already gone. Then I'd see her on the corner of Broadway. She'd taken to hanging out with a tough looking group. They all wore black jeans and black leather jackets. I have no idea where she got a black leather jacket, and I hardly recognized her the first time I saw it. She was with a pale, skinny girl who wore heavy dark eyeliner and stared off into space with a far-away look. Even though I was definitely not one of the cool kids, Maddy didn't disown me. "Hey Frances! Com' 'ere," she hollered. I approached cautiously. "This *he*'eh 's my cousin Frances," she introduced me.

"Hi," I said awkwardly. They were all smoking of course.

"Heh, heh, Frances?" One boy laughed at me.

"Yeah, Frances," Maddy said, punching him in the arm. "Something wrong with your ears?"

"Duh, no," he said, rubbing his arm. He looked to be on the margins of the group.

"I guess I'll see you back home," I offered.

"Yeah. See ya," she said. "Wait," she changed her mind. "I'm goin' home too."

"Where have you been all day?" I asked once we'd walked out of earshot.

"Just hangin' out."

"Won't you get in trouble for cutting class?"

"Guess not," she said with a shrug. "Don't think anyone gives a crap."

"Are you learning anything in your classes?"

"Are you?" she asked sarcastically.

"No. Not even in advanced English. There's nothing advanced about it; I finish the assignments in class and just read library books-at least I try to read over the commotion. The kids make fun of me for reading. They make fun of me when I talk so I keep my mouth shut. The other day a girl tried to put staples in my blouse while I was just sitting in class minding my business. I called out to the teacher and she told me not to disrupt class. What the hell?"

"Tell me about it," she said. "Math is the same way. The teacher passes out stupid work-sheets, the kind we did in third grade. Then he sits with the boys and talks about football. He's the boys' gym teacher too. That place sucks!" she pronounced.

"It sucks," I agreed. I didn't know how I could take two years of it. "After two years at this place...I'll fall so far behind I'll never catch up in high school; that's assuming I can live through the next two years. I'll never go to college," I lamented.

"Just keep on reading. Keep going to the main library and teach yourself. You'll make it, Frances. You're just too smart not to make it."

"You've got to make it too! We should go read together," I pleaded.

"Nah," she said.

"Why not?"

"It's no use. There's nothing out there for me to do anyway. Not in college, not anywhere."

It was the most despondent thing I'd ever heard her say, and it frightened me. "You can't think that way," I said. "Sometime, we should talk to my dad. He's not book smart, but he knows things. He understands people-like your brother Tommy. Maybe he can help." She shrugged. "He might have some ideas, something we can't think of because, well, we're kids."

"I'll think about it," she said. I felt a little better. Then she added, "Frances, don't say nothin' to your dad, OK? Let me think about it a while. Let me ask him myself if I want to."

"OK; I won't say anything about it. But I am going to talk to him about how awful school is for me." She nodded with a slight grunt and lit up again.

16

I got through September and now it was almost the end of October. Even though I wasn't challenged in school, I came home every day exhausted just from coping with the noise and abuse. I did what little homework was expected and spent the rest of the time reading on my own, so I had a lot of free time. One particularly boring, rainy Saturday afternoon I wandered over to see if Maddy was home. We never used the phones because the Malone kids weren't allowed to use the phone; her dad checked the phone bill. She didn't call for me anymore in the morning, and if I didn't go around the block at just the right time, she and Tommy were already gone. I didn't know it then, but school was even worse for her than for me. She and her brother got picked on a lot, but she was too proud to tell me. After school she just hadn't been around much. I don't know where she went, but several times I'd walked around the block and tapped anxiously on the back door, only to get no answer. I was careful not to disturb her mom, or wake her grandmother, but then I wasn't sure if anyone had even heard.

This time she opened the door and smiled at me in her funny half-smirk before she had time to think about it. It was kind of a tired, almost sad smile, but I knew she was glad to see me. "Hey," I said. I felt a sudden happiness, the way kids do at the sight of their friends. I realized I hadn't felt like a kid in a while. It was a sweet, airy feeling, like pink bubblegum.

"Hey what?" she said, looking down at me.

Children don't need a reason to be with a friend, but suddenly I felt kind of foolish standing there without a purpose, as if the gum had popped in my face. "Ah, wanna do something?" It was all I could think to say and I hoped it would be enough. I just wanted to be with her again.

"Sure, why not. Come on in," she said with a shrug. She'd been in the kitchen helping Joanie prepare the vegetables for the big Saturday night boiled dinner. Joanie was grimly attacking a heap of carrots with a sharp knife, and barely nodded when I walked in. She was a hard worker, I'd give her that; she'd worked hard ever since I met her, and now did all the housework her mother no longer could. But she didn't do it out of the goodness of her heart. Maddy told me her dad gave Joanie a pretty substantial allowance-cash, as well as cigarettes, and enough of both to spare if she helped her out in a pinch so she could get out for the evening with her boyfriend.

Maddy explained that Joanie had been 'boy-crazy' ever since sixth grade, and started making-out early, behind her father's back. She got caught once with a hickey on her neck, and Maddy still remembered the beating; you could hear it all over the house. After that Joanie made sure the boys sucked someplace where her father wouldn't see. One morning when the sisters were getting dressed, Maddy saw the telltale marks on her breasts. Joanie had just started junior high school. She threatened to slit Maddy's throat in her sleep if she told on her. She didn't have to say that; Maddy's not a tattletale.

Joanie was never much of a sister, and didn't seem have much use for girlfriends either. She never kept the same friends very long. Now she had a steady boy-friend, and spent all her free time with him. Jack Mack was several years older, and had dropped out of high school. It wasn't clear what he did for work. Maddy said he did some kind of odd jobs. He couldn't seem to find a real job because he had a criminal record; he got into knife fights, and had been arrested more than once before he was eighteen. My mother was appalled, and told me I was not having anything to do with boys until I was sixteen, and then only boys she approved of. But as long as Joanie did all the house-work, Uncle Malone looked the other way and didn't ask questions. She could get all the hickeys she wanted.

I was curious as to what kind of odd jobs earned you enough money to buy the Chevy convertible Jack drove. Most guys his age didn't even have a car, and his wasn't an old beater. It was new when he bought it. He bought Joanie stuff too-clothes and records, and even a stereo to play them on. Maddy told me that sometimes Joanie skipped school and spent time in her room with Jack, listening to the records. It turned out he was the one who'd given Maddy the 'leather', as the kids called the black leather jackets that were suddenly so popular in junior high. When I asked why he'd given it to her, she told me she helped him with a job.

"Like chores or something?"

"Yeah...like chores or something," she said. "Listen Frances...Jack is just a small time punk, but he's bad news. Joanie don't know it, but she's playin' with fire." Maddy sounded upset, so I stopped asking questions.

Between the household drudgery and Jack Mack, I don't think Joanie did much by way of school work. I don't think anybody cared, or even expected her to graduate. Joanie wasn't a likable girl, but I had to feel a bit sorry for her.

"Can I help?" I asked, not wanting to be useless.

"Nah, there's not much left," Maddy said. "We can go on upstairs in a few minutes." She was peeling the potatoes. I don't think they had more than one peeler anyway.

"How's Annie doing in school?" I asked.

"Uh, OK, I guess...she doesn't like first grade as much as *Kindagahten*," Maddy elaborated.

"That's too bad. Maybe she'll get to like it-it's early yet," I added hopefully.

"Umph," she grunted.

The conversation stalled. Except for the slicing sound of the peeler and the thwack, thwack of Joanie's knife on the cutting board, the house was stone quiet-no howling, no head-banging, no Baby Michael. Maddy never talked about her brother. I couldn't tell if she was sad or relieved, but I expect it was both. I was thoroughly coached not to ask, of course. Mom said that he had some kind of "mental retardation" as she put it, but couldn't or wouldn't elaborate, and claimed not to know where they'd taken him. I only know that it broke Auntie Joan's heart, and seemed to unravel her mind. I'd sat by her bed a few times and just listened. It was like watching a piece of thread from a garment that's caught in a fan, whirling round and round until it disappears, leaving the wearer naked.

I don't know what got into me that afternoon. I'd never really spoken with Joanie, not alone anyway, and never about anything personal. But I still had a burning question that no one seemed willing or able to answer, and it precipitated into my consciousness again as I sat watching the two sisters chopping and peeling. In the three seasons since Nana's passing, I found myself growing more curious about my mother's relationship with her own mother. I knew it wasn't good. I suspected that it was somehow tied to whatever happened between Aunt Hannah and her sister. Something nagged at my insides, and suddenly the question just seemed to ask itself.

"Joanie, ah, I was wondering if you knew what happened...between my grandmother and yours. Why didn't the sisters speak for all those years?"

"Maybe I know somethin', what about it?" she said in her icy way.

"Actually, I overheard my dad say that they never got along because Nana was a 'swinger.' She liked to go out to parties and have fun, but her older sister didn't approve." Joanie snorted and laughed through her nose. I was intrigued, and pressed on. "What's so funny? What's a swinger?" I asked. She ignored me, but I insisted. "What does it mean, Joanie?"

"It means...that your Nana was a slut," she said with a malevolent smirk.

139

"Huh?" I asked.

"And a drunk," she added.

"Jeezes, Joanie, you're such a jerk!" Maddy said angrily. "Yeah, you oughta know what a slut is, I guess," she added.

I looked from one to the other, surprised and confused-my usual state.

"Up yours, ya little dyke," Joanie shot back at her.

My stomach flipped over. I could see that my query had ignited a firecracker, but I didn't understand. I knew what a slut was...sort of, but I didn't know what dyke meant. I wanted to tell her forget it-sorry I asked, but I really wanted answers too. I knew I should back off, but I had to know more. The puzzle was slowly coming together, but I still couldn't make out the big picture. "Joanie, what are you talking about? What exactly happened?"

Undaunted, Joanie elaborated. "She went out most nights, got drunk and screwed men-lots of different men."

"Oh," I said. I thought about how Nana slept away the last years of her life, so drunk she forgot she was smoking. She was always slipping into the bathroom to take her medicine...and everybody but me knew she was an alcoholic. How did I miss everything?

Joanie continued to regale me with apparent satisfaction. "She started young-when she was about fifteen or sixteen-that's how your mother got borned," she added. "But it didn't stop after that. And Gramma...your Aunt Hannah...she raised your mum until she was four. Your mother lived right here in this house with my dad when she was just a little kid. My Gramma got custody away from your Nana on account of her being..."

"Just-shut-up!" Maddy pounded her fist on the metal kitchen table that was up against the wall, so hard it rattled Jesus on his cross.

"What the hell's the matter with ya? She's a big girl. She oughta learn a thing or two," Joanie countered, unperturbed.

"Maddy...it's no big deal," I interjected with a studied casual shrug, hoping to defuse the situation. "I already knew all that stuff...about my mom," I lied. "I knew she never had a father," I added. Now I understood why Mom's maiden name was Harahan. She had completely avoided the topic of her illegitimacy, and it went right over my head.

"Joanie," Maddy interrupted, "know what your problem is? You don't know when to close your pie-hole...and I don't mean just because ya talk too much!"

Joanie's lip curled back in a look of disgust, as if she'd walked into a puddle of puke. "*You* think you can tell *me* what to do?!"

"Yeah."

"What are ya goin' to do?" Joanie asked sarcastically, cocking her head and sneering down her pointy nose. "Beat me up?"

"I just might," Maddy shot back.

"Try it...and Jack'll cut you up," she spat out the words with her silver eyes flashing like tiny razors.

"Yeah, but you don't want Jack cuttin' me...'cause then he might go to jail and you two couldn't hump your brains out while Ma's lying sick in bed!"

"You little piece of shit!" Joanie screeched, brandishing the kitchen knife. "I'll cut you myself!"

"Joan Marie Malone!" Gramma Malone was standing in the doorway still wearing her hat and coat. None of us knew how long she'd been listening. She braced herself with one hand on the doorframe. She'd dropped the paper bag with the ham, and it hit the floor with a loud thud. It must have weighed as much as a newborn.

"Hi Gramma," Joanie said meekly. Maddy jumped up and retrieved the ham.

"Don't you 'Hi Gramma' me! What kind of talk is this?"

"She started it," Joanie pouted, pointing at her sister.

"We was just havin' a stupid fight, Gramma," Maddy said soothingly. "Joanie didn't mean it; it's really all my fault."

The stern old woman looked from Maddy to Joanie, and then fixed her eyes on me. "What do you think, Frances? Two sisters talkin' to one another like that?"

I shrugged. "I don't know, Aunt Hannah. Maybe if I had a sister I'd fight just as much." I said it but that's not what I really thought; I thought Joanie was one mean bitch.

Aunt Hannah wasn't fooled. "So you're a diplomat now, are you?" She gave me a wry smirk. I shrugged noncommittally to avoid lying again. "Are you two done with them vegetables?" she fairly barked at her granddaughters.

"Yes Gramma," they chorused glumly.

"Then sit down, all of you. First let me set the pot to boiling..."

"But Gramma, I was going out tonight! I have to get ready," Joanie whined.

"You'll sit down and not be goin' nowhere 'til I'm finished with you!" I don't know how she did it, but Gramma Malone spoke like she expected to be obeyed. Joanie sat and sulked, while Maddy kind of kicked back, ready to take whatever came. I wondered if I should leave.

141

"You sit, Frances. You're family, and you ought to hear it too." I sat. She took off her hat, and Joanie got up to help her off with her coat, then left for only a moment to hang them in the closet. Gramma donned her starched white apron and began to fill the great pot on the stove with water from a smaller pot.

"Gramma, let me get that for you." Maddy got up.

"All right then, Mad'lin," she said with appreciation, holding out the two quart pot. Maddy went straight for the big pot and brought it over to the sink. The old faucet had no aerator and the water pressure filled it quickly. "You'll never be able to lift it." Gramma shook her head in disbelief.

"Yeah, she will," Joanie muttered.

Maddy grimaced at as she hoisted the pot by the handles and made her way across the kitchen to set it down on the old gas stove. "There!" she said with satisfaction.

"Oh my!" Her grandmother marveled. "What a big strong girl the good Lord has seen fit to make you!" Joanie looked as if she were about to make one of her trademark snide comments, but thought better of it. Gramma pulled up a chair and composed herself. I waited expectantly. "I've been thinking about things," she began. "Ever since my sister died, I've been thinking about things I wish I'd done different, but it seemed like what's done is done, and it's too late now to make it right." She looked at each of our faces to see if it registered.

"What things, Gramma?" Joanie asked.

"Hmm," the old woman sighed. "I'm not sure how to put it." We waited. "I heard every word you two said," she came out at last.

"Oh, Jeez," Joanie put her hand to her face.

"Sorry Gramma," Maddy said.

"That's it exactly: if you keep at it, you will be sorry, more sorry than you can know, because you can't undo some things," she said. "Not a day goes by that I don't think of your Nana, Frances. All those years-all those years I could've been with her, helped her. And I was too stubborn and proud, and I thought I was always in the right. Then there was all the time that I missed with your mum too, and I missed out on most of your growing up," she looked at her granddaughters.

"What exactly happened...with you and Dad?" Maddy asked.

"Oh, that...well, we had our differences of opinion; we still do. But he's a grown man and I can't tell him how to live his life. It's not my place to criticize your father, so I can't speak about it. We had a disagreement, and he left. He just took you all and left. I regretted my part in it, but I was too proud to go to him. Let's just say we finally worked it out as best we could. But I never did have the time to make things right with my sister Margaret. I kept waiting for her to come 'round to me, and I was too stubborn to go 'round to her. Hearing you two girls made me think…well, I could at least tell you what an old fool I was and help you not to make the same mistake. You are sisters, and you need each other. We all need to pull together and get your mother through, and help Tommy find his way…and take care of little Annie. God knows we tried hard enough with that poor baby; that's in God's hands now," she said with her eyes on the crucifix.

"I can't get along with her," Joanie cut in, selfishly unmoved by her grandmother's words. "She's…she's just such a weirdo. It's embarrassing!" Joanie spoke with a sneer. Maddy snorted in amusement at her sister's consternation. She was used to it.

I'd never thought of my cousin as a weirdo, but I knew she was different. As my mother always said, Maddy wasn't at all lady-like. She broke rules, swore like a sailor and did things we weren't supposed to do-but in many ways she was better than anyone I'd ever known. Maddy was a fighter but never a bully. She stole her dad's cigarettes, but was otherwise honest and fair-minded. And she was fiercely loyal. Even from a young age, that was her most remarkable trait. Very few people know how to love for keeps.

"Listen to me, Joanie. And you too Mad'lin," their grandmother admonished. "We can't never fully understand why we are how we are-what makes us this way or that-let alone fully understand another. But we must try not to judge. My sister was how she was for a reason. I'll never understand it all, but I could always see how she suffered in her body and mind. And she drank. She lost all control when she drank, and there were…consequences. When I was younger, it looked to me as if she brought all her problems on herself, because she wouldn't behave the right way-like I did. But behaving the right way isn't always right either. Being perfectly good isn't always a good thing."

I was confused, and looked at my cousins' faces to see if they were making sense of it. Joanie looked at the clock and sighed. Maddy was thinking hard; I could see it in her eyes, which looked like smoky gray clouds shifting in a high wind.

Gramma Malone elaborated. "Your mother is so good they should make her a saint someday!" She shook her head and sighed. "But she's let herself be worn away, because she cares so much and tried so hard. The Catholic sacrament of marriage is one of obedience. We're called to be selfless and serve

God and our families...our husbands and children. I wish your mother could have been a little selfish; I wish she'd broken some rules!"

"What rules, Gramma?" Maddy asked.

"Well, I might as well come out and say it: I think it's a damned shame the way the Catholic Church treats women! They don't let us control how many babies we have-it's barbaric! Not that I blame poor Joan," she added. "She's a good Catholic. But if a woman is worn out with one pregnancy after the other, what about the children she has already? How is it fair to them? Some women can take it-they can have ten or twelve and still stay strong. But what about the ones that can't? It's chewing her up from the inside out, but still she's expected to conceive, because her husband and the Pope and God say so! It's a man's world...and they tell us God is a man too; from the looks of things, I can believe it."

"That's what my mother says." I felt like making a contribution. "Not about God, but she says it's all 'in the hands of our fathers.'"

"Well, she's got that right. But I've been watching things change. I have a little television in my room, and watch all the news on my own. I read the *Boston Globe* every Sunday. Now that war is terrible! It's not like the Great War, nor World War II either. I find myself agreeing with the young people; thank God our Eddie Murphy will be starting at the seminary. At least we don't have to worry about him going off.   But it's on account of you girls I've been paying special attention to the women's liberation. At first I was against most of it, but I got to thinking...maybe these women were right. Maybe we did need to be liberated, almost like the blacks, although I don't really understand their ways."

Now I could see where Maddy got her independent spirit, her intellect; but it would be some time before I could fully appreciate the leap that this turn of the century woman had made to free her own mind.

"I had five children," she continued. "I lost two to diphtheria, and one in infancy," as she spoke, her eyes shimmered. "I loved them all, but if I'd had a choice, I wouldn't have had so many. I fell asleep on the floor by the bed the night my last two girls passed," she whispered. Maybe if I weren't so exhausted day and night, if I didn't have them all so close together, I could've saved them..."

"You didn't have anyone to help?" I asked.

"Help? It was the depression. We had to let all the help go."

"What about...grandpa?" Joanie asked. I was surprised she was interested.

"He said that tending sick children was a mother's duty," she answered. "I guess I failed my duty. I always wondered if they called for me when they died. It pained me to think that I just didn't hear," she said.

"Gramma," Maddy broke in. "I don't know anything about diphtheria, and I don't know about grandpa. But he was wrong to leave you alone that night. That's complete bull...crap!" she compromised her expletive. "You shouldn't blame yourself."

My cousins' fight had rattled my nerves. The truth about Nana was shocking and sad. Now the image of two little girls dying in bed with their mother on the floor...it was too much. I folded my arms on the table, laid my face down and cried like a baby.

"There, there, Frances." Aunt Hannah patted me on the back, but went on. "I was never the same after I lost my little girls. All the happiness seemed to go out of me. And then Mr. Malone...passed away, right on the heels of losing them! I still had two boys and my little sister Margaret, but I had nothing inside to give my living children...or Margaret. Think of how terrifying it must have been for the three of them, watching all that sickness and death!"

"I don't know how you did it...all alone," Maddy said with awe.

"But I wasn't alone. I had God and my church. We had Father Mahood. It was Father Mahood that helped us through," she added. "He was a very young priest, even younger than myself, but so kind and devoted. That's why it's so...complicated. I love God and our Catholic Church. I'm just not sure the church is absolutely right about everything. I think we need to work some things out with God for ourselves."

I'd cried myself out and listened in silence. Aunt Hannah sat quietly for a moment, trying to knit it all together. "Joanie," she said, "when my sister got pregnant, I judged her and called her 'everything in the book', as they say. What she did...well, it was even more serious back then, a terrible disgrace on the family. I felt I'd sacrificed my life to raise her right. It made me boiling mad. I understood later that the way I treated her had something to do with how she...behaved, after she had her baby. When I heard you, it brought it back to mind and made me ashamed. You probably heard your father use those words, I expect. But I don't even blame him...he heard them from me first. It is true that I kept your mum, Frances-I don't regret that. I had to for a while. And it's true that we don't really know who the father was...my sister told me she'd gone off with some 'Irish seaman'. She was only fifteen! Ah...it doesn't matter; I should never have said them things. After your mum adopted you, your Nana kind of relived the past. She said it sort of 'come out' while holding you as a baby, although I didn't understand what she was talking about at first...probably

145

because I didn't want to. She came marching over here and told me that I broke her heart to take away her Evie. Told me it was never the same for her afterwards, like she never felt natural being her mother. I was shocked to hear it after all those years. So I defended myself. I told my sister it was her own fault for being a no good drunken so and so. I told her a cat would've made a better mother." She sighed. "Then she told me that I'd been a worse mother sober than she'd ever been drunk, and if I didn't believe it, just look at how my boys turned out! It hurt because she was right. I said terrible things, and told her to get out in the heat of anger. I never even apologized later on. I was too ashamed of myself, I guess, too stubborn and too proud, although I can't think now what I had to be so proud about. I know she loved you Frances, in her own way. I imagine it didn't always seem like she did, but she had feelings. I just didn't see it in time."

I knew I'd been right at my grandmother's wake, when I saw 'Old Mrs. Malone' watching me. I hadn't fooled her one bit with my sorry performance. Now she almost seemed to read my mind.

"Gramma," Maddy said, "it's hard to hold back when you're about to explode...I know that. All them fights I was in, growin' up. And I still get so mad sometimes...I guess you just heard me," she added ironically.

"That seems to be a trait shared by the Malones and the Harahans," she said. "My husband, Michael Malone...he had a temper, not that he ever laid a hand on me. He used words in anger. He drank some too...is there an Irishman that don't?"

"From what I can see, the Italian men are about the same," I interjected.

"You think so, Frances? Hmm...I think Italian men have more of a softness about them. I think they drink and get more tender-hearted. Irishmen get drunk and act like bastards!"

Just then we all heard the great pot reach a roiling boil. Joanie jumped up, turned down the flame and stirred the white frothy bubbles just before they spilled over. "Well," Gramma Malone chuckled, "might as well call a spade a spade. You know, I like your father, Frances," she added. "He's a very good man." I nodded in agreement. "So what I'm trying to tell you is simple, but harder to do than you can ever imagine: be kind to one another, and no matter what happens, don't let anything tear you apart. Don't judge each other's weaknesses, or...differences," she looked from Maddy to Joanie. "And if you do get your Irish up and say things you ought not to have said, never be too proud to say you're sorry. Or you'll end up an old fool like me, all alone with years to think about how right you were about whatever it was that came between you. Life is tougher than you know, and from the looks of things, in some ways it's even tougher than when I was young. But some of the change is good, I believe. You girls have so many choices now. I could only be a wife, or a nun, and then I couldn't even choose to be a nun after my mother passed. It was my duty to marry and raise Margaret. But you girls can go to school and be almost anything," she said earnestly. "You know, Frances, I did watch that Jane Goodall of yours, on the PBS channel. She's a smart lady, but you're every bit as smart, so you keep learning and go on with your education."

"Gramma, I don't have choices. I'm not smart like Mad'lin and Frances," Joanie said rather sadly. "And I want to be married," she added wistfully. "I'm in love with Jack…"

"Now you listen to me," Gramma pointed her crooked finger at Joanie, "you're a smarter girl than you think. And if you want to do something with yourself, if you're willing to apply yourself at school, then I'll see to it you can go on to college-all of you," she added, looking at us each in turn. Then she turned back to Joanie spoke in a lower her voice, "And another thing: you're too young to be in love, and too good for that Jack Mack." Gramma Malone pulled herself up sternly. Joanie sulked, but didn't backtalk.

"But how will you send us to college?" Maddy asked, truly interested. I was astonished.

"Don't you worry about how. I have some…investments. Now none of you say a word to anyone about it." She pointed at her granddaughters and underscored, "Your father, and your mother," she directed at me, "wouldn't appreciate my meddling, and I don't want my son getting any ideas about my money. I'm trusting you, because I want you to plan for a future."

She looked at her granddaughters expectantly, and they both nodded in silent commitment to keep their grandmother's secret. I hoped Joanie could manage it. Then she put her hand on Joanie's arm and said, "Joanie…that boy Jack," she shook her head. "I know you don't want your old Gramma telling you what to do, but…well…you're better than all that," she finished quietly. "I don't want you to ruin your life…but we'll talk more about that in private." I expected Joanie to protest, but she didn't. "And you, Mad'lin," she continued.

"Uh, what about me?"

"You're a special girl, that's plain to see. You've got courage and strength, and you're smart as a whip. You can be anything you want, but not if you don't go to school." She gave her a knowing look.

"Gramma, school is…" she was searching for a word that wasn't rude.

"Our school is a complete waste of time, Aunt Hannah," I ventured. "We learned more last year at Edmunds."

"Well, stick with it for now," she said. "I'll think on it, and see what I can do. Even more important, you two quit your fighting. You stop judging her," she said to Maddy, pointing at Joanie, "and you," she addressed Joanie, "you need to cultivate self-respect. Then you can begin to understand and love the sister you've got. You don't think you'll need each other, but you will. Stick together...all of you! I'm an old woman; I might not be around that much longer."

"Aw, don't say that, Gramma," Maddy protested. "You're too tough to go anywhere...you're not goin' to heaven any time soon. They're worried you'll start runnin' the place. The Pope better watch out for his job too!" She wore her most winsome smirk, and Gramma Malone smiled back. One face was young and the other wizened with age, yet they were so much alike.

That night at the supper table, my mother was in a chatty mood while my mind raced round like a hamster in a wheel. The evening dragged on. The hope of money for college was a secret. I could never let on what I'd learned about my mom and Nana. I certainly couldn't bring up the subject of the Pope and birth control either. Dad would about shit a brick!

When I was finally alone in bed, I searched my memory in the light of Aunt Hannah's words. Had Nana loved me? I thought back to when I was much younger. Sometimes my mother took me to visit her in Charlestown, to the narrow brick row-house where she lived alone for so long. Mom would go into town and shop, child-free, while I sat on the back piazza with Nana. She always seemed old to me-skinny and wrinkled, and she moved slowly, like an old person, but she wasn't sick then. Sometimes we'd take walks in the nice weather to the corner store to get her daily pack of Camels, and she'd buy me a piece of candy. Then we sat on a bench while she smoked and I ate, since neither of us could wait until we got home. I recalled how I held up both hands afterwards, so she could wet a Kleenex with her spittle and wipe the sticky off. I was small, and unused to the traffic in the city, so she always squeezed my hand tight when we crossed at the walk-light. I got to press the button. Nana never exactly expressed love, but when we were out alone together she was protective of me. She was especially concerned with the alley; you could see it from her side-window because Nana had an end-house. I had to wonder if anything bad happened there, because each time we passed she warned me of the danger, pointing her boney finger with a scowl:

Don't never play down in the alley. That's where they put out the ashbins, so it's dirty and there might be broken glass. Only bad girls and boys hang out down there, up to God-knows-what! So stay away, Frances...and always be a good girl."

It didn't seem like much, but I guess that was the best she could do. She loved me in her own way, and I was sorry she was gone before I'd figured it out.

17

Halloween was just a few nights away, and I planned to help Maddy take Annie out for trick or treat. She wanted to be a fairy princess, and Mom had given us some old fluffy curtains to make a costume, along with gold ribbon and some netting that had been part of a tutu I'd worn one year at a dance recital. It was my first and last recital; Mom told me years later that I'd danced like a baby hippo. All I remember was being relieved when she said I could quit the dance lessons and take swimming instead. I'll bet the dance teacher was relieved too.

I fashioned the tutu into fairy wings by tying a ribbon around the middle so it puffed out on two sides, and could be pinned to the back of her curtain-dress. I felt satisfied with my new grownup, behind the scenes role for Halloween. For the first time, I wasn't planning to dress-up and go trick or treating. We were in the den, and Annie was watching TV, something she wasn't allowed to do at home. Their father was afraid they'd wear out the old television, so he kept it for himself to watch the news and ballgames. *The Muppet Show* was on and Annie was enthralled. I was enjoying myself too. In one instant I felt like a kid again, and just didn't feel ready to let go of Halloween. "Hey, Maddy," I ventured. Why don't we get into the spirit of things and dress up for Halloween?"

"No way!" She looked at me like I was nuts.

"Why not? Even grownups dress up sometimes, like when they give out the candy, some of them have costumes."

"Uh-uh," she shook her head. "You do what you want. I don't want anyone from school seeing me in a Halloween costume."

She had a point. Like so many other things we had enjoyed up until just last year, it would be decidedly uncool to go trick or treat in junior high school. Sometimes when I walked by the playground swings hanging lonely and motionless, I wished I could go jump on. I longed to hear the rhythmic creaking as the swings went back and forth, and enjoy the hypnotic pleasure of watching the world go up and down. Now Halloween was gone too. I turned back to the Muppets. One of the puppet characters was a funny monster with two heads; it gave me an idea. "No one has to know," I said. "We could make a costume that's so good, no one will recognize us." Maddy looked intrigued, like she secretly wanted to have one last fling with trick or treat, but wasn't convinced yet. "Look," I pointed at the screen. "We could make a two- headed monster."

"How?"

"We could put a big sheet over us both with two holes for our heads to stick out…"

"That'd be a two headed ghost…"

"We could dye the sheet! Let's say, purple! Yeah, two-headed monsters are definitely purple!" I insisted, even though we were watching a black and white set. "And we'd use Halloween makeup to color our faces all purple, and make some hats out of pillowcases…"

"Dyed purple to match!"

"I'll ask Mom for some sheets," I jumped up.

"I must be out of my mind." She tried to pretend she was only doing it for me, but I could see the tell-tale sparkle in her eyes.

Mom was in a playful mood. "You two must be cuck-coo!" She laughed. "Sure, I've got some old sheets-some old scarves for your head too, and you can use the pillowcases for holding the candy."

"We'll dye them all to match!" I said.

"You'll have to get some Rit Dye. And that stuff makes a mess, so do it down in the basement sink and wear old clothes," she cautioned. "Just be sure to clean up after you're done."

The next day we walked to the Five and Dime on Main Street, right after school. We bought a cheap Halloween makeup set that even came with glitter, and a box of deep purple Rit. We went to my house and got the sheets and brought it all to the basement, filled the old sink and dumped in the dye. I didn't get a stick to poke the fabric down, and used my hands, which quickly turned a light shade of lavender, like an Easter egg. I held them up, looked at Maddy and grinned like a mischievous Jack o' lantern. She knew what I was up to.

"Don't do it!"

"Let's do it, let's dye our arms to match!" I plunged my arms in, almost up to my shoulders.

"You're definitely out of your mind!" She started to laugh.

"I dare you to!" That was all it took. Maddy wasn't about to be outdared by me, and elbowed me over so she could stick her arms in too. After a minute she pulled them out to check the progress-her pasty white skin turned an even deeper purple. We howled with laughter, and held our arms deep in the purple water for another five minutes, until the water started to feel cold. The Halloween spirit carried us back to childhood again, a place we'd only just left and now longed to go back, if only for a little while. When the cloth had set to a deep purple we had to rinse the whole mess. It stained the sink. Then we wrung it out as best we could and left through the bulkhead to the clothesline, dripping a trail across the floor. Outside it was raw and chilly and looked like rain, a typical autumn evening in New England. I hoped it wouldn't pour and wash away the purple. I hoped it would all be dry by tomorrow, and we'd have enough time to put together our creation.

"Frances Jean Orillio!" Mom was shocked when she saw our arms, which were chapped as well as purple from being in the water so long. "That's going to take forever to wear off!"

We hadn't thought of that, and looked at each other, imagining going to school purple for a week. I started cackling like a hen and Maddy snorted with laughter. Then Mom started laughing too. "Well," she said, "if this is your last time trick or treating, you might as well do it up!"

The next day was cold and crisp and clear, and the evening promised to be perfect, with a three-quarter moon and starry sky. Mom helped us align our heads evenly under the sheet and mark where to cut the holes. We poked our heads out. We practiced walking up and down the kitchen, which was harder than we thought. We had to synchronize our movements so as not to rip apart. She was taller and had a bigger stride.

"You have to slow down for me," I told her. She put her arm around me, hooked her thumb in my waistband and pulled me close.

"Walk," she commanded. Now we were marching as one, and even figured out how to turn around. We each had only one usable, purple arm to stick out from the sheet.

"Wait," I said, laughing so hard I couldn't catch my breath. I gotta pee." The monster lost one of its heads for a bit. She looked even sillier by herself, with a big purple sheet hanging off of her.

Before we put on our makeup we dressed Annie, and made a big fuss over her. She had a magic wand with a silver star on the end, and we'd put silver glitter on the star, and some in her hair. She flitted about the room waving the wand, with her white tutu wings and chiffon drapery flowing gracefully around her.

It was time to go into the bathroom and figure out our makeup. After wrapping up our hair to cover it in the dyed scarfs, we decided to smear the thick purple makeup over our faces. We ran out of purple, and had to use deep blue to cover some bare spots, so the two headed monster had a blotchy blue-purple complexion. There was some gold glitter, so we stuck some of that to the makeup.

Mom and Dad were waiting in the living room to see us off. Tommy was with them, since Dad had asked him to follow along and watch out for the girls. "Oh my gosh," Mom declared. "Joe, just take a look at your daughter-get the Polaroid!" Whenever there was a holiday or birthday, or someone special came to visit, Mom would always shout, 'Joe, get the Polaroid!' That way we could be sure at least a few pictures came out, since you never knew what you might get when you sent out a roll to be developed. The special film was very expensive, and it was always an honor to be photographed with the Polaroid.

"Jeez! You two are somethin' else!" Dad had to force himself not laugh long enough to snap a picture. You could hear the mechanical sound as the photo paper rolled out. It was the color of coffee with no image at all and a thick white border to grasp it by. If you touched it even a bit it wouldn't develop in that spot. Dad carefully laid the photo face-up on the marble table that still bore the chip from Nana's drunken pogo-stick debacle. Mom was clicking away on her little Kodak. The square flashcube spun around with each picture, so you had four goes at it. The light was blinding. Everywhere you looked there were bright blue-white spots.

"Now we're a blotchy blue-faced purple two-headed monster that can't see," I said, blinking. I had Annie by the hand.

"And who's the beautiful princess?" Dad was effusive. "The monster captured the princess," he laughed.

"And she has to lead us around and feed us candy so we won't eat her," I joined.

"Be very careful going up and down stairs," Mom said. "Watch that Annie doesn't trip over the drapery."

"We will," I assured her, although I hadn't thought of the stairs.

Our first stop was the Malone's house, to show off to their parents and Gramma. Joanie was going to hand out the candy. Mom said it was the first Halloween celebrated at the old house in over ten years. The last had been when Joanie was just a little girl. The kids had been too young to go out, but Joan had decorated and handed out candy. She'd been pregnant with Madeline. From then on the house had been left in darkness on Halloween nights, and the kids showed their displeasure by throwing eggs. Now that Tommy Malone lived there, there'd be no more eggs, just as there were no additional broken windows. We marched up the stairs with our arms bound tightly about each other's waists, and clomped loudly into the house. Annie flitted in ahead of us twirling and dancing, and our clumsy entrance was made all the more absurd by her grace.

153

"Jesus, Mary and Joseph! Look at you two," Joanie said. "I don't know these kids-no relation of mine," she joked. "Mom's in the parlor," she added.

Auntie Joan was actually dressed for the first time in a while. She was usually in bed, or on the couch wearing a robe when I visited. It was nice to see her in a maternity dress with her hair combed and even a touch of lipstick. I thought she must be getting well at last. "Come and show mummy," she smiled and held her hand out to Annie, who rushed over and hugged her. She noticed that her mother looked well, and it made her happy. "How lovely!" she marveled. "And who made such a beautiful costume?" She looked at me and smiled warmly.

"We both put it together. My mom gave us the curtains."

"Thank you so much girls," she said. "You've done a fine job. And what a pair you make…look at those arms," she reached out and took Maddy's hand in hers. Then she giggled like a girl and laughed until she had tears in her eyes. "Tom," she called. "Tommy dear, do we have a camera handy?"

"I dunno," he growled from the kitchen.

"Come in and see the girls," she coaxed.

He didn't answer, but I could hear the kitchen chair scrape the linoleum and his heavy feet as he came in. His presence in the room was like a wet blanket. A big stinky wet blanket. "Eh?" he grunted.

"Look at the girls!" Joan chirped.

"Ah, nice, very nice," he said to Annie, then looked us up and down and grinned in spite of himself. "Ain't you two a sight?" He shook his head and showed his big yellow teeth.

"Tom, where's the camera?" Auntie Joan asked again.

"How the hell should I know where anything is in this shit-house?" Annie's face fell and she looked at the carpet, and I could feel Maddy's body tighten like a steel spring, but she kept quiet. I tried to put it right.

"My mom took a bunch of pictures before we left. We'll be sure to make copies."

"Fran, Mad'lin," Annie whined, "We're going to miss trick or treat!"

"You kids go on," Joan said, "but be careful."

"We'll be careful," I said.

Outside the air was nippy, the stars were twinkling, and the streets were buzzing with children in costumes. It was perfect. I didn't think we needed Tommy to protect us, but it gave him a way to take part. I think that may be what my dad had in mind all along. We marched off down the street with Annie by the hand. From the very first house, the adults all marveled at our costume.

We were the only two-headed monster anyone had ever seen, and several of our neighbors insisted we come inside so they could have a better look, or snap a photo. One even brought us in to show the grandpa, who was too frail to come to the door. The attention slowed us down some, and Maddy said we'd better make tracks if we wanted to get a decent haul of candy.

We'd been at it for more than a half hour, when we ran into a skinny witch; she looked familiar, even with her face covered in green makeup. The witch was accompanied by a very large ghost-the costume was no more than a sheet with two eye-holes and two thick legs sticking out from underneath. We went for a closer look.

"I'd know those tree-trunks anywhere," Maddy chuckled in my ear. It was Kathy Kelly and Dotty Day, and they didn't even have a little kid with them.

"Hey Kelly!" Maddy's rough voice gave her away instantly.

"Mad-Dog Malone? Is that you? Oh my God!" Dotty squealed.

"I came for the candy," Kathy said glumly from under the sheet. From the look of the sack in her hand, she'd been walking the streets for a while.

"Can I bum a cigarette?" Dotty begged.

"What's a matter with you? There's little kids everywhere-ain't got none on me anyway."

"Happy Halloween," I said, tugging at Maddy.

"Uh, we don't have to tell anybody, do we?" Kathy grumbled.

"You don't have to," Maddy said. "I plan to show off my purple hands with pride," she laughed, holding out her arm. "Do you even believe what this kid talked me into?" She gave me an affectionate squeeze under our purple sheet, and we started on our way again.

"Hey Tommy!" I heard Dotty call out in a lilting tone. I nearly forgot Tommy was following us; he didn't say a word and had an eerie way of just disappearing into the background. Dotty held her fingers to her lips and seductively inhaled an invisible cigarette, trying her hand at feminine charm. "Please," she wheedled. Tommy ambled over and handed her one, and even whipped out his lighter. I hadn't seen him act this way with any girl but his sister, and looked to Maddy to see what she made of it. She just gave me a 'don't ask me' look. I could feel her shrug under our costume.

Another forty minutes or so of marching around in the cold and climbing up and down stairs with Annie in tow, and I was beat. The crowd had thinned, and most of the little kids were off the streets. It was about 46 degrees when we started, not bad for a Halloween night, but the temperature had definitely dropped. Annie was starting to shiver. Of course, she wouldn't wear a coat over her costume, and had only a turtleneck sweater under the curtains to keep her warm. I had my winter jacket on under the sheet, but my feet felt like ice. And I had another problem-I needed to pee really bad. "Hey monster, we gotta go pee soon. Can't you feel it?"

"You always gotta pee! What I need's a cigarette break," she said in her low, gravelly whisper.

"The candy bags are pretty full. I think we hauled enough loot for the night," I said. "Annie, I think it's time to start back..."

"Aw!" she complained.

"Most of the kids have gone home to eat their candy. Don't you want some candy?" My strategy didn't work. She shook her head no.

"We haven't done Harcourt Circle," she insisted. Harcourt Circle was a cull de sac, and it was just around the corner. We had started from the other direction, and skipped it.

"What do you think?" I asked my other half.

"I can hold out for a few more houses...so long as you don't wet us."

We rounded the corner and saw the lights were still on in only three of the houses. "OK, Annie, we do those three and then back to my house." She nodded happily and tugged me along. "I'm not going to make it back to your house first. My dad will drive you home," I informed Maddy.

It must've taken another fifteen minutes or more just to do three houses. One of Annie's playmates lived there, and her mom insisted upon dragging us into the house to take a few snapshots. We were heading back when I heard a siren approaching fast from somewhere close by. "That's coming this way," I said.

"It's coming in from Broadway." Maddy stood tall with her neck craned, listening. I could tell she was concerned. My house was only a few doors down the street and I could see the light on and the back door open. They must be watching for us. Maybe they heard the siren too. We started walking faster. Tommy instantly caught up and was on our heels. Annie was on the other side of us now, clinging to her sister's hand and trotting to keep up.

"You're going too fast, Mad'lin," she whined. The poor kid was tired.

All at once there was pandemonium: bright flashing lights, headlights, red and blue lights, a blaring truck horn and a couple of whoops from the siren. The ambulance had rounded the corner and rolled to a stop just a few feet behind us. I screeched as I let go of Maddy and lurched towards the sidewalk on my left. Tommy had grabbed Annie's arm and dragged her off to the right. Maddy had Annie's other arm and tore off after them-literally; the sheet was rent in two with a loud rip.

"Jesus Christ!" I heard Maddy yell from the other side. The big truck was between us and I couldn't see them anymore, but I knew they'd all made it across. I plopped down on the curb and wet myself, then laughed so hard my belly hurt. I bent over double in peels of nervous giggles. The driver made eye contact with me, checking to see that I was alright, then looked over towards the others. The ambulance rumbled slowly down the suburban block, picked up a little speed and headed off, but definitely not in the direction of the Malone's house. We hadn't really been in danger, but it scared the piss out of me.

Tommy stood on the other sidewalk gripping Annie by the arm while Maddy ran back across to where I was sitting with my hands over my face, convulsing with laughter. She reached down, grabbed me by my upper arms and hoisted me to my feet. I was all wet in the crotch, but it was hidden by what was left of the sheet. I'd laughed so hard I could feel tears rolling down my face. She thought I was crying and hurt.

"Frances! Jesus, Frances, what happened?!" She pulled my hands down to check my face. I found out later I was streaming purple tears.

"I...I...ah...I wet my pants!" I was giggling so wildly I could hardly speak. "You...alright?"

"Fine, just great!" she answered sarcastically. "You scared the shit out of me!"

Then we heard a man's voice bellow. "Frances?!" It was my dad, running up to us with a flashlight.

"I'm fine," I called out, getting a grip on myself. "Dad, I'm fine! We're all OK!" I heard him slow to a walk.

After I'd cleaned up, I went down to the kitchen and rejoined what was left of the party. Mom had made hot cocoa. There was candy spread all over the table. Annie had stopped shivering, but she was exhausted. She stared glassy eyed with her little chocolaty fist holding a melting Hershey bar. Tommy sat silently chewing on some Twizzlers. Dad had his hand on Maddy's shoulder and kind of kneaded it thoughtfully. He had a small glass of whiskey in front of him.

"You still have purple makeup all over your neck, in your hairline; you'll have to soak in a tub and scrub it off," Mom informed me. "You too, Madeline," she added.

The Polaroid photograph taken only hours before was displayed in the middle of the table. Mom's Kodak flash cubes were reflected somehow, and made it look like stars flew round our heads while our eyes glowed like red hot coals. It was perfect.

"What the hell happened with the two-headed monster?" Dad broke in with a smile at last. He had been uncharacteristically quiet. When the kids were around, he usually engaged them in non-stop merry banter.

"One of the heads ran off and wet itself!" Maddy laughed out loud and Dad was quick to join in. Their laughter saved the Halloween spirit that nearly got run over by an ambulance, but I could see he'd been scared to death.

Later on that night I heard him whispering to Mom in the bedroom. "I heard the siren...I ran out with the flashlight, but all I could see was the other kids-no Frances. The damned costume was torn apart! The truck was stopped in the middle of the road...I thought it clipped her for sure. I thought she was gone."

18

One chilly night in late November, I happened to wake up really thirsty from a late snack on potato chips. I nearly ate the whole damned bag, which blew my diet for the week-again. I was premenstrual. It was that kind of thirst where a sip from the bathroom faucet just won't do, so I went downstairs to get a tall glass of ice water. There was a gorgeous full moon, and I decided to shut the kitchen light off and just look at it out the window while I sipped. There's nothing like a wicked thirst to make a glass of water so satisfying. Then I noticed a light in the Victorian tower showing over the hill. I glanced at the clock; it was ten past 2:00 am. I watched to see if it might be a reflection from the bright moon on the windows, the same way as when the sun set at just the right angle. Light can play tricks. One brilliant summer afternoon I thought for a moment I saw flames, but it was just the deep orange sun on the stained glass. But tonight I was sure: there was definitely a light on in there, because it suddenly went out.

19

The Monday before Thanksgiving break, we were in my room doing a big term project for our science class. We had a new teacher; the old one had up and quit, and this one was actually teaching. She let us work with a partner, and I decided we should make a cardboard model of a Skinner box. I'd gone to the library and read all about operant and classical conditioning, way more than we had been assigned. I tried to get Maddy interested, but she couldn't have cared less, so I designed the project and she was busy cutting heavy cardboard along the lines I'd drawn with a ruler. Even with a huge pair of sharp kitchen scissors, it was so thick I could hardly cut through it. It hurt my hands.

"Guess what I did Saturday night," Maddy gave me a mischievous look.

"What?"

"Tried some reefer."

"What's that?"

"Pot...Tommy got some and..."

"Don't touch that stuff! It's dangerous."

"Don't be such a baby. It's cool," she said.

I was terrified. They'd shown us films in school about the consequences of smoking, drinking, and using drugs. I took it all straight to heart. "It's bad enough the way you smoke so much. Didn't you see those black lungs in the jar at the school assembly?"

"Yeah...they'll go with my black heart," she snorted in retort.

"It's not funny," I grumbled. "Honestly, I don't know what anyone sees in those awful smelly things." I'd finally asked to try her cigarette, just once to find out. I didn't finish the whole thing; it was even more disgusting than I'd imagined. "Your mom worries about you too-I can tell. I don't know how you can try pot and hide it from her," I chided. "I felt so guilty about trying a cigarette...well...I told my mother."

"You told your mother? You told on yourself? Unbelievable!" Maddy was laughing so hard she put the scissors down absently. Just when she was about to stop, she'd look at my serious face and laugh all over again, until it ended in a smoker's cough.

"Yeah, I told her I tried it once, just to see. Actually, I went into her room and woke her up in the middle of the night. I had to. I felt so guilty I couldn't sleep. But Mom wasn't even mad; she told me she once smoked a whole pack when she was eleven."

"Your mother did that?"

"Yeah. Some kids in Charlestown offered her cigarettes, and she didn't want them to think she was…'a goody-two-shoes', she called it. So she smoked down one after another. She singed her eyebrows and burnt holes in her clothes. When she got home, my Nana took one look and knew what she'd done. My mom puked half the night, and she thought she was going to get punished, but Nana just said she'd learned her lesson. I guess it worked out, 'cause Nana was a smoker, but Mom never picked up another cigarette. But seriously Maddy…drugs are dangerous. You don't know what it might do to your brain." I sulked.

"Aw, don't worry about me, Frances," she soothed. "I just tried a little, 's all." Then she looked at me with a half-grin and a gleam in her eye. "Now don't you go blabbin'!" she warned. "Mind ya business, or else Mad-Dog Malone's gonna' beat you up!"

We were sitting side by side on the rug, and she grabbed me playfully and pinned me down with one hand while tickling with the other. I started rolling around laughing in a ticklish fit. Suddenly I screeched. Maddy could tell I wasn't playing, and stopped. I sat up and clutched my side, and when I took my hand away to look, there was blood flowing through my shirt near the bottom of my ribcage. I'd rolled over onto the scissors, which were left open on the rug, kind of sticking up from where she'd dropped them amongst the scraps of cardboard that littered the floor.

"Oh God no," she said seriously. "Le' me see, Frances," she pried my hand away and pulled up my shirt. "Sweet Jesus! We gotta get your mom. Don't move." She went downstairs and I could hear her call, "Aunt Evelyn?!" Then I remembered that Mom had gone out on errands to shop for Thanksgiving. She could be back in minutes, or an hour, probably somewhere in between. There was no way to get in touch with her, and my dad was always out on the road.

"Maddy!" I called. "She's gone out." I heard her bound back up the stairs. "It's not that bad," I said, trying not to look again. "I'll go clean off in the shower before she gets back. It'll be OK. Just wash the shirt out for me, get a sponge and clean the blood off the rug, or Mom will have a fit."

"Are ya sure, Frances?"

I nodded. She grabbed me from behind and lifted me gently to my feet, while I pressed hard against my side with both hands. The bathroom was just outside my room. It had a shower stall, and I figured it would be a good idea to flush the wound. I stripped down and dropped the bloody shirt into the sink. I ran barely warm water, but it still burned. Every time I took my hand away to look, it bled more. The blood mixed with water made it seem much worse, like a river of blood splashing over the white tiles, swirling down the drain. The last thing I remember was looking at Maddy through the frosted shower doors. She was at the sink rinsing my shirt, just like I asked.

Then I was lying on the bathroom floor, wrapped in blankets. My head hurt. There were strange men over me, putting a pressure bandage on my ribs. I didn't understand at first, and tried to cover my exposed breast and push away the rough, masculine hand.

"Mom!" I called out, trying to sit up.

"Where's your mother?" a man's voice demanded.

"She went out shopping," I answered, frightened at his tone.

"Who is this?" the man interrogated. Now I could see there was a policeman in my room gripping Maddy roughly by the arm. She had blood all over her shirt and her hands were behind her back. I thought that was strange. Then I realized he'd handcuffed her.

"She's my cousin Madeline," I whimpered.

"Madeline Malone? Tom Malone's kid is your cousin?" he interrogated.

"Yeah Officer, just like I told you," she said calmly. He scowled at her.

"What happened here, Miss Orillio?" the officer asked.

"I rolled over on a pair of scissors," I said. "We were just horsing around. They were left on the floor because we were cutting up cardboard for a school project. It bled a lot, so I tried to wash it out in the shower. I must've passed out...my head hurts."

"That's 'cause you cracked it on the tile floor; lucky you didn't split your head open. And you have a puncture wound, almost to the muscle," the paramedic explained. I felt waves of nausea, but it wasn't only from the concussion or the gash in my side. I realized that they thought she stabbed me on purpose.

"Frances?! Oh my God, Frances, where are you?" I heard my mother scream from down in the kitchen. She ran up the stairs in her high heels, so fast it's a wonder she didn't break her neck.

"Mom! I'm sorry. It was a stupid accident. The scissors were left on the rug and I guess I rolled on them just the right way...or the wrong way...we were wrestling around. It was totally accidental...Mom...tell them Madeline would never hurt me. She'd never hurt anyone," I was crying.

My mother bent down and looked in my face. "Are you alright?"

"I think so. I just fainted when I saw all the blood."

162

"Is she badly hurt?" Mom asked the paramedic.

"It's a pretty good cut, but it didn't go through the muscle. I'm more concerned about her head. She took quite a fall and was still out cold when we got here. I don't think she lost that much blood though; you can donate a pint anytime, and she's a big enough girl, about 130 or so," he added.

"Hey, I'm 128," I said indignantly.

The man chuckled. "It just looks like a lot of blood if you're not used to seeing it. She needs to get that stitched. We need to take her to the hospital."

"Mom!" I whined, "Tell them it wasn't Madeline's fault-I rolled over on the stupid scissors. We were rough-housing, just like you always said not to. Mad'lin was tickling me, all in fun." I was beginning to think she didn't believe me. Then my mother stood up straight and smiled at the policeman.

"I'm sure it was an accident officer," she said. "Just when you think they're starting to grow up, they act worse than little children." She shook her curls and smiled her most charming smile. Then she stepped closer to Maddy and put her arm around her shoulders. "This is my niece, Madeline. She and Frances are best friends. She would never hurt her," she assured. "And my daughter Frances doesn't lie," she added with a touch of firmness. "So there's no problem at all, officer." She tilted her head winsomely.

"Humph," he said. Then he unlocked the cuffs with a click. Maddy stood looking down at me, and I saw her quickly wipe away some tears with the back of her hand.

"One more thing, officer," my mother chirped sweetly. Then she edged a bit closer to him and I heard her whisper. "Her mother isn't well, and she's...expecting. Please don't call around. There's no reason to bother, and we can't risk upsetting her now. We just can't."

The doctor in the ER who stitched me up was entirely without surgical talent. I have a thick raised scar, almost two inches long with a kink that kind of looks like a white worm burrowing into my flesh. Mom was appalled. It was an angry red for nearly a year afterwards, before the color slowly faded away. In the darkness I slip my hand beneath my pajamas and caress it with my fingertips. Even decades later, it can suddenly bring the scene vividly to life. The sensation opens a portal to a place where people I love remain as they were, fixed in time. The scar is pretty ugly, but I don't mind it.

20

"I can't come over as much anymore," Maddy said. "Ma's lookin' worse than ever, and I got to stick around and help out."

It was the beginning of December, right after Thanksgiving break. Mom had invited the Malones to dinner, but Auntie Joan couldn't make it at the last minute. The cousins came over and ate quietly, then Dad drove them home with some turkey and fixings my mother had boxed up for the adults.

I went over to visit Auntie Joan at least twice a week, and tried to help out by doing little things like hanging up Annie's clothes and putting her toys away. Sometimes I just sat with my cousins at the bedside; Auntie Joan had been moved from the couch up to the bedroom. She looked terrible. She was in her eighth month of pregnancy, but her belly didn't seem much bigger than when she was five months along. She'd definitely lost weight. The worse thing was that sometimes she got very confused, and struggled to gather her thoughts. It was like watching someone trying to collect lost feathers from a pillow that had torn open in a stiff breeze.

Father Mahood came every Sunday to bring Auntie Joan Holy Communion, and sometimes visited during the week if he had the time. I knew he was there when I saw the shiny black Lincoln sedan parked in the driveway. It was owned by the parish, of course, but Uncle Malone grumbled that a priest should drive such a fine car. He complained when it was parked in his spot, and he had to put the cab on the curbside until Father left. No one else visited the family. My mother said she just couldn't bear to see her friend like that anymore, but didn't try to dissuade me from going.

Auntie Joan stopped talking about Baby Michael and almost seemed to have forgotten him, just as the doctor and the priest said she should. Now she focused entirely on the new baby, and the family saw that as a good sign. They attributed her strange ramblings to physical exhaustion, and expected she would spontaneously recover after she delivered. As I listened to her narratives grow more bizarre with each passing week, I wasn't so sure.

"Mama wanted to be a nun, but changed her mind when she met my papa. He died fighting in France when I was just a baby. He was a war hero.

Mama always said that someday we'd go visit his grave...but we never could put aside the money...he's buried in France. Mama was left all alone, and I think she regretted that she didn't go into the convent," she sighed. "She gave up so much, and all she got out of it was me. I tried to be so, so very good for her. She always expected me to become a nun, and I thought I would. But I loved children, and then I met my Eddie," she said dreamily. "I believe God is going to send me a daughter. I'll call her Immaculé after Mama, because she's going to become a beautiful nun. She's going to belong to Jesus."

Whenever Auntie Joan drifted that far out into the sea of her fancy, Maddy just fixed her gaze on the bedspread or out the window. Annie looked on her mother's strange revelry with sorrowful eyes, probably wondering at how she could be more absorbed in a daughter who wasn't yet born, while she sat by living and breathing.

"I could be a nun too," she said tentatively that afternoon.

Joan regained her bearings and looked at Annie, almost surprised that someone spoke aloud. "You can be anything you want, my darling," she said, reaching out to caress her daughter, who was reassured for the moment.

After their mother dozed off we went back to the girls' room. Annie played silently with her Barbie dolls spread on the floor. Maddy smoked with her head hanging out the bedroom window. I pretended to read an assigned chapter in the history book. We were having a test this week, but I didn't need to study. The teacher couldn't have cared less about teaching, so he assigned the stupid questions at the end of the chapter, then gave the exact same questions for a so-called test. Funny thing was, half the kids flunked anyway.

"Did you ever meet your other grandmother?" I asked Maddy

"Huh? Ma's mother? No, she was dead long before I was born."

"And her husband-your grandfather-passed away...it must have been so hard growing up without a dad."

Maddy checked to see that Annie was occupied, then motioned me to come over. "Her dad didn't 'pass away' when she was a baby," she whispered. "Her ma got up one morning and found a note and a five dollar bill on the kitchen table. It was the depression, and he just split."

"How did you find out?"

"Your Nana used to live around the corner from my ma. Gramma heard it from her a long time ago, when they were still speaking. I heard her tell your mother a while back when she came to visit. I listened from the hallway. What're ya gonna do?" She shrugged. "They don't tell us nothin'- it's the only way to find out about anything."

"I get most of my information sitting on the staircase."

"Ah. Anyway, Gramma said Ma's mother was kind of...out there. Her Irish neighbors in Charlestown thought she was strange because she came from France. I never met her, but I don't think that had much to do with it. Her maiden name was Honoré; she was Immaculé Honoré. Can you imagine naming your kid Immaculate Honor?"

"Wow. I have enough trouble with Frances."

"Back in France, her mother was all set for her to be a nun, but Immaculé met a man and ran off to America. Her mother never spoke to her again. About nine months later, the guy just up and left. It was before my mother was born...and he never even married her. That's why Ma's maiden name was Honoré. After she found the note, Immaculé ran all around asking people if they'd seen the guy, or knew anything about it. Nobody knew anything about 'im, but then everybody sure knew that Immaculé got ditched. Gossip spreads fast in those row-houses. You didn't even have to leave your house to pass it along because everyone was crammed close together. Neighbors talked right through the wall. Gramma didn't like those row-houses; she said you could hear your neighbor fart through the wall. Anyway, Immaculé had to leave her baby all day with a woman who took in lots of kids, 'cause she had to earn a living doing fancy laundry for rich ladies. Did you know that French ladies have a special way of doin' laundry...ironin' and all?"

"I hadn't heard."

"Yeah, Ma told me that. Anyway, she had to make up a story to get by. You couldn't tell people you had an illegitimate kid, and get a job. So she dressed in black and claimed to be a widow. She told everyone her husband had died fighting for France in a war, and was buried over there in a military cemetery. That's the story my mother grew up with, and that's how her mother managed to cover up that there was no grave for her to visit. The story got bigger and bigger over the years. She told Ma that her father was such a hero that the French put up a monument to 'im...someday they'd make a trip over and see it. She never married again, and dressed all in black for the rest of her life. Gramma said Immaculé went kind of dotty towards the end. She died real young."

"How'd she die?"

"She got sick-don't know with what."

"And your mom never found out the true story of her father?"

"I don't think so, but you can't be sure. All I know is that the story is real to her now."

I knew just what she meant because I lived it, but I had to wonder. If stories become real, was there any such thing as truth? Is truth even all it's cracked up to be? I guess Immaculé thought it preferable for her daughter to hold a false gilded image of a father who loved her, a brave casualty of war. Better to believe he was an honest man and a hero to boot, rather than the despicable cad who abandoned them in poverty and shame. Maybe the lie was a good thing. After all, that's why my mother told me the story of how much I'd been loved; how my real parents put me up for adoption because they wanted the best for me. Problem was, she was so uncomfortable with the truth. I'd always sensed the discord between the lie meant to spare my feelings and the state of her innards; you could almost see her intestines writhing. It just didn't work, and the anxiety it aroused was probably much worse than if she'd come out and said, "Your unwed mother couldn't keep you. Your biological father abandoned you both-and that was that. Sad, but it happens all the time." I guess they just couldn't do it. I was conceived in sin and born out of wedlock, and that was one helluva big deal for Catholics in 1958. No matter which words my mother chose to tell the story, the only feeling I got was shame. They insisted that being adopted was special, but all I got out of it was that squirmy feeling in my stomach you get when you know someone's hiding something they really don't want to talk about. Special my ass! I was coming to understand that in the grown-up world, truth was like the Mass Transit, with dozens of subway trains traveling to various destinations. If you don't like where the truth is heading, just pick one that suits you and hop on, even if it takes you far out of your way. Personally, I don't think it's worth the trouble. I'd rather be an honest bastard, and just ride it out to the end of the line.

21

Eddie Murphy came home for the Christmas holiday, and I got asked over especially for the occasion. I hadn't seen him since sometime last summer. He looked strikingly different, serious and manly in his dark suit, but it was more than the clothes. It already felt like there was a priest was in the house. Uncle Malone put down his paper and stared awkwardly. Then he actually stood up and shook Eddie's hand, as if he were greeting a stranger.

I did catch a glimpse of the old Eddie, the tender boy-not-quite-yet-man that I first met last winter. The five of us went into a little back parlor, just Eddie and us girls. He asked us to tell him everything about his mother and Gramma, and wanted to know how we were all getting on in school. He had a way of making you feel important, not like a kid, but as if your opinions really mattered. I was happy to be included, like one of the family. Maddy openly displayed affection, and even Joanie seemed relaxed when Eddie was around. I'd spent more time with her lately, and she was a tough nut to crack. Sometimes she spoke with surprising sensitivity about her mom, or her brother Michael. Usually, she reminded me of a porcupine with its quills erect, ready to defend itself.

"And where's our Tommy?" Eddie asked after a while.

"Who knows?" Joanie answered sarcastically. "He doesn't spend much time around here."

"Mad'lin, what's going on? What about his studies?"

Tommy had begun to drink beer and smoke pot on a regular basis, and he cut school a lot. Maddy wasn't about to snitch, but she didn't want to lie either. She cleared her throat and answered evasively. "Not much." Joanie smirked, and Maddy gave her an evil eye that warned her to keep her mouth shut. "He gets kind of moody. School su...ah...stinks," Maddy added, catching herself.

"We don't learn anything...it's a mess," I added. "The new science teacher I liked so much lasted barely a month, because the kids were so disrespectful!"

"You should all be in Catholic school," Eddie said seriously, looking and sounding priestly and pedantic.

Annie had been sitting on Eddie's knee, staring off in space. She hadn't outgrown her tendency to float between two worlds, one the rest of us inhabited and the other back deep somewhere in her mind. It was hard to tell how much, if anything, she took in. But just when you thought it was all going over her head, she fooled you. "Tommy is just grouchy because he gots his period," she piped up in her little girl's voice. Eddie looked embarrassed.

"What?" Maddy looked at me questioningly, hoping for an explanation. I shrugged.

"Joanie gets grouchy when she gots her period," Annie insisted. "I know, 'cause I seen her panties in a bucket down the laundry."

"Oh, Jeez Annie! You don't go tellin' that to our brother. What's the matter with you?" Joanie was mortified.

Eddie set her gently on her feet and stood up. He spoke over her head. "I think you girls need to explain...ah...something to Annie," he said softly. "It's time I went to sit with Mum."

Art Linkletter's kids had nothing on Annie. She went way beyond the 'darndest things' and seemed to have no notion of what not to say, or when not to say it. Children her age were wising up, and she sounded much younger than her years. The others were starting to notice, and ridicule her. Annie made the most embarrassing observations with pure ingenuousness. Some were funny. This time she was seriously confused.

"Annie, boys don't get periods," I said gently.

"Your mom said you get them when you're older," she explained.

"Ahh," Maddy and I said collectively. Last summer when Maddy had her first menstrual fiasco, my mother had comforted Annie and explained that it was just her period. It wouldn't happen until she was much older. Apparently, she hadn't been detailed enough with her explanation. We looked at one another, astonished that Annie had never picked up on it being a female specific phenomenon.

"Sweetie, only girls have babies..." Joanie explained patiently, perhaps to make up for her previous rebuke.

Annie frowned with indignation and interrupted. "I know that!"

"Well, only girls get periods. It's how...later when you get married and grow a baby..."

"Nooo...you're wrong," she shook her head. "I know Tommy gots his period too." Then she left.

22

I couldn't sleep one night and suddenly remembered the chocolate cream pie we'd had that evening for desert. I wasn't supposed to get up and eat, but I couldn't stop thinking about it. I decided that no one would miss a little tiny sliver...umm, with a sip of milk too. The hell with dieting! I crept downstairs like a cat burglar and snapped on the kitchen light. "Ahh!" I put my hand over my mouth. "Dad, you scared the crap out of me." He was sitting in the dark with the pie in front of him.

"Ha ha ha," he laughed, then put his finger to his lips like a mischievous child. "Shhh." I got a spoon and we went at it from two ends, until our spoons met in the middle. We divvied up the last bites.

"Mom's gonna' have a bird," I said.

"I'll take the rap," he offered with a conspiratorial grin.

"OK," I agreed. "Just make sure I'm not around when you do. I'm a terrible liar; I'll crack." As we were cleaning up, I had an urge to look out the back window. I'd recalled that on my last late night foray into the kitchen, I'd seen a light in the tower. I didn't really expect to see it again, and sucked in my breath audibly when I did.

"What's a matter?" Dad asked.

"Look. There's a light on in the tower," I said.

He looked out. "Yeah, I seen it too," he answered. "I get up sometimes to take an aspirin, and one night I noticed it. Sometimes it's on, sometimes..."

"Dad, it's moving! It's a flashlight; someone's climbing down the stairs with a...ooh, it went out!" I had goose bumps.

"Who do you suppose is up there?" he asked.

"It'd have to be their grandmother," I answered. "Maddy said no one else is allowed. But I don't think she knows her old Gramma's wandering around up there in the middle of the night. If she did, she probably would've told me."

"Ha! What a couple of nosy Nellies," he scoffed. "Better not tell your mother..."

"I know. I'll hear about minding my business," I whispered. We snuck back upstairs one at a time so as not to make too much noise.

23

A few days before Christmas, Uncle Malone took Gramma and Eddie out shopping in the cab. Joanie was taking advantage by watching soap operas on TV, something that she wouldn't normally be allowed; it wasn't because they worried about her viewing habits, but because Uncle Malone still guarded the old black and white TV. He was certain the kids would wear it out prematurely. "You should go over to my house," I quipped. "Mom spends the afternoon ironing in front of back to back soaps."

With nothing much to do, we trooped upstairs. Tommy was in his room, and Maddy banged on the door. "Hey Tommy, what's up?" she hollered. No answer. "Tommy?" She tried the door and it opened. The bedroom window was open a couple of inches, and it was freezing in there! It was four o'clock and almost dark too. She tiptoed inside, and I followed. No one was there, and she shrugged as if to say, 'don't ask me.' Then she went over to the window, pushed it up and stuck her head out. She leaned way out and looked around.

"Be careful!" I said in a strained whisper.

"I'll be damned!" She pulled her head back inside.

"What?"

"Go see."

I looked out and saw the roof-line, and the gable with the third half-story. The tower stood above it, but you couldn't see inside the windows. "What am I looking at?"

"The window-over in what used to be a maid's room; it's open just a smidge," Maddy said slyly. "I know where he's got to-crafty sonovabitch," she added with admiration.

"Oh," I said, catching on. "He must have crawled across the roof and found the window unlocked...that's dangerous. What do you think he's doing in there anyway?"

"Up to no good, I'll bet." She looked at me with her best mischievous smirk, then stuck her head back outside. "Hey Tommy! We know you're in there!" She fairly sang it out, good-naturedly teasing her brother.

"What the fuck's a matter with ya?" His voice came from across the roof.

"Hey, watch it, the kid's here," Maddy shot back. I heard a scraping, clambering sound, and then he appeared at the bedroom window. She helped him push it up and he climbed in.

"What're yas doin' in my room?" he snarled. "Get out!" He seemed seriously mad at her, but I thought he looked more shaken than mad.

"What's the matter with ya?" Maddy asked softly. "We was just wondering where you was...what have you got over there anyway?"

"Never mind! Just keep your damned mouth shut about it...and get outa here before I throw you out the fuckin' window!"

"Jeez, real nice! Merry Christmas to you too." She tried to laugh it off, but I thought she seemed a little worried.

I looked around and was glad to see Annie had left the room. I hoped she hadn't heard. We went into the girls' room expecting to find her, but it was dark and empty. I turned on the light, figuring she was hiding. Maybe Tommy scared her. "Annie? Are you in here?" We looked at each other, and I checked under the beds while Maddy opened the closet. She shook her head no. We heard Joanie come up the stairs.

"What the hell's going on? The kid came running downstairs and ran off outside without a coat."

"Why didn't you go after her?" Maddy yelled as she tore off down the stairs. I followed carefully; I do not run down stairs, and by the time I grabbed my coat off the peg, Maddy was already out the back door.

"Annie?! Annie, where are you?" I called, soon as I was outside. Maddy had run around to the back, so I went the other way towards the front. I didn't have to worry long. Even though it was dark, I could see Annie standing close by the side of the house, under Tommy's room where we'd discovered his secret and pissed him off. She was craning her neck to look up at the window. I ran over and pulled off my coat and put it around her. She just kept staring up, straining to see. "What are you doing out here?" I asked.

She glanced at me nervously, and then took one more look up as if to make sure of something. "I'm waitin' for Tommy to throw Mad'lin out the fuckin' window," she explained calmly. "I'm gonna catch her."

When we got back inside we thought the excitement was over for the evening. Our big concern was not to upset Joan. "You mustn't tattle-tale; it'll only make him madder," I said. "Tommy was just being grouchy. He didn't really mean it."

"OK." She shrugged. "I gotta go pee!" She ran off upstairs. Joanie had gone back to her soap operas, and we plopped down on the couch and watched because we were too tired to do anything else. I decided it was about time to go home. Then I thought it might be better if I waited until the adults got back. Tommy had been pretty nasty up there. I heard Annie come back downstairs and she appeared at the entryway to the parlor. Her little blue corduroy pants were soaked from the crotch to her knees. She was crying.

"Oh-oh," I said sympathetically. "What happened?"

"Mommy won't come out of the bathroom...she made me wet my pants," she cried in embarrassment.

For a moment the three of us froze like rabbits. Maddy jumped up and tore off back up the stairs, with Joanie after her. This time I remembered to watch out for Annie. I took her hand firmly and followed them. I could already hear Maddy banging on the door.

"Ma! Ma, are ya OK? Ma, please...open the dowah!" She shook the old crystal doorknob violently. It rattled, but wouldn't open.

"None of us ever bother to lock the dowah," Joanie said. She bent down, trying to see through the keyhole, then stood up with her hand over her heart. "Jesus-God help us...Ma's layin' on the flowah!"

Tommy was suddenly at my elbow with an old metal toolbox. He tried to stick a screwdriver in the keyhole, but it was too big, so he whacked the doorknob with a hammer. It broke off and fell to the floor, and we heard the inside knob hit the tile with a crack. The door was still stuck, but now we could see into the bathroom better. I bent down and looked. "Joanie, dial 911!" I said, and then grabbed Annie by both shoulders. "Annie, you said you could crawl through to the linen closet?" She nodded. "Let's go!" We headed for her room. "She's crawling in!" I yelled out from the bedroom. It seemed to be taking forever. I went back to the hallway.

"Tommy, if you kick the door will it hit her?" I asked. Maddy peeked in through the hole where the doorknob fell out.

"No. There's enough room."

Tommy kicked so hard I expected it to bust open, but the door was solid oak, and only vibrated loudly. "Damn!" he said, and started kicking with all his might. Bang! Bang! Bang!

I put my hands over my ears, but took them away to listen. "Wait!" I said, holding my hand up like a traffic cop. "Annie, are you in there?"

"Yes."

"What happened?"

"Mummy fell off the potty and pooped on the floor. I can't wake her up."

I held my breath and stayed calm so as not to alarm Annie.

"Do you see the skeleton key hanging on the hook?" Maddy asked evenly.

"Yes."

"Get it and open the door."

"I can't reach it."

"Use the chair," Maddy told her. "Drag it over...be careful."

We heard the chair scrape. "Got it," she said. We heard the sound of the metal key in the lock.

Joanie came back and told us the ambulance was on the way. Then the door creaked open. We tiptoed in while Tommy hung back in the hallway. Annie wasn't crying anymore; she stood silently by and watched as we hovered over her mother.

"She's breathing!" I pointed to her chest, which rose and fell, barely. The fecal odor was horrid, like something rotting. Joanie took a bath towel and covered her.

"Frances...is it the baby?" Maddy whispered. She crouched by her mom and took her hand as if it were made of glass. Her face was gray-white like the old porcelain.

I examined the contents of the toilet. It was full of dark sticky excrement mixed with blood, and more blood oozed from her body. There was no sign that her water had broken. I still didn't understand exactly how sex worked, but I'd read enough about pregnancy and birth to know this wasn't a miscarriage, at least not yet. "No, I don't think so," I said, hoping I was right. "Get some blankets," I turned away and started to leave.

"Please don't go, Frances," Maddy begged. I'd never seen her so frightened.

"I'm going to get my mom; I don't want to tie up the phone in case someone calls back. I'll cut across the yard and through the fence. We'll be right back in the car." She nodded. I went downstairs and Tommy followed after me.

"I'll watch for ya," he said simply, grabbing a flashlight off the shelf in the back entryway. He stood in the yard and shone the light on me until I scrambled through a missing board in the fence and was safe at home.

My mother was already with them when we heard the ambulance arrive, and she was there when Joan regained consciousness.

"My babies," Joan said weakly. "Please...Evie...take care of my babies."

"Don't you worry," Mom said. "I'll take care of everything."

When the others came home, my mother was there to break the news, and she stayed so they could all turn around and go back out to the hospital. She'd already taken upon herself the practical task of cleaning the bathroom. Joanie helped her. Mom bathed Annie and fixed some toast and Campbell's

Soup, and she made sure that we all ate at least a bit before she put Annie to bed. My dad came by in the other car, and I went home with him reluctantly. Mom slept on the couch until Aunt Hannah and Uncle Tom and Eddie returned; it was almost dawn.

Joan had carefully hidden the symptoms of her colon cancer for the last six months, when she began to suspect something was very wrong. She was afraid they'd insist on operating to save her life, and she wouldn't risk losing the baby. Little Immaculé was stillborn on Christmas morning. Mom kept Annie that Christmas, and Maddy stayed too. Somehow my parents had presents for them, wrapped and waiting under the tree, while the surgeons removed most of Joan's bowel, along with her uterus. It was far too late to save her now. It would only buy some time before the cancer ate away the rest of her insides. The doctor remarked that it must have been agony, and didn't know how anyone could hide that much pain.

After the surgery, Joan came home surprisingly soon and in remarkably good spirits. She had a colostomy bag, and plenty of pain killers. When anyone asked how she felt, or if she needed anything, she explained simply. "I'm happy. I'm happy this is all happening to me and not to someone else. It's God's will." Her smile was so radiant it seemed to come from another world. "I'm so happy Immaculé will never suffer on this earth. She's with Jesus now, and that's where we all want to be."

24

"What a crock o' shit," Maddy scoffed.

We were over on the side porch, sitting on the half-rotten stoop under cover of darkness. It was frigid. January 1971 had rolled around. It was almost a year since my grandmother's wake, a year since I was ripped through a door by the alley and into the world of the Malones. Suddenly I had a whole new family to love, and just when I did, one of them was dying. It hurt like hell, and the worst was yet to come.

"Huh?" I asked, unsure as to which crock she referred. There was no context; we'd been sitting in silence. Tommy had a flask with some sort of booze in it, and they were passing a joint.

"I don't believe in a God who gives one person cancer so he don't have to give it to someone else. And if He does, then screw Him!"

I wasn't very religious, but my stomach flipped with angst. Talking that way about God seemed like asking for trouble. I shut my eyes and prayed silently. "Dear God, she doesn't mean it; please don't punish her. Her heart's just broken."

Tommy didn't seem to have an opinion on the matter as he toked away. He had quite a stash of marijuana in the third half-story, and of course, I had to keep my mouth shut and mind my business about it. Last year I wasn't supposed to tell about a stolen pack of cigarettes, which seemed pretty silly now. Even though I customarily passed, Maddy held the joint out to me and I suddenly snatched it and sucked hard, just like I'd seen them do. I couldn't hold it in; the back of my throat burned so bad I choked and hacked. "Sorry," I croaked as the smoke escaped.

"Here, try some of this." Tommy passed me the flask. I took the tiniest sip possible. It was awful, but it helped sooth my throat. Maddy passed the joint again.

"Take it easy," she coached.

"Ah..." I was successful. We passed it round and I took a hit each time. I did it because I just wanted to feel close to them. I wanted to feel exactly like Maddy was feeling. I did it because I hoped it would fog over the terrible sadness. It seemed to work. "My feet feel funny," I said after a while. "They feel all tingly." Maddy started laughing hoarsely and even Tommy chuckled through his nose. Then we all had a laughing fit that died as suddenly it began and turned to stone silence. We stared at the stars in the sky. It was dark, with almost no moon.

"I can't believe it," Maddy said after an indeterminable time that could have been ten minutes or an hour. I searched the sky looking for whatever it was she couldn't believe.

"What?" I asked, confused.

"I can't believe what Ma pulled. Gramma's right-being good isn't always a good thing. How is it good to be so sick and in pain, bleedin' out your ass every day and hidin' it from your family? How is it good to leave your kids? She knew it was something bad or she wouldn't have hid it. She must've known it was the cancer. Poor Annie. Know how I feel, Frances?"

I just shook my head no. I could feel my mouth kind of hanging open, and I couldn't think of anything to say.

"Pissed off, that's how! She did it to herself, for herself. What Ma did was just...selfish."

I hadn't thought of that, but now I did I could see her point. Still, it felt wrong to be angry with poor Auntie Joan. I was too wasted to speak, which was a good thing, because I probably would have said something stupid. I just listened, and like their grandmother had taught us, tried not to judge.

"Dad drove us out to the cemetery," she continued quietly. "He waited in the cab while Gramma walked out with us big kids-that was the afternoon we left Annie with your ma. We had trouble findin' the gravesite. There was hard crusty snow on the ground, all slippery, and I told Gramma we should go back-I was afraid she'd fall, but she wanted to go on. I hung onto her. We found the little white stone with the baby's name. You should come see it Frances...it's kind of nice. There's a little sheep lying on top, carved out of the marble. Gramma bought it for her, and a plot next to that...for Ma. She wanted us to know it was all taken care of-everything, the funeral and all. Jesus...it's just waitin' there for her, like the frozen ground is just waitin' to open up and swallow her. And the worst thing about it is...she can't wait go! She talks on about it like she's goin' on some sort of a goddamned vacation! A one way vacation-without us. The only thing she wants is to see Annie make her first communion this spring." She sighed and sniffed loudly. "I think it's the only thing she's ever asked God...for herself. She prayed for the baby to live, but that was for the baby. All she's ever asked for herself was another six months, and...do you think she'll make it, Frances?"

I wondered if I should just say yes-it'll be alright. But that wasn't what she wanted, and the question deserved an honest answer. Then I knew Maddy didn't expect me to give a prognosis. She wanted to know something else, something my foggy brain couldn't drive through, but fortunately my heart just took the wheel. "I...I don't know. But when it does happen, I'll be right here," I choked out before breaking down completely. "I'm sorry," I sobbed. "I'm so, so sorry." Maddy slid over on the stoop and for the first time, hugged me tight. She cradled my head with one big hand, pulling it to the breast of her leather jacket. I'll always remember the feel of cold leather on my cheek, leather permanently infused with the scent of Marlboros, and a hint of cannabis. She wanted to know what I thought because I was important; it was her way of saying she needed me. I'd never had anyone need me before, and it made me feel strong, like I could stand up to anything so long as she was there. My head rose and fell with her deep breaths. She may have been crying, but I couldn't say for sure. It was too dark.

25

Tom Malone had always been a quiet man, but it was not a gentle quiet. He reminded me of Gramma's Saturday night boiled dinner. You couldn't see all those skinned potatoes and carrots, cabbage and ham churning around in the giant pot of scalding water, but you could smell it in the greasy clouds of steam escaping from under the lid. He hardly said 'two words,' as Dad put it, but he got his message across with a raised hand and barks of hyperbolic threats. I'd seen him riled; at the slightest provocation he bellowed dire warnings, like, "You touch that TV and I'll break your godamn neck!" The first time I heard it I nearly ran for my life. Maddy just laughed; "He don't mean it," she said. Still, it terrified me, and I could see that Annie somehow took it literally. I couldn't tell what was roiling back behind Tom Malone's narrow eyes, but something about the very way he walked unnerved me. The way his thin upper lip curled back to show his yellow teeth in a crooked smile made me avert my eyes. Worst of all was the acrid stench of his 80 proof sweat; one whiff set me to vigilance.

After the initial shock of his wife's illness and the loss of their baby, Tom had been more attentive, even tender with his family. For a while he stayed closer to home, often checking in at lunch to sit with Joan. By February he was staying out later and coming home drunker, even more so than he used to, Maddy told me. He'd been sleeping on the couch since early in Joan's pregnancy, and had shunned the marital bed ever since. Now he stayed locked in the little side parlor late into the morning, even after noon, and God help the kids if they woke him. He came home one night with a used color TV, installed it in his lair and declared that if anyone bothered it, he'd "Fix them good!" Of course, that only made the kids all the more determined to watch it, but they kept a careful lookout when they did. They tried to get me to join them one afternoon when their Gramma was out doing errands, but I declined. I could watch anytime I liked at home without fear for my life. Besides, I would never come out and say it, but the parlor was nasty. It stank like a stallion's stall.

One evening Annie slipped in and decided to watch the thing all by herself. Her dad had just left-she saw him drive off. When she'd settled down to the *Muppet Show*, Tom came back for something he'd forgotten and heard the TV in his parlor. She was so engrossed she didn't hear him coming. Annie was like that with the TV, and I once remarked that she wouldn't notice a bomb going off when she watched.

Maddy heard her sister scream, so loud it woke the ghosts and reverberated with the echoes of every child's cry that ever filled the old house. She feared Annie had found her mother unconscious, or worse. But as she came charging down the stairs, she heard the sound of a hard hand slapping flesh, a sound she knew well. From the parlor doorway she could see the upper half of her sister's small body bent over double, screaming in pain and fear and shame, twisting around to free herself. She tried to reach back and pull her pants up, but her father just kept at it, striking her hand if it got in the way. He had her legs pinned between his knees, and with his left hand on the back of her neck, forced her head almost to the floor while he struck with his right. One side of his upper lip was twisted in an odd grimace, a look which in another context might be mistaken for a sardonic smile. With each blow he raised his arm in a high arc, and the force of his open palm already left deep red handprints. The image was so overpowering that Maddy's ears filled with a ringing sound, and for a moment she heard nothing, as if someone had turned off the volume in the middle of a movie.

"Stop it! Stop it!" Her high pitched hysterical voice sounded foreign in her ears, as if it came from someone else. He didn't slow down or even look up, so she hurled herself on him and tackled the offending arm with both of hers. He flung her off effortlessly and she hit the floor hard, but jumped up and went back at him. This time she wrapped herself round the arm with two arms and a leg, and clung on as if wrestling a giant snake. "Tommy," she cried, "Tommy, help!" But Tommy didn't come. He was off somewhere.

Then Tom Malone lost interest in beating his six year old daughter and turned on the elder. His face was blanched, and the white scar on his chin stretched thin as he grimaced in malicious anger. "I'll fix you!" he roared, and reached for her throat with his other hand. She hunched her shoulders and tucked her head in like a turtle, all the while watching Annie slowly crawl away, sobbing hysterically with her pants tangled at the ankles. When the child was clear of the room she let go and rolled out of his reach. Then she sprang up and stood with her back to the doorway. Tom was taking off his belt.

Mad-Dog locked eyes with the beast, engaging him until her sister escaped. She couldn't run for it, couldn't risk leaving her sister alone in the house. Her father was stinking drunk. Right then the front doorbell rang. It was one of the few things that actually worked around the place, probably because it got so little use over the years. It distracted Tom, and Maddy decided to dash for the door and ask whoever it was for help. He lurched after her, but she was too fast. She got to the door first and flung it open. It was Father Mahood, come to look in on her mother. He stepped inside and started to take off his black hat as usual, but his pale wrinkled face took on a puzzled expression as he looked past Maddy into the hallway. She turned to see her father standing behind her with crazed eyes, and the doubled-up leather belt in his hand. She noticed with disgust that his fly was unzipped.

Tom Malone's lips moved as if he would speak, but no words came; or perhaps they were drowned out by the piercing cries of the terrified child. Maddy wasn't sure if her father was still furious, or if he was ashamed of what he'd done. He looked at once like a scared little boy before the priest, a little boy who's gotten himself in trouble- and a ferocious bear about to maul.

"Oh, hello Tom," Father said awkwardly. "It, ah, appears I've come at a bad time. I'll just come round tomorrow," he said, replacing his hat.

Maddy wanted to reach out and grab him by his black cape to stop him from going. She wanted to call out, "Father help us, don't leave, please help us!" Somehow she couldn't. She just couldn't air the family's dirty laundry, couldn't spill the bucket of shit they were riding on their way straight to hell. Once the secret got past the front door, it couldn't be hidden away again. Only silence would let it die, and tomorrow, be buried. Tomorrow they would all act like nothing happened.

The priest let himself out and the door shut behind him, leaving a cold blast of March air in the entryway. Mad-Dog turned to face her attacker, but he was already lumbering off, and was soon out the back door. She listened. The engine of the old cab coughed, and wouldn't turn over. "Dear God," she prayed, "start the car." It started. Then she heard the cab peel off down the street with a loud squeal. "Please don't let him kill someone," she prayed again.

"You gotta promise me, Frances. You're the only one I trust."

"Does your grandmother know...he abuses?" I croaked, barely able to speak. I was sickened.

"Yeah...and no. I'm not even sure he knows."

"What?"

"I mean, I don't think he shaves in the mirror and says, 'Tom, you son of a bitch, you're a child abuser.' I think he thinks of it as discipline. For a long time I thought the same thing. Like when Tommy threw the fire cracker at a nun and we caught hell, we figured we had it coming. When he lit the fire in the janitor's closet...yeah...but when Dad whaled on Tommy for gettin' bad grades, I thought that was pretty messed up. Maybe that's how his own father treated 'im...it's all he knows. But there's something else. I don't know how to explain it; there's something about the way he…gets off on it. That's sick! That's what scares the shit out of me. I mean, I'm not worried about me, but what kind of sick bastard beats a little girl for watching a goddamned TV? Frances, I almost told on him. I almost told Father Mahood, and if he stayed another second I think I would've. But he just freaked out and left, almost like he was afraid of my dad. The old guy isn't stupid either…he saw what was going on."

"You've got to tell someone!" I said. "What if he hurts her seriously? This is serious enough, but what if…" I thought of all the horrible wounds a drunken brute could inflict on a child. My head was spinning, and I felt nauseous. The last time I got hit was the cuff in the head for asking too many questions about black people. When I was little I got spankings. I can't remember what they were for, but it made me feel like they hated me, though it wasn't nearly as painful as when Mom threatened to send me back to the orphanage. Maybe it was because I wouldn't go to bed, or perhaps I defied them one too many times. They both seemed outraged at my propensity to argue back, something neither of them would have dared to do. Their parents were even more exacting; my mother got spanked for putting up a fuss because she was scared at a wake. That's how they disciplined children back then-but this sounded very different. Now I knew why Annie was so quiet around him. I always suspected something was wrong. I remembered the little red sneakers with the holes, and how frightened she was he'd be angry if she lost them. The poor little kid wasn't sure what might set him off. She must really have wanted to watch that Muppet show. I hated Tom Malone! I wished he would drop dead. Dear God, why did Auntie Joan have to die instead of him?

"Frances!" Maddy interrupted my tumultuous thoughts. "You won't tell, will you? It'd probably make 'im worse. What could anyone do? No one can talk to 'im. I'm afraid he'll take us away from Gramma again. Maybe this is why they fought, why he left her last time. And now Ma's gonna…she's gonna be gone soon. We need Gramma." She looked at me imploringly.

"OK. I promise I won't tell-for now. If something worse happens, I may change my mind. I may have to. That's the best I can do."

"It'll all blow over," she reasoned. "He's probably upset about Ma. He hasn't been this bad for a long time. I don't think I ever seen him on Annie that bad. He used to do Joanie like that, but she got too big I guess. He used to do me like that all the time, but I fought back…and I won."

"What do you mean?"

"Uh, ya know that scar he's got on his chin?" She cocked one eye at me questioningly.

"Yeah, you can't miss it. It's like a dented car fender; then it gets thin and white when he...smiles, if you can call it that. What about it?"

"I did that," Maddy smirked as she told me.

"What? How'd you do that?"

"He was whaling the shit outa me for somethin'-again. I was nine. I got away and he come after me. Lucky for me I had on my school uniform; it was a dress, so I didn't get hung-up like Annie with the pants around her ankles. He was lunging down to grab me again from behind, yellin' 'I'll fix you.' He was comin' right in and I grabbed the first thing I could. It was a table lamp-an old heavy brass thing-and I just swung it back without turning to look, just swung it with two hands like I was up at bat while he was headin' straight for it. Bam!" She smacked her fist into her palm with a loud crack. "It was like two trains colliding. Fuckin' chin split wide open. I thought he was gonna murder me for sure, but I didn't care. I'd rather be dead than afraid all the time. I ain't never been afraid of him since, but now I'm scared for Annie."

"Jesus," I said quietly. "What did he do?"

"Funny thing is, he didn't do nothin' to me. Just ran out with his handkerchief over his chin and drove hisself off to the hospital. That night when they thought I was asleep, I heard him tell Ma that he fell on the ice-just slipped and hit the curb while he was gettin' outa the cab. It was winter. After that we never said nothin' about it. Not even once."

I wondered how that worked. How do you beat your child so bad that she fights for her life and sends you to the hospital? How do you just munch toast and drink coffee next morning at the breakfast table? How do you pretend it never happened, while the child sits on her bruised buttocks and the father chews painfully with stitches in his swollen face, from a gash that would scar him for life?

26

"We should try the dress on Annie. We'd better make sure it fits in case you need to alter it. Then she could at least model it for her mom-we could take pictures," I suggested.

"It's not until June. I don't think she's going to make it to the First Communion," Mom said, shaking her head sadly.

Joan had gone into the hospital twice, once at the end of March and again in mid-April. She got infections around the stoma. None of us thought she'd come back, but she did. She fought to hang on, and it seemed bitterly unfair. Even if she lived until the end of June, she was in no shape to go to Church, no shape to leave the house.

I admired my mother's devotion. She was the only one who visited regularly, aside from the family priest. She helped Aunt Hannah clean and sponge bath the patient, and even learned to change the colostomy bag. It seemed ironic that when Auntie Joan's mind was ailing, my mother avoided the place like the plague. Now that Joan was terminally ill, she bore up like a trooper. For me the most difficult part was the overpowering odor that oozed from her permanent wound in fluid and feces, as if she were already beginning to decompose. No matter how many times Mom changed the sheets, or doused the room with Lysol, it smelled like death. But now Joan's mind was quiet, grounded by morphine and whatever else they gave her. She no longer had strength for the rambling streams of consciousness my mother found so disturbing. Joan was right and properly sick, and had a good excuse for it. My mother found that acceptable.

I had an idea. "Why couldn't Annie receive First Holy Communion early? Why couldn't Father Mahood celebrate the Eucharist in the home, with the whole family present?"

"I never thought of that." Mom was intrigued.

It seemed a simple solution; I wondered if there was some reason no one had suggested it already. Perhaps there was some religious prohibition, some cannon law that forbade it. Of course, it wouldn't be the same as watching all the first communicants walking down the aisle, all in white, kneeling at the railing with their little hands folded, waiting to receive the body of Christ. The priest would be in his best vestments, the little girls looking like tiny brides with their white lace veils. There would be a full mass, and the church would have lilies. It was every Catholic mother's dream, that and being mother of the bride. It certainly wouldn't be the same, but this was no time to nit-pick.

Mom brought my idea to Aunt Hannah, who consulted her priest. Father Mahood was happy to oblige, and they rushed to prepare the communicant. Annie had yet to make her first confession. Though her grandmother had seen to it that the child went regularly to catechism class, it wasn't clear that Annie understood any of it. Father Mahood stood her in front of him in the best parlor and quizzed her, asking what it meant to receive the sacrament of Reconciliation. The frightened child fidgeted, dug the toe of her little shoe into the carpet and finally shrugged. At the same age I had memorized my lines, and could tell you that it meant to confess your sins and receive absolution. But I didn't really know sin, or understand how the priest could wave his hand, mumble in Latin and wipe it away. It was definitely all about the dress, and the little party afterwards. Come to think of it, I wasn't sure I really understood it much better now.

Father was patient with her. He sat her down and explained the sacrament of penance and communion all over again. When he asked if she understood, she nodded. Good enough. She was brought to confession the next Saturday, and only God and his priest know what she said in there.

We were on for a week from Sunday and the preparations would be a scramble. The house had to be cleaned, food prepared, and the whole family gathered together, perhaps for the last time on earth. Mom had to take the white dress in at the bodice, and a good three inches at the waist. Then it was perfect. It was hard to get Annie to stand still while Mom put the pins in. She kept flouncing the skirt, and trying to do pirouettes. I would have been smacked on the bottom by the third time, but my mother was older, and had grown more patient. She seemed to understand children better now, and was definitely much more accepting of Maddy.

For the first time, I realized that growing up wasn't something that happened all of a sudden when you were twenty-one, or even twenty-five. My mother was almost fifty, and was settling into a calmer, more confident woman. She mentioned to me that the 'change of life' was finally over and done, and while I knew what that meant biologically, it would be decades until I could fully appreciate it. Throughout menopause, she had lived with her sick and difficult mother, right up until finally burying her. Now I understood why my mother had gone out of the house so much that last year. No wonder she feared mental illness! In her compromised state, Nana nearly drove her crazy.

"What are you going to wear?" I thought to ask my cousin, who hadn't put on a skirt since sixth grade, not even for mass-when her grandmother managed to get her there.

"Huh? Whada ya mean?" she said absently after exhaling. We were sitting up by the lilac bushes again. The weather was fine. I think Mom knew she was smoking up there, but she turned a blind eye.

"For Sunday, silly! You can't go in jeans and the leather jacket."

"Aw, crap. I hadn't thought about it," she sulked. I could see the topic was a sore spot. "Why can't I wear what I want?" She didn't sound as if she really meant it, but gave it a try.

"Everybody will be in Sunday best. There'll be pictures-come on, you know you've got to dress right."

"Yeah, I guess. Maybe Joanie has some old thing I can put on. Yuck!" she said, just like a little kid.

I was never one of those girls who lived for clothes, even when we wore dresses to school every day. But I still liked to dress up and go to church. It gave me an excuse to wear nylons and look pretty. During school this past year, it was the fashion to not care about clothes, or at least look like you didn't care. Still, the blue jeans, or dungarees as we called them, had to fit right. You had to look cool. I couldn't pull it off, and I stopped trying. In hip-hugger jeans and the leather, Maddy embodied cool. She was tall and lanky, and I tried to imagine her in one of my Sunday outfits, in a dress and nylons. It seemed strange, unnatural, but I couldn't think why.

"Why don't you ever like to wear dresses?"

"Frances, don't be such a dope," she said. I felt embarrassed. She was right; I was a dope—about some things anyway. Only I couldn't figure out what it was I was being so dopey about this time.

"Sorry," I said, because I couldn't think of anything else to say.

"That's my Frances." She smirked. "I call you a dope and you're sorry. The truth is, I don't have a good answer. I just feel funny...I feel all wrong wearing a dress, even before sixth grade," she said seriously. "I feel...naked, or at least like I walked out by mistake in my underwear."

"I think I know what you mean. I remember how when school started back at Edmunds, and we wore knee socks instead of tights. When the cool September air blew up your legs, you felt half-naked." I hadn't really thought about it, but girls' clothes left you feeling vulnerable. There was nothing between your most private parts and the world but a thin pair of panties. Panties with a short skirt hanging barely to your knees! We were trained to sit carefully, lady-like by Kindergarten. When winter came we wore tights, and it was almost like wearing pants. Then spring came and it was knee socks, ankle socks and back to feeling drafty and exposed. We always changed into slacks and shorts for play, but my mother told me she wore dresses all day when she was young. She even had to act lady-like at play.

    "Yeah, I guess that's it," Maddy said absently. "But I want everything to be right for Ma. I don't want Dad griping at me in front of everyone." She assumed a disdainful sneer and mocked in a low masculine growl, "What the hell's a matter with ya anyway? Why don't ya ever fix ya self up like Joanie?" I giggled at her performance, but there was nothing funny about Uncle Tom. "I don't want anything to upset Ma...I guess I'd better ask your mom what to do about an outfit," she resolved, as if that were the lesser of two evils.

27

The big day came off perfectly. The weather was perfect. Annie looked perfect. Uncle Malone seemed relaxed and sociable, thanks to Dad. He usually had that effect on him. Tommy had to wear his suit from last year, since nobody thought to see about getting him a new one. It was so small he couldn't button the jacket, which barely went past his waist, so they decided he should abandon the jacket altogether. The pants were a little tight, but most of his growth had been in the upper body, and his Gramma was able to let the cuffs down so they weren't flood-pants. He wore a nice shirt and tie, and looked passable. Aunt Hannah was frugally dressed in the same crisp blue suit she'd worn when I met her formally, just over a year ago. Joan wore a loose flowing dress with pale, multi-colored flowers. It had puffy sleeves that were sheer chiffon, the same fabric as was layered over the solid pink sateen underneath. My mother had gone shopping and selected it for Joan, since she couldn't go out anymore. The look was amazing; it was just...perfect. Joan had lost so much weight, but somehow my mother managed to make her look beautiful. You couldn't tell how thin she was, couldn't tell where the dress ended and she began. It was like a gentle waterfall of flowers washed over her, covering her sickness for one last day.

My parents brought a real First Communion cake from the bakery. It was like the one I had, with pink and yellow rosettes, and *Congratulations Annie* written in icing. There was even a little plastic Jesus on top. Annie's eyes lit up at the sight of it, and I could see she had scant understanding as to the magnitude of what was happening, both the mystery of the Eucharist and the significance of receiving it in the family parlor, rather than with the other communicants at mass. It was all for the best. She looked very happy.

It's funny how you miss some things when you're standing right in the middle of it all. Dad took at least a half dozen Polaroids while Mom had to change the flashcube several times on the Kodak. There was a candid shot of my cousin Maddy, only marginally in the frame. She wore a simple but elegant beige dress my mother had pulled from her own closet, and altered to fit, practically at the last minute. It was a straight A-line, with short flouncy sleeves. She looked strange with her bare, muscular arms hanging awkwardly by her sides. She hunched her shoulders forward in an unconscious attempt to conceal her bosom, and her eyes were cast down like a prisoner about to be led off to the gallows. There were plenty of snapshots of Annie, some fuzzy and out of focus as she flitted aimlessly about, others with her staring off into space when she was supposed to be looking into the camera.

I absconded with one of the Polaroids when no one was looking, and squirreled it away in my purse. It had just developed before my eyes, and was so remarkably sad I had the sudden impulse to shield the rest of the party. The customary beatific, transcendent smile had left Joan's face, and a look of crushing sorrow, however fleeting, had stolen its place. She held the tips of Eddie's fingers tentatively, as if they were about to slip from her grasp like a balloon from a small child's hand. All you could see of Eddie was his lower half; he was standing as if to move away. As she gazed up at him, her face revealed the raw certainty that they would soon part for an indeterminable time. I thought I saw a wash of something else, of fear, or doubt, perhaps even a tinge of anger, as if her firm grip on faith and the promise of resurrection had faltered, if only for just one moment.

Those photographs are the mistakes-the ones that get stashed away in a box with the negatives and stored somewhere on a back closet shelf. Only the best are chosen for the family album. But someday when you clean out the closet and sort through again, you might discover that many of the discards were far more interesting than the pictures on display, with everyone saying cheese, nicely centered in the frame. From the vantage point of time, many of the pictures we saw as mistakes were truly works of art. They reveal who we are when we think no one is looking. They capture the pathos that makes joy so sweet, like the fleeting New England summer after a long hard winter.

But most of the rejects are just shots of people caught in awkward poses and looking plain silly. There was even a goofy picture of Father Mahood, poised with a fistful of cake about to be stuffed into his wide-open mouth. He was sitting on one of the best parlor wingchairs. Tommy happened to be standing in front of him, as if he were speaking to someone outside the camera's lens. It was so close-up you could see the whites of Father's eyes, which seemed oddly fixed on the back of Tommy's ill-fitting suit.

28

Sometimes a New England spring eases in gradually, but usually it has a mad tug o' war with winter that can last until June. You might get days or even weeks of warm sunshine that breathes life back into the dormant earth, followed by a spate of raw chilly rain more suited to the end of February. Late in the month of May, we had a freak snowstorm-freaky even for New England. Large sticky flakes fell in the night, and we awoke to a blanket of snow on the tender green shoots, on leaves that had only just unfurled. The lilacs on the hill were in brilliant bloom. Now each cluster of blossoms wore a tall snow hat, stark white on lavender. They looked strangely beautiful and at the same time sad, since the cold prematurely withered the flowers, bent their heads and snapped some right off at the stem. I ran out and took some pictures with Mom's Kodak. I made sure Dad took a couple of Polaroids, just in case.

By afternoon the snow had melted away in the spring sunshine, and Auntie Joan had slipped off to be with her beloved husband Eddie, little Immaculé, and Jesus. Gramma said the spring snow was a sign from heaven, a rare sight for a rare soul. We gave her a small framed photo of the snowcapped lilacs.

At Auntie Joan's wake, all of the neighbors who'd kept their distance from the Malones, from the seedy family rumors, the mental illness and dreadful wasting disease, now poured out full of respectful condolences, with cards and flowers. I think my mother had a hand it. She told me privately that Gramma had arranged the wake and paid for everything.

I saw in a heartbeat that it was a grand send-off, nothing at all like my grandmother's wake. The Mapleton Center Funeral Home was a great white house on lush green grounds, with flowering shrubs all around. Inside was like a palace. Even the ladies' room was all plush covered elegance, with a little velveteen settee in the anteroom, and great shining mirrors on the walls. Everything looked and smelled so delightful that it was almost hard to grasp the sadness of the occasion. There was a pervasive sense of peace, and relief that their mother's pain was over. Joan looked far better in death than she had in such a long time, all plumped up somehow. She wore the dress that my mother had just brought for the communion celebration. Aunt Hannah told her that Joan had expressly asked to be buried in it. She felt it would be a shame to wear it only once, and confided to her mother-in-law that she wanted to look her best for Ed, when they finally met again in heaven.

Out back there was a little private patio covered in flowering vines, where you could sit on wrought iron garden-seats and smoke. That's what I remember most about those two days-sitting in the garden while Maddy and Tommy puffed silently. You could hear multitudes of songbirds. It was adjacent to the beautiful cemetery, replete with the stately old Maple trees that gave the town its name.

I think the hardest part of a funeral is when the casket is lowered into the ground. You suddenly realize that your loved one is not going to be spending eternity resplendent in a bed of white satin, surrounded by flowers forever blooming. You're suddenly brought up short, faced with a hole in the dirt, thoughts of decomposition, worms and bones. The priest was praying. My head was bowed, my hands were folded but I wasn't listening to him at all, wasn't saying my prayers as I ought. I raised my eyes furtively and searched the sky, trying to imagine a final resting place other than this lonely spot beneath our feet. I stood at Maddy's side, so close our bare arms pressed together. Hers was strangely cold even in the warm sunshine. She'd put on the dress, but it would be for the last time.

Then I felt a gentle but urgent nudge from her elbow. I looked up, and Maddy whispered her sister's name, more like mouthed the word, 'Annie' with her palms up in a questioning gesture. I looked about quickly, and flushed with a wave of panic. She'd been standing right by my side, but had slipped away somehow and was gone.

Beyond the group of family gathered by the graveside, I saw her. The sweet child skipped lightly over the dead, bending down to pull the wildflowers that grew between the stones. Relieved, I signaled with my eyes, and pointed inconspicuously with my finger close to my breast, so no one would notice and think me rude. Maddy sighed, shook her head and smiled her funny half-smile, with one corner of her mouth twisted ironically.

Annie wore my first communion dress, had asked to wear it for her mother. She began to spin pirouettes, then paused to lift one leg high and turn out her toe like a ballerina; I saw that she'd discarded her shoes. She waved her little bouquet as she spun, then all at once tossed it and flung herself hands down onto the soft grass. I put my hand over my mouth to stifle laughter. Annie's bare feet rose, and her full skirt and petticoats flared gracefully in an arc as she turned a perfect cartwheel. The scattered flowers fell gently to earth.

S. Rose

Part Two

29

The spring of the snow-capped lilacs died of thirst and quietly collapsed. From the fourth of July to the third week of August, precious drops of water stubbornly hung in the air and refused to rain, shrouding the sun with a searing white haze that hurt your eyes. A sweltering summer rose from the dust-every green thing beyond the reach of a garden hose burnt and dried up. For a time it seemed as if all the flowers and tender shoots and even the color blue had abandoned the earth.

I was exhausted. The suffering I had witnessed left me wrung out like a dishrag, and provided a sobering kick in the pants that admonished me to grow-up and quit whining over small disappointments. I compromised; I moped in silence at what was turning out to be one long dull sorry-ass summer. Dad's overtime got cut back, and my parents decided it wouldn't be prudent to go to the lake, not even for a one week stay. I was too old to run outside and play, but still too young to get a summer job. Though stupefied with boredom, I didn't mention it. You really miss complaining about everyday things when they're swallowed up by the genuine tragedy of others, sickness and death and loss that renders the common place gripe an absurd self-indulgence.

Mom had been stuck in the hot summer doldrums right alongside me. One morning over coffee and an issue of *Ladies' Home Journal*, she suddenly perked up. Apparently wallpaper had become passé; we would strip the old paper that had hung since before I was born, and paint all six rooms. The article explained how to do it yourself, so the cost would be minimal. I was more than happy to help. Mom rented a wall-paper steamer, a heavy steel propane powered monstrosity that took both of us just to lug it into the house. The gas tank was grimy with an oily substance that turned out to be flammable; we nearly set the living room on fire before we got it under control. It singed the rug. After a couple hours of struggling we developed a technique: Mom wielded the steam wand while I attacked the faded patterns of paisley, ferns, and tangled vines with a flat metal scraper. The house filled with steam and the temperature rose above 80 degrees. We had no air conditioning. When the walls were finally bare and prepped, the two of us painted away, accomplishing the entire project without so much as a squabble. I got to choose the color for my bedroom, and watched in wonder as the dull white plaster turned a vibrant periwinkle blue that matured to a soft hue with a subtle sheen, almost like possessing a piece of bright summer sky. Whoever said it wasn't fun to watch paint dry must've been far too busy. After the last brushes were washed and the mistakes scrubbed off the floor, there was nothing much left to do.

Labor Day weekend heralded a blessed tropical downpour that lasted nearly eight days with hardly a pause. Since no one could mow in the rain, lush grass soon grew up and turned suburban lawns to verdant pastureland. Neighbors began to joke with one another that it was about time to build an arc as they scurried about beneath umbrellas. The welcome deluge was followed by a relentless drizzle that droned on 'til mid-October, punctuated only by intermittent rainfall. Our basement flooded. Damp drippy days slowed to a sluggish crawl, and slogged on for the duration of a tepid gray autumn.

Although I had hated seventh grade, I'd anticipated the first day of school with optimism. Eighth grade might be better-it couldn't possibly be worse. Before I even set one foot in the ominous brick building, I was alerted to the fact that the old school bells had been replaced with an ear-burning electronic buzzer, to herd us about like cattle. This was definitely worse. They blasted it once to end each period, then we had four minutes to change classes before the late signal. There were three lunch periods. The stomach-churning and downright demoralizing blare was better suited to lockdown a federal prison, than to bring order to a junior high school; but considering the behavior of the student body, I supposed that it might be intended as ironic foreshadowing.

The eighth graders scrambled to establish dominance over the incoming class, as well as any teachers not strong enough to control them. Overcrowding had rendered discipline next to impossible. There were fights before school, after school, and in school. During one free-for-all, the little bald principal strode boldly into the fray to establish law and order. He was promptly knocked down and swallowed up in a testosterone fueled slugfest. A burley assistant principal and Mr. Donald, the boy's P.E. teacher, had to wade in and haul him out.

The hallways on the main floor by the office were, if not quiet, at least free of mayhem, but the lower floors were jungle law. The basement level, home to gyms and locker rooms, echoed with primitive primate calls, loud hoots and howls emanating from somewhere in the brain that evolved prior to spoken language. Their limited oral lexicon consisted of homosexual slurs and swear-words that were bandied about so liberally they became blah and banal. The harsh clang of slamming lockers and the occasional rhythm of fists beating a loud tattoo on the metal doors provided instrumental accompaniment, a sound like primeval war drums.

The half-grown children who ran amok in school were even more out of control when school let out. It was as if they had no parents at all, and the consequences were predictable. That year my class counted its first casualty. One of the pretty popular girls who partied with the wildest crowd was killed in an accident. They were drinking and staggering down a highway, and she got clipped by a car going sixty, by a driver who never expected to see children in black leather emerge from the darkness of well past midnight. Her body was flung high into the air and landed face-first on a guardrail in front of her drunken friends. The wake was closed-casket. I didn't attend the wake, but Maddy told me about it. The girl who died wasn't a close friend, but she'd partied with her like she partied with just about everyone; besides, it was the Irish thing to do. I couldn't even recall what the girl looked like, and I'm sure we never spoke. She was just one of many I'd passed, nearly indistinguishable from the throng of girls in black leather jackets with long, flat-ironed hair bleached out to the color of straw, yellow on black like a bumblebee. I was very glad Maddy wasn't out with them that night.

While I was decidedly even more miserable this year than last, Maddy somehow dove head first into the sea of chaos and swam like a big fish. Naturally we spent less time together. To spare my feelings, she thoughtfully explained that it was because she just did stuff, stuff I wouldn't appreciate, stuff she didn't want me getting into. That much I'd figured out. We were in the same biology class, but since I had advanced English and she had advanced math, we had different schedules and even different lunch periods. I ate alone. Between classes, Maddy would scan the crowded halls and when she caught sight of me shout, "Hey, Frances!" through hands cupped like a megaphone, and just about as loud. It was reassuring, and let everyone else know that she was watching out for me. We still walked home together-on the rare occasions she was going straight home, and then the conversation avoided talk of her family or anything too important. Mostly, it centered on getting high-the last time she got high, who she got high with, and the latest reefer that Tommy just got in, or was getting in from Middlefield...for the next time they would get high. As for me, I indulged a couple of times when I was alone with Maddy and Tommy out back of the Malone Mansion, as she sarcastically referred to the dilapidated structure. I was sure my parents would kill me if they found out, and that proved to be quite a deterrent. Besides, it seemed a fifty-fifty chance as to whether I would catch a buzz, or a headache with a sore throat.

For logistical reasons, our relationship took an inevitable detour, but I think there was more to it than the stuff Maddy did or the company she kept. The bonds between people are like living things, and it was only two years since our friendship had emerged from a tender cocoon of preadolescence. It had scarcely unfurled its wings when harsh winds from the grown-up world blew it off course, and tore us from one last happy dance with childhood. When the storms passed we bumped and bobbed like two boats in the harbor loosed from their moorings, and nearly floated off in opposite directions. I suppose we might have drifted apart forever if it weren't for my mother's dedication to hold the families together.

Ever since last spring, Mom had maintained a weekly mac 'n cheese supper for my cousins-even Tommy when she could round him up. Maddy dutifully arrived every Thursday at 6:00 pm, with Annie in tow. She relinquished the leather jacket without a fuss and allowed Mom to put it away in the closet for the duration. Otherwise she wore the thing inside and out like a protective outer skin, even in summer's heat. Mom always sat with us and asked about school, and always served ice cream with Betty Crocker Brownies for desert. Dad was home in time for dinner most nights, and though dog-tired, managed to joke and banter and coax smiles from the bereft children. It was a fine gesture on their part, and the predictable routine provided an anchor, if only a light one.

At dinner Maddy was polite, sometimes a bit reserved and at other times almost, almost just like her old self. Then we went upstairs to my room and ostensibly did homework, while we watched the small black and white television I'd inherited, since my parents replaced the kitchen set with color. Once we were alone she closed up like a clam. I knew I had to be patient. No doubt being with me reminded her of it all-not that I ever brought any of it up. It was more of an association, like Pavlov's dogs salivating over the dinner bell. I know because Maddy had the same effect on me. Alone in a quiet place, the sound of her voice, or the look in her eyes seemed to conjure up the ghosts of memories, so recently buried that the grass had not yet grown over their graves. Disjointed images suddenly flashed before me, like an unwanted snapshot lodged painfully in my mind's eye. When she was with off with those other kids doing her 'stuff,' she could forget everything, at least for a while. None of them could ever know Maddy Malone like I did, and that's just how she wanted it.

30

Nineteen Seventy-one finally marched away all wet and mushy, and washed down the gutter with nothing much good to remember it by. It was a brown Christmas. I don't think I'd ever been so excited to see a New Year come in, but as the first few weeks rolled out it was decidedly anticlimactic. Nothing new happened. I'm not sure what I expected, but then I supposed it might be like reading a fat novel: it takes a while to set up the exposition before the action begins to rise.

It began at last with an editorial column in the Mapleton Daily News; the topic was desegregation. I followed with interest as the letters to the editor flowed, drawing commentary from folks who had clearly never written a formal letter in their lives. I listened as the neighbors flapped and squawked with general outrage at the idea of busing black students into Mapleton High School, which I would attend next fall. It was almost March.

Even without official segregation, there were still no black people living in town. Of course, the schools were all-white. My mother wasn't happy about the idea of forced integration, as most people called it, but said she'd accept it so long as no one tried to bus me off somewhere. Dad was irate; he declared that if the town tried to "pull that crap," he'd send me straight off to Catholic school next fall. Mom wasn't in favor of Catholic school. I'd asked once more to transfer at the beginning of the school year. I tried to impress upon them that I was receiving a dismal education, but Mom brushed it off. I tried to describe how badly the kids behaved, but she insisted that Catholic school kids behaved twice at bad when school let out. I seriously doubted it. The final argument was that it was just too expensive. Mom asked me if I wanted Dad to work himself to death for tuition money. "Let me get back to you on that," I retorted.

Since it looked like I was stuck in public school, the idea of integration actually appealed to me. If my parents were upset about it, that meant I had to be all for it. I was for the most part well-behaved and pathetically compliant. I needed a way to grow, something to push back against them like a diver uses a springboard, but rebellion was not my sole motivation. I was also genuinely liberal in my thinking, and truly welcomed the chance to get to know some black kids. African-Americans were still mysterious to us, and since we had no experience with black culture, it was a vague concept at best. I imagined they must be like anyone else I knew, only darker.

The Jim Crow laws of the south were something I had only read about in a book. It meant that blacks couldn't sit at the lunch counter or use the same toilets; otherwise, their business and money and cheap labor were welcome. In my world, the culturally dictated segregation of blue-collar, suburban New England created an absolute divide. When a black lady from out of town came to shop at the Mapleton Center Woolworths, several people stared with open hostility. I even heard an old lady mutter to her companion, "What does she think she's doing here?" I was going on fourteen and had never met a black person. That was about to change.

You never know what small thing will influence a child and for better or worse, change the course of her life. It may be the most insignificant event or words spoken offhand. Sometimes the little things pile up to build one big thing- and then there's the domino effect. I'm not entirely sure into which category I'd place my personal situation. It may have begun years ago, when I'd asked from the back seat of the car why there were no black kids at the park on the Mapleton side of the river, and Dad answered me with a backhand on the side of my head. The fact that I had to hide Martin Luther King's biography so as not to upset my father probably had something to do with it. I can state with certainty that it was my run-in with the first black girl ever to enter a Mapleton Public School that got me packed off to St. Anne's. But it was Dad's vignette of the German shepherd and the six foot nigger that pulled me into an invisible riptide of racism, sucked me down into the dangerous undertow with Beulah May Bone.

My father had a way of being kind and noble, rough and offensive, as well as sagacious and stunningly ignorant. He never would have harmed anyone, and would have driven his eighteen wheeler off a bridge to miss any stray pedestrian, without regard for skin color. But when the subject came up, he freely voiced his opinion on the inferiority of the black race. It wasn't that he had anything against them-so long as they stayed in their place.

One night he came home from work with his buddy Stan. I'd met the man before, and he was a good sort, a hard-working family man, Catholic of course, like us, like all their friends. It was Friday so they had a couple of drinks and laughed about the news of the day, which involved a stowaway in the trucking terminal and a loose German shepherd. I thought they would split their sides laughing over the story of the guard dog, and the "six foot nigger." When Mom heard, she shook her head and rolled her eyes as if they were a couple of naughty children. She didn't talk that way, but she wouldn't correct my father, and certainly wouldn't say a word in front of his workmate.

"Aw, come 'ere Ev," Dad said, getting a cordial glass to poor her a little whiskey. She sighed and sat down. Dad couldn't wait to tell her all about it, but first he coaxed, "Frances, be a good girl and go watch a little TV, OK honey?"

"Sure," I said with a shrug and left the kitchen. After I'd clomped up the stairs, I tiptoed back down half-way to sit out of sight and listen.

Dad and Stan had gone into the terminal as usual, unlocked the door and found themselves face to face with a guard dog, an enormous German shepherd. The handler usually collected the dog before anyone came in, but his van had broken down and he was late.

"Holy shit," Stan said, "Run Joe, run for it!" They beat it down the loading dock. My dad jumped off the platform, hit the ground running and made it to his car. "I never seen a big guy run so fast!" I heard Stan laugh. Dad was getting rather portly. From the safety of his car, my father turned around and saw that Stan was knocked down on the platform. He was a tall lanky guy, and the big dog stood with his front paws planted on his chest and growled in his face.

"I thought you was right behind me," Dad continued in an animated voice, "and then I seen you laid out flat with that dog on you, and I was gonna go look for something to club him with..."

"Yeah, you were a real big help," Stan said sarcastically. Just then the van tore into the parking lot. The dog handler leapt out and whistled, and the dog bounded away with no harm done to Stan. "I almost crapped myself!" Stan roared with laughter. Mom was giggling by now.

"You should'a seen your face-white as a sheet!" Dad exclaimed. "Then the poor guy comes up and says, 'Gee, I'm sorry,' and POW, Stan pops him right in the nose! And then he goes, 'Whad ya do that for? I said I was sorry!"

"Sorry my ass!" Stan had told the dog handler. "I didn't hit him that hard," he added. Mom was giggling like a girl at their antics. I could picture it all, and stifled the laughter behind my hands to keep from giving myself away; but that was just the first part of the story.

"Then we go inside and hear somethin'," Dad continued. "We think, what now? Is there another dog? So we go to the sound and it's comin' from a storage cabinet under a counter. We think maybe it's rats, so we open the door real slow-and there's a big nigger hidin' in there! Musta been six-foot tall! He was all bent up like a pretzel in this little cabinet!" Both men were howling with laughter now.

"Oh my God, what was he doing in there?" Mom asked.

200

"Broke in to steal, of course," Stan said. "Guess he didn't know the dog was inside. They train them dogs not to bark, ya know; no warning. If someone breaks in they just hold 'em there! So the dog must've stood guarding that cabinet while the six foot nigger 'd been crammed in there all night!"

While the men guffawed, my mother indulged them with some feminine laughter, before countering, "Oh, that's just awful." Then she burst out laughing again, and I suspected the rare drink of whiskey had something to do with it.

"So we go, 'What the hell are you doing in there?'" Dad said. "And the nigger says, 'Is he gone? Is da dawg gone?'"

"He was shakin'!" Stan added. They took turns mocking the man, his Negro accent and his terror. They decided to shove a wrench through the handles of the cabinet and hold him there until the police came.

"Then the cops told him to come on out and he says, 'I can't sah.' 'Why not?' they wanna know; and he says, 'I can't move, sah." It was my father speaking, affecting the man's accent. It was followed by general hilarity. I felt ashamed.

I gathered that would-be thief had been in there so long they had to pry him out, and he couldn't stand up straight for quite a while. While Dad and Stan laughed even louder at the punch line, I didn't hear Mom anymore. Apparently, the police had a laugh too. I was relieved to overhear they had been patient and didn't harm the prisoner. I have to say in my father's defense that he wouldn't be laughing now if they had; he really wasn't a cruel man.

I went quietly to my bedroom. "That does it! I'm never going to be like them," I pledged in self-righteous indignation. I wouldn't bother to challenge my parents with another futile argument. I'd just choose how to act in my own way, and show by example how we should treat one another. My superior morality would speak for itself.

31

The rough laughter at that poor man's expense resonated throughout the weekend. I returned to school resolved, just itching to get me a black person to be nice to. I didn't have to wait long. The first and only black student in town enrolled in Junior High East, the very next Tuesday, as if God had dropped her off special delivery for me. She was also the first black person any of us had sat in the same room with. It was sixth period when the dean escorted the new student to Mr. Donald's math class. "This is your new classmate, Beulah May Bone," he announced curtly, then turned and walked away. All eyes fixed on the new girl; you could have heard a pin drop.

She was a tall, broad girl. I couldn't tell if she was fat or muscular or how she was shaped, because she wore big pants and a bulky coat that made her look all lumpy-it wasn't a leather jacket. Lots of kids kept their coats on in school. I think it made them feel safer, or perhaps made them feel as if they had just stopped in and wouldn't be staying long enough to take off their coats. Beulah just stood looking at us, unsure of what to do, and the first thing I noticed was how big and white the whites of her eyes looked. It was the same impression I'd had when I was four. She had her hair straightened, so it didn't stick up all wooly, but lay flat down the sides of her head and then stopped in jagged edges. Her clothes exuded poverty. The rest of the kids just stared. Then a few boys started looking at one another and made faces.

"Well, don't just stand there posing for animal crackers! Take a seat!" Mr. Donald snarled with undisguised distain. He'd tossed the ball out and the boys ran with it; the room resounded with cruel laughter.

Someone mocked her name: "Who's this? Boolah? Boolah My Boner?!" Mr. Donald grinned like an evil jack o lantern to egg them on. A big jock who was one of his favorites blurted out, "Suck my boner," while several other boys mooed like a cow. Somebody squawked, "Faggot!" You didn't have to be perceived as gay to be called faggot. It was an all-around insult, good for any occasion.

I was sitting alone in the back of the room with one empty desk in front of me. Beulah anxiously scanned the room and made a B-line for the spot. I'm sure I looked like the safest among the rows of white faces. As she approached I offered a shy smile, but she didn't stop to smile back-just sat quickly and ducked her head low over her books.

I already knew that one of the worst crimes you could commit in the eyes of these kids was to be somehow different. Black was definitely different. The dominant group constantly bullied and picked on the weak or odd like a flock of mindless chickens. Some of the teachers were just as bad. Mr. Donald was the worst.

Mr. Donald taught math in addition to boys P.E., since we had separate classes. He was the quintessential jock, tall and squarely built with muscled up arms and a six-pack showing through his polo shirt. He had a shock of sandy hair like a thatched roof, and big white teeth that should have looked nice when he smiled, but somehow made him look even meaner. Most of the girls thought him handsome, and sucked-up pathetically. He wasn't married, and shamelessly flirted with any willing young female teacher. Boys that were rugged and masculine and good at sports loved Mr. Donald, and he acted like their best pal, like one of the boys. If he didn't like you, he was one mean son-of-a-bitch.

Beulah was not the first student I'd seen subjected to Mr. Donald's juvenile abuse. I had witnessed an assault on a boy in his class, carried out by children but orchestrated by the adult who was there to guide and instruct us. I was one of only three girls in that math class. One day when the other two happened to be absent, I came in late with a note from the office. Mr. Donald must have thought I was out for the day, because I walked onto a scene that looked like of a pack of hyenas tearing at some dying thing. His name was George Goldenberg.

George had a soft feminine fanny and a wiggle in his walk. To make matters worse, he favored tight-fitting plaid pants. No one wore plaid pants. All the boys called him Georgette, in addition to the usual slurs-queer, faggot, or homo, usually predicated with the F word; the most sickening thing they said was "Die Faggot, die!" Then they tripped him; or threw his books on the floor and kicked them down the hallway; and pushed him around and otherwise tormented him day in and day out, even in Mr. Donald's class. Mr. Donald not only allowed it, he relished it. Every day he greeted George Goldenberg by calling him 'Goldenboy' in a tone rancid with contempt. It wasn't just a play on his name, but because George had shining, naturally gold curls. He also had big blue eyes with lush lashes, and plump pink lips.

When I arrived late that day, they had George laid out on a table in the back the room, out of the line of vision should someone pass by in the hallway. They held him down and took turns smacking his pretty face. They'd got his plaid pants almost off. George was crying hysterically and struggling unsuccessfully to escape, while Mr. Donald jeered and taunted, "What's a matta' Goldenboy?" George's tears only fueled their sadistic lust. Mr. Donald was obviously not pleased to see me walk in; my presence spoiled all the fun. "All right!" he barked, "All of you back to your seats, enough!"

I dropped the note on his desk, retreated to my place in the back row and sat rigid with fear. I could hear George sobbing quietly behind me, but I didn't turn around. Mr. Donald avoided looking in our direction all period.

Teachers who were different got picked on too. Miss Spinner taught girls' P.E., and everybody said she was a lesbian, a 'big dyke,' but not within her earshot. Unlike the timid old English teacher who suffered from shellshock, she didn't let the kids bully her. She'd get in your face, blast her whistle and make sure you got detention if you stepped out of line. Mr. Donald monitored detention.

Miss Spinner ruled the gymnasium and girls' locker room like a Sargent Major. Outside of her natural habitat, with the silver whistle hanging silently on her flat chest, she looked vulnerable and a bit lost. Unlike all the other female teachers, Miss Spinner wore no makeup. She was in her late thirties and unmarried, which was also unusual for the time. When she walked the hallways, her plain, close-cropped hair, bandy legs and awkward masculine strut left her open to constant, if clandestine ridicule from students. I even saw a few teachers making faces behind her back, just as bad as the children. Worst of all, the thirteen and fourteen year old girls giggled and twittered that you had to watch out, because Miss Spinner would 'feel you up' if she got you alone. It was a cruel, baseless remark, and I certainly didn't believe it. I don't think the gossips truly believed it either. It merely served as a way for a girl to establish that she was definitely not a lesbian, which I took to be the general purpose behind all the slurs-in addition to the general enjoyment of just being mean. While I hated P.E., I was fine with Miss Spinner. She was always nice to me, even though I made all the outs, dropped every ball, and was otherwise hopeless at physical activity. I think she felt sorry for me.

I had no idea if you could really tell if someone were gay or lesbian just by the way they looked, and only a vague idea what it meant to be gay. Boys who seemed girlish and girls who seemed boyish were perceived as gay, that much was established. It was abundantly clear that being gay was not accepted, especially among males. Miss Spinner was spoken of in an offhand, joking manner. She was pathetically laughable. Poor George was treated as if he were crud on the bottom of someone's shoe.

My question was, why? Why was so much energy expended to define and assert oneself as masculine or feminine? What was behind the overarching concern with what kind of genitals one had and where one wanted to put them? Why did everyone but me seem to care so much? The topic hit close to home. For one thing, boys still disgusted me, and I didn't even want to think about touching their *mm-mms*. Did that mean I might be a lesbian? Yet I loved any excuse to dress up. I wanted to be a mom, and I'd always played with dolls-I still hadn't parted with my Barbies. But there was another consideration far more important than dresses and dolls; I wasn't anything at all like my cousin Maddy.

I found out that last year, some of the kids called her a queer the moment we arrived at Eastie. When they found out we were related, they even bullied me with, "Your cousin's a fuckin' faggot!" I didn't get it at first; I thought they were just being mean, and I was scared to death, but I needn't have worried. Maddy had all the wit, people skills and street sense that I lacked. She quickly and cleverly dodged the homophobia bullet with the help of drugs. By Christmas break she and Tommy had become major suppliers of booze, and the most awful weed imaginable. Not that I was a connoisseur, but it was kind of like smoking lawn clippings. The quality didn't matter. Pot provided this unruly pack of teenybopper-wannabe bad-asses a whole new venue. They worshipped her. By the time we started eighth grade, she was greeted like an old pal by most of the boys, and was equally charming with the girls. She knew how to 'pahty hahty' and look tough in a black leather jacket. It was the defining article of clothing that established one as a cool kid who did stuff; its absence marked one as a dork and a loser, like me. Maddy really pulled it off. I was the only one who knew that the jacket also served to disguise her figure, and create a new upper torso to replace the one she secretly loathed.

The kids stopped calling her names, but not before I'd heard them all. I learned that dyke meant lesbian. I recalled Joanie's tirade in the kitchen, which seemed like a life-time ago, and finally understood why Joanie thought she should be ashamed of her sister. I still didn't understand why Joanie was such a mean bitch.

It hadn't yet occurred to me that while I was confused about gay people, what they were really like and how they lived, the gay kids were just as confused, and far more anxious. With the possible and rather uninspiring exception of Miss Spinner, there were no role-models. I could only imagine how terrible it felt to hear all those ugly words, and know they were all about you. Poor George must have been afraid for his life.

As for Maddy, I feared that she was in a precarious position, skating on a thin ice of prejudice that could crack anytime. Sometimes I secretly hoped she would grow out of it, shed the crusty butch exterior like the leather jacket and end up married with kids. It wasn't that I didn't love her as she was; I was worried about what would happen next. After all, where were all the gay people? Where did they put 'em? It was the same question I'd asked about the black people when I was little. With no other information to go on, it looked as if lesbians wound up odd and alone, the butt of cruel jokes, like Miss Spinner. I decided to ask my mother if you could tell whether or not someone was homosexual just by looking at them, and for that matter what it really meant. I secretly hoped for reassurance that it was OK to be gay. Mom answered thoughtfully by telling me a story about a friend named Pauline.

"Everybody called her 'Paulie,' and she was...*different*," Mom said with emphasis, "noticeably different from the time she was just a little kid. All through high school, Paulie didn't date any boys at all. She seemed to always have one girlfriend she hung out with, just the two of them. There was, you know, talk, but no one came out and said anything to her face. No one would ever come out and ask about such a thing; it wouldn't have been polite," she explained. "Then one time a group of us went to an amusement park-we were out of school, eighteen or nineteen by then. There was a 'tunnel of love' with little boats going down a man-made canal. It was dark inside, and if you went in with a boy, you expected to get kissed. You only went with someone you trusted, a boy you knew wouldn't get too fresh," she added, though I wasn't sure how fresh was "too fresh." I decided to just listen and try to understand from context. "Anyway, Paulie hopped on a boat with some fella-I don't remember his name, but she came floating out the other end alone! We all looked, and there she was, just sitting in the boat with her arms folded across her chest, looking all put-out. Then the boy came slogging through the water soaked from head to foot. It was hard to walk in about three feet of water! He didn't want to talk about what happened, but whatever he tried in there, Paulie didn't like it one bit. She pitched him overboard, head-first! Now that was the talk of the town for a while. Everybody knew then that it was absolutely true." Mom spread her hands in a gesture of finality, and I was left with the impression that if a boy tried to kiss you too much or got "too fresh," and you shoved him off or threw him out of a boat, you were definitely a lesbian. It was the *love-boat test*.

"Of course, Paulie never tried anything with me," Mom added. "They know their own kind. They're not bad people, just different. If you think someone is...like that, you mustn't mention their differences," she warned. "You just don't discuss it at all." It was yet another rendition of the theme of minding your business. "You probably don't remember, Frances, but Pauline showed up at Nana's wake with her...ah...the lady she lives with," Mom added as an afterthought. "I hadn't seen her in so long, and it was really nice of her, very thoughtful. They just popped in, said their prayers, offered condolences and rushed off."

"Why did they rush off?"

"They don't generally mix with people they don't know well, because some people just don't like them, don't accept gays and lesbians at all. Frances, I hate to say it, but what I'm trying to explain is-adults can be just as cruel as children towards people who are different. Technically, Catholic teaching calls it a sin; I guess there is something in the Bible about it...but it seems to me there are far worse sins people commit all the time and everybody accepts them just fine. As for me, I can't say that I'm completely comfortable-I just can't imagine living like that and I don't even want to think about, you know, what they actually do together," she rolled her eyes as she spoke. "But Pauline was my friend, and I don't believe in treating people like outcasts because they're...like that," she said. "By the way, what makes you ask?"

"For one thing, the girls all say Miss Spinner's a lesbian," I answered truthfully without adding unnecessary information, not yet anyway.

Mom had met Miss Spinner at parent's night. "I can see why," she giggled. "You know, we had a lady gym teacher just like that. She was called Miss Thyng, T-H-Y-N-G, if you can believe it! The kids went wild over that name, and her odd ways. She wore one of those short gym skirts with tight fitting bloomers that went half-way down her thighs-we couldn't help but see them; she sat in her office at a table with her legs spread like a man... "

"Actually, the kids at school are preoccupied with the subject of homosexuality," I interrupted.

"Preoccupied?" Mom raised her eyebrows.

"Yes, always calling names like faggot, homo, queer...and it's the way they say it! Like it's the worst, most disgusting thing in the world to be gay." Then I told her about George. As I related the details, I choked up a bit with unexpected tears of anger that I'd been too frightened to feel while it was happening. I despised those boys, and especially Mr. Donald. I felt ashamed that I didn't have the courage to stop it, to say a kind word or even speak to George. But I was afraid they might go for me.

"That's just terrible," Mom sympathized. "The poor boy didn't ask to be that way." She considered a moment then remarked, "Goldenberg, you say? Hmm...something tells me that teacher has a problem with anti-Semitism too."

I hadn't thought of that, mostly because no one taught us the relevant history. My only first-hand experience with anti-Semitism was when Dad scrutinized the bill at the Kosher Deli, insisting that all Jews were swindlers.

"What an awful man that Mr. Donald must be," Mom concluded. "Your dad's a manly man, but he'd never hurt anyone...in fact, he told me a funny story about a gay man," Mom said with a bemused smile. "Daddy was out driving and he saw a car pulled over by the road with what looked like a woman in distress, peering nervously at a flat tire. It was a back road with nothing around for miles, so he stopped to help her. Well, she was a *he*, a man, and he was as queer as a July day is long, all...you know," Mom affected a limp-wristed imitation, batting her eyes, etc. I have to admit that it was pretty funny. "Dad said he was more helpless than ten women!"

"What happened?"

"He changed the flat tire! He said it was worth it for the laughs-but not in front of the fellow. But seriously, you need to understand something, something very important." Mom looked at me intently.

"What?"

"Frances, you're a kind, very morally conscious girl- you've been that way ever since you were a small child. I never had to tell you how to treat people. What you need to understand is that all this hatefulness towards gays, or Jews or blacks or anybody is very dangerous-and I don't mean just for the targets, like that poor Goldenberg boy. It's a dangerous thing for anyone to mix up in. People get hurt. Dad helped that man, but he only told me and his sisters...he had them in stitches, laughing about the "stranded fairy" by the side of the road. But you don't think he'd go into the terminal and tell the other truck drivers? A couple of them might understand, but most probably wouldn't. So don't you go saying anything around school," she warned. "Don't try to be some...what do they call it? Activist. You don't want them labeling you. You don't want to become a target. It's one thing to treat everyone decently, and another to try and tell people what they should do, how they should think-that's where it gets dangerous. It's like I always tried to tell you when you asked about the Negro people; just mind your manners and your business. Stay out of it."

32

Beulah May Bone didn't open her mouth in Mr. Donald's class that first day, which was no surprise, considering the reception she got. I felt terrible about it, and couldn't wait for the period to end so I could talk to her. When the buzzer went off, she bolted from her seat and managed to get out before the pack of boys. One tried to trip her but she saw it and stepped over him. I didn't have a chance of beating the boys out the door, and always lingered at the back of the room hoping they wouldn't notice me. The strategy usually worked. Then I had to go down two flights of stairs and navigate the crowded halls, jostled and even shoved out of the way, to get to the basement on time. I made it to P.E. by the final blare. Beulah was still standing by the doorway to the girls' locker room, clearly anxious and reluctant to enter. This was the moment I'd waited for.

At five foot one, my head was at the height of her chest. I looked up and announced, "Hi, I'm Frances."

She eyed me skeptically. "Mah name's Beulah," she said. Her voice was very deep, with what sounded to me like a southern accent.

"We'd better go in or Miss Spinner will mark us late for class and give us detention," I warned.

"Mmm hmm," she nodded, and followed me inside.

Miss Spinner gave me a stern look so I explained, "I was showing the new student to class." She ignored me and blew her whistle.

"Hurry up girls, change up!"

As if P.E. weren't horrid enough, we had to wear the most ghastly gym suits. They were one-piece affairs that zipped up the back, with blue shorts and blue and white horizontal stripes on top. We looked like a gang of convicts. It was so degrading, but it was one thing I had in common with every girl in the school. We all hated those gym suits. The suits also had an equalizing effect: absolutely no one looked cool in them.

"Do you have your suit?" Miss Spinner directed at Beulah.

"Uh, no ma'am," she answered.

"Why not?" she demanded.

"I dunno...where'd you get a suit at?" she drawled.

Some girls started giggling. Miss Spinner blew a shrill blast and glared at the girls. They didn't want to get detention, so they shut up. "Do you have your schedule?"

"Yes ma'am."

"Well bring it over here! I've got to add you to my roster," Miss Spinner said, in her usual brusque manner. Beulah shuffled to the front of the crowded locker room trying to avoid bumping the other girls, and handed over the paper schedule, almost at arm's length.

I lived through one more P.E. class. I always dressed slowly and seemed to come out after most of the girls had gone. When I emerged from the curtained dressing cubby, Beulah was standing alone. She'd waited for me. I smiled, and this time she smiled back. We walked a bit in silence then I asked, "What's the matter?"

"Nobody want me *he'eh*!" she said emphatically. "Da teachers don' like me."

"Oh, I don't think that's true," I lied. "And Miss Spinner's just...like that; she's strict with everybody."

"Dat math teacher...ooh Lord," she shook her head, "he sho' don' like me!" Beulah rolled her eyes and stuck out her lower lip. This was the first conversation I'd ever had with a black person. I tried to study her face without staring. She had full lips and a broad nose, and her skin was very dark brown.

"Mr. Donald? He's just a jerk!" I said. "He's mean to me too. He only likes boys that are good at sports." At the time, I didn't know enough about men to understand, but Mr. Donald was also a sexist pig, and as it turned out, even more reprehensible than any of us could have imagined. "He's a real jerk!" I insisted.

"Maybe," she said, "But I know he don' like me."

"Where did you transfer from?" I tried to change the subject. I was so involved in conversation that I hadn't noticed how quiet it was in the hall. Kids had stopped in their tracks and just stared. Beulah May didn't miss it. I noticed the whites of her eyes as they rolled around in her head. She was trying to signal me, get my attention. My stomach flipped when I realized a group was gathering around us. "Where's your next class?" I spoke up boldly, trying to ignore them. "I'll walk you there." Apparently my confidence threw them off for the moment. They let us pass, but someone mumbled nigger; the others giggled, and I pretended I hadn't heard.

We had P.E. on Tuesdays and Thursdays. By Thursday Miss Spinner had found Beulah a used gym suit. It was an extra-large and still kind of tight.

Without her bulky jacket, I could see she was big busted, like a mature woman. "Great outfit," I laughed good-naturedly. She cocked her head to one side and studied me through narrowed eyes, trying to determine if I was making fun of her. I guess she figured out I was making fun of the gym suits, of all of us. She smirked and kind of huffed in acknowledgement.

After P.E. we got a chance to talk again. I greeted her with a friendly, "How're you doing?" She looked around to see if we were alone.

"I scahed, Frances," she spoke in a low tone. "I ain't never been to no school like dis before."

"Where did you go to school before?"

"Some school in Delaware."

"What was it like?"

She shrugged. "Mostly, kids was black!"

"What are you scared of," I asked.

Beulah pushed out her lips and made a funny face. The look told me I'd asked a stupid question. "Everybody he'eh is white! Everybody! An' dey don' like me! Nobody he'eh talked to me but you-in two days!"

"I like you," I chirped. "I'll be your friend." Pollyanna had nothing on me. I'd learned so many adult things, yet when it came to relationships, I was as ingenuous and naïve as I'd been at Edmunds Elementary.

"Thanks, Frances," she said. "You a good girl."

By the following Tuesday I knew something wasn't right. Beulah didn't say hi. She looked over my head and acted as if I were invisible. When I came out of the dressing area after P.E., she was gone. I went into the hall and there was no sign of her. She still sat in front of me in Mr. Donald's class, and he treated us both like dirt. I was never a favorite, but he'd at least acknowledged me, and smiled when he passed me back a paper. Now he dropped it on my desk like he might catch cooties if he lingered too long. He sneered down at us with disdain-and I thought math class couldn't get any worse.

The next time I saw her she was standing with a group of the toughest, meanest kids around. The girls in this bunch were especially vicious, and there had been some serious fights where they hurt other girls so bad they needed stitches. Even Maddy and Tommy avoided that crowd. Beulah was whooping it up with them, all full of raucous laughter and absurdly foul language; I mean, just how many times can you insert some variation of the verb 'to-fuck' into one sentence? I stopped in my tracts and stared with my mouth open. They looked back at me as if they'd seen a cockroach, and she spat out, "What the fuck you lookin' at girl?" I felt like I got kicked in the stomach, and their mean laughter chased me down the hall as I ducked my head and scurried away like a mouse.

That was only the beginning. It seems that Beulah quickly found out I was one of the most unpopular, not-cool, dorky kids at Eastie. She wanted to make it plain to her new associates that she wasn't accustomed to stooping to my level. We hadn't been friends. It never even happened. I was definitely not the sort of girl she'd hung out with back in Delaware. Once she got the feel of the place, the lay of the land, she turned on me. It wasn't enough just to dump me; she had to bully me to secure her new status with these girls, and make sure her secret was safe. Beulah had told me she was scared: scared of being black in an all-white school, scared because nobody liked her. I thought she'd rather kill me than have anyone find out.

Over the next week she progressed from scathing looks and curses to threats. I didn't tell Maddy. I was afraid she'd get into a fight with those girls, a fight she'd lose, because they had no scruples. They weren't even civilized. They did terrifying things-like jump a girl, ten against one and tear her up with fingernails, bottle tops or whatever else they could use to maim, without actually killing her. One girl had some braces torn right off her teeth.

I was also ashamed. How did I get myself into this? How could I be so blind-sided? Why was I always so stupid? I just tried to lay low and hoped Beulah would go off with her new friends and forget all about me.

The following week was worse. Beulah told me she was 'gonna git me,' and she did. While her new posse looked on, she tripped me on the stairs and I fell hard. Of course, there were no teachers anywhere. I just sat on the floor in the stairwell and sobbed with my books strewn around me. "Why, why are you being so mean to me?" I asked pitifully. As she leered down at me, her black face began to appear uncommonly ugly.

"If you tell anybody, I gonna fix you good," she threatened. The skinny white girls laughed in approval. That spelled trouble. They'd found a new victim, a new source of amusement.

I went to school the next day sick with fear. I was afraid to tell my parents, afraid they would complain to the principal, and Beulah would retaliate as promised. It would also mean admitting that I hadn't listened, and I stubbornly hid my predicament to avoid the inevitable, 'I told you so.'

It had been only two weeks since I had extended the hand of friendship to Beulah May Bone. Now I spent all my energy trying to avoid her. I took circuitous routes to class, traveling down one flight and across a hall, to go back up the stairs to a room only two doors from where I'd started in the first place.

All this to dodge Big Bad Black Beulah, as I'd come to call of her in the privacy of my own thoughts.

Wednesday I cut school for the first and only time in my life. It wasn't planned. At the sight of the building, I felt so sick I just turned around and fled. If I'd thought about it, cutting school on a Thursday and avoiding P.E. would have made more sense. I hid out alone in a park for hours before deciding to slip into the public library. Nobody noticed me or asked why I wasn't in school. Nobody called my mother. I was hoping to get caught so I could get their attention and ask for help.

Thursday I decided to tell Maddy and Tommy. Pride didn't matter anymore. I'd make it clear that I didn't want them to fight, just tell me how to handle it. I wish I'd done that in the first place. I saw them on the corner before school, embedded in a noisy, amorphous sea of smoking teenagers, but couldn't bear to draw attention to myself. It would have to wait until after school. I entered the prison-like building with my eyes glued to the floor, as if avoiding all eye contact would render me invisible. I had more than the usual amount of dread. If only I'd listened to my mother when she told me to mind my own business...

Beulah went out of her way to unnerve me in math class. Whenever Mr. Donald was facing the blackboard, she turned in her seat to cast searing malevolent looks tinged with a cruel smugness. I knew something very bad was up, and determined to tell my parents that night. I'd make them listen, even refuse to go to school if they didn't take me seriously. I dreaded P.E., but thought I could make it through one more day. I should have skipped out and run all the way home.

Beulah ignored me all through P.E.; she didn't dare antagonize Miss Spinner. After the final signal for dismissal at the end of seventh period, I poked my head out from behind a curtain in the girls' locker room and listened like a deer in the forest. It looked as if everyone was gone, but to be on the safe side, I crouched down and scanned beneath the row of curtains to check if anyone was still in the cubbies. I'd seen Miss Spinner do that before she locked up. For a moment I thought I heard something, like maybe rustling or a whisper, but no, all was quiet. Too quiet. I gathered my books and dirty gym suit and emerged from the cubby. Then I froze, afraid to leave the locker room, afraid Beulah might be waiting for me out in the hallway. I decided that the sensible thing to do was to go to Miss Spinner and ask for help. The thought filled me with relief. Miss Spinner would listen to me; she'd walk me to the office so I could call my mother. She wouldn't let anything happen to me. But my relief was short-lived. Her office was dark. So that's why she hadn't blown her whistle and yelled at me to hurry-up… I turned to leave, praying that Beulah was long gone. I didn't get far.

She jumped out from behind the last curtained cubby in the row, the one nearest the exit. I gasped, and my hand shot over my mouth. Suddenly there was a commotion behind me and peals of razor sharp laughter. There were four other girls who'd been hiding in the same way, up on the benches so I couldn't detect their feet. I didn't know their names, and they hadn't even been in our P.E. class. Whatever they had in mind was clearly premeditated. I tried to simply walk around Beulah and head for the door, not at a run but walking fast. I hoped that if I pretended I wasn't too scared, it would take some of the fun away. I wanted to scream, but I was afraid nobody would come, and besides, it would be like throwing gasoline on fire.

Whichever way I moved, she stepped in front to block me. I panicked and tried to run around her, but it was futile. She just moved her bulk into my path again and again. "Where you goin' girl? Why you in such a hurry?" Beulah taunted to the amusement of the assembly. I gave up and stood still. It didn't do any good to let them play with me like a trapped rat. I breathed as evenly as I could, resolved not to cry, and attempted to reason out what might be the most effective thing to say. Nothing came to mind. I'd already learned that begging in these situations made it worse; that's how Kathy Kelly came to sit on me in the fourth grade. What I wouldn't give to be back at Edmunds Elementary! Kathy was a big old marshmallow; in fact, she'd been bullied so much last year that her mom had sent her over the river to St. Clément's, on a scholarship for poor Catholics.

While I was lost in contemplation with my life flashing before me, one of the coconspirators must've decided she wanted to see some action. I was suddenly shoved from behind with such force I crashed right into Beulah, dropping my stuff on the floor as I instinctively put my hands out. I landed face-first with both hands against her ample, matronly bosom. She reached down and grasped my left breast, dug in her fingers as if it were a doorknob and then slammed me backwards onto the cement floor. Pain shot up my spine, and I felt the tears come despite my effort to hold them back.

"What-choo think you doin' touchin' my boobs?! You wanna start somethin' wi' me girl?" Beulah May Bone screeched like a banshee in mock indignation. She was an accomplished bully; she jutted her lower jaw and scowled like a gorilla in a display of dominance. I heard the shitty little girls behind me hoot with laughter, like a troupe of white-faced capuchin monkeys.

I stared back into Beulah May's eyes, searching for some light, but could barely distinguish her pupils from the muddy pigment of her iris. The dull eyes evidenced neither reason nor mercy. It was like being attacked by a wild animal. All of the racist speech I'd ever heard, the prejudice I'd staunchly opposed rushed up to kick me while I was down. At that moment I was sure they were right all along. I'd seen brighter, kinder eyes on a dog. I felt hatred, pure hatred at this betrayal. It filled me up and crowded out fear. If I was going to get the shit kicked out of me, I was going down fighting.

I couldn't think of a single intelligent thing to say, but I hadn't been immune to the social power of homophobia and racism. I spoke deliberately and with studied distain. "Why would anyone wanna touch your boobs?" The words bubbled up from my anger. I heard more hooting from behind me. It sounded like the girls might be laughing at Beulah, and it bolstered my resolve. "Did you ever see them flabby things when she was changing into her gym suit?" I addressed the others boldly. Wild laughter ensued, and I built to my crescendo: "Even Miss Spinner wouldn't wanna touch those!" I wrinkled my nose in disgust and looked to the girls for continued approval. "Even if she was hard-up; she wouldn't wanna' touch your fat, stinkin' ugly black boobs!"

Beulah's eyes went wide in genuine surprise...the whites looked so big and so white! Her mouth hung open a bit. The other girls broke out into such shrill laughter I thought they'd pass kittens. "Stinkin' black boobs!" one repeated, and inflamed the others even more. For a moment I felt relief. It seemed like they might be about to switch sides. But to lose the respect of this group now would have put the only black girl in unspeakable danger, far more than I could appreciate.

Beulah jumped on me so hard I thought I might break. She punched me a few times in the head and face while the other girls stood laughing. Then she started to tear open my blouse. I heard fabric rip, buttons popped. "I'll show you whose boobs is gonna be ugly," she snarled, clawing at my bra. She couldn't tear it off, but pulled it down on one side, whipped an Afro-pick out of her back pocket and raked it over my exposed breast. My scream echoed through the mostly empty locker room.

"Enough!" a girl yelled from behind me. "She didn't do nothin' to you-you started it!"

"Shut the fuck up!" Beulah snarled, and the girl was cowed.

I shielded my breasts with my arms across my chest and Beulah struck me in the face with her other fist. Then she dropped the comb, wrenched open the snap on my jeans and managed to get at the zipper while I grabbed her thick wrists and tried to pull her hands away. No chance! Beulah shifted back off my hips, trying to get my pants off, so I rolled over to crawl away, get away anyway I could manage. I tried to kick, but my legs were pinned under her weight. I felt my jeans go down, underwear and all. Then I felt the sharp metal comb tear down one buttock. I looked up at the girls and cried out, "Please help me!" But they were looking past me and Beulah, right over our heads. Suddenly they screeched an alarm and ran off squealing like piglets. They just bolted down the locker room, around the rows of cubbies and out the back door. Then I felt the weight come off my legs. Miss Spinner must have walked in...funny she hadn't blown her whistle...

"Ahhrgg!" Beulah May Bone roared like an angry bear.

I rolled over to look and saw that Mr. Donald had her locked in some kind of wrestling hold, pinned tight with both arms behind her back. The others had seen him come in and run off without warning her. He looked down at me with a horrified expression, then lifted his head to avert his gaze as he bellowed across the room, "Janet! Janet, are you in here?!" Miss Spinner wasn't there. I quickly pulled my pants on and covered my breast with the torn blouse. "You OK Frances?" he asked, looking at me now that I was decent.

"Uh, I think so." I didn't think so at all. I felt a burning pain on my breast, and my head throbbed.

"Go up to the office-see the nurse!" he ordered. "They'll call your mother." Then he yanked Beulah so hard that her backside pressed flush to his body; he bent his head close to hers. "You and I are going to have a little talk." Mr. Donald spoke menacingly with his mouth barely an inch from her ear.

"Lemme go! Git your hands offa me pig!" Beulah hollered and thrashed, trying to wrench her arms free. She put up a good fight, and I could see it took some effort for Mr. Donald to hold her. He was grimacing with clenched teeth, grunting and enjoying the sport of it as if he were tackling a two hundred pound tuna.

"Go!" he yelled at me, and then propelled her over to Miss Spinner's office, still thrashing and kicking, but powerless to stop him. I got one last glimpse of her before the door was closed.

"Frances! Hep me!" Beulah looked at me with wide, terrified eyes. Her tough talk had vanished like smoke. Then Mr. Donald kicked the door shut behind them. The door was so loud. The whites of her eyes looked so big.

Help her? Fat chance! Even if I wanted to, how could I help? I figured she was going to get yelled at, written up, maybe arrested for assault and hopefully expelled. I got up and tried to button my blouse. A couple of buttons were still attached, but my hands were shaking so bad I couldn't do it. At the sight of the blood pooling in my bra I almost fainted. I stumbled into a dressing cubby and sat on the bench, panting with my head between my knees, to wretched to cry.

"I'm gonna teach you, nigger. I'm gonna teach you! You think you're so tough? Pickin' on a little bitty white girl?!" I heard Mr. Donald's voice and my heart caught in my throat. He must have felt sure I was gone.

"No suh," I heard her whimper. "Please suh...I didn't mean nothin'! I sorry..."

"You're gonna be sorry! You don't even belong here! You're never gonna mess with one of our girls, not ever again! I'll show you what happens to niggers like you!"

He spoke in a lowered voice, but it carried through the door. Then I heard something like a chair scrape...no-too loud...it was that big metal table. I heard more struggling, then grunting. I thought it was Beulah, but then it sounded more like Mr. Donald. I thought I heard Beulah trying to cry out, but it was muffled...it sounded like he had something over her mouth. Bang! The heavy oak office chair must've hit the floor. I instinctively covered my own mouth to stifle my cry, so I didn't give myself away. I wasn't supposed to be there. I wasn't supposed to hear any of this.

I scurried from the locker room into the hallway. It was empty. I ducked behind a row of lockers in case Mr. Donald came out; I didn't want him to know what I'd heard. What had I heard? I tried to think. I knew he was a bully. He was always hurling threats, and I'd seen him rough-up boys when they misbehaved-practically every day. He'd grab an arm and whip them around, slam them against lockers or throw them into their seats if they didn't sit the first time, but this went far beyond discipline. It had a bad smell. It was the rancid meat of race hatred. I knew it, because I had my first bite only moments ago, and spat it back out. Something terrible had happened, something my reason couldn't quite put together, but I must have sensed it in some primitive part of my brain. It was the sound of rape. No one had ever explained it to me, but my stomach knew it was rape by the way it bent me over double and made me vomit.

***

Maddy was at the back door that afternoon. It didn't take long for the gossip to reach her-everyone around East Mapleton heard that 'a nigger beat-up a white girl at Eastie.' We had just got back from the local emergency room. It all seemed unreal. The police had been called in, and I scarcely remembered their questions or what I said before Mom told them to back off. They'd already searched half the town for Beulah; she was probably half-way back to Delaware.

"Why the hell didn't you tell me what was goin' on?" Maddy's query was predictable.

"I dunno. At first I thought she might lose interest and just leave me alone. Then I felt so dumb for getting myself into such a mess. Then I guess I was afraid you'd end up getting killed in some fight over me," I said.

"If you told me right away, I just would have smoked her up, made like we was friends, even if I hated her guts-that is if I'd got to her before she started in on you. If I knew what she was up to, I woulda kicked her black ass! Me and Tommy and my friends, we woulda..." Her gray eyes smoked like lava that just ran down the side of a volcano, but hadn't quite cooled off yet. It was a look I'd seen before. "And those little sluts she hung out with too!" Maddy kept her harsh talk low so my mother wouldn't hear downstairs. She was on the phone with Dad.

I had bruises on my face and my breast, which also bore three distinct gouges. "Lemme see," Maddy said gently, pointing at the bandage. I peeled back one corner of the non-stick tape and winced. "Jesus Christ," she whispered.

I looked down at the angry red marks that went from my breast bone to my right nipple. All at once the sights and sounds and smell of blood washed over me like an instant replay. I cried like I'd never stop. "Why, why would anyone be so mean to me?" I choked out the words between sobs.

Maddy's explanation was direct and compendious. "'Cause she's a nigger. I coulda told you this would happen." I was truly surprised. In the years I'd known her, Maddy had never used the N word in front of me. Now I understood that she'd hidden her prejudice out of respect for my views-she even handed me the Martin Luther King biography! "Some of 'em may be OK, but you can't ever trust 'em," she went on. "I'd about like to kill her! I'll fix her if she dares show her face around town!" Maddy was all fired up again.

"Don't! You've got to stay out of it," I said urgently.

"What? Why?"

"I don't think she'll ever come back anyway, but...Maddy, you've got to promise, promise me you'll never tell..."

"What is it? Did she do something else to you?"

"No. It's what I think Mr. Donald did to her. I couldn't see, but he dragged her into the office and kicked the door shut..." I told her the words he used and described the sounds I wasn't supposed to hear.

Maddy looked away, and exhaled audibly. "Jeezes...I need a cigarette," she said.

"Do you think...?" I began. The feeling in my gut was coalescing into a conscious thought that was just too horrible for words, as if I said it out loud, it might really be true.

"Listen to me Frances," Maddy interrupted forcefully. "Just forget it. Keep your mouth shut and for once don't worry about someone else. Take care of yourself and forget all about it. There's no tellin' what happened behind that door. Mr. Donald's not tellin', and if Beulah told, no one would believe her anyway. Maybe he beat the crap out of her, maybe worse; maybe she just fought him so hard the chair got knocked over...you don't know! In any case, you can't do nothin' about it, so just mind your own business!" Maddy paused to catch her breath, and finished more calmly. "Otherwise, you'll only wind up gettin' hurt more...and you already got hurt too much."

Mom and Dad wanted to know every detail. Mom especially wanted to understand how this girl came to single me out for such violence. I explained that all the other kids had been mean to the new black girl, so I decided to show everyone and be her friend.

"But it just doesn't make any sense! Why would she turn on you like that?" Mom was in anguish.

"Because I've always been picked on!" I yelled back. "I tried to tell you how horrible school is... I'm only barely tolerated because I'm Maddy's cousin and she's popular." I collected myself and lowered my voice. "Beulah was ashamed when she found out her new white friend-the only kid who'd even talk to her-was a big loser."

"Don't you say that! Don't you ever say that!" Dad directed at me, then turned to Mom and slapped his palm on the table. "Listen to me Ev! It had nothin' to do with Frances. You're lookin' for some reason, but there ain't no reason! It's just the way they are. They're like animals!"

My father was all red in the face and he looked like he could've killed someone. I'd never seen him this angry before; it reminded me of Mr. Donald. I realized then that a man's heart was just made differently, beat differently from mine. Even the warm heart of my father held within it a potent rage, ready to let loose if need be to protect his family. The charming WWII stories he'd told of his tour in the Philippines suddenly took on new meaning. It wasn't an Eagle Scout adventure...it wasn't a hilarious half-hour romp with McHale's Navy. I understood that when it was absolutely necessary, my father, the loving man who fed and sheltered me, had also fought and killed other men.

That night I awoke screaming with the first of many nightmares. Both parents rushed in to comfort me as if I were a small child. I couldn't explain it, but mostly the nightmares were of Mr. Donald. I was more afraid of him than of Beulah, but I was even more afraid of myself, of the bitterness that took hold and sunk its roots deep into the soil prepared for it long before I was born. I had been swimming for a lifetime in the insidious sea that was northern racism, struggling to keep my head above water. Beulah May Bone knocked me under and I sank like a stone. It's not that hated them: I just didn't want to have anything to do with black people, ever again.

"Now you see?! We tried to tell you, but you had to learn the hard way!" My father was still shaken the next day. We'd had a rough night, and in the morning my bruises looked even worse. For the first time in my memory, Dad called in sick.

"You were right, Dad. I was ignorant." I was sorry for the pain I'd caused him. "Niggers belong over the other side of the river!" I suddenly shouted the forbidden word as if I could keep harm away by saying it. He looked satisfied.

My mother shook her head sadly and said, "Frances, you have to take each person as they come. They're not all like that...I just wish you'd listened. Next time be polite, but mind your business."

"There ain't gonna be no 'next time'!" Dad bellowed. "You're not goin' back there, not goin' to public school ever again!" Mom and I looked at each other questioningly. "They think they're gonna' bus those people in next year? I know what's been goin' on with all them riots in the cities; out in Detroit...down south...I read the papers. They act like a pack of animals!"

I took my cue from Mom and waited silently for his anger to die down. "Frances," he said almost calmly, "is going to St. Anne's. I was gonna wait 'till next year, 'till high school, but now..." He sighed deeply and stopped himself from rehashing the catalyst for my sudden transfer to St. Anne's. "I don't want any argument from you," he warned me, then looked up at my mother, "you either," he told her quietly but with authority.

"Whatever you say, Joseph," Mom said simply.

"I'm not going to argue, Dad. I'm so happy! St. Anne's is a great school; but can we afford it?"

"Don't you worry about that; I'll do what I have to. I'll work nights, but my girl isn't goin' back to that place. I'll go fill out the application and pay the tuition today-that's why I stayed home. As soon as you recover, you start," he dictated the plan.

"Will they let me start this late in the year?"

"I told you, don't worry...you just rest and get better. I'll talk to them. I'll explain everything."

"We'll have to order a uniform," Mom added. "Frances, you'll wear a uniform from now on."

"I don't care what I wear. I want to learn," I said.

If I ever tasted bitter irony, this was it. Here I'd been complaining since last year about the poor education, the horrendous behavior...maybe Beulah did me a favor, I thought, then shuddered at the price each of us had paid.

Beulah May Bone just seemed to disappear that day. Mr. Donald reported that when he went to lock up, he discovered her in the act. He admitted that he physically restrained her and conducted her to Miss Spinner's office, but said she ran off as he was writing the incidence report. He allegedly searched the school grounds, but she was gone.

There was no one at her home address, nothing but some vacant rooms over a butcher shop. Turned out she never even lived there; the police suspected she had been homeless.

I wasn't questioned any further. They were only concerned with what happened to me. I knew if Beulah came forward and charged Mr. Donald, there'd be more questions. For a while I waited anxiously, but the call never came.

33

I needn't have worried about the tuition for St. Anne's Catholic School. For the first time in his life, Dad sought legal help. His local Teamsters' Union sent him to some tough lawyers, and they filed a suit against the district. Since the principal had called the P.E. teachers away to a meeting before final dismissal, the locker room was left unattended; they settled out of court without admitting negligence. It was a substantial settlement, more than enough for my tuition, straight through high school graduation. The rest would be put aside towards college-all but a bit we would use for one week at the lake that summer, a week for just me and my Mom and Dad.

It took over a week to look presentable. The teachers sensitively explained to my new classmates that I had been a victim of violence, and instructed them to make me welcome without asking personal questions. They did as they were told. My mother insisted upon driving me to and from school. My parents were afraid for a long time that 'horrible black girl' might be out there looking for me. I was pretty sure she was gone for good, but couldn't explain why.

When I entered St. Anne's, I was desperately behind academically and socially. I'd always been a strong reader, but I was unpracticed at writing. My math ability was back somewhere in the fifth grade. I'd taken Spanish, but learned nothing. I didn't know much about history, at least not according to their curriculum. I'd studied animal behavior because it interested me, but that didn't count for much towards science. I was supposed to know about the earth's crust and different kinds of rocks. We hadn't been taught about rocks. My teachers spent the rest of the year figuring out how to get me caught up. I focused intently on academics and rendered myself emotionally numb. It was just what I needed. It seemed no time at all before another milestone had passed. I was finished with my junior high school years. I made a 2.0 G.P.A., and would have to study over the summer.

Summer break came fast after a dizzying few months at St. Anne's, and we took our week at the lake. Time seemed to stand still by comparison. I had long quiet hours to think. Late one afternoon I sat alone in the old wooden rowboat, looked down at the permanent scars from an Afro-pic showing above my new bathing suit and came to an inescapable conclusion: I was very fortunate to be white. I'd just turned fourteen.

I had one cruel injustice perpetrated upon me by a black girl, and everyone rallied to support me. I had a father with a good job and money for legal help. The school district upheld my human worth. They placed great value on my pain and suffering, on my scars. Beulah had perhaps suffered even more, but nobody seemed at all concerned. I really didn't know what happened behind that closed door, but if I accused Mr. Donald of anything, there would be outrage. He was my rescuer. Besides, Maddy was right: no one would believe it. Even the victim confirmed that with her silence.

The monstrous engine of racism had been roaring along for hundreds of years before I was born. I didn't set it in motion, but wondered if I'd helped to drive it forward, right over the bridge. I finally had to accept that it was far too powerful for me to stop. I already tried that; it was like trying to stop a truck by standing in front of it.

***

Light danced on the lake in the setting sun. Behind me, the mountains cast great quavering shadows. In the shadow of the mountains I could see clear down to the bottom. I plunged into the cool water, dove deeper than I'd ever dared, and nearly touched the mud before turning to kick and pull my way up again. The last few yards were a struggle. How strange it is to keep from breathing when your lungs cry out, breathe! I loved to see the sun from beneath the surface, shimmering like a living sheet of glass. I broke through and gulped the pure air. Behind me, the boat bobbed and rocked gently, waiting patiently for me to bring it to shore.

34

Fall semester at St. Anne's High School began, and my anxiety slowly drifted away with the autumn leaves. My parents decided it was safe for me to walk alone, so I left home early each day and walked with a light step all the way to Mapleton Center. I slowly shed that stubborn ten extra pounds and actually grew, one final inch taller. Last year in the middle school we'd worn plaid jumpers, which made me look fat and feel self-conscious. This year we got to wear chic skirts of maroon, gray and navy plaid along with navy blazers over a regulation white blouse, complete with a maroon tie. Dad even bought me a little gold tie-pin with the St. Anne's logo. As a freshman, we still had to wear matching knee socks or solid tights, but next year the girls could wear nylon stockings. I'd never worn a blazer before, and felt very grown up. Everything about the uniform delighted me; not only the way I looked, but the crisp scent of the wool blend, and even the way the pleats of the skirt brushed my knees when I walked. Some of the girls lamented that they couldn't wear the sexy new styles, but I loved the fact that no one at school could make fun of my clothes or the way I wore them.

Mom was wrong. The Catholic school students behaved themselves, even after school. Not that they were perfect, but there were no fights in school or on school grounds. There was no foul language in the hallways. Amongst the girls you might hear the name of the holy family invoked-Jesus, Mary 'n Joseph-or an occasional hell or a damn uttered in the bathroom. It was very risky, since you never knew when a sister might barge in to check-up on us. If a boy even let a minor swear slip in front of a girl, he excused himself. I could walk the halls without fear of being shoved or called some disgusting name.

I actually became rather popular. It wasn't dorky to be a good student, and a group of us met regularly at the school library to study. The teachers, nuns and priests all, worked diligently, and by the middle of freshman year I had attained a 3.0 according to St. Anne's high standards. I developed a flair for writing, and just managed proficiency at math.

Our family life began to change fast. Now that I was in high school, Mom finally got to have her part-time job. After all those years, her old boss was glad to have her back, which made my mother especially proud. As for my father, so long as his supper was ready every night and his uniform ready every morning, he didn't complain. The argument just seemed to wear itself out.

Between my school involvement and Mom's job, mac 'n cheese night fell by the wayside. My cousins were always welcome to stop by, and Annie tended to wander over to our place frequently. Sometimes she talked, but mostly she liked to draw quietly. Annie was in the third grade, but she still loved the *Muppet Show* and *Sesame St.*, so I had the pleasure of her company while I did homework and she watched my little black and white TV. But without the obligation to bring her sister for a weekly visit, I saw a lot less of Maddy. It was Christmas break before I finally had time to sit down and ask how things were going at Mapleton High.

"It's kinda like prison run by the prisoners." Maddy told me how kids tore the doors off the stalls in the bathrooms, so she held it all day, or else left campus and went over to the Woolworths. She laughed as she described how some boys unbolted a toilet and pitched it down a flight of stairs. Someone smashed up the principal's car. The campus sprawled across several multistory buildings, and there were remote stairwells where kids sat smoking pot. You could buy just about any kind of drugs, and there were places you didn't go unless you were there to do business. There was serious violence over territory. They didn't bus black students to Mapleton High after all, and it was still all-white. Maddy couldn't imagine why any black students would've wanted to be there anyway.

No one wanted to be there. Teachers turned over fast, and the ones who stayed were there because they couldn't get jobs at a good school. There was one exception: a small group of advanced placement students in a baccalaureate program. It was a school within a school. They got special classes, their own teachers, and even their own cafeteria, all in a new building wing accessed by a single hallway. It was guarded by a private security company, paid for collectively by the wealthy parents of the privileged students. No one who came from Eastie, from our end of town, had a prayer of making the grade for the program. For everyone else, Mapleton High was hell and they all wanted to leave as soon as possible. Tommy was going on sixteen, and planned to quit school after freshman year-with his father's blessing. Maddy cut school a lot, and was already counting the days until she would turn sixteen. She doubted she would finish sophomore year.

"I'm so sorry," I said.

"What are you sorry for now?" she asked sardonically.

"I wish you could come with me to St. Anne's."

Maddy looked towards my school uniform that was hanging on the closet door, airing. Mom touched it up with the iron every day, and I always wore a clean white blouse. She gave me that funny half-smile, half-grimace that I missed so much. "You think you could get me into that?" She pointed at my uniform and snorted in derision.

"I suppose not," I conceded humorously, though her lack of education and future prospects was no laughing matter.

For the first time ever I was happy to go back to school after Christmas break. Sometimes a new year feels truly new, like starting all over again. This year I felt at home at St. Anne's. The gossip died down, and I was no longer, "That new girl from public school-you know, the one who got beat-up." I was, "Frances Orillio-she's kind of quiet...studies a lot, but a really nice girl."

The months sped by. Almost every weekend I did some activity with classmates, and Mom was relieved that I had begun to develop what she called a normal social life. Sometimes we went bowling, or to see a school-approved movie. I visited the homes of some of the girls from school, and brought a few home as well. They were well-mannered and better educated than Maddy, but I noticed that none of them could think like she did. Even with their superior vocabularies, they couldn't communicate on the same level. By comparison, they seemed like polite, happy children.

So I had a social life at school, but still felt alone. There was no one I dared confide in, no other girl I could count on not to gossip or laugh at me as I tried to grow up. I wanted to know more about relationships with boys, but was afraid to ask anyone. When I went on outings with mixed groups of boys and girls, I still didn't understand the flirting, the unspoken secret language that came so easily to the majority. I learned to fake it, to smile and laugh with the others as I hung on the edge and tried to figure it out from observation. One thing was clear: all the other girls liked jocks-muscles, athleticism and competitive male swagger. It did nothing for me. I had a penchant for quiet, thoughtful boys, the ones others sniggered about and called 'sissy.'

At St. Anne's Catholic High School, I discovered that the homophobic remarks were whispered instead of shouted, but they were there. It was the same old battle to identify as solidly masculine or feminine, albeit in a more civilized manner. The girls gossiped about two particular boys and even a priest they perceived as gay. I saw some boys flash the limp wrist behind the backs of certain fellow students, upperclassmen who had already decided on a priestly vocation. They were the serious, intelligent young men that reminded me of Eddie Murphy.

Now I knew what my wretched uncle had meant by calling him a 'fruit'-or at least I knew it meant gay. I hadn't seen Eddie in so long, but I still sighed when I conjured up a memory of his soft voice and gentle ways. I had to keep my preferences to myself. None of the other girls seemed to go for that type, and I began to worry that there might be something wrong with me. I'd already been asked which boys I liked, but managed to put them off. "I'm not telling," I said modestly. Since the only boys I found appealing were bound for the priesthood, I wondered how I'd ever get a husband.

It's a wonder any Catholic girl figured out how to get a husband-or rather what to do with him once she got one. We were taught to worship the Blessed Virgin, Holy Mary, Mother of Jesus Christ. Her submission to God's will and the Immaculate Conception was the model of virtuous womanhood. The antonym of immaculate is filth. Sex was filth. Our mothers and Catholic school teachers joined forces to steer us clear of opportunities to even be alone with the opposite sex, while the sexual revolution of the 70's roared past like a missed train. All desire was supposed to be put on stand-by, until it was sanctioned and sanitized by the sacrament of marriage.

Even though the road to Catholic womanhood was all laid out for me, I felt awkward, confused, and terribly anxious. It wasn't only about the inevitable sexual intercourse that was mysteriously waiting for me far off in a snow white marital bed; I was afraid of my own body. It wasn't enough to deny us any form of sex education, to pretend that sex didn't exist. As part of our Catholic upbringing, little girls and boys caught touching themselves were shamed and slapped. We weren't even supplied with a proper word to label our genitals. One three-year old boy I babysat called his tiny penis his 'uh-uh', because whenever he reached for it he was rebuked with a sharp, 'uh-uh!' The lessons stuck. Our sexual awakening was confined to furtive sidelong glances at the boys in order to explore in solitude which ones tickled our fancy, a guilt provoking battle between biological necessities and early aversive conditioning.

I suffered in silence. The thought of speaking to my mother made my face hot with shame, and I certainly couldn't ask Maddy to explain it-the stirrings inside, or lack thereof in response to most of the young men around me. She was on the other side of a great divide. I knew it, but couldn't say anything about it. I worried about how she would manage to find her own way. Who would answer the questions she must have? There was nothing for gay kids-no one to ask and no place to go. Their teenaged years were spent learning how to construct and live in a closet, how to pass. Kids like Maddy Malone and George Goldenberg couldn't build a closet big enough to hide their queerness.

Since we were all indoctrinated to understand the carnal act as a regrettable marital duty, Catholicism had a double-whammy effect on homosexual youth. Their sex didn't serve to fulfill God's commandment to be fruitful and multiply-an act so dreadful that we girls needn't go over the details until just before the wedding. In the eyes of the church and most of society, relationships between gays could never be sanctified. Homosexual relationships had to be shoved far out of sight and forced to hide in dark shabby places, away from all the rest who thought themselves decent people. Given the options, many young Catholic men sought refuge from their homosexuality in the priesthood, by which time a fair number of them had become sickened from formative years of internalized self-loathing. Then their sexual desire took the form of disease and spread like a cancer through the church, eating away at the very soul of the families they touched, even unto the seventh generation. It would be decades before we knew it, but we were mired in an era of pedophile priests.

35

"In some ways, she's seems bright enough. In other ways she's...kind of a dumb bunny," Mom said.

"What's a dumb bunny?" I had to know.

"It's an expression my mother used to describe a pretty little girl who isn't very bright. What I mean is, sometimes you tell Annie something and she just stares like she can't hear you-they even checked her hearing. They say there's nothing wrong with her ears...well, I sure gave them an earful over that horrid woman! To think that all year she humiliated Annie, punished her for something that any fool can see is beyond her control. That's just what I said: 'any fool can see!' I mean, why didn't she just whack her with a hickory stick while she was at it? Miss Blodget should have retired a long time ago! That's what I suggested to the principal-right in front of her. And I said we might file a law suit for child abuse too!"

Mom was irate. The school year was nearly over, but she had called a conference with the principal and superintendent to have Annie transferred to another class immediately, and to lodge a complaint against her teacher. Miss Blodget was a woman nearing retirement, trained sometime back before WWII. Mom suspected she hadn't taken a refresher course since, or if she did, it sure didn't stick. No one had ever dared to take her on; the old battleax was accustomed to inspiring fear in children and parents alike.

When Aunt Hannah had attended a midyear conference alone, Miss Blodget informed her that Annie's grades were poor because she 'just sat and daydreamed and refused to pay attention.' She likened it to a bad habit that could be eradicated with a firm hand. The surly spinster asserted that Annie's obvious immaturity stemmed from a lack of self-discipline, a problem that must first be corrected in the home. She admonished Aunt Hannah for spoiling the child, and added that the loss of a mother was no excuse. Hannah Harahan Malone told Miss Blodget that her business was teaching and she ought to stick to it, and not meddle in the lives of families, especially seeing as she had no children of her own.

Miss Blodget retaliated. Whenever she caught Annie in a 'daydream', she roused her by clapping loudly in her face, or banging on the desk with a ruler and shouting, "wake-up!" The class laughed uproariously, and Miss Blodget encouraged them to point their fingers and laugh in an effort to shame her into compliance. Then she made Annie stand by her desk, sometimes for an hour or more to 'train' her to pay attention, while the other children gloated and tormented her with ugly faces.

Naturally, we didn't know anything about it. Annie wouldn't or couldn't speak up for herself, and Miss Blodget took complete advantage of her helplessness. I'd seen Annie drift in and out of awareness many times over the years. She was often confused, even frightened after the lapses. The thought of how she must have suffered made my heart break. Now it made sense that she never went out to play with other children. Ever since first grade she'd had trouble making friends, but the actions of this teacher made her a social outcast, completely untouchable. At the sight of Annie, other little girls called her 'weirdo' and 'retard' or just made faces and said, 'eeehw!' If Annie stepped on the green linoleum squares, they all jumped on the white ones. No wonder she preferred to play alone, or stay in the house with Mom and me. She often came over to watch TV, or just sit in the same room coloring with her crayons. Sometimes she carried on long, one-sided conversations with one or both of us, scarcely requiring an, "Oh-I-see," or an "Uh-huh," to ramble on. Other times she remained silent, coloring for hours on end, lost in a world of her own making.

We were all right there, but couldn't help because she didn't tell anyone about the trouble at school. Instead, she began to get sick every morning, and vomited so fiercely that they had a complete gastro intestinal series done at Children's Hospital. We were all very worried, considering her mother had died of colon cancer. An attentive nurse picked up a drawing Annie made while in the waiting room. It was a girl standing by a desk, raining copious tears while every child in the rows surrounding her pointed what looked like arrows and spears. Annie explained they were going to shoot her. The nurse coaxed the whole story out, and informed her anxious grandmother. The GI turned up nothing.

"Why didn't you tell Auntie Evelyn, honey?" Mom spoke very gently, as if she were talking to a much younger child, even though Annie was going on nine years. The poor kid squirmed uncomfortably, twisted her toe absently into the kitchen linoleum, looked past my mother and shrugged. It was hard to tell if she didn't know, or didn't know how to explain.

The principal moved Annie to another class and put the teacher on administrative leave while they investigated. Mom hoped that would fix the problem. It was a great start, but didn't undo countless hours of psychological torture. I sensed that something more needed to be done, but nobody knew what to do.

The debacle at Edmunds Elementary brought to mind how Auntie Joan had been blamed for Baby Michael's bizarre behavior, his 'mental retardation' or whatever it was-the family still didn't talk about it. I didn't understand it, but I was sure the doctors had it all wrong. I'd witnessed time and again as she lavished love on that child, and cared for him with the patience of a saint. If I had to put up with him day and night, I think I would have tossed him out a window and run screaming stark naked down the street. Joan took their accusations straight to heart, and it killed her long before the cancer took her life.

I was sure Gramma Malone didn't make Annie immature, or cause the difficulty at school. We all tended to baby Annie because she arguably needed careful watching-but why? My inclination was to blame her detestable father and his heavy right hand. Yet Maddy had the same father, and she'd been as tough and streetwise as Annie was childlike and naïve. She was about the same age when she turned on her abuser with a brass table lamp! It was exasperating. I felt as if the 3000 pieces of the jigsaw puzzle were all there, right under our noses, only we'd lost the box cover with the picture on top.

In the new class Annie was far less miserable, but didn't seem any further along at making friends. My mother came up with what she imagined was a marvelous antidote. For her ninth birthday, she decided to go all out and throw the biggest kid's birthday bash East Mapleton had ever seen, and invite every little girl in Annie's new class in an effort to make her popular. I knew my mother's heart was in the right place, but I wasn't so sure this was the right approach.

"She just needs a chance to shine! After what that awful teacher...that...excuse me...sick bitch did, no wonder Annie has no friends. I'd like to go give that woman an ass-kicking!"

"Good for you. I'll help," I said approvingly. "But seriously, Annie is so shy, and I don't think she's ever been invited to a kid's birthday party before. I know she never had one, what with all that happened...but..."

"That's why we've got to do this. Trust me. And unless you can come up with a better idea, just help me out and try to be positive about it."

I didn't have any better ideas; I just thought that freaking Annie out with a bunch of squealing girls who'd probably reject her as soon as the ice cream melted might be worse than doing nothing at all. I know that's how it worked for me when Mom threw my big birthday party back in the fourth grade, for the very same reason. I didn't even need help from a sadistic teacher to be unpopular. Either she'd forgotten all about it, or perhaps substituted a new and improved ending for what turned out to be a painfully awkward day. I decided to keep my mouth shut and let her try to work her social magic.

Mom worked Monday through Thursday, from 9:00 to 3:00. She went to the library after work and came home with an arm-load of books on how to throw a successful children's party.

"Have you asked Aunt Hannah?" I inquired.

"Yes, of course I discussed it with her, and she's very appreciative. She's a proud woman, but she's more concerned about Annie than with pretending she can handle everything by herself. It's about time."

"Uh, have you asked Annie?"

"Oh, this sounds like a cute game. You release balloons outside, and the one who chases them down and collects the most wins!"

"Mom?!"

"Yes, I told her...I said we were going to have a nice birthday party at Auntie Evelyn's house this year. I asked if that was OK-she smiled and nodded. I've got three weeks to get her used to the idea. Next week I'm going to bring the invitations to her class and hand them out to the girls myself."

"So you haven't explained that all the little brats who've been so mean to her are coming to the party?"

Mom looked at me annoyed. "These are girls from the brand new class, not the ones who laughed at her."

"Maybe, but none of them were very nice to her...didn't you listen? She couldn't walk down the hallway or eat in the cafeteria without some kid making a face, or putting their thumbs up so you didn't catch her cooties!"

"Frances, what are you talking about?"

"Cooties! They did it to me and it's so mean. They gang up and say, "Everybody put your thumbs up or you'll catch Franny's cooties! I know it sounds silly, but it really hurts when you're a little kid. So you haven't told her?"

"No, not yet. Isn't it funny that she doesn't even ask...I mean, unless you explain every little thing..."

"Exactly. So she thinks it's going to be just us. Please don't tell me you're going to wait until the last minute."

"No. I'll let her know well before I go into her class. She'll be nervous, but I know how to handle those girls. I'll build it up as the event of the year. They'll be eating out of her hand." She smiled, fully confident in her ability to manipulate little girls.

Mom took Annie to shop for a new birthday outfit, since she was still wearing my hand-me downs. The styles had changed drastically since I was her size, but Annie didn't care or even seem to notice. She still adored the full skirted dresses we wore in the sixties-one of the kids had remarked that she looked like Alice-in-Wonderland. Mom picked out a mini-dress, only it had shorts underneath so she could play and bend over. It was a miniature version of something a teenager might wear, polyester of course, in a bold flower-power pattern and sleeveless for springtime. She got a pair of clunky, square toed shoes that were all the rage to complete the outfit. Aunt Hannah insisted on paying for the clothes, and tried to give Mom some cash for the party, but she wouldn't take it. Annie enjoyed all the attention, and when we got home she was still admiring her new look in the mirror. That's when Mom broke the news.

"Wait 'til all the girls from school see your stylish new outfit. You look so grown-up! I'm sure they'll love it. You'll be the best dressed girl at your birthday party."

"What girls?" Annie was pulled from her affair with the mirror.

"All the little girls in your new class," Mom chirped.

Annie looked confused, then alarmed. "They're coming here?!" she asked in disbelief. "Why?"

Only a moment before she'd been twirling and flitting about in her new outfit. Now she stood awkwardly with her arms held stiff by her sides, and her shoulders hunched as if ready for a blow. I gave Mom a smug 'I told you so' look. She didn't appreciate it.

"Of course they're coming, dear. You can't have a birthday party without other girls."

"I only want Fran and Mad'lin and you and Gramma. You're girls," she pleaded.

"We're too old to play games...don't you want to play birthday games, like pin the tail on the donkey, and..?" Mom was too flustered to recall the silly games she'd spent so much time researching. The answer was all too predictable.

"No. No thank you, Auntie," she corrected, mindful of her manners.

"Not even to make Auntie and Gramma proud?"

"Mom!" I practically hissed at her. "Don't do that!" It went right over Annie's head. Mom looked a bit sheepish.

"Annie, what do you want most for your birthday?" Mom asked in a tone that made me suspicious. "Is there something special you want this year?" Annie thought a moment, then a big smile spread over her face. "Well," Mom coaxed, "tell me what it is."

"A bunny rabbit! I want the white bunny they have at the pet store!"

There was a grimy little pet shop downtown by the Woolworths. Annie dragged us in there whenever we took her out for ice cream or more crayons. She'd asked Maddy for a rabbit last Easter, when there was a boatload of baby bunnies in a window display. "We can barely look after ourselves, never mind a pet," she grumbled. "Besides, rabbits poop a lot. You have to clean it. See!" She pointed to the bottom of the cage. "Yuck!"

Annie just looked sad and said, "I don't mind if he poops." We hoped she'd forget about it, but just the other day we went by the store and there was one, fat white rabbit left all alone. The others had been bought up when they were little and cute, for children's Easter baskets. "Oh, look," she cried. "He's all by himself...he's so sad...please," she choked up, and tears ran down her smooth cheeks for a plain albino rabbit with lackluster fur and dull pink eyes, probably destined for some laboratory. She almost got me crying. We coaxed her away and bought her some colored pencils. She stopped talking about it, but clearly hadn't forgotten.

"Oh, I don't know about that...I'm not sure your grandmother would allow a pet." Mom looked defeated. I could see she had planned to offer a bribe, a special gift for the birthday girl's cooperation. It was her ace-in-the-hole. But a rabbit? It would need a hutch or something-we weren't really pet people, so I wasn't sure. Even though I'd warned Mom, I felt sorry for her. She really went all out for this party. She bought party favors and paper hats with matching napkins and a table cloth. There were streamers and balloons. She'd gone to the principal and asked to see the class roster, to be sure not one little girl was left out. The invitations were written and sealed in pink envelopes. My mother had the best of intentions. She wanted to undo the damage done by that draconian teacher, but she also wanted to give Annie a social makeover, as if one party could suddenly win her popularity. I recalled my mother's continual lament that I didn't have lots of friends like she did as a girl, from the time I was in Kindergarten to when I met Maddy. Then I guess she gave up. I'd just about forgotten how painful it was-not my unpopular status, but her deep disappointment in me.

"A bunny rabbit? Sure, you can have a bunny, sweetheart!" Dad came home in the middle of the party discussion.

"Joseph, don't tell her that! You can't give her permission when we haven't even asked my aunt." Mom was mortified.

"So she can keep it here," Dad argued. "What's wrong with that?"

"Oh, I don't know..."

"Hey, I never got a pet rabbit," I was half serious. "And you wouldn't let me keep the duck!" I swear I remembered that duck, and how sad I was when it was taken away. Mom insisted that I was too young to understand at the time. I just thought I remembered because of the picture and the story she told me.

"Ducks quack; loud! You don't remember, but you could hear them whole blocks away, every morning, bright and early when she fed them," Mom argued with me.

Annie stood there looking from one of us to the other. "But rabbits aren't loud," she informed us.

"That's right," Dad said, "rabbits don't quack, ha-ha-ha!" Annie joined him in a peal of giggles.

"Where would we put it?" Mom whined.

"We got a whole back yard that hardly gets used. I can put one of those wooden...rabbit boxes out there," Dad countered.

"I think it's called a hutch," I corrected.

"Fine, we'll build it a rabbit hut..."

"No, it's a rabbit...never mind," I said. In the space of a few minutes, Dad had made Annie happier than I'd seen her in years with the promise of a simple rabbit.

"Then it's OK if the other little girls come to your party?" Mom asked, sounding exhausted. I'm not sure whether Annie had figured out that this was the right answer, or whether she was so overjoyed at the prospect of her new pet that she would have agreed to anything.

"Yes. Yes Auntie," she added politely.

Dad was able to take us to the pet shop the very next morning, since it was Saturday. On the way he explained that he would buy the bunny, but have the man keep him for Annie until we built it a house.

"Are you sure this is the one you want?" Dad asked when he saw the forlorn creature sitting in a stinky box of sawdust. It looked like a lump of fur with a nose on one end and a cotton tail on the other. It didn't react at all when Annie stroked it. I knew rabbits weren't known for their intellect, but this one looked as though it didn't have a brain in its narrow skull. Annie grinned and nodded vigorously. "OK," Dad said. "You wait here." He went over to the man and began the bargaining ritual. "I'll give you a buck for the rabbit."

"What? Sir, the price is five dollars, but for her, I'd go four-fifty." He smiled at Annie.

"For that? You gotta be kiddin' me!" My father turned abruptly and walked to the door.

"Wait! I'll go four even, but that's it!"

Dad paused but didn't turn back. "Come on, kids," he said. Annie looked devastated, but started to follow him out obediently.

"OK. Three!" The man held up three fingers. "My final offer!"

My father turned around to face the man and puffed himself up. I knew he was going to haggle with the shopkeeper-who was also Italian. I hadn't seen this in a while, and nudged Maddy with my elbow. "Watch and learn," I whispered.

"Listen, Pal; I know that ain't worth even one dollar. What will they give you for it at the dog-food factory, fifty cents?" He spoke in Italian, but I understood enough to get the gist.

"Fifty cents? Are you crazy?! Look at the meat on 'im!" The man pointed at the rabbit. "For that I'd get at least a buck-fifty!" The pet store owner gesticulated indignantly and looked very put-out.

My father's expression suddenly changed from mild belligerence to smug satisfaction, as he whipped out his wallet and held forth two dollar bills. "Then Sir, permit me to be generous: two dollars," he said in his most elegant Italian.

"Bah!" the man said as he walked over and took the two dollars. Then he went and got a box.

"What about the bunny hutch?" I whispered when he'd gone into the backroom. Dad was so busy bargaining that he forgot we needed to build something to put the rabbit in before we took it home.

"Oh, ah...we'll come by day after tomorrow," he addressed the store owner. "I gotta go get some lumber...don't got a place to put him yet." Dad had reverted back to English, and he looked a bit sheepish.

"What?! You want me to feed your rabbit another two days?!

"Ok-we'll get it tomorrow."

"For boarding the rabbit I charge another two dollars," said the man. His beady black eyes sparkled with triumph.

"Put it in the box. We'll take it now," Dad said.

The man reached over the display window and unceremoniously hauled the rabbit out by the scruff of his neck. It hung there piteously without even kicking. "See? Gentle as a lamb," the man said. "And look at the meat on 'im!" He plopped the rabbit into the orange box and jammed the lid on. Dad carried it out without saying thank you.

We all piled into the back seat with the rabbit on the floor, happily chewing his cardboard box. "He's the most beautiful bunny! Thank you Uncle Joe!" Annie beamed with happiness.

"You're welcome, sweetheart. Whada ya gonna name him? Or is it a her? Hey Frances, do you know anything about…"

"How would I know? I never got a pet bunny," I teased.

"Aw, come on…"

"Actually, when the man held it up I couldn't help but notice…how shall I put it," I said delicately.

"That thing had one big pair of pink balls," Maddy broke in.

"Ha! Ha! Ha! Is that right?" Dad laughed. I didn't think he'd find it so funny if I'd said it. He always had such a soft spot for Maddy. They laughed together, and Annie seemed oblivious to the comment.

"Your bunny is a boy," I explained.

"I know," she answered.

"How do you know?" I asked.

"I saw his big pink balls too," she said sweetly.

"Oh, ho, ho! Now see what we did," Dad said humorously. "What's his name?" He hoped to change the subject.

"Flopsy, like in <u>Peter Rabbit</u>." She had his name all picked out.

It was a long day. We stopped at the lumber yard and got plywood, two-by-fours, and heavy wire mesh. I remembered the hinges and a latch. Maddy waited in the car with Annie, who wouldn't leave the rabbit.

"I thought it was coming in a couple of days," Mom looked mildly annoyed when we traipsed in holding the big box.

"It…ah…I mean…we had to bring it now. I'll explain later," Dad said. "I'll put him in the basement for the time being. Don't worry-we won't make a mess."

"Better not," Mom warned.

It took all afternoon to build the hutch, especially as there was no blueprint. I suggested that we make it with short wooden legs. That way, Annie could reach inside easily, and we wouldn't have to worry about it falling over on her. When Annie asked Mom for a carrot to give Flopsy, we all realized we hadn't bought any rabbit food-or bowls to put it in.

"Stupido!" Dad popped his palm to his forehead.

"I'll go," Mom said bemusedly. "It's got to eat…see, this is what I mean," she whispered to Dad. "What a big pain in the…never mind." She grabbed her purse and left.

237

Mom went to the Woolworth's pet department. It turned out that a bag of bunny chow and two heavy crockery bowls cost more than the rabbit. When we took into account the tab from the hardware store, we might as well have got her a puppy. I pitched in five dollars of baby-sitting money, and the gift was from all of us. Just as it was growing dark, we placed the hutch at the foot of the hill and settled Flopsy into his new palace. It was hard to tear Annie away, but at last we convinced her that the bunny needed to go to sleep. We took her home.

Early the next morning, Dad went out in his pajamas to pick up the Sunday paper from the front lawn. The grass was still wet with dew, but Annie was out back, sitting in it. She stroked the placid creature that lay across her lap, and spoke softly to it. Mom brought her in for breakfast-she hadn't eaten. After breakfast, Dad went to the basement and got one of those short folding sand chairs you use at the beach, to put by the hutch.

Later that morning, I saw an odd sight that alarmed me at first. Annie was walking down the sidewalk towards our house, leading a strange man by the hand. He was wearing flannel pajama bottoms and a t-shirt, and shuffled along in slippers. What was left of his hair stuck out in greasy clumps, as if he'd just got out of bed. The man allowed himself to be led by the child, looking dazed and blinking in the bright sun. When I realized it was Tom Malone, I was even more alarmed. He'd lost so much weight, I scarcely recognized him. He didn't look well at all, but that didn't concern me. Ever since Maddy had told me of her father's temper and abusive outbursts, the sight of him made me sick. What the hell was he doing here? I called my father to the door. "What do you think?" I asked.

"Beats me! He ain't come by in years," Dad said, then stepped out onto the back stairs. "Hey, Tommy! How the hell 'ave ya been?" Tom looked up as if he wasn't sure who'd spoken.

"I'm bringing Daddy to show Flopsy," Annie explained.

"Oh, that's nice," Dad said.

Tom Malone shrugged bashfully and shuffled into the yard. He looked so pathetic and weak. It was embarrassing; I almost felt sorry for him. I watched as Annie led her father to her special chair, where he sat down awkwardly. She hauled the rabbit out of his cage and placed it in her father's lap. "This is Flopsy," I heard her say. The broken man just stared down at the animal, and seemed to have no idea how to act. Annie knelt by his side and took his right hand, the same hand that had so cruelly struck her, gently in both of hers and placed it on the rabbit's back. "He's soft," she explained, smiling up at his vacant eyes. I ducked into the house.

After a bit, Dad went out and brought Uncle Malone in for coffee. Mom made him some toast. He nodded and mumbled some thanks, and slurped the coffee loudly. He dropped crumbs in his lap like a child, and like a child, didn't seem to notice.

"She figured out how to clean the cage with a garden trowel," Dad made conversation. "I showed her how to her sprinkle it's…"

"Joe, please," Mom said, "not at the breakfast table."

"Those little brown pellets…around the base of the flower beds," Dad said. "See Ev," he added with a merry twinkle in his eye, "it makes free fertilizer!"

Mom laughed in spite of herself. "I'm glad she's so happy with that old bunny. It's rather homely, don't you think?"

"Don't let Annie hear you say that," I warned. She was back outside.

"Did you do that, Joe?" Tom's voice quavered as he suddenly interjected the odd question.

"Eh, Tom?" Dad was puzzled, not sure what he was talking about.

"All that…you made all that…for her?" He spoke softly, almost tenderly as he pointed towards the backyard. I couldn't believe this was the big brute I'd met a few years ago, the man that sent shivers through me when he entered a room.

Dad figured out that Tom was referring to the rabbit hutch. "Oh, it ain't nothin'," he said, and swept his hand through the air as if brushing away a fly. Tom looked as though he meant to say more, and his lips began to twitch as he struggled to speak, but couldn't find the words. Then he blinked rapidly and sniffed like he was about to cry. Dad looked away, uncomfortable. I was staring awkwardly down at the linoleum when the coffee cup fell to the floor, followed with a loud thud by Tom Malone. I was sure he was dead.

36

Tom Malone didn't die of his stroke. The doctors said he'd likely had a series of smaller strokes in the days before he collapsed in our kitchen. That explained why he acted so strange. It was a miracle that he survived, but he'd never work again-not that he'd ever worked much. A life-time of hard drinking had left him too sick to drive a cab for almost a year now. He was sixty-three, but since he'd reported only a fraction of his income all his working life, the social security disability check was paltry. The only other income was Aunt Hannah's social security. I finally asked Maddy about that college money her grandmother spoke of all those years ago-not for college, but for survival. It was gone. Apparently, her grandmother had spent it all on Auntie Joan's wake. Maddy stated it as fact, neither bitter nor complaining.

I figured it couldn't have amounted to that much money after all. Aunt Hannah probably didn't understand how expensive college was; old people seemed to think the value of a dollar hadn't changed since they were young. I guess funerals were a lot more than she'd imagined too. My mother said it was a family disgrace that she shouldered the entire burden, emptied her bank account to honor her daughter-in-law, while the husband was still alive and kicking. By now, I understood that my mother hadn't dug very deep in the pocket when it came time to plant Nana; my grandmother's wake was bargain basement. I heard it from Maddy who heard it from her grandmother. Even the wilting flowers had been recycled from the previous guest.

Over the years, the Malone Mansion had gone from needing a bit of work to run-down. Now it was truly falling apart. Even when he was well, Tom Malone hadn't done one damned thing to fix up his mother's house, not in the three years he'd lived there. He certainly wouldn't be any help now. The house had a few more plywood windows, not because kids broke them, but because the ropes that worked like pulleys on the double-hung windows were rotting away. If you didn't replace them, they suddenly snapped and the window crashed shut, shattering the glass. Some rotten wooden gutters had fallen down, and one hung menacingly overhead, barely anchored to the house. We were warned not to walk under it. The roof sagged precariously, and leaked in a few places. The weathered clapboard hadn't been painted in my lifetime. Mom grumbled that it was an embarrassment, and wondered aloud that no one turned up from the city commissioner's office to issue a condemned notice. Only the old tower stood straight as an arrow, pointing towards heaven just over the hill beyond our back yard.

Tom Malone crumbled along with his childhood home. The last stroke had turned him into a feeble old man overnight. Although he was seventeen years younger than his mother, he could have easily been mistaken for her husband, and ten years older at that. He shuffled along with a walker, and could hardly use his right arm. Much of the limited speech he'd possessed was lost; much, but not all. Just when you least expected it, he'd tell you in a faltering voice about things that happened long ago, when he was young or even a boy. Other than that he was silent. He couldn't tell you what happened yesterday if he wanted to.

About six months earlier, Tom had sunk what little money he'd stashed away and started a family business with Joanie's longtime boyfriend, Jack Mack. Joanie worked radio dispatch from a back room. She had dropped out of school after her sophomore year. Now she was eighteen, and it was a source of shame that Jack hadn't married her, but nobody said anything. Jack drove the shiny new black cab and worked long hours, ferrying folks day and night under the auspices of Malone's Quality Taxi. Most of the passengers were regulars, sketchy guys up to God-knows-what, and Jack knew who to pay off so police would look the other way while they did business. Although he was incapacitated, Tom Senior was still on the books as owner, a position that didn't seem to provide any income. Jack kept a tight lid on the cash, and told Gramma Malone that it all went to pay off the loans he took out to buy the new cab, the radio equipment, and all the necessary city permits. He attributed the financial losses to the higher costs of insurance for commercial drivers, and claimed to make only a few dollars an hour himself. Joanie got paid minimum wage. Funny thing was, Jack always seemed to have plenty of money for booze or drugs or whatever he wanted. When the family's old washing machine broke down, he phoned Sears and ordered a new one. How else could Joanie wash his clothes?

Maddy stopped attending school without finishing freshman year. It was a complete waste of time and besides, the family was broke. They could offer her only a roof and a meal at suppertime. She didn't care about herself, but sometimes there was no cereal or anything for breakfast and she'd scrounge for some leftovers to feed Annie. At school, Annie was on the free-lunch program.

Maddy didn't want any part of Malone's Quality Taxi, even though she needed money. She told me she wanted to earn an honest living like my dad-maybe even drive a truck someday. She said it was bad enough that Jack ferried

241

drug dealers around the back streets of Middlefield, but the prostitution really disgusted her. When she spoke offhandedly about it I was shocked, then annoyed with my own naivety. How can you have drugs without a little prostitution? They go together like hotdogs and Boston baked beans. I learned that Jack was a dealer and a charmer. He managed to find a few poor girls from the projects in Middlefield, girls with no family to turn to, and make them feel like he was doing them a favor. They had next to nothing, and could be bought cheap. Some of them even had kids.

Poverty wasn't Maddy's biggest concern. Her father's incapacitation left the family vulnerable, at the mercy of Jack Mack. He was a tense, secretive little man, and suspicious to the point of paranoia. He could deliver the most acid remarks with a smile on his face, and it was impossible to discern his true intentions. They were all afraid of him-even Joanie. Maddy said she'd caught a glimpse of a 'shit-load' of cash and drugs in the trunk of the black cab, when she happened to walk up behind Jack in the driveway late one night. He'd slammed the trunk, whipped around and pulled a gun on her in one easy move. In the safety of my room, Maddy reenacted the whole scene, affecting his voice and pantomiming the action. It would have been hysterical if it weren't so deadly serious.

"What the fuck do you think you're doin?" His gun hand was shaking.

"I live here," Maddy told him with an offhand shrug.

"Listen baby dyke, don't you ever sneak up on me like that again! Next time you might get hurt."

"Well, next time don't be so sloppy," she told him, and then walked calmly into the house without looking back, like she wasn't afraid.

"Oh my God, weren't you scared?" I was horrified.

"I was scared shitless! It didn't really hit me 'til later, but as soon as I got inside I started shakin' all over. Frances, you gotta keep quiet about it," she warned.

I tried to think of a solution. "Why don't you call the police?"

"Are you crazy?! For one thing, Jack pays some of them off-over in Middlefield. And he'd probably wipe out the whole family when he got out of jail-if he even went to jail-these guys know all the angles. Besides, Tommy's kinda stuck in a...situation. I don't want him goin' to jail," she added, then explained the situation.

Tommy had inherited the old yellow cab, a rusted hunk of metal that barely ran, with an engine so loud it roared like a diesel truck. It backfired frequently, and a sound like gunshots could be heard from a mile away. You always knew when Tommy was coming or going, day or night, even though he'd spray-painted the car with dull iron gray primer, bumpers and all. Many times we were all startled in the middle of supper, and Dad remarked sarcastically, "Jeez, it sounds like Al Capone is livin' behind us!" Tommy was too young to legally obtain a license to drive a cab, but he delivered packages, and sometimes the people who carried them. The orders came in code over the radio, and Jack was behind all of it. He even took over the pathetic marijuana trafficking that Tommy started back in junior high school, replacing it with higher quality pot and harder drugs. He took most of the money, and promised Tommy a brand new car when he'd saved enough of the profits. Meanwhile, he claimed Tommy somehow owed him money for paying off cops or something.

"Well, what about Tommy then?"

"Whada bout 'im?"

"He's man of the house now-can't he do something about Jack? Tommy's a big guy, much bigger than Jack...why doesn't he just throw him out?"

"For that matter, I'm bigger than Jack; one time he had his boots off to nap on the couch, and when he stood up I seen I was an inch taller. But nah, Tommy can't do nothin' about it; he doesn't dare. I hate to say it, but Jack's got Tommy whipped. Listen Frances: with men, it ain't just about who's bigger-it's who's got the bigger balls."

"Huh?"

"I don't mean the actual size of their testicles." She grinned at my naivety. "Although...there's something to all that-they're pretty wrapped up with what they got in their pants, but it's more about the way a man handles himself. Acting tough! That's how he makes other men think he's got big ones. What you gotta understand about guys like Jack is how they'll fight over it...like if they think another guy is gonna make 'em look small. And if one guy kicks another guy's ass in front of everybody...it gets even more dangerous. He might just crawl away. But maybe he's gonna come back at 'em and do whatever it takes to prove he's got big balls-even if he has to kill someone."

Oddly enough I understood the explanation, thanks to watching the male chimps Jane Goodall filmed chasing and biting each other to establish dominance. But what a nightmare! The only plus side to all this was that it turned Maddy off to drugs. She still smoked like a fiend, and drank some, but had backed away from all but the occasional joint. I was afraid for my cousins, but wouldn't risk telling my parents. I worried that Dad might attempt to intervene, and I didn't want him tangling with Jack Mack.

37

The following September, we all pushed Maddy to enroll in school again and at least finish sophomore year. When she found out she could take driver's education, she agreed to give it another try, but still wanted a part-time job. I'd been meaning to speak to my father about her job search, but I didn't quite know how to explain the problem without revealing secrets. She couldn't get the unskilled work girls usually did, like running a cash register or waitressing. When she applied for a waitressing job, they told her they only hired girls. She told them she was a girl, and they sent her away. When she turned up for a job as a stock boy, they told her they wanted a boy. Maddy struck out every time, and she was getting desperate.

One Saturday evening in early autumn, Dad gave us a ride home from the movies. I was busy with school, but I always made a point of rounding her up for a night out when I could. It gave her a break from home. It gave me a break too. She was the only one I could truly be myself with. With my St. Anne's friends, I always felt a bit like I was acting in a play. Maddy and I were so different on the outside, but she was still my only real friend.

I asked Dad to take a detour through Mapleton Heights so we could gawk at the ritzy houses where some of my classmates lived. I insisted that Maddy ride shot-gun and I climbed in the back. At five foot nine, she was so much taller than me; I fit better in the backseat. Besides, it gave her a chance to talk with my dad. They enjoyed each other.

I'd been inside a few of the Tudor style manses, and described the layout of all the rooms and how many bathrooms they had. One had five bathrooms.

"Damn!" Dad remarked. "The women must spend all day cleaning; by the time you got done with the fifth, it would be time to start over! Look at all those windows! How do they keep them so clean?" I explained that most of the people in these neighborhoods hired help to do their windows, mow their lawns-even clean the bathrooms.

"I don't know about bathrooms, but I wonder how much they pay you to do the lawns and windows?" Maddy asked.

"I have no idea how much they pay, but I know how to find out," I said.

"You gonna ask your friends?"

"No, even better. We'll look up window washing in the phonebook and I'll call a few companies, say I'm looking for estimates. I'll describe a house like one of these with dozens of windows. That way you could offer a bargain and get business! For lawns you'd need a lawn mower and a truck to get around in, but all you need is buckets and rags and paper towels for the windows."

"Maybe for just the inside," Dad interjected. "For the outside you need ladders-big heavy extension ladders. It's dangerous."

"What about a long pole with a brush on the end...and a garden hose!" Maddy countered enthusiastically.

"That might work for the lower story, but look how high up the second story windows are. You'd need one hell of a long pole!" Dad chuckled. "And them double-hung windows stick. You need to take down the storm windows too, and they're heavy. It's hard work."

"I can do hard work," Maddy challenged.

"You'd need a truck and a ladder."

"I'll learn to drive. I'll get my license next year. For now, maybe Tommy will go in on it with me. He's got the old cab. We can start our own family business."

"Yeah, I think you're on to something-for Tommy anyway. But he'd have to do all the heavy lifting. Maybe you could wash the inside windows, but..."

"I can do anything Tommy can," Maddy insisted.

"Aw, you shouldn't do such hard work, up on ladders and all. Just help your brother for a while and don't worry; someday you'll have a husband who'll take care of you."

Maddy went stone silent. I froze, hoping she wouldn't have a fight with my dad. I waited a few anxious moments, but no retort came. I needn't have worried. She loved and respected him too much. With only the streetlamps for light, I surreptitiously scanned her features from the back seat, looking for some clue to decipher her feelings. She wasn't fuming with anger. She was pensive, perhaps even a bit sad.

"Uncle Joe...I'm not going to have a husband," she said quietly.

"Oh, 'course you are! A smart, handsome gal like you..."

"Uh, thanks for the compliment but..."

"In just a few years now..."

"Uncle Joe!" Maddy's voice was urgent, pleading. "I ain't gettin' married...I...just look at me," she trailed off quietly. "That ain't for me."

Dad rolled up to a red light at the intersection. He turned and looked across his broad shoulder, tilted his head a bit and studied her carefully, as if he could see something from that angle he'd previously missed. In the warm glow of the traffic light I could see his face, thoughtful and kind. "Hmm," he mused, "I guess you're right. Oh well." He shrugged. "Then I guess you gotta learn to work!" He smiled at her, then turned his eyes back on the road. The car eased smoothly onto Massachusetts Avenue, heading east.

38

For Thanksgiving, Auntie Angela invited all the Orillios to celebrate at her place. It stood out in my mind because she served lasagna and meat sauce along with the turkey, and I basically ate two dinners. I found out later that Aunt Hannah hadn't made a turkey; she was just too exhausted. The kids only got frozen turkey pot pies. Jack took Joanie out to a restaurant.

In reciprocity for Thanksgiving, my parents planned a big Christmas Eve party with all of the relatives from Dad's side of the family. The Malones weren't invited; Mom explained that it was a grown-up party, but I think she secretly felt that the Orillios and Malones just wouldn't set well together. Nonetheless, Maddy and Tommy unexpectedly brought Annie over with some carrots for Flopsy, and then came to the door, ostensibly because Annie wanted to visit with us. I think they smelled the food. Mom said later that she could practically see them drooling. She invited them to join us. I guess my cousins had never seen a real Italian Christmas feast before. They ate like pigs.

The following afternoon when Christmas was winding down, we made a dutiful family visit to the sick and elderly, to see Aunt Hannah and Uncle Tom Malone. We met him shuffling around the house, confused and disheveled in foul smelling clothes that he'd slept in for days. Gramma told us in private that when the doctor made a house call, he'd remarked that as far as he could tell, the patient's will to live was the only thing that kept Tom going. Gramma countered sarcastically that her son was too ornery and stubborn to die, and if that was a will to live, then she had to agree. Uncle Tom was surprised when we turned up with some little gifts, and mumbled something like, "Whas 'll this?" He'd forgotten it was Christmas. Aunt Hannah looked like she'd hit an iceberg. She wasn't sinking yet, but she'd begun to list. My parents came away concerned, and whispered quietly that night behind the bedroom door. I couldn't make out what they were saying, but it had something to do with Annie.

After the holidays I hunkered down for the worst part of the year, that time when spring is still so far off that you forget the sound of birdsong, or the feel of sun on your skin. But I didn't have time to dwell on it. As second semester sophomores, we were frequently reminded that we would be upper classmen next year, so we might as well start to get used to it. The academic expectations suddenly increased exponentially.

It was April vacation before I finally disengaged my nose from the books long enough to come up for air. I blinked in the warm sunshine like a sleepy groundhog and sighed with relief. So far, 1974 was a lucky year. The U.S. involvement in Vietnam was over-as was the registration for the draft. Nobody in the family got sick or died. Best of all, the New England spring truly arrived with a warm wind that chased away winter for good.

Now that the weather was fine, we all came out of hibernation and started doing things again, going to movies, or taking the trains into town just to sit in the Boston Commons. But until school let out, my time and attention was divided between academics and my St. Anne's social obligations. It was right around then that I noticed the passing of time sort of shifted into a higher gear. I remembered when a school year lasted forever, and the space between birthdays seemed like two years apart by comparison. Sometimes it seemed to be moving too fast. In the month of May, the smell of the lilacs blooming on the back hill made me wish I could slow it down, and become a child again if only for one season.

39

It was a glorious evening in June, but I was dutifully studying for my final exams. Suddenly Maddy turned up in the driveway and whistled under my open bedroom window. At the old familiar sound, my heart felt light, as if it suddenly forgot that four years had passed and it now beat much closer to adulthood. I jumped up and waved out the window, then flew down the stairs.

"I'm going to sit in the backyard for a short break. It's gorgeous outside," I called in anticipation of the question, 'Where are you going, it's a school night?'"

"Take a sweater," Mom called. "The night air..."

"Uh huh," I said, ignoring the imperative, and skipped out the door. It was almost sundown. There was a magical moon in a deep blue sky, so bright it hid all but the brightest stars. Maddy had already walked out back and was climbing the hill, looking over her shoulder to make sure I was following. Her face fairly glowed in the light. We neared the top and crouched down to burrow behind the lilac bushes, like children playing hide and seek. They had grown enormous, and the burgeoning purple blossoms nearly covered the rotting wooden fence, between the crumbling Malone Mansion and our back yard. After she'd lit up a Marlboro, we settled against the fence and I just waited.

"What's up?" she began.

"Nothin' much-the nuns and priests keep us snowed under with work. If they keep us busy enough, we won't have time to sin." I chuckled, enjoying my own Catholic school humor, but she didn't seem to hear me.

"Hmm. I went to our old dentist today, all the way over in Middlefield."

"Oh," I replied to the nonsequitur. "How'd it go?"

"Not great. I had a shit-load of cavities. I hadn't been in years."

"Oh, that's too bad. I hope you feel better."

"Jack was supposed to be driving me home from the dentist, and he ended up making a run on the way back...I can't wait 'til I can drive myself places."

"Me too. I'm taking my road-test this summer, after I turn sixteen," I said, wondering where this was going. I felt pretty sure she didn't come by to talk about the dentist.

"Anyways, on the way back from the dentist I ended up in the back seat with one of the girls," she dropped casually.

"What girls?" I was really confused now.

Maddy gave me a 'you dope' look and elaborated, "The girls that depend on Malone's Quality Taxi to get where they need to go when they need to get there."

"Oh...those girls," I answered, even more puzzled.

"Yeah," she said. "I could tell she was new to the business. She had her little boy with her too, and he was asleep. She looked kinda scared, like a scared kid, and I was thinkin' maybe she was scared of me...so I says, real quiet, so I don't wake the boy, 'Don't mind me, I just look like shit 'cause I came from the dentist.' I tried to smile, but I couldn't tell if I was smilin' or not 'cause of all the fuckin' Novocain. So she says, 'Oh, I'm sorry.' It reminded me of how you're always saying that. She was all fidgety. I could see somthin' was botherin' her-the poor girl was so nervous she couldn't even light her own cigarette. I took the matches from her and tried to light it, but her hand was shakin' the cigarette all over...I had to hold her hand still so I could light it. She had these big brown eyes and she just looked into me, like a baby deer. Christ, she couldn't 'ave been more than eighteen! The window was open, and I leaned in close to light her cigarette so the match didn't blow out." Maddy puffed a few times, collecting herself before going on. "Up close, I could smell her cheap perfume...I could still smell some old goat on 'er too."

I saw Maddy's nose wrinkle unconsciously at the recollection, but then her face melted into a blissful smile.

"Underneath all that I smelt somthin' sweet. I swear it was so sweet and spicy too...kinda like lilies mixed with incense at the altar on Easter Sunday." Maddy spoke in a hushed awe, as if she'd discovered some priceless holy relic while picking through the trash. The full moon looked as if it had balanced on the tip of the tower over the hill. It was bright, but her eyes were shining even brighter than the moon. After a moment she went on.

"I got her cigarette lit and she took a long drag and turned her face away to blow the smoke through her lips, real classy-like, then she looks back at me and says, 'Thanks sweetie'. Her voice was so high, almost like a little girl. You'd never even know she was...I mean, the girl's gotta eat, don't she?"

I considered whether I should agree, or say anything at all, but I could see there was more. Whatever it was, it was fragile as glass. I feared that one wrong word from me might shatter it, or frighten it away like a scared rabbit. I held my breath. Maddy inhaled the Marlboro, exhaled, coughed then swallowed before she continued.

"She put her hand on my face. It was kinda rough, like from a dishpan, but so soft...I mean her touch was so soft and gentle. It smelled good too, like that soap you wash babies with. I took it and just kissed it, even though my lips were still pretty numb from the dentist," she said with a sardonic smile. "Then she slid her little hand behind my neck and pulled me in close to her. Next thing I know we was makin' out, makin' out like crazy! Then I started shakin'!" Maddy chuckled bashfully with her hand to her face and blushed like a debutante. "I mean," she said, "there was Jack in the front seat, and I'm thinkin', holy crap, what's he gonna say?' But he was cool-acted like he didn't see nothin'. So I just took her little body into my arms-she had this tiny waist-and I kissed her face, her neck, all over. Then she took one of my hands and pressed it to her breast, snuck it behind my jacket where no one could see, just long enough to give me this big wet kiss. I never done it before...it felt so nice... then we had to stop," she explained. "After all, the kid was sleepin' and Jack was there," she sniggered some smoke from her nose, then went on to share each precious detail of her magical moment.

"She straightened her blouse, and opened her purse to check her lipstick in a little mirror. When she smiled at me and wiped some lipstick off me with her thumb, I just about died! I wished we coulda stayed there all night," she sighed. "Her stop was comin' up and she was getting ready to go, but before she woke the kid she took a pen out of her purse and wrote this..." Maddy withdrew a little scrap of paper from her inner breast pocket and carefully unfurled it, as if it were a map to buried treasure, written on gold leaf. I looked closely and saw it was a phone number. I made out the name, Linda. "Ain't it a pretty name?" It was a rhetorical question. "When she put it in my hand she made these big eyes at me, like, 'don't tell him nothin'. I ain't gonna tell Jack nothin'. I ain't tellin' Linda's business to anyone...'cept you Frances. Tellin' you isn't really like tellin'."

"Of course not," I said. "I'm happy for you," I added, looking at her. "I hope next time you don't have a mouth full of Novocain." I laughed.

"God, can you believe it? I hope nobody ever finds out about that!" Maddy had bared her soul, but hadn't yet dared to look at my face. Finally she turned to me. "Frances, you're the best."

"No, you're the best...my best friend, like a sister-or brother, or both...God, I've missed you!"

"Missed me? I've been right here all along. I'll always be right here."

I snuggled down and put the back of my head on the padded shoulder of her black leather jacket. "I'm almost jealous of her," I said absently after a moment.

"Huh? You couldn't be jealous of that poor girl," Maddy said seriously.

252

"No, it's not really about her...but I can't be your girl anymore," I said. "I think I wanna be a lesbian too!" I was joking, yet there was a tiny kernel of truth in it. I felt left behind somehow.

"What?! A lesbian? Yeah, I guess that's what I am, but no, you really don't wanna be gay," she said incredulously. "Jeez, you're a funny kid Frances; you always were such a funny kid." She laughed at me gently and ruffed up my hair with the affection of a big brother. "You are my girl. Right from the start, ever since I first saw you back in that alley. You'll always be my girl."

40

I turned sixteen that summer and got my driver's license on the first try. Dad had been teaching me since I was old enough to see over the dashboard, teaching as we went along by commenting on the condition of the road, or the actions of another driver. Lucky for me we didn't have a nice garage like the folks up in Mapleton Heights. It's a pain in the ass to have to switch the cars when the one you want to drive is blocked in by the second car, especially in the bitter cold. As a result, I was taught to start the car and warm it up by age twelve, and at thirteen, I learned to back out and park. Since I'd been whipping the cars in and out of the driveway for years, I was confident behind the wheel, and not in the least intimidated by the state trooper in his broad-brimmed hat, sitting right beside me for the road-test. He remarked that I took to the highway like I was born driving. I did great, even though the road was slick with rain.

Now Mom let me borrow the car once a week to go out with friends for the whole day. It was the best summer I'd had in years. I took some girls from St. Anne's shopping at the new mall, two towns over. I took Maddy and Annie to the beach. Annie still couldn't swim, and she still loved to play with my sand pails. The ocean is beautiful, but I never really liked to swim in salt water. My favorite place to swim was Walden Pond, and since it wasn't far, Mom often let me use the car just to spend an hour or two. Whenever I could, I brought Maddy. We practiced swimming; once Maddy got the hang of it she turned out to be a strong swimmer. Sometimes we goofed around and acted like a couple of kids again, but mostly we talked. Walden Pond wasn't crowded then. You could always find a quiet place, and it was always cool under the trees.

Little by little, Maddy told me about Linda; she was in love with Linda. She called her from a phone booth at least once a day, and if she was home, walked all the way over to Middlefield and crossed the bridge on foot to be with her. When the weather was fine, they took the boy to the park. His name was Johnny. I learned that Linda had a job as a waitress, but from time to time needed a way to make more money. She had no family here, only a mother in Florida-they didn't get along. Linda had to pay a woman to take care of Johnny, and when there weren't enough hours or the tips were bad, there wasn't enough to live on. During one of those times, she met up with Jack Mack. He had his feelers out for vulnerable girls. We would learn much later that he paid off the owner of the shabby restaurant to cut back Linda's hours, something he did regularly. Single mothers were easy prey; that's why so many of 'his girls' seemed to have kids. Maddy's dream was to make enough money to get her own place and take care of Linda.

Finally I got to meet her. We picked her up at the crack of dawn and drove all the way to Provincetown. Linda hardly spoke the whole way. She was shy and modest, not at all like I imagined. I think the fact that I was a Catholic school girl may have freaked her out. Maddy was right about her eyes: they were so big and golden brown, she reminded me of Bambi. Her pale face freckled in the sun, and with almost no makeup, she looked like a little girl. When Linda finally opened up, she spoke lovingly of her son Johnny, and remarked how sweet Maddy was with him-he'd been left with a trusted friend for the day. The boy was almost three years old, and Linda had just turned eighteen.

I'd never been to P-town, and neither had Maddy. I told my mother we'd gone to Cape Cod. It was the only big lie I ever told her, and I hated to do it. We sort of went through the Cape anyway... It was amazing to see so many gay people out having a great time, just being themselves. There were a few flamboyant looking men in women's clothes, but most of the people looked like anyone else, except that the couples were the same sex. Now I knew what they must feel like: I was the odd-ball here. There were plenty of straight people that came to gawk, but Maddy didn't care. This was their place. She held Linda's hand openly in the street and practically walked on air.

Over the summer of our sixteenth year, Linda welcomed Maddy into the world she didn't know was waiting for her. She knew who was who among the working class, and helped Maddy find a job at a warehouse where it was relatively safe to be gay. After work, Linda took her to the bars in town where only gay people hung out. She showed her how to bind her breasts with an elastic band, so she could look butch even without the leather jacket to disguise her figure. From what I gathered, that's how it worked-masculine butches and the femmes, or 'lipstick lesbians', who looked like any other girl. I was probably the only girl in St. Anne's privy to such inside information. Anyway, it must have been a relief to take the heavy jacket off when it was eighty degrees. Linda even brought Maddy to a gay barber to have her first really short boy-haircut. I guess it was easier for girls like Maddy to just pass as a boy, to become invisible when necessary. When the barber finished, he spun the chair around to face the mirror, and Linda introduced Maddy to herself.

Except for the haircut, the details of Maddy's life were a secret from the rest of the family-not that I knew all of her secrets. She was too classy to tell me the details, and I certainly wouldn't have asked, but I caught on that she and Linda had moved beyond kissing. I didn't quite know how it worked between them, but hell-I didn't even really understand how it worked between a man and a woman. I learned what little I knew from pen and ink anatomical drawings and a dry explanation in a textbook on human anatomy and physiology, which was tucked away down in the basement of the town library. I sat out of sight and tried to grasp the section on reproduction. The prone female looked like an orange with a big wedge missing; the headless male torso looked like it had a little hotdog sticking out of it. I didn't know if ejaculation involved a scarcely noticeable mist of tiny seeds, or a flood, like a stream of urine. From Maddy's off-color remarks, I guessed that it smelled bad, but none of the girls at school discussed any of it. I'm sure most of them were as worried and confused as I was.

41

My well-nigh perfect summer was rudely punctuated by a snub-nosed Irish boy named Patrick Shanahan, and his equally stubby penis. I'd never been on a date before, and hardly knew Patrick at all. We went to St. Anne's together and occasionally attended movies with a large group of classmates. When he phoned and asked me out for a date, I automatically said yes.

Patrick was a typical specimen, a blue-eyed, fair-haired, baby-faced Irish Catholic boy. He was neither homely nor particularly handsome, but definitely full of the male swagger that didn't appeal to me. He didn't strike me as dumb, but he wasn't what I'd call smart either. In short, I wasn't at all attracted to Patrick, but reasoned that I ought to make an effort and perhaps he'd grow on me. I had to start somewhere; dating was part of becoming a young lady. It was very exciting, especially as it wasn't just any old movie date; it was for a party at the house of one of his good friends, up in Mapleton Heights. I was nervous and at the same time relieved. I was beginning to think no boy would ever ask me.

Patrick Shanahan drove up in his own car, an old station wagon his father had passed down to him. He stood up straight, stepped into the house and greeted my folks properly. He called my father sir and looked him in the eye as they shook hands.

We made pleasant small talk on the way to Mapleton Heights. I wore a light summer dress, pretty but modest, and when I got there discovered that all the girls were wearing tight jeans and revealing low cut tops. Oops. I was also surprised to learn that they were all at least a year or two older than me. Patrick's friend was actually his older cousin Harry. It was a graduation party. None of the other guests even went to St. Anne's.

The parents were out. It was loud. A boom box blared out the omnipresent popular rock music that every American teenager worshiped-everyone but me. I liked things very quiet, and only listened to classical music on a phonograph I'd had since childhood. It was one more thing that set me apart from my peers; even my mother remarked that I was a bit stuffy. The hits of the seventies sounded like a cacophony of unintelligible whining and wailing, to the accompaniment of a pounding, drumming, grating noise. It was a sound that made me want to put my hands over my ears and scrunch my eyes to shut it out.

I'd already learned back in seventh grade that to do so got me labeled as a freak, so I managed to grit my teeth and hide my freakishness when necessary.

Patrick was no sooner in the front door than someone rushed over and put a beer in his hand. I didn't like beer, and sat sipping a Coca Cola as he pounded down a few more beers. By ten o'clock he was pretty drunk. The house was full of smokers and I was choking in a thick fog. Upstairs they had pot. I had the sense not to go upstairs, near the bedrooms.

After eleven, the living room was full of couples slow dancing, hanging on tight to one another to keep from falling down drunk. Patrick grabbed my hand and led me into the crush without asking. We danced, and he slid first one, then both paws down to my bottom. I froze. He pulled me in until I was mashed against his pelvis; I didn't know what on earth to do.

At school dances, the nuns had lectured us to always leave enough room between dance partners for the Holy Ghost. The girls practiced dancing together in P.E., and Sister Agnes would come over and measure the space with a balloon, just to make sure we got the point. Sister Agnes certainly never explained what to do if a boy grabbed your ass. Why hadn't Mom told me that you just reach round and pull his hand back up on your waist?

The music stopped and I retreated to a corner, trying to decide if I should tell him I wanted to go home, or just slip out and take the bus. Maybe I should call my mom? Oh God, how humiliating! Patrick saw me sitting there and swaggered over. "Whasa matter, baby? Aren't you havin' a good time?"

"No, I'm not." I decided to be direct.

"Wanna go?" Patrick smiled.

"Yes, please." So that's all I had to do to get out of this? I felt relieved.

We left without saying goodbye and no one seemed to notice. My stomach was in knots and my eyes were burning; it was a relief to get out in the night air. The cars were lined up along the curb, and he'd had to park way down the street. As we walked, I noticed that Patrick staggered. I stopped at the passenger side door.

"I don't want to trouble you," I said.

"Whah?" Patrick was confused.

"Well, I don't think you're OK to drive…"

"Course I am. Get in!"

My face felt hot, and my stomach fluttered in fear. My heart was pounding. I thought I was going to cry. I wasn't ready for any of this. Why was I such a baby? I got in the car. The old Chevy station wagon had big bench seats. Patrick hopped in the other side and revved the engine. He reached under the seat between his legs and fished out a little bottle, uncapped it and took a long swig. "One for the road!" he said. Before he pulled out, he reached his arm around my waist like a giant hook and just reeled me in, until my body was pressed up close. He had one arm around me and the other hand on the wheel as we took off down the street going northwest. I thought he must be going around the block to turn around, to head east down Mass Ave. He kept going.

"I live in East Mapleton. You're going the wrong way," I said nervously.

"Ha! Very funny!"

"What's funny?"

"We're not going home yet, you dope. I took you out to a great party, showed you a goodtime..." He turned his head sideways towards me-instead of the road- with an angry look contorting his baby-face. I gripped the seat and stepped on an invisible brake. After a few turns, he suddenly swerved over to a deserted street, overlooking a park. He cut the engine and things happened fast.

"Come on, baby, give Patty a little kiss."

"What? I don't even know you!" I said rationally. He seemed to have grown an extra pair of hands.

"Jus one lil kiss..."

"Alright, just one and then we go," I negotiated. He was right: I was a dope.

"Sure, sure baby! Jus one..."

He pressed his mouth on mine, opened it like a mason jar and jammed his tongue down my throat. I'd heard all about French kissing. This was it? I gagged; his breath stank of beer. I pushed his face away, turned my head and managed to break the airtight seal. "OK, let's go now," I said, thinking I'd kept my part of the bargain.

"Whah-the-hell? Com' on, Franny! You're an Italian girl, ain't ya?" Patrick said with a leering grin.

It was dark, but I could see that the hard liquor he'd just guzzled had kicked in. He was even more out of control. He ignored my request and dove in for another round, this time putting all his weight on me until I was almost lying on the bench seat. He groped my breast but quickly lost interest, and decided to get straight to the heart of the matter. He wrested up my dress and got his hand between my legs. I felt his stubby, fleshy finger poking aimlessly around my thighs, like a little blind mole. Then I knew it wasn't a finger. Patrick Shanahan had a penis that was barely the size of a man's thumb-not that I had any basis for comparison. I thought of the anatomical drawing of the male torso with the tiny hotdog sticking out of it.

"No!" I yelled, and started slapping him on the head so hard it hurt my hands.

"Chris...I'm only havin' lil fun," he slurred. "Ss-naw-lik I-wss gonna do it."

"If you don't stop I swear to God I'll bite your nose off!" I screamed at him.

Patrick pulled away sharply and flopped back against the driver side door. I caught a glimpse of his pathetic pink thing, and what little I saw reminded me of a hairless newborn rodent. He quickly put his hand over it and did what I assumed was jerking himself off. It took about four seconds. I could tell because he made a funny face and then panted a bit. "Stupid bitch," was all he said as he fumbled for the door handle in the dark, and then tumbled out of the car onto the grass, puking like a dog on his hands and knees.

I clutched my purse and jumped out of the car. The park was at the top of a hill overlooking the Boston skyline. I couldn't run. It was too steep, so I walked quickly, looking back over my shoulder. I made it two long blocks to the bus stop on Massachusetts Avenue, but I didn't feel safe until I was on the bus heading towards Boston. I needn't have worried. Patrick had passed out in his own vomit, although I wouldn't know until much later that night.

Meanwhile I sat on the bus, unconcerned with where it was going so long as it took me in the opposite direction of Patrick Shanahan. I was still shaken and disgusted. I was also utterly and completely bullshit. I was bullshit with that pig, Patrick, with the other jerks at the party, and with my own naïve stupidity. I was mad at my parents too, for not knowing Patrick was a complete jackass, and for not telling me what to do or even what to watch out for. I was even mad at Sister Agnes! Patrick only wanted to take me out because he thought Italian girls did things Irish girls wouldn't do-or maybe because he had more respect for Irish girls and wouldn't try something like that with one of his own. It was blind prejudice. When he was eager to leave the party, I mistakenly, stupidly thought he wanted take me home. I didn't see it coming. I missed all the signs.

Now what? If that was what dating was all about, I never wanted to go on another date again. There really must be something wrong with me. I tried to reason it out. Patrick was vile, but then I wasn't attracted to most boys-only the boys that everyone else seemed to think were gay. Well, not all of them; I hadn't been attracted to George Goldenberg-but that was back in eighth grade. I was a kid then. My thoughts ran round like a hamster in a wheel, and were just about as pointless. One thing I knew for sure: boys' *mm-mms* were nasty.

Oh my God! I'd flunked the love-boat test! I came to the conclusion that I must be a lesbian after all, and almost cried right there on the bus. What would I do? I wasn't cut out to teach physical education! My parents would be so disappointed...maybe I could become a nun?

The air brakes puffed and squeaked as the bus stopped to pick-up passengers. I was sitting by the window with my head sharply angled, looking at the traffic so I wouldn't have to look at people.

"Hey, Frances!"

I turned towards the familiar voice. Maddy sauntered down the aisle as the bus pulled back into traffic, walking like a sailor onboard a swaying ship without hanging on to the poles. I had to smile. If I tried that I'd fall on my ass. She slid in beside me.

"Where're you off too, all alone?" She was in good spirits.

"I'm going home. You?"

"I'm goin' to meet Linda in town, have a few drinks. Ah…Frances? What the hell's the matter? You look like shit." She spoke softly and with genuine concern. I looked into her face and the tears welled up. I wiped them with the back of my hand and sniffed.

"Oh Maddy," I whispered. "I went on my first date, and it was ter…ter…terrible!" I hid my face on her shoulder and wept.

"Jeez, Frances," she patted my hand. "That date must 'ave really sucked. Wait; did some asshole hurt you? Ya know, try anything…"

"Nooo…well, sort of." I sniffed. "I can't talk about it here," I whispered.

"Who was the guy?" she demanded.

"Patrick Shanahan, but…"

"Shanahan…hmm; don't know 'im. But you point him out and Tommy and me can pay him a call."

"Shh." I shook my head no.

"You sure? You sure you're alright?"

I nodded yes, and tried to look alright.

"OK…whatever you say." She shrugged. "Hey, why don't you come into town with me? Linda likes you a lot-it'll be great!"

It was providence. My first date was a fiasco. I was sitting alone on a bus, contemplating whether I could enter the convent to avoid becoming a lesbian, and my dear queer cousin turns up and invites me to a gay bar.

"Sure…why not! What the hell!"

The bus went to the train station, and we took the Mass Transit into town. When we climbed the stairs and emerged from the subway, Linda was waiting under the starry night sky. The mood was festive. There were people everywhere out to have a good time. Maddy rushed up to Linda but came to an abrupt stop, just short of the embrace I could all but see in her heart. They discreetly clasped hands for a moment then broke free.

"You remember Frances?" Maddy asked Linda.

"Sure I do." She smiled sweetly. "How are ya doin' sweetheart?"

"Fine, thank you," I said formally, out of habit.

"Com' on," Maddy propelled me along with one hand on my back and the other behind Linda. "Frances had a rough night," she told her quietly. "Some asshole gave her a hard time on a date."

"Oh, I'm sorry, hon'" Linda said.

What a sweet girl. I could only imagine what kind of experiences she had with men, and here she was comforting me. We walked a ways and turned down a few streets, and I didn't know exactly where we were or where we were going. Then we arrived at a green painted door with a sign over the top, *Alley Katz Bar and Grill.*

Inside, the hits of the seventies played from a speaker, but at least the volume wasn't too loud. It was fairly packed, but the social hubbub was relaxed and subdued...even mellow. The smell from the grill made me realize I was very hungry.

"It ain't much, but it's home," Maddy said in my ear so as not to offend anyone. The tiny front room had a bar and was packed with people, mostly gay men, and a few large masculine-looking women; I thought they were women, anyway. Maddy exchanged smiles with most of the people she passed, and warm greetings with a few as we made our way to the back room, where there were some grimy red-vinyl booths with high backs. It was full of women, women who looked like women, and I think I saw some men in drag. The booths were all taken.

"Hey Maddy," a young woman called, motioning us over with her hand. She was with another girl, finishing a meal. The food was served on plastic plates with a blotter, and a couple of cold French fries lay in the grease. "Come and sit with us!"

"We're a friendly group," Maddy said as we squeezed in. "Room for everyone!"

"Who's your new friend?" one girl asked in a spicy voice. She wore a mini-skirt with a tight-fitting stretch top, and lots of jewelry. Her face was heavily made up.

"Sandy, Betts." Maddy looked at me and gestured to each girl in turn. "This is Frances; my oldest friend, from when we was just kids...my best friend, who happens to be straight-and also happens to be my cousin, but don't hold that against 'er either!" Everyone laughed and I joined in. Maddy continued. "She's adopted, thank God; she's not a Malone!" The girls looked at each other and laughed some more. I searched their faces; I didn't quite get the point. Maddy gave me her most winsome smirk, that funny half-grin I'd always loved, leaned in close to the company and spoke with an air of mystery, as if she were about to let us all in on a deep secret. "Us Malones are kinda screwed-up." She soon had the girls in fits of merry laughter.

A waiter in tight black jeans swished over. "Hi girls," he spoke in an overtly feminine voice and smiled sweetly. "Well look at you!" he addressed Maddy, putting his hand on his hip in hyperbolic amazement. "Four girls all to yourself-you dawg!" They had hardly finished laughing and now started up again. The waiter laughed along, then asked, "Whad'll it be?"

I suddenly realized I had only a few dollars on me. I'd thought I was going to a house party, then home. I discreetly opened my purse on my lap, and peeked into my wallet without taking it out. Maddy saw me. "I hadn't planned to go out on the town," I told the others, embarrassed.

"Your money's no good here!" she announced gallantly.

"You order for me, please," I said.

"OK Frances, what you need is a drink...let's see; I know you don't like beer." She looked at the waiter and smiled knowingly. "Bobbie, Frances will have a Kahlua and cream, please...she had a rough night with some jerk at a party," she added in an undertone.

"Oh, I'm sorry to hear that honey," he said, wrinkling his nose, and making the most marvelous gestures. "Straight boys can be such pigs!" Everyone laughed and I felt better all ready. "Are you all eighteen?" Bobbie winked at us as he asked. In 1974 the drinking age was eighteen, but it was pretty easy to go out for a drink if you were sixteen-some started at fifteen if they looked grown-up.

Before I could open my mouth Maddy broke in, "Of course she is-I can vouch for her. She left her ID in her other purse." Linda decided to have Kahlua too, and Maddy ordered a pitcher of beer to share with Sandy and Betts.

"What's Kahlua?" I asked.

"Oh, it's delicious. Very mild, like a coffee milkshake," Linda told me.

Bobbie brought the drinks first. We toasted Maddy. It was delicious! There was even whipped cream on top; I was hungry and thirsty so I guzzled it down. When the burgers and fries came, Maddy ordered another round of Kahluas for Linda and me.

The food was horrid-even worse than it looked. I nibbled politely on some French fries and took a few tiny bites of the burger. "You gonna eat that?" Maddy pointed to my plate after I'd stopped picking at the food.

"I think I'm finished...sorry, I guess I wasn't that hungry."

Maddy reached across the table, grabbed the burger and took a big bite. "Jeez, Frances! What are you always sorry for? Stop saying that!" She admonished me gently with her mouth full, then washed it down with more beer.

On the next round we drank to my first time at Alley Katz. Then Linda suddenly piped up, by way of conversation, "Frances is so smart! She gets real good grades at St. Anne's Catholic High-it's this real nice school!" Sandy and Betts looked at one another, speechless for a moment. Linda hadn't intended it, but the juxtaposition of my status as a Catholic school scholar and the celebration of my first time at a gay bar struck everyone as hilarious.

By the time Bobbie put the third Kahlua and Cream in front of me, I had a warm glow all over. I had no idea that one ounce of Kahlua contained as much alcohol as a glass of robust red wine; I'd never had more than a four ounce glass of Merlot with dinner. Multiple factors converged to bring the evening to its inevitable conclusion. I was unaccustomed to drink, and I hadn't eaten a full meal all day. Bobbie liked Maddy-she was a good tipper. The shots were generous.

Sandy and Betts said goodnight. I was sucking the last yummy drops of my drink through a straw, slurping loudly. I kind of waved bye-bye at them without coming up for air. Linda started giggling. Bobbie swished over again and smiled.

"You want another?" Maddy asked.

"No, she doesn't!" Linda said. "You already got the kid pie-eyed...she's shut off."

I looked from Maddy to Linda, then down into my glass of melting ice, which I poked with the straw. "I hate penishes," I blurted out.

"What?" Maddy grinned, not quite sure of what I'd said.

I licked my lips, swallowed, and tried again. "*Penisssez!*" I said too loud. "They're...yucky!"

"Do tell!" Bobbie said, as Linda pressed her hand over her mouth to suppress the giggles, and sputtered into her hand. Maddy wasn't laughing. She pulled out a twenty dollar bill and told Bobbie to keep the change. He took the hint and left.

"Com' on, kiddo," Maddy got up and hoisted me out of the booth. When I reached for my purse, I noticed that my bare legs had left sweaty impressions on the sticky seat.

"Oh, isn' tha' funny?" I pointed at the booth. I was unsteady on my feet, a whole new sensation, and Maddy put her arm around my waist to lead me outside into the beautiful summer night.

We sat on a bench in the Boston Common, with Maddy on one side and Linda on the other, looking at one another questioningly like a couple of concerned parents. "Frances...ah...what exactly happened with this Shanahan?" Maddy asked seriously.

"I dunno; he ashed me if I wanted to leave, and I thought he was takin' me home...then he stopped at the park and stuck his tongue down my throat-eeeehw! Then he pushed me backwards and rubbed his penish on my legs...I was afraid he was gonna put it imme...but he didn't 'cause I said I'd bite 'iz nose off!" After I finished the iteration, I promptly pitched forward and vomited violently onto the cement pathway, splashing my feet a little. I was wearing summer sandals. Linda got some Kleenex out of her purse and wiped my mouth, then dabbed the bits of vomit off my feet.

"What a piece of Irish crap!" Maddy was fuming.

"Yeah...there was somethin' about thah too," I interjected. "He thought I did...stuff...because I was Italian. He said, com' on, you're *I*talian, ain't you?'" Then I hid my face in my hands and cried it out.

"The thing of it is...Frances is...ah...special." I heard Maddy speak to Linda in a low tone, as if she thought I was probably too drunk or crying too much to follow. She rubbed my back as she talked. "She's real smart about some stuff, but with people, this kid's always been as innocent as a baby! My little sister's just the same-even worse. And they both got the biggest hearts-never would hurt no one. Frances was with us all through...when my mother...anyway, I hate it when people do dirt on her 'cause they think they can get away with it! This ain't the first time someone's hurt her." Maddy leaned over me towards Linda and lowered her voice to a whisper. "There was that nigger I told you about, and now this bastard...it was her first date too. It's the same with our Annie; kids always pickin' on 'er, and even that teacher-my Aunt Evelyn got that wacco canned, but Annie took it hard. Now there's a sin, if you ask me! Some people would say you and me was the worst sinners...maybe I am; but I never hurt no one for the hell of it. People like Frances and Annie are just...special; better than the rest of us. It's almost like they was too good for this shitty world. I'd like to go find that miserable prick and kick his sorry Irish ass."

I sat up, suddenly sober. "What time is it?!" No one had a watch, but there was a clock tower in sight.

"Oh, crap...it's two-twenty; what time did your folks expect you Frances?" Maddy asked.

"Not long after mid-night! Oh my God, they're going to kill me! And they'll be so worried...and disappointed...I'll probably be grounded 'til I'm eighteen, but it's the look on Dad's face that I can't bear to think about."

"Jeez, I'm sorry Frances; it's all my fault. I'll tell your Dad it's all my fault. Hey, maybe we should stop at a phone booth and call?"

"Oh, let's just go home. That way there'll be one big blowout instead of two."

We hurried down to the subway. The train was ready to leave, and our luck held out. We caught a direct bus at Alewife station and made it home in under a half-hour.

As Maddy walked me up the back stairs, I noticed that there was only one car in the driveway. My mother saw me coming and flung the door open. "Frances! My God, where have you been?" She pulled me inside and gripped both shoulders, peering into my face. I can't imagine what I must have looked like in the harsh light of the kitchen.

"It's all my fault, Aunt Ev..." Maddy began, but my mother couldn't have cared less what she was saying.

"Your father's been driving around Mapleton Heights looking for you since just after midnight. He found that horrid boy, drunk as a skunk at the park. Daddy shook the truth out of him and put the fear of God into him, I'll tell you! We're lucky he didn't break the kid's neck!"

I was dubious as to what sort of truth Patrick had come out with, but just then the phone rang.

"Joe, she's home! She's alright." Mom took her mouth away from the phone and told us, "Your father's at the police station." Then she spoke into the receiver. "Yes, tell the police it's OK, they don't have to come out...nothing happened." Then Mom cast me a worried look and covered the mouth piece with her hand so he couldn't hear. "You *are* OK, aren't you Fran? That boy swore on his life that nothing...*happened*."

"I'm OK, Mom. Nothing happened. Patrick got drunk and really fresh, and I kinda freaked out." I minimized the incident; there was no point in upsetting my parents any further and besides, I felt sure I'd never get into a situation like that again. I'd learned what to watch out for.

"She's fine, Joe. Come home."

Maddy tried to take the blame, but I wouldn't let her. "She didn't make me go into town, and she certainly didn't make me drink three Kahlua and Creams."

"Frances was kinda upset when I met her on the bus, so I thought I'd cheer her up. I didn't know how bad it was...didn't find out what a jerk the guy was until afterwards. Then the time just got away from us...I shoulda took her straight home in the first place. I'm sorry Uncle Joe...Aunt Evelyn."

"Where'd ya go drinkin'?" Dad wanted to know.

"A bar," I said timidly.

"Well, that much I figured out…where?"

"Alley Katz," I said.

"What kind of bar serves sixteen-year-olds?" Dad was indignant.

"A gay bar," I said in a tiny little voice. Dad's jaw dropped. "Don't worry," I said, "everybody was really nice to me."

"I'll bet!" he said sarcastically, but he wasn't as mad as I'd expected.

"I don't think that's what your father's worried about, Frances," Maddy said wryly.

"Oh…don't worry Mom and Dad; I'm not gay…not a lesbian…I don't want to have sex with girls." I still had a residual effect from the Kahlua and it made it easier to speak my mind. This was the first time I'd ever said the word sex in front of my father, and he looked a little uncomfortable. "I'm just not ready to have sex with boys either. Not for a long time," I said with surety. I loved Maddy, and I had great fun with those girls, but somehow I just knew. Someday when I was ready the right man would come along, someone quiet and kind, thoughtful and smart. I definitely wasn't gay.

"Not 'til you're married!" Dad insisted, picking up on the part about sex with boys.

"Of course, Dad." I wasn't a hundred percent sure about that, but I'd caused him enough grief for one night. "And when I get married," I assured him, "I'm going to marry a sweet, good, caring man…like you." It sounded sappy, but I meant every word.

Dad walked Maddy home. She told me later that he thanked her for taking care of me that night, for helping me forget all about that "slimy little mick." Then he told her it better not ever happen again. Then he hugged her goodnight.

42

As the beautiful summer waxed into a rare Indian summer, I entered my junior year at St. Anne's. I tried to reason with her, but Maddy was definitely not going back to school. She had fulltime work at the warehouse in Boston, and after work hung out in bars a lot-there was no other place to socialize. It didn't seem like much of a life to me, but Maddy was happier than she'd been in years, maybe in her whole life. Linda was really a great girl too, thoughtful and smart in her own way. They were fine people, and I thought they should be allowed to live out in the open like they did that one glorious day in P-town, maybe even get married someday. Then I laughed inside at what Sister Mary Katherine, who taught Catholic family life, would say if I ever expressed my views. What would she say if I told her about my night out at Alley Katz? That is, after I revived her from of a dead faint.

The semester was moving along unremarkably. Then just before Halloween, Annie contracted the mumps. Childhood mumps is not remarkable, but I remember it vividly. Two things happened. I got to experience what it was like to have my own pet rabbit. And I accidently found the old skeleton key that unlocked the door to the tower that had made me so curious for so long. Sometimes I wish I could go back and leave it under the radiator...if only it had slipped through the floor boards.

The doctor said Annie wasn't allowed outdoors for at least a week. I didn't mind feeding Flopsy. I did not enjoy crawling half-way into the hutch to scrape out the poop with an old paint scraper, but it was the stench of acrid, viscous male-rabbit urine that really got to me. Yuck! I couldn't wait until she was well again. By Halloween she was over the worst of it, but still had a sore throat and missed trick or treat. She never even complained about that, and only begged to go see her stinky old bunny. I actually tried to catch him-I thought maybe I could put the rabbit in a box and carry it over for a visit. He kicked wildly, scratched my arm, ran to the far end the hutch and stomped his back feet with a loud thump. I definitely did not have a way with animals.

Instead, we bought a real oil pastel crayon set at an art store, along with heavy paper and a little book, <u>Learn to Draw in Pastels</u>. We originally had it in mind for a Christmas present, but thought she really needed cheering up right now. Mom was concerned because Annie had lost a couple of pounds from her slender frame, so she made a big bowl of chocolate pudding.

When we arrived around the corner, I was relieved to find that Jack and Joanie had gone out for the day. Those two were so much alike; I always felt a vague chill in the air when they were at home. Before settling in the kitchen, we stopped and greeted Uncle Malone in his hovel of a little back parlor. He surprised us by grasping my mother's hand with his still functioning left hand, looking straight into her eyes and asking, "Hss my gal? Hss my gal been?" We were all flustered at this sudden burst of affection, and thought he must be very confused. It almost seemed as if he'd mistaken my mother for one of his daughters. Annie stood by him and smiled. It was perplexing; after he'd become ill she was inconsolable for a time. Now she often sat by him, talking and showing her drawings. I'd even seen him stroke her hair with his good left hand. Go figure! Well, sick or not, Uncle Malone still gave me the creeps.

At the sight of the rows of brilliantly colored pastels, Annie was awestruck. She was so taken with the gift that she opened the plastic wrapper, tore off a sheet of paper and started to draw straight away without a word, even forgetting to say the customary thank you. It was as if she lost sight of everyone in the room.

"Aren't you going to thank cousin Frances and Aunt Evelyn?" Maddy asked. Annie looked embarrassed at her omission, and thanked us politely before asking the general company if she might go to her room and draw. "Sure," Maddy said with a shrug. Without further ado, the child left with her new treasures, abandoning the bowl of pudding and leaving us standing there amused and a bit puzzled.

"Well, how do you like that?" Gramma said with a hint of a chuckle, but I could sense the underlying concern. "That child'll always need watching over," she added, looking from Maddy to me and back at Maddy. "Seems kind of odd...maybe we should've told her 'No, wait 'til later'; she doesn't seem to know how to behave-not that she means to hurt anyone's feelings," Gramma remarked.

Maddy's gray eyes always looked smokey, like storm clouds gathering, when she was worried or getting angry. She'd never come out and tell you how she felt, so you had to watch for the signs. "She just doesn't get it. You have to explain every little thing," she said.

"I think she's got an artistic nature," I offered. "She's thoughtful, and very caring in her own way. I remember back when I cried at my twelfth birthday and she got so upset, because she thought I was sad."

"Remember when she thought Tommy was going to toss me out the...window," Maddy said pointedly omitting the expletive.

"What's this now?" Gramma asked, naturally confused. My mother raised her eyebrows.

"We was havin' an argument-a long time ago now; it was nothing. I don't remember what upset him so much, but you know how Tommy gets. Ah...he told me to get out of his room or else he'd throw me out the window," Maddy explained. "Annie heard it and ran out the door, straight out into the cold without a coat. So Frances finds her there, staring up at the window-she got the right one too, even with all the windows in all the rooms in this old place!" I hadn't thought of that, but now it was pointed out, I saw it was very clever, and fast too.

"Glory be!" Gramma exclaimed. "She didn't want to miss the show, eh?"

"No! That wasn't it at all," I explained. "She was concerned, afraid to even take her eyes away from that window. I asked, 'What are you doing?' She glanced over at me and explained calmly that Tommy was going to throw Mad'lin out...I've got to tell you," I said, looking at Mom and my aunt with a smirk, "she repeated, 'Tommy's gonna throw Mad'lin out the f___ing window. I'm gonna catch her.'"

"Frances!" Mom admonished, even though I didn't actually say the whole word.

"Oh, ho-ho! Oh my!" Gramma Malone laughed like a Santa Clause.

"It's not like she doesn't care about others," I finished.

"No, no, that's not it at all," Gramma agreed. "She loves deeply-very deeply; she reminds me of her poor mother, God bless her soul."

The conversation paused, and I decided to ask a blunt question, poke my nose a little bit into my extended family's business. "Does Annie ever talk about her mum?"

"Sometimes, but not how you'd think," Gramma said. "She doesn't cry, or say she misses her mother. She just talks about her like she was in the next room-talks about what her mum might be doing in heaven with her little sister. Come to think of it, she told me that little Immaculé gets to go out and play with baby Jesus now."

"Oh, isn't that sweet," Mom said, but I think she was trying to be polite. It sounded like something a five year old would say.

Gramma continued, "So I asked her, 'Where do they play? In the clouds,' she says, pointing up at the sky-we were comin' out of mass, and there were big white clouds. So I says, 'Are you sure? How do you know?' And you know what she says? 'Oh, I see 'em sometimes, playin' up there. Jesus can fly, and baby Immaculé too, because she has wings now. She's an angel.'"

Maddy and I excused ourselves to go see what Annie was up to. She lay stretched out on the floor and worked her new crayons, blending the colors together with her little fingers, and oblivious, or at least unconcerned with our presence. I hadn't been upstairs in the girls' bedroom for a long time. Everything looked a bit smaller; thankfully, the potty chair was gone. Ever since Eddie moved out, Maddy had her own room, but still had to get up for Annie's night terrors, sometimes more than once in the same night. That's how she discovered the ghost at last, the one Annie had been frightened of all these years.

"I almost crapped myself!" Maddy exclaimed. "You should have seen her-all in white with long flowing white hair sticking out!" Maddy gestured with her hands for emphasis. "She just stared off past me like I wasn't there!"

It wasn't a ghost at all. It was Gramma Malone roaming the house in her full-length white nightgown, with her long hair unleashed from its customary bun. She was a sleepwalker. That explained why she always slept so much during the day. After that, Maddy got up to watch her whenever she heard her out of bed. Gramma had a brass ring with a couple of skeleton keys to let herself up to the third half-story, locking the doors behind her. They could hear the keys rattle like the chains of a condemned spirit.

"Jesus, Mary 'n Joseph! How does she manage the keys in her sleep?" I asked incredulously.

"Beats the hell out of me! I tried following her once and she whirled around and pointed a flashlight in my face and just stared like some devil. Christ, no wonder the kid was scared!"

"That's the light I see sometimes when I look out our kitchen window! Your grandmother must climb up that tower in the middle of the night. My dad even saw it," I said in an awed whisper.

"Why didn't you tell me before?"

"I didn't know for sure who was up there. I figured you all knew what you were doing. Besides, it was none of my business."

I sat down on the floor beside Annie and peered over her shoulder to admire the drawing. She was gripping a scarlet crayon, and her fingers were caked with pigment. The picture was of a child with something red in her hand. I couldn't make it out.

"Is it an apple?"

"Nope."

"A red ball?"

"Uh-uh," she shook her head no.

"What is she holding?"

"The girl got her period, and took off her panties to hide them in the closet," she explained.

Maddy and I looked at each other, and she said, "Jeez, not this again," so softly Annie didn't seem to hear.

"Oh, she doesn't need to do that," I comforted. "You just wash them in the sink and put them into the washing machine. If they won't come clean, you just throw them away. It happens sometimes."

"Nooo you can't," she insisted. "Daddy will get mad if you throw out your panties. That's why Tommy hides his in the closet." After making this startling revelation, the child who saw Jesus and her dead infant sister playing hide 'n seek in the clouds blithely continued to color. I suddenly felt like I was listening to Auntie Joan all over again, and my stomach fluttered with angst.

Behind her, Maddy signaled confusion, turning both palms-up while silently intoning, "Whah-the-hell?"

I shook my head no, to indicate that we should think very carefully before we said or did anything. Now there was no doubt in my mind that something was wrong with Annie, something that needed expert attention. I'd speak to my mother later in private. For the time being, I decided to sit quietly and watch her for a while without further comment.

From my vantage point on the floor I could see under the furniture. It was unbelievably filthy. Whoever cleaned up seemed to forget that it might be necessary to pass a broom or a mop under the dresser or bedstead once a year, whether it needed it or not. There were long lost articles of clothing caked with dust, as well as bits of things like parts of toys or stray pencils. Across the room I saw a coin under the radiator. It was a tall, iron-gray forced hot-water type, and made a sound like ballpeen hammers on a steel drum when the heat went on. It had thick layers of black dirt caked in between the coils, while the dust underneath looked as though it had rested peacefully undisturbed for decades.

Indeed it had; and if it weren't for the light shining through the window at just the right angle, it might have remained untouched until the Malone Mansion itself turned to dust. But Maddy decided at that moment she needed a smoke. She shoved back the curtain and banged the double-hung wood-framed window a few times with her fist. Whether from heat or cold, they always seemed to stick. Then she leaned back out of the draft to get it lit, and when she did, I saw the key. The blackened old skeleton key balanced almost vertically against one of the radiator coils, camouflaged to match with a patina of grime. If

I had stood up only seconds earlier, I wouldn't have seen it. I quietly rose and moved closer to look.

"What are you doing?" Maddy asked, although she didn't sound very interested.

"Ah, I think there's a quarter or something under there," I said casually. I didn't want Annie to know what I'd found, so I determined to tell Maddy later.

"Uh-huh," she said, blowing smoke out the window.

I squatted down to stick my fingers carefully in-between to grasp it, but before I reached the key I saw another. It was lodged adjacent to the pipe that came up through a hole in the floorboards, wedged right in behind it, in what looked like a deliberate hiding place. I caught my breath, and decided to go for the coin instead, to buy time. It was a nickel, so worn and black I couldn't make out the year.

"Well?" Maddy asked.

"I found a nickel," I said cheerfully as I stood up and displayed the filthy coin.

"Great. Now you're rich," she said sarcastically.

"Very funny. I've got to go wash my hands," I added, holding up my dirty hands. I could scarcely contain my excitement. As soon as Annie got over her mumps I'd get Maddy alone and tell her what I'd found. I hoped one of the keys would unlock the door to the tower. I hoped Maddy would let me in on the adventure if it did. For a moment I felt just like a kid again.

43

The mild October had sent a glorious autumn, bursting orange and red with everything cast in a golden light, like a sunset in every tree. That made it all the more sorrowful when a harsh wind blew up from the east and snatched it away, stripping the branches cold and naked by mid-November. Winter snuck up when no one was looking and smacked us with a solid frost, even before Thanksgiving. We were in for a rough ride, one helluva cold winter. We didn't know it yet, but this year the frigid weather wouldn't break until February. As soon as the sun went down the temperature plummeted; at barely five-thirty it was already pitch dark. The darkness would only descend earlier each day from then on, 'til late December. To me it always felt suffocating, like being rolled up in a rug.

Maddy looked like a three day old birthday balloon when she turned up at the backdoor one Friday night, shivering in the sudden cold snap. Dad welcomed her inside and asked, "Why the long face?"

She mumbled something about failing the road test...again. Last spring semester in tenth grade, Maddy had stayed in high school for the sole purpose of taking driver's education for free. The instructor was an asshole. The man obviously didn't like the looks of her. When they went out on the road, he let the two boys in her group have practically all the driving time. She hardly got behind the wheel, and they laughed at her mistakes besides. She'd failed her first road test. She also made good on her promise to quit school for good without finishing her sophomore year.

"Don't worry," Dad said, patting her on the back of her leather jacket with a hearty slapping sound. "Lots of people flunk a few times-it don't mean you won't turn out to be a good driver."

We were having hot-dogs and beans for supper. Mom got right up and set a place for Maddy, but instead of digging in with the usual gusto, she chewed slowly, and absently made patterns in the baked-beans with her fork. Then she sat up straight and cleared her throat to speak. "Uncle Joe, will you teach me to drive?" I never heard her ask my folks for anything. It sounded like it meant the world to her.

"Sure, sure I will!" Dad said enthusiastically without the slightest hesitation. "We'll start tomorrow. I'll teach you on the Mustang...when we're done, Mario Andretti will have nothin' on you!"

"Wow! The Mustang? Standard transmission and all? Cool!" Maddy jumped up and threw her arms around my Dad's broad shoulders. "Thanks Uncle Joe, you're the best!"

I was so happy for Maddy I wasn't even jealous, though I did wonder why I never got to drive the Mustang; come to think of it, I'd never asked. I guess I just assumed I wouldn't need to learn the standard. I drove the Buick, Mom's car. It still ran great and looked gorgeous, but it was a Buick, a middle-aged gentleman of a four-door sedan.

The Mustang was Dad's car, and brand new last spring. This year, instead of the usual trade-off with Mom getting a new car and Dad using the old one for work, they bought Dad a Mustang. Mom said that in their entire marriage, he'd never asked for anything just for himself. She was only too happy to see him enjoy it. Mom was getting worried about Dad, and remarked that he seemed down in the dumps sometimes. He was showing his age and tired more easily. The work he'd done all his life was growing harder. I overheard him remark to his buddy Stan that compared to when he was young, it was like doing it all with a fifty pound sack on his shoulders.

Dad lit up like a teenaged boy over that sea-foam blue Mustang, and it energized him a bit. He had cheered up Maddy with his generous offer, but I think he was just as excited. He was already talking the fine points of the Mustang, how it handled, kind of warming up for tomorrow. They were having a great time. When Dad explained that driving an automatic wasn't really driving, I decided I just had to learn to drive a standard too. I'd ask him to teach me how to drive the Mustang, but it could wait. At least I already had my license.

The next day Maddy turned up at 9:00 am. Dad hadn't even finished his Saturday breakfast before she was on the back stoop, shivering in the frigid morning. I guess they hadn't established a time, and she didn't want to keep him waiting. Mom let her in, and offered her some bacon and toast. Dad was grinning from ear to ear at her childlike enthusiasm. He was exhausted, but gearing up to go out in the cold for her. Mom rolled her eyes behind Maddy's head in a look that said 'can you believe this kid?' Dad gave her a sly wink.

"Madeline, dear, why don't you let me lay that on the radiator, lining-side down, so it'll be warm when you go out?"

"Thank you Aunt Evelyn," she answered politely as she shed the jacket and trustingly handed it over. Underneath she wore a couple layers of t-shirts and a heavy flannel. My parents never mentioned Maddy's penchant for male clothing. After the dress incident of 1971, Mom dropped the subject once and for all. We didn't discuss my cousin's obvious butch presentation, and they didn't ask prying questions about girlfriends. Mom truly lived by the credo, 'Treat people decently and don't talk about their differences; mind your business.' Of course, I would never divulge Maddy's personal confidences to me, and my parents respected my privacy.

"All set to go?" Dad asked, coming back from the bathroom. He seemed to go a lot now. Time was when he was always ribbing me and Mom for stopping to tinkle before we went out anywhere, or right when we got back. Once I tried to turn the tables and joked, 'Again Dad?' as he got up during a commercial break. When his back was turned, Mom made a serious face at me and shook her head 'no'. I felt sheepish, but wasn't sure what I'd done wrong. How was it different from his teasing? I mouthed the word 'sorry' and never mentioned it again. I didn't understand, because nobody spoke about prostate health. To mention the functioning of men's *mm-mm*s was completely taboo, so poor Dad must've been mortified.

Maddy got all zipped up and ready for her adventure. "You comin' Frances?" she asked. Dad looked over her head at me. I'd known him all my life, and though it would be hard to describe it, he let me know nonverbally that it might be better for Maddy if I sat this one out. It made sense; she'd been so embarrassed in front of those boys, and her confidence needed building.

"Gee, I'd luv to, but I'm slammed with homework," I said truthfully. The little bit of apprehension dissipated from her face.

"Oh, I forgot!" Dad said, as he was about to open the backdoor. "Fran, could you back the Buick out?" In the game of musical cars, it was hard to keep track of what went out last. Sometimes you just looked out to the driveway, which was flush to the house, to see what was parked where.

"OK," I said, moving towards the door.

"Get your coat."

"I'm coming right back in..."

"It's cold; you'll need it."

"OK." I grabbed a wool jacket out of the closet and had it half on when he opened the door. There was an arctic blast. "Holy Crap! It's below freezing already? I gotta have gloves-Maddy, I'll get some for you. Dad, have you got your gloves yet?"

"Don't need 'em, thanks, and she's gotta grip the wheel. No gloves...but don't worry, we'll get the heat going. She's got a great heater," Dad said, referring to the car like a new girlfriend. As we filed out the door, he handed me the keys to the Buick and said, "Wait 'til we get out, then bring it back under the carport and let it warm up a bit for Mum; she's got some errands."

I jumped into the cold leather front seat and it sent shivers from my ass to my skull. I hated the cold with a passion. I'd always hated the cold: the cold, damp, gray, rainy, shitty New England weather. I usually spent at least eight months of every year complaining about it.

Even though it was just below freezing, the Buick revved up without hesitation. Dad kept it finely tuned, with all its fluids checked, stuff I knew nothing about. I roared backwards down the narrow driveway with scarcely a look over my shoulder, and parallel parked by the curb in one smooth move. I heard the Mustang's engine turn over, cough and go silent. It happened again, and I realized that Dad must have insisted Maddy drive from the get-go. She was so nervous that she was having trouble starting it. Then there was the inevitable stall-out as she tried to let off the clutch. Yikes! Now I felt like a jerk for showing off. After all, I didn't know how to use the clutch either. The Mustang's engine stalled so many times I thought he'd have the sense to give up, and at least take it out for her, but finally, she started rolling backwards. Then the car bucked as her foot came off the clutch too fast, and it stalled out again. Maddy must've been dying of embarrassment. I was just about to get out, sashay up to the window and with all the feminine finesse Mom had taught me, smilingly ask if perhaps maybe it just might be a little more comfortable if they kinda began the lesson driving forward? Just then the Mustang zoomed down the drive, sailed backwards across the street and up into the neighbor's driveway before screeching to a stalled-out stop. Thankfully, the neighbors only had one car, which was pulled up close to their house and so avoided collision. Thankfully, I'd remained safely in the Buick and didn't get run down in my own driveway. I smiled and waved as if nothing unusual happened when I pulled past them into the driveway, and ran into the house without looking back. I forgot to leave the engine idling to warm it up for Mom's shopping.

44

"He's comin' home. Danny's comin' home at last...I...I was afraid I wouldn't live to see the day." The Malone Matriarch addressed my father with the weak voice of a frail old woman. Then the great wall of stubborn stoicism gave way at last to an avalanche of tears. It marked the end of an era.

She was eighty-three, and I'd seen her stand strong for nearly five years, holding the shaky family together with her Irish teeth. It was unsettling to see her like that-not that she didn't deserve a good cry. The poor old soul had lost her husband and daughters long ago, and spent so many years alone. She shared her roof with a surly alcoholic son and his ailing wife, tended the sick and buried the dead who should have been burying her someday instead. Now after more than sixteen years in prison, Daniel Maddox Malone was coming home. He had been her favorite son, the one who'd always looked after her. The separation had hurt like death. His imminent return was met with joy, as if for the Resurrection itself.

"You'll still have plenty of time with 'im...you're not going anywhere for a while." Dad hiked the kitchen chair closer with a scrape and comforted her with his arm around her shoulders. "Look on the bright side," he added. "Danny will be home for Christmas!" At this Gramma burst out crying all over again, whether from happiness at the thought or sorrow at all the Christmases he'd missed, I couldn't say. Mom presented a lovely floral box of scented Kleenex and hovered by, looking uncomfortable. Gramma sniffed and wiped her eyes.

"Joseph, I hate to impose, but...can you take me over to...to bring him home? I'm too old to go alone; there's no one else I'd even think of asking."

"Of course, Aunt Hannah! Be glad to-no trouble at all," Dad assured.

"Thank you, God bless you." She blew her nose loudly and sniffed a bit. "Oh, isn't that nice? These tissues smell like flowers...I'd forgotten how good flowers smell. It's so damned cold this year. We've been locked in a hard frost since November! Did you hear the Middlefield River is covered in ice this year? I don't remember the last time that happened. The kids tried sliding on it. One fell through and drowned." She shook her head sadly.

"Yes, I read that in the paper," Mom answered. "That's so sad. The kids aren't used to seeing the river iced over. Most years it doesn't stay cold enough, it's usually a pattern of freeze-thaw-freeze-thaw. They don't understand that the ice is still thin over moving water…"

"Yeah, it's froze solid by the riverbank. White solid; but it's all black down the middle. You can see the water running under the ice. You don't ever walk out on black ice," Dad carried on the conversation.

"Feels like there's no end to this cold-snap in sight. Feels like spring will never come," Gramma said. "It's so sad he missed the warm weather. Think of all those years with no flowers." She began to weep again.

I was standing in plain sight, so I guessed the news was no secret. I considered whether I should leave the kitchen, like I had all my life when grownups discussed serious things. On impulse I quietly pulled up a chair and sat like I intended to stay. When no one asked me to go to my room, I wondered a moment if they hadn't noticed me.

Then Dad said cheerfully, "This isn't a time to be sad; he's coming home. This calls for a drink." He rose and went to the cupboard.

"Oh, you know I don't drink, Joseph," Aunt Hannah said, forcing a smile and carrying on the longtime banter between them.

"Well it's about time you started!" he retorted, trying to buoy her.

"Humph. I hadn't looked at it that way. I suppose it's never too late for one more bad habit," she said with a chuckle.

"That's the spirit, Aunt Hannah!" Dad got the little bottle of fancy whiskey and set it on the table, followed by three tiny cut-crystal shot glasses. "Sit down, Ev." He motioned to my mother.

"It's not even five o'clock yet," Mom groused; she wasn't much of a drinker.

"It's Saturday. Besides, it's after five somewhere," he said mischievously as he poured one full glass and two half full.

Mom didn't sit. I had a funny feeling that it was out of protest. She was uncomfortable at the idea of welcoming home a convicted felon. I could understand her point-there was a child living in the home; but Mom didn't know the half of it. I hoped Danny's homecoming would be an improvement. I looked to Dad for guidance. If he rejoiced with Gramma, it must be the right thing to do. Dad met my eyes across the table, as if he'd just noticed I was there. He slid the little glass that held a thimble full of drink in front of me with a wink and a smile, then raised his high. The whiskey glowed warm amber in the kitchen light. I followed suit, and Gramma grasped her glass and lifted it carefully. I noticed a slight tremor.

"To Danny Malone! A warm welcome home and a many years to come!" Dad's robust voice rang out and I felt secure, sure he'd always be there and always know just what to do.

"To Danny Malone," I said proudly, and tossed it back as I'd seen done many times. It was my first real taste of whiskey; that dreadful stuff Tommy had in the flask didn't count. The smooth spirits went down easy, and a warm glow spread over me, though I doubt it was from the few drops in the glass.

"To Danny!" Gramma blinked back the tears and took a sip. "Hmm, that's not bad at all." She held the glass to the light to study it before finishing off the rest. Then she turned to me with a smile, and reached over to pat the back of my hand. The chiseled features had softened like weathered stone, but she was still unmistakably herself. Her pale blue eyes seemed ancient as she looked me up and down, through my insides and back again. "What a fine young lady you turned out to be, Frances," she determined with surety.

"Ain't she?" Dad affirmed.

"Yes," Mom interjected. "We're very proud; we couldn't have asked for more."

My mother's words flew straight into my heart and it almost skipped a beat. I'd waited my whole life for them, for what every adopted child longs to hear. I wasn't the consolation prize any longer; I was the coveted convertible behind door number one. It was like coming home again for the first time.

45

W e usually don't get snow in November, unless it's just a dusting. This year we were in for a white Thanksgiving. Mom said she wasn't really in the mood to cook for the whole clan, but felt it was the right thing to do. Aunt Hannah just couldn't manage it. Without Mom, the kids wouldn't have a turkey again. "I'd feel guilty all year if I didn't have them over," she sighed.

I helped her stuff a twenty-four pound turkey the night before, so we could start it cooking early in the morning. We had to; the thing was so big it would take all day to cook. After performing a team-lift to get the heavy roasting pan to the oven-rack, we found out it didn't fit into the oven.

"Shit!" Mom hissed. "I can't get the damned bird into the oven!"

Dad looked up from his paper, surprised and tickled at her outburst. "Ha ha ha!"

"I think we have to take some of the stuffing out," I offered.

"It's the height of it-the breastbone is touching the top, but I guess you're right. It'll probably go down if we un-stuff it a bit. What a pain in the ass!"

Dad was still chuckling as he got up and lifted it off the rack, and carried it with ease back to the countertop. After we pulled some stuffing out, we were able to mash it into the oven. Mom said that it had better shrink as it cooked, or else we couldn't get in there to baste it.

At two-thirty, Dad drove around the corner to fetch Gramma and Uncle Tom in the Buick. I guess Maddy thought it would be fun to climb through the back fence and roll down the snow covered hill. Annie followed suit, and surprisingly, so did Tommy. We watched out the window as they had so much fun, they did it again. Then Maddy and Tommy had a snowball fight while Annie was over tending Flopsy.

"Honestly," Mom said. "You'd think they'd be too old for that...and now they're going to traipse into the house with all that snow..."

"Shh; they're coming to the door," I whispered. "Mom, is something the matter?" I hadn't seen her that grouchy since Nana lived here. I'd almost forgotten how irritable she used to be. Mom just shook her head no, and then quickly assumed a broad holiday smile. Dad was back. The Malones were at the door.

Jack Mack was with them; we hadn't been sure if he would come along. Jack wasn't specifically invited, but Dad had extended the invitation to "The whole gang," as he put it. It was a bit awkward. My parents did not like the man, and they were scandalized by what appeared to be going on with Joanie. One night at the supper table, Dad even stated outright that he disapproved of Joanie, "Behaving as man and wife...living in sin." I think he didn't want me getting any ideas.

Disapproval notwithstanding, once Jack was in the door, Dad treated him like family. He took all the coats and asked them to be seated. "Whad'll ya have?" Dad offered Jack a drink. "We got Budweiser, red wine, white wine...I got some Four Roses too..."

At that Jack raised his index finger and nodded curtly, a gesture better suited to a waiter than a host. "Straight up!" he demanded, making matters worse.

"Comin' right up!" Dad said jovially. Mom and I made eyes at each other. Joanie jumped up and approached Mom, looking embarrassed. She surveyed the stove, and gestured towards the many pots holding the gravy, squash, turnips and boiled potatoes.

"What can I do, Auntie?"

"No, you're my guest."

"It's too much! I want to help," Joanie spoke with sincerity.

"Well, it isn't all going to fit on the table, so I guess we'll have to fix the plates at the counter and bring them over."

Our eat-in kitchen barely accommodated the clan. Even with the extra leaf in the table, there was just no room for anything but the dinner plates. We had to serve them restaurant style. Maddy jumped up and offered to help too. "Thank you, Madeline, but we'll be tripping over each other," Mom explained. It was very true.

"Then Tommy 'n me 'll wash the dishes, right Tommy?" She slapped him on the back.

"Sure," he said with a shrug. His face was still red from getting hit with snowballs-Maddy had a good arm for throwing. Tommy looked happier than I'd seen him in a while; come to think of it, I hadn't seen him at all for some time.

Even though we went regularly to mass and I attended Catholic school, we weren't overtly religious at our house. Nonetheless, we always said grace at holiday meals. When Dad asked Gramma Malone to do the honors, Jack reluctantly laid down the fork he'd been shoveling into his mouth with an audible clink. He folded his hands, but looked blatantly annoyed. I was royally pissed now. It was bad enough that he was a foul-mouthed, gun-toting, tyrannical, lying, cheating, pimping, drug-dealing bastard; now he'd insulted my parents in our home. I decided that I disliked him more than anyone I'd ever met in my life. I was too busy hating Jack Mack to hear a word of the grace performed by my Aunt Hannah, and just mumbled amen along with the others.

Before she had anything to eat, Maddy cut up the turkey for her father as if for a small child-he couldn't manage it himself anymore. Uncle Tom chewed with his mouth open and dropped food on his lap.

By the time I sat down to eat I was exhausted. We'd been making Thanksgiving happen all morning, and ever since last night. We served apple cider, and Mom and Dad had a glass of white wine. Dad made the mistake of asking if everyone had enough to drink, and Jack spoke up. "Hit me," he said. Before everyone else was half-way through with their meal, Jack had put his away. He stood abruptly and announced he was going outside for a smoke. I think I actually saw Mom bite her tongue. "You comin'?" Jack directed towards Tommy and Maddy. Joanie was in the middle of serving, so he ignored her.

"Ah, no thanks," Maddy said, trying to convey a look of disgust. Tommy looked to her for a cue, then silently shook his head no. The back door was right behind Dad's chair, and when Jack opened it a blast of cold air swept across the table and blew his paper napkin onto the floor. Jack didn't even shut the door behind himself. I jumped up to close it and slammed it much harder than I'd intended. Everyone went silent. I stood there and hoped Jack might fall on the ice and break his neck, or with any luck catch pneumonia and die.

During the uncomfortable lull in the conversation, we could all hear Uncle Tom chewing. Throughout the meal he'd been intently focused on his dinner; he was never much of a talker, but his complete silence was decidedly awkward. He didn't even compliment the food. "I think that white meat is a little dry for him," Mom remarked to Aunt Hannah, probably because of the loud chewing. She got the gravy boat and walked around to his side of the table. "Here Tom, let's try a little gravy," Mom addressed him in the tone reserved for infants and invalids. He looked up from his dinner and into her face, as if surprised to see her there. He swallowed, and wiped the food from his mouth with the back of his hand. Maddy snatched the napkin from his lap where she'd placed it, and stuck it in his left hand. Her father didn't use the napkin. He smacked his lips and struggled to speak. Mom stood patiently, considerately waiting-perhaps he didn't like gravy?

"*Mahrget*?" It was garbled, hard to make out. "Margret?" he asked again. This time we understood; he was looking for my dead grandmother, his own aunt, with whom he hadn't spoken over the last ten years of her life.

Mom looked flustered. "It's Evelyn, Tom."

283

Tom looked baffled, and studied the company seated round the table, slowly checking out each face as if expecting to find her. "Where's Margret?"

"Ah, she's not here..." Mom trailed off.

"Tom," his mother addressed her son. "Margret's passed away. Years ago now...don't you remember?" He appeared stricken by the news. "Margret's dead," Gramma said firmly.

Tom's lips worked silently for a moment, as if trying out the syllables before using them. "Margret's dead?" He suddenly dropped his fork to the floor and sobbed, drooling a little, too distraught even to cover his face with his good left hand.

46

Dad seized upon the early snowfall to teach Maddy and me one of the most important lessons of our lives: how to drive in it. The timing was perfect. I was on school break, Dad had the Friday after Thanksgiving off, and Maddy wasn't scheduled to work that long holiday weekend. As we'd wrapped up our very interesting family dinner, Dad lightened the mood by announcing the plan for the following day.

"You up for it?" He grinned.

"You bet!" Her face lit up.

After the shaky start in the driveway just a few weeks earlier, Maddy had mastered the manual transmission. She passed her road-test easily, after only half a dozen or so hours of intensive instruction from my dad. "She's a natural! She just needed to have her confidence built up a bit," he had remarked modestly.

I appreciated her accomplishment even more when it was my turn to try it. It was touch and go for a while, and I wasn't so sure the stick-shift was for me, but Dad pushed. I was glad I stuck with it; driving the Mustang was a blast!

The weather cooperated that night, sending sheets of freezing rain onto the existing snow; then the temperature dropped, forming a solid crust of ice over everything. "For the luva Mike!" Dad laughed when we got our first morning look out the window. Now the snow was packed with a hard, shiny shell that looked almost blue as it reflected the sun-rather like the pictures of the North Pole in National Geographic.

"Oh Joe, you're going to have to cancel this driving lesson-just look at that mess!" My mother was adamant.

"Naw, this is great! It's the whole point-just what the doctor ordered. We'll be fine, don't worry," Dad told her. She knew when he'd made up his mind about something.

We bundled up and went carefully out onto the snow covered stairs. I cleaned them off right away and then started to help Dad shovel the driveway, but not before I tried walking in the front yard where the snow was deepest. It was crusty on top, but still soft underneath. In some places it bore my weight, but in other places my feet randomly broke through. I remembered walking on this type of snow when I was little, still light enough to stay on the surface unless

I jumped hard to fall through the crust. The icy sheet over the driveway was so solid we had to stop and pour ice melt over it. Ah, winter in New England... Maddy turned up before we were finished, took the shovel from my hand and started scraping the ice. She dislodged a bit more than I had, but still not to the asphalt.

"To hell with it! Dad decided, plunging the blade of the shovel into a pile of snow. It was already after noon. "If we leave it sit a while, the ice melt will work better. Then I can scrape the sludge down to the tar with the heavy metal, curved shovel. I didn't think I'd need to bring that thing up from the basement this early in the year." He got into the driver's seat of the Mustang. "I'll get us out of here," he said. Maddy and I climbed into the back together.

My father drove us out of the neighborhood, past the projects and over towards the Middlefield River Bridge. I was already mentally prepared for the lesson; every winter since I could remember, my father had lectured from the front seat on the art of driving in New England weather. He told me how to drive in the pouring rain or a snowstorm, and how to drive on ice and snow. I'd heard all about driving on soft snow, packed snow, wet snow, and snow mixed with various kinds of ice, whether in daylight, dusk or in the blackest darkness.

"The worst kind of ice," my father told us as we neared the bridge, "is black ice. You have to watch out for it because you can't see it."

"How do you watch out for it if it's invisible?" Maddy asked.

"You learn what to look for. You have to watch for signs-not road signs, but clues, like when the road is wet from rain, or even exhaust in heavy traffic, and then the temperature drops like crazy around 5:00 o'clock; or when the snow piled by the side of the road melts a little during the day and leaves a puddle. Then it snaps cold and the edge of the road gets patches of black ice. And you always watch out on bridges! The pavement on a bridge will get slick before the road, because the cold air goes over and under-there's no ground underneath to hold the heat. So when it's wet or cold, you gotta let off the gas and be ready to maneuver. There used to be a sign on that bridge," he said, pointing up ahead. "It warned: Bridge Ices Before Road. Somebody crashed into it! Guess they didn't read it...and they never put up a new one. Now, in any kind of ice, the worst thing you can do is jam on the brakes. If ya do, you'll lose control, fish-tale, and next thing ya know, ya spin out like a top, just like drivin' a Zamboni! Ha ha ha!" There was almost no one else on the road, and he slowed to a stop as we approached. "I want yas to see somethin'," he explained. "The road's been plowed, but it's still slick. I'm gonna get 'er up to about thirty, put 'er in third gear right at the speed limit, and just drive over without slowing down, like some dumb you-know-what who don't know how to drive in weather," he added, looking over his shoulder at us with a wink and a smirk. "Watch what happens." He did just like he said and we started over the bridge. When we came near the arch in the bridge where the wind swept underneath, the back end of the Mustang fishtailed a bit. If you picture a fish swishing his tail wildly from side to side, that's what a car will do on an icy road. "Whoa!" Dad exclaimed in mock surprise. "What's happenin'?" He jammed on the brakes and the back end started to swing around. Maddy's eyes went wide and my heart kinda jumped, even though Dad knew what he was doing. Long before there was any danger of hitting the cement wall, he downshifted. The engine purred low as he slipped the clutch a bit to get even more torque, then instead of applying the brakes like you'd think, he gave her some gas to drive out of a potential wipe-out. The Mustang obediently straightened out, and rolled smoothly across the icy bridge that spanned the frozen river between West Middlefield and East Mapleton.

"Wow!" Maddy was impressed. I smiled proudly; I really had the coolest dad.

As soon as we were on the other side of the river, we passed *Pete's Last Stop,* the last bar as you left Middlefield, and an oasis for working men living in Mapleton, which was a dry town. Some liked to call it *Pete's First Stop*. It was also the place for underage smokers to score, since they had a cigarette vending machine that was outside by a backdoor, and the management didn't care. Mapleton was also one of the first towns to ban outdoor cigarette vending machines, something Maddy grumbled about from time to time. She could find her way to Pete's vending machine in her sleep.

"Now we go someplace safe where you can practice," Dad said, as he headed down obscure streets. As we went further into Middlefield, Maddy pointed towards a long row of triple decker flats, a dumpy looking rundown place full of kids running and sliding on the sidewalk.

"Linda lives down that way," she told us.

"Who's Linda?" Dad asked to make conversation.

"Just a friend of mine-someone I know from work."

"Hmm," he replied.

The residential area abruptly thinned out and we drove behind an old abandoned brick factory with smashed out windows, the kind of place you didn't want to go at night, or even in daytime. No one was hanging around that afternoon, probably because of the weather. The lot had been driven on as recently as last night, but hadn't been touched by a plow. It was a hard-packed slick surface, rather like an ice skating rink. Dad showed us some driving techniques, far more daring than on the bridge. There was really no danger if you stayed away from the building, and didn't go too fast. He warned us never to go faster than about forty miles per hour in similar road conditions on the high way, especially in poor visibility.

My father dispensed wisdom to match his skill behind the wheel. "Now, if ya can avoid goin' out when it's bad, do it! But if you're out already-and that's what will eventually happen-don't ever go faster than what's safe. What's safe is what you can handle comfortably. Never mind what other people are doing, and don't pay attention if some jerk is honkin' at ya. Put your flashers on and drive at the speed that feels right; just pull over and stop if you have to and let them go past. If someone wants to slide off the road, it's their tough luck."

We took turns driving the Mustang. I went first, and kept forgetting I was driving the shift, which was the whole point; you had so much more control, especially in snow and ice. My extensive experience driving the Buick actually got in the way as I struggled to maneuver on the snow. Dad insisted that I lose control on purpose to see what it was like, so I wouldn't panic if or when I skidded for real. Even though I had a clear area with nothing to hit, the skidding and fish-tailing unnerved me. I did finally get the hang of it.

"I'm done for today," I said. "Let's give Maddy a chance before it starts to get dark." It wasn't even three p.m., but in late November the sun only travels in a lonely little arc on the distant horizon. At about four-thirty-seven, it craps out completely; it's as dark as midnight.

The fact that Maddy had the benefit of watching me struggle might have had something to do with it, but she hit the gas and drove around like she'd been born driving on snow. She went in and out of fishtails, then Dad made her feel what it was like to jam on the brakes hard. We spun like a top. "Now do it again, but drive out of it," he instructed. She did it perfectly the first time. "Can you do that again?" he asked, thinking it might be beginners luck. She did, again and again. "Wow," he said. "Now keep goin' straight, like you was drivin' down a regular street, and when I say *now*, pretend a kid ran out in the road."

"What?!" I asked from the back seat.

"About how far in front of me?" Maddy understood right away that it was a test.

"Let's say…thirty feet. Any closer than that and it's in God's hands," Dad said.

"From which side?" She was eager for the challenge.

"Good question…say he's comin' from your right; it's always worse if somethin's comin' across your passenger side." She nodded as she gripped the wheel and bore down on the surface of the road with her smokey gray eyes. She was doing a bit over thirty, which seems fast in an empty lot.

"Now!"

Maddy jammed on the brake and the car went into a skid. She cranked the wheel hard to the right and the back end swung out-the opposite of what my dad just taught us. I thought she must've panicked. We were traveling nearly sideways when she downshifted and hit the gas, quickly pulling out of the spin and heading to the right at a sharp angle, almost off the imaginary road, before finally straightening out and coming to a complete stop. Then my stomach caught up with me.

"What the hell happened?" Dad exclaimed good humoredly. "The way we was swirling around on that ice...I felt like I was ridin' in a Zamboni while it was cleanin' off the skatin' rink! We gotta get you a job drivin' the Zamboni! Ha ha!"

"I missed the kid," Maddy calmly interjected. Dad stopped laughing and looked at her quizzically. "I knew I couldn't stop that quick on the ice," she explained, "I could feel it-so I drove around him. Almost went off the road-if there was a road, but I think I made it."

"Hmm; let's get out and have a look," he said. She shifted into park and they got out. I waited in the heated car. "Well I'll be damned!" I heard him declare. I cut the heater so I could be nosy and listen. "Here's where you hit the brakes," he pointed at the skid marks. "Then we swung over here, and around sideways...let's count. One, two, three, four..." Dad paced the steps to where the Mustang idled patiently. He reckoned that if it had been a road, she would have stopped only a couple of feet from the child, a little off to his right. She'd turned the car sideways to slow it down, but didn't let it go off the road. "Nice going, Mario-or maybe we should call you Zamboni!" Dad said with a hearty laugh as he shook Maddy's hand like a man, and clapped her on the back of her leather jacket.

She got to drive us back over the bridge that joined Middlefield and Mapleton, back home where Mom would be waiting with cocoa, worrying a bit, wondering why we'd been so long out in the cold.

47

After his mother was buried, Eddie Murphy gradually slipped away from the family. He saw his half-siblings and step-grandmother infrequently, usually only at Christmastime and Easter, though not on the holiday itself. After Tom Malone's stroke, Eddie had visited his step-father in the hospital, and once again when he was settled back at home. But in the year since Jack had installed himself in Tom's place, Eddie hardly ever came home; it probably didn't feel like a home any longer. Then he stopped coming altogether, and didn't even phone on his grandmother's birthday. Maddy tried leaving a couple of messages with the secretary at the seminary, but they weren't returned.

"I don't care about me, but you'd think he'd at least give a crap about Annie. She's blood, after all. We had the same mother." Maddy scowled and spat in the dirty snow as we stood in the cold out in back of her house-so she could smoke, of course.

"I'm sure he cares; it's just that your father never made him feel very welcome, and now the way things are...well, with Jack and all that..." I tried to make an excuse for Eddie.

"Bullshit! That's the point I'm trying to make. He's the older brother-the one that's a legal adult. Look at the family! He oughta strap on a pair and do something about it. And he ignores my messages...that dumb rabbit Annie loves so much has bigger balls than Eddie Murphy!"

"Oh Maddy...Eddie's going to be a priest. He'll be ordained soon, won't he?"

"What the hell's that got to do with anything? All the more reason he should look after his family...not that I care for myself, but Tommy always looked up to him," she insisted with pride. "And you're right about the ordination; that was supposed to be sometime this fall, and still no word from Eddie. I don't expect we were invited. I guess I can't blame him. He's probably ashamed of us."

I shut up before I made her feel worse. Maybe Maddy was right. Eddie Murphy was probably gone. He had his own life now, and ironically, other people's families to look after while his own house was falling down on the heads of his sisters and brother.

Not long after that conversation, a strange letter turned up in our mailbox. It was addressed to me, and it was strange because the return address read Lac du Bonnet, Manitoba, Canada. I didn't know anyone in Canada. I'd certainly never heard of Lac du Bonnet. Even though it was freezing outside, I stood on the front steps and opened it with some trepidation.

My Dearest Frances,

I hope this letter finds you and your dear mother and father well. I hope you can forgive me for leaving without saying goodbye, and for burdening you with my sorrow. I feel you are only one who will understand.

I have left the seminary-run away is more like it. Yes, like the coward I am, I have run away from everything. I am too afraid to go to war, too afraid to become a priest. I am too weak to tell the truth, and unable to live with the lies.

I can't face my family. All is not as it seems. In the church I learned that righteousness may serve as only a thin dark cloak to cover evil. The very people we believe to be of God visit harm upon those who trust in them. They are vile, betraying the lambs they are charged to protect, committing terrible sins in the name of Jesus Christ. I am the worst sinner of all.

Even now I do not have the courage to speak of it. I pray that God and the Holy Spirit will bless Tommy, restore him in mind and body, and heal his wounded soul. I beg his forgiveness. If I suffer for the rest of my life it will not be long enough to atone. I throw myself at the feet of Christ Jesus and beg for divine mercy. Give my sisters and brother my love! I pray for God's blessings upon them, and my step-father, and especially my dear Gramma Malone.

God bless all of you!

Eddie Murphy

Alone in my bedroom, I read the letter three times before carefully folding it and placing it back in its envelope. No street address-how could I even write back? I opened the big geography book and found Lac du Bonnet, over the Canadian border north of Minnesota. The nearest city was Winnipeg. How did he wind up there? It sounded like poor Eddie was in trouble, like maybe he had some sort of a nervous breakdown, just like his mom did in the end. It pained my heart. Maddy thought Eddie didn't care about the family, but he cared so much it broke him. I assumed he was referring to Tommy's 'situation'-Maddy must have told Eddie when he last visited, after her father's stroke. I could only guess that Eddie felt unworthy of the priesthood because he'd been unable step in and shepherd his own family. But what did he mean about the war? It was over. If he left the seminary, would he still be eligible for the draft? Had he stayed in seminary just to avoid it?

It was a lot to think about. Above all I wondered why he chose to tell me. I decided to wait a while before showing the letter to anyone. I hoped that he'd write to his sister or grandmother now that he'd found the courage to contact someone. For now, it seemed like I was the only one who knew what became of Eddie Murphy, or at least knew that he was alive somewhere in Canada.

48

Dad said later it was like something straight out of an old black and white movie. The rusty metal gates creak open and a gray-haired man steps though and stands unceremoniously on the other side, holding a small bundle of belongings. The frail elderly mother embraces the middle-aged son who'd been imprisoned behind the gates, since he was a young man and his mother was a strong, middle-aged woman.

Daniel Maddox Malone was a quiet man then, and he was still a quiet man. He had been away since before I was born, since Maddy was an infant. It was hard to grasp the idea of spending what for me was a lifetime in prison. Now he'd been home for a week, and I still hadn't had so much as a peek at him. I was decidedly curious. I'd never met anyone who'd killed a man, except for in war-not that I knew of anyway. Considering the effect Uncle Tom Malone always had on me, I imagined he would be scary and sinister, scarred and ugly.

"Dad?" I ventured. He was watching a ballgame, and I'd waited for a commercial. "Ah, I was wondering if you knew anything about...Daniel Malone. I mean-how did it happen?"

My father looked thoughtful. "Well, it was a bar fight; he didn't go in lookin' for trouble, but it sure found him. He's a helluva big guy-he worked down at the loading docks: rough work with rough guys. I think he got so mad he just didn't know 'is own strength. The butt load of booze didn't help, but they all did that stuff, drinkin' and brawlin'. He was an amateur boxer too, and I think that's partly why they came down so hard on 'im. Like, he should've known when to stop. The judge didn't think he showed remorse either. I know they got that wrong; he felt terrible. Thing is, Danny isn't the kind of guy who's gonna come out and cry about it. He sort of drew into himself...but I know he felt real bad. It's sad how it only takes a couple of minutes to screw-up your whole life."

"What did he get so mad about?"

"Ah, it was somethin' another guy said...somethin' really insulting, and it just got to 'im, I guess. It was especially tragic on account of he was finally getting married. He was about thirty-eighty, and he took a bit longer than usual to find a girl...he just waited for the right girl, that's all. She was an older woman, never married...and there was a rumor that she was, ah, expecting," he whispered. "I don't know if it's true or not; I never asked. Anyway, Danny was out celebrating with some buddies, and some wise-guy made a crack about..." Dad shook his head, and clearly wasn't comfortable going on. "The other guy really started it, but Danny threw the first punch and...what a shame his friends didn't pull 'im off in time. There're just some things ya don't say to a guy."

"So you don't think he's at all...dangerous...to the kids?"

"Danny? Hell no! He's not a hothead like his brother; it took a lot to get 'im that mad, and he never laid a hand on any woman or child. He's a lot smarter than Big Tommy too, between you and me."

"That's all I needed to know. Thanks Dad."

Mom made a carrot cake, and dutifully climbed into the car, balancing it on her lap for the short drive around the block while she openly expressed her reservations about the family situation. "Maybe we should offer to have Annie come stay with us-just for a while, until things settle down."

"The kid is always welcome, but...settle down how?" Dad wanted to know.

"Well, is he going to stay there for good?"

"That's how I heard it-just in time if you ask me, the family is going to ruin, in more ways than one," Dad added, leading me to consider how much he really knew about Malone's Quality Taxi.

"And this is an *improvement*?" Mom's voice had been rising in pitch, until the final syllable on 'improvement' could be heard by dogs a mile away.

"Hold on to your hat, Ev! I mean, hold on to your cake!" Dad said with a laugh. "Danny's a good guy. Always was. Sometimes good people make mistakes-big mistakes, even do bad things; but that don't make 'em bad."

Mom sighed as though she was not convinced. I was picturing the judgment scales we all knew from our children's catechism when we stopped in front of the old Victorian house.

As we went around to the side-porch door, I remembered the first time the three of us made this uncomfortable journey, almost five years ago now. Mom clutched the same crystal cake plate; funny how no one had managed to drop it in all that time. I was a child then. When Uncle Tom had greeted us at the door, my mother had looked like a frightened child. This time we were greeted by Maddy, now my oldest and dearest friend. Uncle Tom Malone was too frail to come to the door, and it was a marvel he'd even made it to another Christmas.

The place was noticeably clean, cleaner than I'd ever seen it-even had some Christmas decorations in the entryway. When I stepped into in the best parlor, I was surprised to see a big Christmas tree. It was strung with old fashioned lights, not the popular blinking lights everybody used in the seventies. They looked as though they'd been hauled out of the attic, cleaned up and lovingly restored. The Malones hadn't had a tree or lights in all this time, ever since Auntie Joan went to the hospital that terrible Christmas. I guess the holiday had been like an anniversary of the tragic event, rather than a holiday. Now a Blue Spruce stood tall and defied sorrow, bringing the years of mourning to a close at last.

Uncle Daniel was standing by the tree with the colored lights illuminating his face. My first impression was one of great warmth, with a merry twinkle in his eye; but then I thought it must have been the Christmas lights. Annie pointed up to the top of the tree, chatting merrily about a star or an angel or some such thing she'd seen up in the endless crawl space of those bedroom closets. It was a touching family scene, worthy of the cover of *Good Housekeeping*. I'd never seen Annie so at ease with any man except my father. She acted like Uncle Danny was an old friend. Tommy was standing silently by, looking awkward as usual, and had to be prompted to wish us Merry Christmas. After all these years, he still seemed dumb as a post, poor kid.

"This is your Uncle Danny," Gramma introduced us in animated voice. The first thing I noticed was his hand-it was huge, the biggest hand I'd ever shaken. He barely took mine between his fingers, as if afraid he might break it.

"I've heard so much about you Frances-all good!" He smiled and fixed his blue eyes right on me, and I suddenly felt like a shy little girl, more awkward than I had in years. His gaze was penetrating, as though he could see through layers of social pleasantries and know just what one really felt. I was struck by the family resemblance, the scrutiny of that look. It was a Malone trait, and not only confined to Maddy and her grandmother. But it felt different when coming from a man, not exactly threatening, but far more powerful. This definitely warranted further consideration. I stepped back and greeted the others, and pretended to admire the tree while studying Uncle Danny. He was over six feet tall, and had obviously kept himself in shape. His face looked older than fifty-nine years, but his body was straight and strong and he had a full head of thick wavy hair, salt and pepper, but mostly salt. Uncle Danny was built like Tommy, or rather Tommy was built just like him, though not filled out as much. He had a broad round face that might have resembled pie-dough when he was young, but now it was deeply furrowed. There was something about the man that drew my interest. I think part of it was the thoughtful way he considered things before he answered a question, but it was more the expression on his face, and his eyes. They were blue like his mother's, but the way he looked at me reminded me of

Maddy. It took me a while because I hadn't expected it, but I recognized it at last as a formidable intelligence, albeit unschooled; it was a raw, keen intelligence.

Meanwhile, Mom was sitting by Maddy and Gramma and Uncle Tom, asking polite questions and making pleasant conversation. Everything felt very different from last Christmas. Uncle Tom sat washed and combed in the bosom of his family. He didn't say anything, but at least he wasn't isolated in the back room. He even smiled a bit and seemed genuinely glad to see my mother. Gramma looked like she was the one who'd just been let out of prison; she stood straighter, laughed out loud and suddenly seemed ten years younger. She was actually wearing a new dress, and blushed like a coquette when Dad told her she was looking awfully pretty.

We had some cake, and after a respectful amount of time elapsed, Maddy started making eyes like she was just dying to tell me something. I thought she probably needed a cigarette too; she looked as if she was about to climb out of her skin. As soon as we got a moment we excused ourselves and went up to her old room, the one she usually ended up sleeping in because Annie was still afraid to be alone. We shut the door and the story nearly burst out of her.

"It was great! He just threw the bum out! He says, 'OK, punk, the pahty's ovah!' Then he told him to hand over the keys-to the house, the cab, the safe...he even patted him down and made him turn out his pockets. Then he handed Jack a chunk of cash this thick!" Maddy exclaimed as she measured about two inches between her thumb and forefinger. "And he says, 'Here's yer sev'rence pay. You're fired!' Uncle Danny did it in front of all of us-me and Tommy and Gramma-even Joanie. So Jack stuffs the money in his jacket and snaps, 'Com' on, Joanie!' But Joanie just stands there, so he says, 'You comin' or what?' And she says, 'No Jack, I'm stayin' right here.' For a second I thought Jack looked almost sad...like he might cry or somethin', but then he looks at Joanie and says, 'Suit yourself, bitch.' Then Uncle Danny gets all red in the face. He grabs Jack by the arm and marches him right out the front door-all the way to the curb like he was puttin' out the ashbins! I ran upstairs to watch and opened the window so I could hear too. Uncle Danny yells, 'You're not to come within' sight of this house, understand?!' Jack didn't say nothin', so Uncle Danny shakes 'im up a bit and he says, 'I'll break your goddamn neck if you ever show your miserable face around here again! You got that?' Jack says, 'Yeah, I got it'. So Uncle Danny turns him loose. Then Jack happens to look up and sees me watchin' the whole show out the window. We kinda locked eyes for a second...he looked so mad I swear it was like there was bullets shootin' right outa his eyes. Then he got into his little convertible and drove off. I guess that's the end of Jack Mack!" Maddy was all fired up as she told me the story, and the glow in her eyes reminded me of the tale of 'old Iggy and the firecracker' I'd heard so long ago. Only this was a lot more serious.

"Thank God," I said. "But are you sure it's over-is Joanie really done with Jack?"

"Seems like it." Maddy shrugged. "Uncle Danny is talkin' to her...talkin' to all of us, Tommy and me, that is, about getting a GED. It's kind of like a diploma. He never finished high school, but he got his GED in...while he was away," Maddy said discreetly. "I never even heard of a GED, but Uncle Danny says it's important for getting a good job, somethin' better than a warehouse. I'm getting pretty sick of that, and they don't ever give me more than minimum wage. They give the guys twice as much, but I'm lucky to have a job at all. Don't seem right. Uncle Danny says we can start that window washing business too. He's gonna trade in the cab and get a sturdy truck and the ladder, all the stuff we need-maybe even go to a print shop and make little cards with a phone number to give out to people."

"That sounds great! My Dad was right again," I said with admiration.

"Right about what?"

"Mom was worried about your uncle because...well, because he just got out of prison."

"I can understand that," Maddy said.

"My father told her not to worry; he said Danny was a good guy-he always was a good guy. I wondered how he could know for sure. When I saw Annie by the Christmas tree with Uncle Danny, I just knew Dad was right."

"Your dad's sharp," Maddy said.

I was sitting on the edge of the bed thinking about all the hard times the Malones had gone through. It looked bad for a while, nearly hopeless, but now everything was changing for the better. As usual, Maddy decided to open the window a bit and have a quick smoke. It's funny how you associate things, like the cold air coming in from outside and the smell of Marlboros in the bedroom. It made me suddenly remember the lost skeleton keys; they were probably still hidden under the radiator. I'd completely forgotten about them.

"Oh-my-gosh!"

"What?"

"I can't believe I forgot all this time-I didn't say anything last time in front of Annie. I didn't want her blabbing."

"Blabbin' about what?"

"I'm getting to that; I hope it's not totally anticlimactic, but..."

"Frances, what the hell are you talking about?" Maddy interrupted. "I'm just a dumb-shit who dropped outa high school! What's an 'anticlimate'?"

"You're not a dumb shit," I said, getting up and going to the radiator. "I just mean maybe I'm getting all excited for nothing but..." I knelt down and fished my hand around in the grimy dust, and extracted one of the keys; it was just where I'd seen it last time. I held it up. "Look."

"So?"

"It's one of the old keys to someplace in this house. It's been there forever, and there's another. Come see."

Maddy got down on the floor and I pointed to the key still lodged by the pipe. "Ah," she said, reaching for it. It was stuck, and she had to wiggle it a bit.

"Don't let it go down between the floorboards," I cautioned.

She pried it out, rubbed the thick dust off on her jeans and examined the key more closely. "They could open any of the bedroom doors," she suggested. "For all we know, this might only be a spare key to the bathroom." She was trying to suppress her excitement.

"Or..." I made a playfully mysterious face, like we were in a detective movie, "... it could unlock the...da, da-da da-the dark tower!"

"Only one way to find out."

"Right now? With everybody downstairs?"

"Sure-they're busy. Let's go."

We tiptoed out of the room and down the hall to the staircase that led up to the third half-story. "You first," I told her.

She put the key in the lock and it opened with ease. We went through some tiny bedrooms that were built for servants; before the depression, that's where the maids slept. Maddy had been in there before, had climbed out of Tommy's window while he was away, and crawled across the roof to see what he had in there. Now his stash was long gone. There was only the typical old stuff you'd find in an attic: musty books, an open chest of old clothes, a moth-eaten dress-making form, and an empty bird cage. "I always find empty bird cages sad," I said wistfully, touching the rusting metal with my fingertip. "I wonder whose bird it was...how it died?"

"Yeah-well, do we stand here and be sad, or do we try your key?" I nodded and went to the little door with the rounded top. I fit the key in the keyhole and twisted one way to try the doorknob. Nothing. "Told ya-it's probably the key to the bathroom," Maddy grumbled.

I turned it the other way and the lock clicked, then the door swung in and opened with a creek. A chilly air that smelled of dust and old wood swept into the room. It sent shivers through me; I even thought I saw Maddy shudder involuntarily. "Ooh…look!" I squealed, pointing at the winding staircase. "And there's the stained glass window! This is where I see the light go on and off from my house; I'm so nervous I have to pee!"

"Not now you don't! Quick, let's get up there and see what's what before someone comes and catches us…then we may never get a look."

"Oh, I don't know…now that I'm here, it's just too scary! You go on without me."

"Aw, you gotta come up Frances! We've wanted to do this since we was little kids! Don't be scared. I'll go ahead." Maddy took my hand and led me up the creaky stairs. She paused on one particularly squeaky step; it almost sounded like a human voice whining. I giggled nervously with my hand over my mouth. "This is what we hear some nights…I can't believe ole Gramma's been rattlin' around up here all these years," she whispered.

"Wait!"

"What now?"

"It's nearly dark-we need a flashlight!"

"No time to find one-let's go," she tugged me along. The staircase spiraled sharply. After the first loop around, I looked back down but couldn't see the door we'd just passed through. Another two loops and we emerged into a small round room with only one tiny window for light. It was up high, way too far up to see out. We waited for our eyes to adjust to the darkness. The room seemed nearly empty but for some long low object, smack in the middle, perhaps an odd piece of furniture.

"What's that?" I pointed nervously.

Maddy strained to see, then let go of my hand and fished her matchbook out of her pocket and struck one. In the flickering flame, she edged closer, being careful not to trip on anything. "Just a table," she said, bending down to touch it. She bumped into something that scraped on the wooden floor.

"What was that?" I whispered.

"A chair; it's a long low table with one wooden chair in front of it…ouch!" Maddy blew out the match that had just singed her thumb, then struck another. "Com' 'ere," she whispered. "There're things on the table," she reached out carefully. "They're framed pictures; and something else…" Then Maddy accidently knocked whatever it was over with a sharp thwap of wood on wood. I sucked in my breath audibly.

"What was that?"

"It's just a crucifix," she said, holding the object in her hand. She blew out the second match before it reached her fingers.

"OK, let's go...we can't even see anything," I urged, feeling anxious with guilt. After all, this was her grandmother's private room. "Wait, what was that? I thought I heard a stair creak," I whispered. We listened a moment, then Maddy groped the table like a blind person, trying to set the crucifix back carefully the way she'd found it without lighting another match; instead, she managed to knock something else over. "Maddy," I whispered, "you'll wake the dead..." I was in the middle of fussing when I suddenly saw a great dark shadow looming across the floor from a bright light directly behind me. "Jesus, Mary 'n Joseph!" I jumped and scurried over to Maddy. When I turned around, I realized I'd been scared by my own shadow.

"No, it's not Jesus or Joseph, nor the Blessed Virgin," Gramma's voice was sharp with sarcasm. It's herself, Hannah Harahan Malone. What in blazes are you two nosy-Rosies doin' up here, I should like to know?"

"Gramma always sounds more Irish when she gets riled," Maddy whispered.

"Ma? Is everything alright?" A man's voice called out from the bottom of the stairs. It was Uncle Danny.

"Now there's a good question," Gramma Malone said thoughtfully. "No; I don't think things have been at all right for a long time now, a terrible long time. I think it's high time we put it all to right, put all the ghosts to rest. Lord knows I'll be joining them soon enough. Come up here Danny," she called over her shoulder.

We heard him climb the stairs, then he stood behind his mother. Gramma made her way over to her chair and sat, placing the flashlight on the table like a lamp. She looked from us to her son and motioned us all to sit down. There was only one chair, so we sat on the floor. Some of the heat from the lower rooms began to rise through the open door below and creep up the staircase, but it was still very cold. "Ma, you'll catch your death up here," Uncle Danny said with concern.

"Oh, I'm quite used to it," his mother answered with a sly smile.

"I'm sorry Gramma; I know we weren't ever supposed to come up here- it's your business," Maddy interjected.

"Aunt Hannah, it's all my fault...I found some old keys stuck under the radiator. It was my idea to try it," I admitted.

"Oh ho, so that's how you got up here?! I thought you picked the lock," Gramma pointed an accusing finger at Maddy, but the wry smile gave her away. She wasn't really mad at us.

"Well…uh…I actually tried that, years ago-more than once. We all did, 'cept Annie; it didn't work," she admitted. "If it worked, I would've come up here way before Frances found the keys, so…"

"It don't matter." Gramma shook her head and sighed deeply. "By the way, Frances, your folks went home. Told me to tell you to stay and visit as long as you like."

"I told them I'd bring you home when you girls were done doing whatever it was you were doing up here," Uncle Danny said. Then he addressed me with surprising emotion. "You've got wonderful parents, Frances. I'm happy for you. I never really knew your mother that well, but she's a fine woman. Your dad and I go way back. He's a gem, your father is, a real gem. You're a lucky girl…I hope you know that."

"I know that Uncle Danny," I said in befuddlement. "But why do you ask? Did I do something wrong? Oh, maybe you think I'm a bad girl 'cause I, uh, basically broke into your mother's private rooms? You're right; it was a terrible invasion of privacy, now that I think about it. I acted like a little kid…I don't usually behave that way though. It was very inconsiderate…"

"No, no, Frances; I don't think you're a bad girl at all…I," he fumbled for words.

"Danny," Gramma interrupted. "I have some things I need to get off of my chest before we freeze up here-you're right, it's pretty raw. I'm glad Frances and Mad'lin got a bit of the devil in them and decided to break the rules. Otherwise I mightn't have found the courage. You would have come up here when I was dead and asked, 'What in hell was that old woman up to anyway?'"

Her spunkiness made us all chuckle a bit, then Danny asked, "Well then, what is it Ma? What do you want to tell us all?"

Gramma Malone sat with the flashlight illuminating her face from below, casting odd shadows on the round walls of the strange room. Above us there were wooden rafters, and a ceiling that came to a sharp point. All these years I'd wondered what it looked like inside…it made me feel like a kid at summer camp telling ghost stories in a tent. "First, let's get a bit more light," Gramma said, opening a little drawer in the table. She took out a box of kitchen matches and struck one to light a big old fashioned kerosene lamp that sat on one end of the table. It was made of glass; it's a good thing Maddy hadn't bumped it. The lamp cast a warm golden light, and she laid the flashlight on its side.

"Gosh, Ma, you been comin' up here all alone at night, lightin' kerosene? In this old tinderbox of a house?"

"Danny, I've been lightin' kerosene since you were in diapers, and don't you forget it!"

"That's my Ma!" Uncle Danny said. Maddy smiled warmly at him.

"I been comin' up here ever since my husband passed. I found everything just like this...the pictures, the cross, and this." She reached underneath the table and dragged out a heavy metal box.

"What's in it Ma?" Uncle Danny asked.

"Just about all my money; you don't think I'd trust the banks with it, do you?" Gramma took a little key out of the single drawer in the table and unlocked it. We all peered inside.

"Jeez, Gramma! That's a shh...whole lotta cash!" Maddy exclaimed. I thought of how poor they'd been-the broken windows, leaky roof...no breakfast cereal.

"That it is!" Gramma said. "And you don't think I could let your father find out about it? He would've run through it a long time ago...wouldn't have had any drive to work at all, not that he ever did much."

"Probably woulda drank it away by now," Maddy said wryly.

"Then there was Jack Mack, that wretched devil of a man." Gramma shuddered at the mention of him. "If Danny hadn't come home and thrown him out-well, I might 'ave had to kill him myself!" Maddy chortled out loud, and then noticed how her grandmother was looking at her, dead-pan silent. She stopped abruptly. Then a broad smile came over her grandmother's wrinkled face; she began to cackle like an old hen. "I had you there!" She pointed her finger at Maddy.

"So you came up here to hide your money?" Daniel asked, shaking his head incredulously. "Well, I can see why, but you don't need to worry anymore; we can put it right into a savings account in your name. No one's gonna take it from you Ma. If you'd like to use some to fix up the house, I can help. It's up to you."

"Yes, I'd like to see the old place repaired. I've been feeling kinda sorry for it, but I couldn't do anything about it without revealing what I'd stashed away-Tom woulda asked questions."

"'Cept you cracked into your stash when Ma died," Maddy said.

"That I did. At the time, I told Tom that I'd emptied my savings account. I lied," she said, with a sly look.

"Gramma," Maddy began, "I never thanked you right for all that...for my Ma. It was so beautiful...the headstone and the trees and flowers and all. I stop there sometimes when the weather is nice, and it don't even feel like a sad place," she finished thoughtfully.

"I went out to the cemetery right away-soon as I came home," Uncle Danny said. "Your mother was a dear friend. You know, for a long time she was one of the few who came to visit me...then she had to take care of all her little ones and I understood, but I missed her." Uncle Danny spoke with a strong current of feeling that moved quietly from deep within, barely rippling the surface. It was powerful, almost palpable, and yet I suspected that it was invisible to most people, like water flowing under thick ice.

In the silence that followed I asked a burning question. "Aunt Hannah...why do you keep these pictures hidden up here?" I could see the pictures were of children, and a man I assumed was Mr. Malone Senior. "Why not keep them in the living room...or your bedroom, if you want to look at them in private?"

"That's the other part of the story. In private, you say? Yes, that's a good way to put it. Frances, you really do have a way of making things plain," she said. "I wanted to look at the pictures and think about things in private-even private from myself, from my daily doings if you follow what I mean. It's not like I wanted them looking back at me every morning when I dressed myself, every night when I went to bed. So when I wasn't sneaking money from my social security and widow's pension into the box, I was...visiting loved ones. You see, I just couldn't bear to go out to their graves any longer. You'd think it would get easier with the passing time, but no."

"I thought you were sleepwalking," Maddy said.

"When you came sneaking up on me that's just what I wanted you to think. I didn't want you asking questions I wasn't ready to answer. It's not sleepwalking that troubles me. It's the insomnia that I got-ever since little Mad'lin and Dorothy passed away...ever since they died in their sleep with me lying fast asleep on the floor beside them. I never slept right again. That's why I always take them naps. No matter how hard I try to stay up all day, I still can't sleep half the night. I usually wake up just after midnight and get the urge to wander around the house, almost like I might find them hiding somewhere. I usually don't fall back to sleep until just before sunrise. It don't escape me-that's when I woke up and found them."

"Good God, Ma! That's awful rough. Did you tell the doctor?" Danny wanted to know.

"Well, I said I had trouble sleeping, but I never went into it-never explained it. He gave me some pills, but they made me feel drunk! I had children to care for, sleep or no sleep, and I couldn't be drugged. Then you grew up and at least I got rest during the day, but I never did feel rested." She was silent a moment. "Ah...isn't there somethin' you wanted to ask, Mad'lin?" Even in the soft light, Gramma had noticed her questioning eyes.

"Uh...yeah; how come Ma and Dad named me after...your little girls?"

"It was your mother did that for me," Gramma answered. "I don't think your father even remembered his sisters. Your mother thought it would be a help to me. It was a lovely thought. We kept in touch for a while, behind your father's back. She helped us to reconcile; otherwise I mightn't have ever known you."

"It's all gonna be OK, Ma. My little sisters are with Jesus, for a long time now. It ain't your fault. You did a great job! None of it's your fault," Danny insisted.

"There's more I got to tell you. There's a reason why I picked this place to come and think on it all. I warn you, it's going to be a shock, but...maybe I shouldn't burden you girls with this," Gramma faltered.

"It won't be a burden," Maddy said. "Whatever it is, you need to get it out in the open. Then maybe you can sleep again."

"Danny, I never told you the truth about how your father died. You and your brother were only little boys, and it wouldn't have been right. You just don't tell children some things," she spoke quietly, and struggled to go on. "Then you grew up, and I didn't see the point in bringing it up after all those years. It's hard enough for boys to become men without a father, without having to think of...such things. I mean, the old adage was, 'What you don't know can't hurt you.' It was popular wisdom-it made sense to me then, but it stopped making sense a long time ago."

"I think I know what you're getting at," Uncle Danny said. "There're only so many things it can be. But whatever it was happened a long time ago. Look at me Ma: I'm an old man now. I've seen so much. Whatever happened, it can't hurt me. It seems it's only hurting you to hold it back."

"By now you've probably guessed it; your father, my husband-Michael Thomas Malone, took his own life." Even after all these years we could see it was hard for her to say it.

Daniel nodded solemnly and said, "I should have guessed a long time ago. Something always seemed...not right somehow, as if the secret took on a life of its own and was always there, even if it had no words, even if we couldn't see it. Tell us about it Ma, tell us so you can put it to rest."

"After your sisters passed, I was inconsolable," Gramma began. We had them waked right in this house, down in the good parlor. All the friends and neighbors came, and I wailed and keened in the old Irish way while your father just sat silent as a stone. I thought he must have a heart made of stone. I was angry with 'im too. When the children were buried and everybody went home, I took to my bed and thought I might die; I almost wished I could. That's when father Mahood came to us, in what I thought was my greatest hour of need, but that hour was yet to come. It was only three days afterwards, and I'd finally fallen into a deep sleep. I awoke at the crack of dawn alone in our...ah...marital bed," Gramma spoke modestly in the old fashioned way. "I had a terrible feeling right from the start, and called out, 'Michael?' I felt his side of the bed, and it was cold. The coldness of it sent shivers through me. The house was so still," she said. Then she turned to her son and spoke with emotion, as if it happened only recently. "I didn't want to wake you and your brother and Margaret, so I got up quietly to go look for him. I checked the bathroom, and looked in on you children. Then I tried to tell myself he must've gone downstairs early for breakfast-maybe he was hungry; but I didn't believe it. When he wasn't there either I felt my heart sink. I'd been terribly angry with my husband; I blamed myself for falling asleep, but I blamed him for not helping me. I guess I just had to blame someone. I panicked-thought he must have run off and left us, thought I'd driven him away with my harsh words. I only wish he'd run off instead of..."

"Gramma...uh...was it up here? Did Grandpa Malone..." Maddy uncharacteristically lost her nerve and couldn't quite get it out.

"Yes. Right here it was...directly over our heads." Gramma pointed and we all looked up to the rafters with a start, as if expecting to see him there, but there were only the crossbeams under the cavernous pointed roof.

"For the luva God," Uncle Danny barely whispered as he peered upwards. I gasped audibly in spite of myself and shot my hand over my mouth. I could vividly imagine how he must have looked hanging there. To think that I'd seen this tower from just over the hill in my backyard, ever since I could remember; I'd never be able to look at it the same way again.

"And these pictures of the children, of little Mad'lin and Dorothy were sitting right here by the crucifix; that's just how he left them. It was a message to me. You see, everyone thought he did it because of the stock market, because he lost all the money he'd invested in business over in Ireland. He did lose a great deal of money, but it wasn't about that at all! Michael Malone was a stern man, and a man of few words. I was only seventeen when we married-didn't know a thing about men. I didn't understand, didn't know how much he cared for us until I saw him there." She pointed up again, and her hand trembled with emotion. "We were together nine years and had five children, but I don't think I knew him at all until it was too late. That's why I come up here. It was so terrible that the only thing to do was stare it down. I could handle it better that way. I got into the habit of talking things over with him. Then I'd light a candle and pray for his soul, and ask his forgiveness. I wasn't worried about the girls anymore; I knew they were safe." Hannah Harahan Malone closed her eyes and sighed deeply with her hand over her heart. We reflected a moment in respectful silence as she finally laid her husband and daughters to rest.

Daniel got to his knees and gently took both her frail hands in his enormous ones. His old mother opened her eyes, and he looked straight into her with a sad smile. "Dear God Muther! To think you climbed up here alone in the night, all these years...what if you'd fallen? And with a kerosene lamp too! What a terrible burden to keep to yourself-it's a wonder you didn't go stark ravin' mad! Why on earth didn't you tell us after we'd grown up? It would have been better to rid ourselves of this old place a long time ago...there're too many unhappy memories; far too many." He sighed and rose to his feet. "But for now, I think it's time we all go back downstairs and join the living; go back down and take care of poor Tom, and keep a Merry Christmas for little Annie."

We stood up and Uncle Danny took his mother's hand. "You're right, Danny; I'm too old to be climbing up here any longer," she said. Then she let herself be led down the spiral stairs, even though she'd done it without any help a thousand times. Maddy and I went ahead and lit her way with the flashlight. Just before he turned to leave, Daniel Malone looked up at the crossbeams and said quietly, "I forgive you Daddy. May you rest in peace, and may God have mercy on your soul, as I pray He will upon mine.

49

"There was no way I could stop...just no way! It wasn't my fault. The kid did it on purpose!" Stan was so shaken he had to down two shots before he could get the first words out. "I was on that rural stretch, right after you come off route two, nothin' but trees. It was just getting dark and I flipped my lights on. That's when he came walkin' out from behind some trees, like he was waitin' there for me. For a minute I thought he was goin' to try and hitch a ride, so I didn't even slow down-it was cold, but we can't violate company policy. Then all of a sudden he turns and steps right out into the road-stood there with his arms out just like this!" Stan stood up and spread his long arms like the crucified Christ. "For a second I could see his face, plain as day in the headlights. He had big blue eyes and the face of an angel. Then-bam! It was over; but that face is just stuck in my head. Why the hell did he have to pick me? Right before Christmas too! Goddamn that crazy kid!"

Stan had come over to tell my father of the apparent suicide that had taken place late that afternoon. It had been on the news, but we didn't have the TV on. Although nobody blamed Stan, the company suspended him from driving until the investigation was complete. He was in no shape to drive anyway.

"Course it ain't your fault," Dad said supportively.

"Do they know who the boy was?" Mom asked. Stan shook his head no. Mom sat down and patted the back of his hand. "Stan, that poor kid didn't pick you on purpose. He just needed a way...he clearly had it all planned and it was just bad luck you were out driving." Stan had more than a little bad luck recently. His wife had died suddenly of a cancer not two years earlier, leaving him with a young daughter and son.

"That's right," Dad said. "It could have been me; it could have been any of us."

"Thanks Joe," Stan said. "I didn't think of it that way."

"Can we do anything to help? Have you got all your Christmas shopping done for the kids?" Mom asked with concern.

"Yeah, thanks Evelyn; my sister's got it all under control-don't know what I'd do without her. Thanks for asking. You're great pals! I just needed to talk it over with someone else. I already burdened my sister with it enough. I hope I didn't make you too upset, or spoil your Christmas..."

"Naw, don't mention it Stan," Dad said. "Anything you need, you let us know."

"Ain't that a shame?" Dad said after Stan had gone home.

"Let's put the news on; I want to know what happened," I said.

"Guess we might as well." Dad shrugged.

We didn't have to wait long before they updated the story. The newscaster stated the dry facts, the time, the weather and condition of the road. He said the driver was not at fault-I thought Stan would be relieved to hear it. It was an apparent suicide, but the motive was unknown. He left no note. They hadn't identified him earlier, until they'd notified the family. Then the reporter said that the victim was a young man of seventeen, survived by his mother and father. There were no brothers or sisters. His name was George Goldenberg.

"Oh God no! That's so terrible!" I felt sick. I was flooded with the memory of that scene in the back of Mr. Donald's math class. What if I'd opened my mouth and protested? What if I took George aside and told him…I don't know what; anything would have been better than nothing. I started to cry.

"Did you know that boy?" Dad asked in surprise.

I nodded. Mom looked at me quizzically. It had been almost three years since I'd told her about George. "You remember, I told you about George-the swishy kid with the big blue eyes, back in eighth grade?" Mom shook her head no. "How he was constantly bullied at school? When we were talking about your friend Paulie, talking about gay people?" I sobbed.

"OK; now I remember," Mom said.

The real kicker was-Maddy had seen Mr. Donald in a gay bar. "Donny," as he was known down town, had used homophobia like an offensive weapon to guard his own secret from students and faculty. After all, who would suspect a big queer-bashing jock? It was far too late to do anything for George Goldenberg, but the tragedy suddenly brought to mind another troubled soul. I still hadn't told anyone about the letter from Canada. I'd been waiting for Eddie Murphy to write his family, but apparently he hadn't. Now I wished I hadn't waited so long.

"Mom, Dad…I just feel so awful. I gotta go talk to Maddy…I gotta go get something first-be right back.

"It's almost suppertime," Mom said.

"I'm sorry. I'm not hungry." I ran upstairs to my room and got the letter, stuffed it in my pocket and ran back down.

"What's wrong, Fran?"

"I'll explain later, I promise. Right now I need to go."

"Why don't you call first and see if she's home?" Mom suggested.

I hadn't thought of that; the kids hadn't been allowed to use the phone, and I was used to just running over unannounced. But I was too upset. "If I try to talk, I just know I'll start crying."

"I'll call," Mom said, as she dialed the phone on the kitchen wall. "Hi, Aunt Hannah. Sorry to bother you, but Fran wanted to stop over and talk to Mad'lin a bit...something serious. No, she's OK. She's just upset. It's about an old classmate who was just...killed. OK, thanks so much."

"I'll take you over," Dad offered.

"Thanks Dad, but I need the walk."

I got my coat and made sure the gloves were in my pockets. They walked me to the door and Mom hugged me goodbye even though I was only going around the block. I stepped out into a cold air tinged with the smell of the sea. Dad picked up his head and sniffed. "They say we're in for a nor'easter. Just about in time for Christmas; it figures," he said with a shrug as he waved me off.

When I walked around to the Malone's back door, I was greeted by Uncle Danny. Maddy stood right behind him. "What is it, child?" he asked tenderly, as he took my coat. I looked into his searching blue eyes and got all choked up again.

"Com' on kiddo," Maddy said with a sigh. She put her arm around me and led me past Uncle Danny, turning her head to speak to him over her shoulder. "Don't worry-I got this."

We climbed the stairs. "Let's sit in my room so Annie don't barge in," she said. I nodded. We sat on the bed. She waited while I pulled myself together.

"First, I have to tell you about George Goldenberg," I began.

"Who?"

"Remember that really queer kid we knew at Eastie-with the plaid pants? I told you how Mr. Donald used to bully George-stood right there and watched while the boys beat him up in math class. It was just before that black girl...you know...in the locker room?"

"That I remember. What about Goldenberg?"

"Then you told me a while ago how you saw Mr. Donald in some gay bar."

"Yeah, Donny...what a douche bag. This about him too?"

"No...not really...well sort of. I don't know if you watched the news, but...George killed himself. He walked out in front of a truck," I said breathlessly. My eyes smarted with tears.

Maddy sighed and shook her head no. "I hadn't heard. That sucks...that really sucks. It ain't the first time-and it ain't gonna be the last." She got up and opened the window, which meant she was going to light a cigarette. She pulled a wooden desk chair over and straddled it backwards. I waited until she lit up and took a drag.

"I know exactly how it happened," I went on.

"How do you know?"

"I know the poor man who was driving the truck-his name's Stan; he works with my Dad. I was sitting right in the kitchen when Stan described it." I related the story.

"Jesus!" Maddy shook her head sadly when I was finished. "The poor bastard! Stan too-both of 'em."

"I feel like it was all those kids that did it to him, them and Mr. Donald," I said. "It's like they killed George, or at least set things in motion. They were so mean...it's like they shoved him into the road. And I feel it was partly my fault too, because I didn't say anything."

"God Frances, not this again! You're always sorry for somethin'. Did you do one single mean thing to George, or even laugh when the other kids did those things?"

"No...but..." I shook my head no.

"But nothin'! If anyone should feel guilty-it's me. I saw the same shit you saw-maybe not in the math class, but all the rest of it-every day...and I didn't do one goddamned thing about it-didn't try to stick up for him 'cause I was just as queer. And I was scared. So please don't give me any guilty crap."

"I'm..." I almost apologized. I shut my mouth.

Maddy smoked in silence for another half-minute. "I'm sorry," she sighed. "I didn't mean to chew you out; I just feel bad for the poor kid." She took another long drag and blew the smoke out the window. "By the way...ah, so long as we're talkin' about how tough it is to be gay...Linda left town."

"Really? When? Where'd she go?"

"Yeah, it's pretty real...it was kind of sudden-just after Uncle Danny came home-right after he sent Jack off, come to think of it. Anyway..."

"Why didn't you tell me?"

"I'm tellin' ya." Maddy shrugged. Then she looked out the window and spoke at length. "Linda seemed upset about something last time I saw her. I called a few times but she didn't answer. So I just showed up and the apartment was all torn apart 'cause she was in the middle of packin' up. First I thought maybe I did somethin' wrong, but she says no-she got fired. So I says don't worry-I started tellin' her about our plans for the window cleaning business-she

311

could work with us. But she says she had to go...'cause life's just too hard this way," Maddy said with finality. "Linda's gone out of state, to live with her mother down in Florida. They made up. Her mom's got a big house with a yard for the kid," Maddy explained with a shrug as if it were no big deal. "Only thing I feel bad about is-she was about to leave without even telling me...without even saying goodbye...after everything we..." She couldn't go on.

"Did you ask why?"

"Nah, I guess she had her reasons. She was pretty upset, and I didn't want to make it worse."

"What'd you do then?"

"Helped her pack," Maddy said with another shrug, as if I'd asked a dumb question. "Then I called Uncle Danny and asked if he could come by in the cab and take a good friend to the airport-her mom sent them tickets. So he comes right over and Linda was real relieved. She starts hugging me and crying and all. Then Johnny starts up too...guess he kinda liked me. Linda cried most of the way to the airport. We waited until she was on board-thank God the flight was on time. I don't think I coulda stood it much longer."

"Did your uncle ask about Linda?"

"Not really. He just bought me a beer at the airport bar; then he drove me home."

"Do you think you'll ever see her again?"

"Nah, 's over. It's better this way. Who am I kidding? I can't ever be with her...take care of her like I coulda if I was a guy. Linda deserves better. There's just somethin' wrong with the suddenness of it all...I know she was holdin' something back. Linda coulda told me anything. I wouldn't ever get mad at her no matter what-she must've known that. Well, I guess whatever happened was her business," she finished with her trademark cigarette butt flicked out the window.

Maddy didn't fool me one bit, and I think she knew it. Losing Linda hurt like death. George's suicide provided the emotional context that worked it up from somewhere in the pit of her stomach; I could feel it from three feet away. We silently agreed to pretend that she didn't feel hurt, and that I believed it.

"This is really bad timing," I said. "I came over to tell you about George because I was upset, and I knew you'd understand, but there was something else too. I wish it could wait, but I don't think it can. I'm not even sure why...I just wish I'd said something earlier," I began. "First I have to ask-has anyone heard anything from Eddie Murphy?"

"Not that I know-Gramma hasn't said anything. Why?" Maddy's eyes clouded with worry. "Did you hear somethin'? Did somethin' happen to Eddie?"

I reached into my pocket, took out the letter and walked it over to her.

"He wrote this to me; I waited to see if he might write you himself."

Maddy took the letter and read it quickly. Then she turned over the envelope.

"Where in hell is Lac-du-Bonnet?" She pronounced it phonetically.

"Turns out it's just north of Minnesota."

"Why do you suppose he wrote to you?"

"I have no idea. Did you tell him about Tommy?"

"What about 'im?"

"The stuff about selling pot. Isn't that what Eddie's worried about in the letter?

"I never said nothin' about it when I seen Eddie. I wasn't goin' to rat on Tommy."

"Then what's all that about Tommy 'healing in body and spirit' supposed to mean?"

"Beats the hell outa me! Sounds like Eddie Murphy's gone nuts, right off his rocker, just like my poor Ma, God luv 'er."

"That's about what I thought-not in so many words, but basically, yeah. Then when I heard about George, especially the way Stan described it...sounded like he went nuts too. It made me think of Eddie in more ways than one. Maddy...I know your father was always making insinuations...ah...rude remarks about Eddie being...well...do you think Eddie is gay?"

"I dunno. He never said anything about it one way or the other. He never had a girlfriend that I knew of-never saw him with a boyfriend either. Now that I think of it, he was always a mama's boy. When he was younger, he didn't seem to have friends or play with other boys much. Ma told me Eddie was always different...that he wanted to be a priest since he was a little kid. I know my father called him names, but then that's how he is-or was. The stroke kinda improved him." She snorted ironically. "Sure, I wondered if Eddie was gay," she concluded. "But I never came out and asked; it wasn't any of my business."

"If he is, that may be part of what drove him over the edge," I said. "It must be brutal for a Catholic boy to realize he's gay. Thank God he decided to run away to Canada instead of..." I stopped.

"Jeezes...yeah." Maddy shuddered with dread, although it might have been the cold from the window. She got up to close it and had to pound on the sash a bit before it slammed shut. Then she stood looking outside and spoke without turning around. "I mean, what the hell does it take to make a kid waltz into the road and dance with a truck?"

We were silent for what seems like a long time when two people who know each other well are alone in the same room. I don't think she expected an

313

answer to her question, and I hadn't intended to supply one; the sound of my own voice surprised me. "Hopelessness... like you're just all wrong somehow. Like no matter what you do, or how hard you try, nothing's ever going to change...you're never going to be happy...or loved."

"Hmm," Maddy considered thoughtfully. "Can't say as I've ever felt like that...it must really suck."

"It does. I used to feel that way Maddy, for the longest time. When I was a kid with no friends, or sisters or brothers...and my adopted mother didn't even seem to like me...and then there was Nana. Nana made me feel...worthless. I guess it was because she had such a hard life herself, but at the time I thought it was because there was something wrong with me. I don't think I ever would have killed myself...but I felt almost dead inside. I don't know what would've happened to me if you hadn't turned up."

"I didn't do nothin' special." Maddy shrugged, still speaking out the window.

"Yes! Yes you did!"

"What?" She turned and looked at me skeptically.

"You told me I was alright when no one else seemed to think so. I could tell that you meant it, and after that I started to believe it too. Maddy...there must've been no one to tell George Goldenberg that he was alright."

She looked straight into me with her quirky half-smile and answered the question I'd pondered for weeks. "That's why Eddie Murphy wrote to you," she said. "You understand everything...and you're not afraid to say anything."

Just then an engine that sounded like a 747 revved up in the driveway, followed by a couple of cannon shots. I practically jumped off the bed. Maddy chuckled. "Damn! Tommy's got to get a new muffler for that piece of crap! On second thought, maybe it's better this way. Otherwise we wouldn't know if he's in or out of the house. Tommy still don't say two words to any of us." At the mention of Tommy's odd, silent ways, I thought of the letter. Eddie sounded particularly concerned about Tommy, but yet was so vague. Something just wasn't right.

"What are you going to do now-about the letter?"

"It's your letter-do what you want with it."

"Maybe we should tell your grandmother. She'd probably like to know he didn't just run off without even thinking about her."

"Yeah, but she'll feel just as bad-get all worried that he's gone crazy or something; at least he sounds pretty crazy. Gramma's been through so much. Uncle Danny's home now- she's finally got something to be happy about. Nah!"

314

Maddy shook her head. "I wouldn't want to upset her with it. Crazy or not, Eddie's gone off and left us. Hope he likes Canada."

"OK then. But you keep it," I said. Maddy shoved the letter unceremoniously in a desk drawer.

There was a light tap on the door. "Yeah, com' on in!" Maddy hollered. Uncle Danny opened the door part-way and poked his head in.

"Everything OK up here? Ma's been worried about you Frances. She's 'bout got supper on. We're waitin' on Tommy to get back from the corner store with fresh bread-don't know what's keepin' 'im."

"Yeah, we're OK...it's just some poor kid we knew in junior high school went and killed hisself-walked into an eighteen wheeler. Frances knows the guy who was drivin'. Her Dad works with him, so she got to hear him tell it firsthand."

"Aw, I'm sorry Frances. I know all about that tender heart of yours. Why don't you stay for supper?"

"Thanks for asking, but I kind of rushed off and my parents were worried about me. I told them I'd explain everything when I got back." I got up to leave.

"All right then, another time." Uncle Danny smiled. "Oh, by the way-have you seen Annie? I thought she might be up here with you all this time, but..."

"No, she's not with us," Maddy answered. "We hid out in my room-Eddie's old room-on purpose to make sure she didn't hear anything she shouldn't. Did you check her room?"

Uncle Danny looked concerned. "Just did. I looked in there first, then thought she must be here...she's not downstairs either," he concluded.

"She's probably over at our place feeding her rabbit!" I announced. Uncle Danny shook his head no. I thought perhaps he hadn't heard about Flopsy. "She goes over at least twice a day to..."

"She'd already come back from taking care of her rabbit-told me all about it and then disappeared upstairs," he interrupted.

"Don't worry. It's a big house, but there're only so many places she could be," Maddy said as she started for the bedroom door. Uncle Danny stepped back so she could lead the way. I followed them. At the top of the staircase I paused. I really wanted to go home; today had been upsetting enough already. But ever since Annie's strange drawing and the even more troubling explanation...I shuddered at the recollection of her little hand caked with crimson pigment. Mom didn't seem to think it was all that important. She thought it was just immaturity, but I knew then I was looking at the quintessential apex of some iceberg. I'd been trying to warn everybody, but nobody seemed to understand. After all, Mom thought she could fix everything with a nice birthday party. Tired or not, I just had to know what Annie was up to so I could go home and actually relax. I turned back from the staircase and followed them into the girls' old room.

"Annie! Are you in there?" Maddy's voice came from deep inside the closet. She had already crawled in quite a ways. Uncle Danny stood by. We listened.

"Yes." Her little voice sounded far away.

"She's crawled all the way through to Tommy's room," Maddy called back over her shoulder.

"Ah-ha!" I said, relieved. I thought about going, but something held me back.

"Annie, you know you're not supposed to go in there...come out come out wherever you are!" Maddy called in a sing-song voice.

"I'm trying to get the angel out! She's stuck," Annie whined. Uncle Danny and I looked at each other.

"What are you talking about? What angel?" Maddy was getting exasperated.

"For the Christmas tree!"

"Oh, that's right!" Uncle Danny exclaimed. "She told me about that days ago and I forgot. I'll go get a flashlight; that child's not going to let us rest 'til she's satisfied." He smiled indulgently and went off. He reappeared with the flashlight and passed it in to Maddy, who had to back out a ways to get it.

"Thanks," she called back. "Holy Crap! It's freezin' in here. And I'm starved!" Maddy grumbled as she groped her way through the knee walls. Then we heard her voice from so far back she had to shout. "Yup, there's an angel in a big old box with Christmas stuff in here! What a filthy dusty mess!" We heard her talking with Annie, but we couldn't make it out. She was trying to reason with her about something. "Hey, is Tommy back home yet?" Maddy shouted.

"No, I don't think so. I didn't hear that old junk heap come up the street yet," Uncle Danny laughed. "Why?"

"'Cause it's right here by his closet; the only way to get this all stuff out is through his room. It's way too big to drag it back the other way, but he'll be bull...he'll have a holy fit if we go through his room. He'd be mad if he knew we was even this far into his part of the closet. I was goin' to have you ask him if it was OK. But since he's not here...God, I don't want to crawl in here again. I'm gonna shove this stuff through his closet door and get out of his room quick before he gets back. Anybody gonna rat me out?"

"Not me!" I said.

"Then go 'round by his door so ya can help me get it out fast!"

"I don't know nothin' about it," Uncle Danny said with a conspiratorial smile. "All I know is ya better be quick!'

"I'm tryin'," Maddy said. She was shifting some boxes around.

Uncle Danny went back out to the hallway and over to Tommy's door, with me right behind him. Of course it was locked, so we stood in the hallway waiting. Now that I was in on the mischief, I figured I might as well stay and see the grand finale.

The light snapped on in Tommy's bedroom; we could see it under the door. We could hear them in there, but no one came out. "See! I tried to tell you Mad'lin, but you just wouldn't listen to me." Annie spoke in the universal tone of 'I-told-you-so.' Then she came to the door and opened it. The little girl looked up at me and shrugged. "Fran, didn't I try to tell you?" Then she pointed to where Maddy was sitting on the floor with a couple of beat-up looking cardboard boxes, open at the top. We shuffled into the room to look.

There was a golden angel with her halo hanging off to one side. There were ropes of shiny foil Christmas-tree garland that had seen better days. There were some old clothes-kid's clothes, as if they'd been stuffed in around the decorations. There was Tommy's altar-boy robe I'd seen all those years ago. There were a couple pairs of boy's briefs, stained dark brown with something. Maddy scrutinized a pair that she held in her hand; her face was blood red.

"What is it, Maddy?" Uncle Danny looked confused.

Maddy seemed to collect herself. "Nothin'," she said, stuffing everything back into the boxes. "You silly little goose!" she addressed Annie. "Tommy must've got a nosebleed-that's all!" She tried to force out a chuckle but it caught in her throat. "Guys, help me get this stuff outa here fast before..."

"What the hell's going on here?!" Tommy yelled indignantly from behind us; his voice struck with the ferocity of a jagged, three-foot icicle falling from the roof. Uncle Danny had been about to pick up a box, and even he jumped up. Tommy had come up quietly. He still had snow in his hair, and his thick winter socks were soaked. I guessed in a heartbeat that the car had broken down; he'd tried to get it going, then gave up and walked several blocks in the snow. That's why his arrival hadn't been heralded by the usual backfire that sounded like a bank robbery in progress.

Tommy's pale doughy face went red with rage, but when he saw the boxes on the floor he blanched white as snow, and even the blue seemed to drain from his eyes. Then he colored up purple and rushed in like a bull to kick the box right out from between us, barely missing Maddy with his foot. The box with the angel and stained undergarments rose into the air and sailed into the opposite wall. The angel smashed.

"I'm gonna fuckin' kill you!" he said as he dove for Maddy, but Uncle Danny intercepted and blocked with his body. Tommy was knocked to the floor, but sprang up and came back at his uncle instead of his sister.

"Take the girls and get out!" Uncle Danny shouted as he took a wide stance in front of Tommy with his back to the door. Maddy didn't need to be told twice. She leapt from the floor and snatched Annie's upper arm as she dashed for the door, shoving me ahead with her other hand all in one move. I rushed out. The door slammed shut.

As we hurried down the stairs we were met by their grandmother. "What on earth's going on up there, I should like to know?" Before we could answer, the sounds of two men fighting made it abundantly clear.

"We just need to sit tight and wait," Maddy explained to her distraught grandmother. "Uncle Danny won't hurt Tommy-he's just lettin' him wear hisself out; then maybe they can talk."

"What?" Gramma asked. Then she looked at me. "Frances, do you understand what she's talking about?"

"Sadly, yes. Aunt Hannah, Maddy...I'm going home," I announced. "I'm taking Annie with me until things have quieted down," I said firmly. Annie clutched my hand and her face streamed tears, but she didn't say a word.

"Yes...that's a good idea. Go. And thank you Frances," Gramma said, just as something went thud over our heads.

"I'll walk you," Maddy offered.

"No thanks. I think you should stay with your grandmother. I think you should get that letter out of the drawer and talk with your uncle. You need to get to the bottom of all of this." Maddy nodded.

I ushered Annie to the doorway and stuffed her into her coat. "Don't worry," I said. "Sometimes boys get mad and fight, but Uncle Danny will take care of everything."

It had stopped snowing and the stars were out. The snow crunched under our feet as we walked.

"T...T...Tommy, ba..ba..bahroke the aaangel!" We were just about home when she suddenly wailed with her mouth open wide and the snots running into it.

"I know, darling, I know. That was really mean of him. Know what? Tomorrow we'll go to the Woolworths, just you and me. You can pick out any angel you want, OK sweetheart?"

"But I wanted that one!" Annie was inconsolable.

"I know you did, but she's gone. I promise we'll find another one that you'll like just as much."

"One with gold on her?"

"Yes! I'll find you an angel with gold! With gold and silver and stars and..."

"Oh, thank you Fran!" Annie stopped and threw her arms around me. She pressed her wet face into my jacket, snots and all. I hugged her tight. "I love you!" Her gentle voice was muffled.

"...and sunshine and the moon too, if you want it," I stroked her hair, and my eyes filled. "I'll buy you a whole box of angels, my darling," I whispered. "I'll buy every angel in the whole goddamned store," I thought.

50

The night of the broken angel we fed Annie a hotdog and beans supper. Then I made popcorn with real butter and we watched Christmas specials on TV. She was in Annie-heaven as she poked bits of popcorn into her mouth with greasy fingers, and hardly took her eyes off the television. Then Mom called Aunt Hannah and asked if she could stay the night. After I got her off to sleep in a cot by my bed, I sat with my parents.

"Well? What's going on over there now?" Mom asked.

"Lord only knows," I said. The whole evening I'd been trying to think what I should tell them-how much should I tell them? "A few weeks ago Eddie Murphy sent a strange letter to me from Canada. He sounded distraught...more like really messed-up, rambled on and made no sense. When I heard about poor George, I got worried. It hit me that sometimes people can feel so bad that they..." Mom nodded so I didn't need to say it out loud. "So I showed Maddy the letter and told her to keep it. After all, he's her brother...half-brother. Anyway, she didn't seem too worried about it, so that was that-it was out of my hands. Then Tommy came home and..." I didn't really know what happened with Tommy. I decided to leave out the details so as not to upset my parents. "Ah...he got totally crazy-mad at Maddy because she went into his closet-just to get some Christmas stuff. His room is off-limits. He almost hit her, but Uncle Danny stopped him. So I left and told Aunt Hannah I was taking Annie, because it sounded like a boxing match up there." Maddy was right: them Malones was kinda screwed up.

"Jeez! I gotta say it: I'm real disappointed," Dad said. "That's kid-stuff! He's about to hit 'is sister 'cause his room's off limits? Tommy's gettin' way too old and way too big for that crap. Damned hot-headed Irishman! I sure hope Danny can straighten Tommy out before he does somethin' really dumb, somethin' he'll regret for the rest of his life."

"I know what you mean Dad, but don't worry. Uncle Danny had it under control. He just needs a little more time with Tommy. I think everything is going to work out just fine."

"I certainly hope so," Mom shook her head. "It's a disgrace! Annie should not be seeing this sort of thing-no child should."

"That's why I brought her home. Oh, I almost forgot...just so you know, in case she brings it up. Tommy kicked a box and broke some old Christmas angel that had been stored back in the closet for the last fifty years; that's what upset Annie. I told her we'd go to Woolworths tomorrow and pick out a new one."

"Good luck finding a Christmas decoration this late," Mom warned. I hadn't thought of that.

We made pancakes for breakfast next morning. Annie chatted merrily with her mouth full and afterwards wanted to take some out to Flopsy. Mom fixed her a little plastic plate and let her believe that rabbits enjoyed pancakes. I watched out the window as that extraordinary child I'd come to love with all my heart trudged through the crusty snow towards the rabbit hutch. I decided then and there that when Christmas was over, we would all sit down for one big fat Malone-Orillio family discussion. Mom had summed it up: Annie should not be subjected to that sort of thing. I really wasn't convinced that Uncle Danny had it under control. Putting the Malone family to rights was going to be like putting Humpty Dumpty together again. I hoped we could convince them that it would be best for Annie to live with us, at least for a while, without making any hard feelings. The idea gave me comfort-I even thought about asking if she could spend Christmas, but decided I should wait. This had to be handled carefully. That's where Mom would come in; she'd know just what to say, and exactly how to say it.

I borrowed the car and we went downtown to Woolworths. We picked up more rabbit-chow, and then looked for a new angel. The only kind they had left was a tacky solid plastic model, with a hole in her back so you could stick a light in the halo that was molded onto her head. It was an indoor-outdoor decoration with a slick golden finish. Annie thought she was beautiful.

51

In the early morning hours on the day before Christmas, we were whacked by a nor'easter that would dump eighteen inches of snow before it finally stopped-snow on top of snow that had already accumulated. It started falling before dawn and just kept coming. The gusting winds blew up knee-deep drifts in pretty peaks and valleys, like white icing on a cake. It piled about four foot high over the front stairs and along one whole side of the driveway. The plows worked all day and into the night, trying to keep up. Flights were canceled and parties put on hold. We'd hear later on the news that a few stubborn souls refused to listen to advisory warnings, and perished on the treacherous roadways, all because they wanted to be with family on Christmas day. We'd learn that out there somewhere, strangers lost loved ones to the very storm that saved one of our own.

I started helping Dad shovel right after breakfast. We began with the theory that if we kept at it all day, it would be easier than letting it build up. After nearly two hours in the wind and sleet, we developed an alternative hypothesis: it might be better to let nature have her way and then deal with it later. But just before it got dark at 4:00 pm, Dad decided to take another crack at it. The plow had already barreled down our little street several times, and each time it pushed up another wall of hard-packed snow at the foot of the driveway. We were hopelessly blocked in; it was almost as tall as me. Dad was afraid it might freeze solid if the temperature plummeted as predicted. It was about thirty degrees, not counting wind-chill; when the sky cleared it could get much colder.

I got a pair of fresh gloves and followed him outside. As I stood in dismay, surveying our own personal glacier, I heard a familiar whistle. We peered through the white-out to see a procession of snow-covered Malones, marching determinedly down Mulligan Street. Maddy and Annie were out front, bracing into the wind. She held on to Annie, and carried a brown grocery bag that turned out to be some half-frozen lettuce for Flopsy. Uncle Danny and Tommy were right behind, each with a shovel on their broad shoulders. I could have cried with relief. Dad was looking exhausted, and Mom and I were worried about him. There was a round of hand-shaking and back-clapping and wishes of Merry Christmas. Then Uncle Danny told Dad to go on into the house-he'd put

Tommy to work; it'd be good for him. Dad thanked him and told him to be sure and come in afterwards for a drink.

"Fran! Mad'lin! Flopsy's gone! His house is all gone too!" Annie stood thigh deep in the snow at the foot of the little hill, and her cry carried over the wind.

"Dear Lord no," I thought. I waded through the snow and stared in disbelief; a great white drift had blanketed the hutch. You wouldn't even know it was there. "Tommy! The bunny is buried in snow! Help!" I called like a damsel in distress. "Don't worry," I told Annie. I was optimistic; Flopsy had a lot more meat on him than when we first brought him home, and his white fur had thickened from the cold.

At over six feet tall, Tommy strode easily through the deep snow. We stepped back as he deftly wielded the shovel and had the whole mess dug out in about two minutes. The metal latch was frozen shut. I took my glove off and warmed it with my hand, then jiggled it open. I held my breath and stuck my head inside. Whop! Whop! The ornery creature thumped his big feet soundly at me. Flopsy had been hiding back in his covered wooden box, snug as a bug in a rug in his bed of straw. Crisis averted. I gave Tommy two thumbs up. He turned away with barely a nod and went off to attack the snow heaped at the end of the driveway. If the rabbit had been dead, I think Tommy would've simply commenced digging a hole to bury it.

The men got the driveway cleared, and came inside for something to eat. My mother had baked up a storm, but now their party was canceled. Even though it was almost suppertime, we all felt like having desert, so Mom put out a couple of pumpkin pies, a plate of fancy cookies and a custard cream cake. She used over a whole quart of milk to make a pot of hot cocoa. I unwrapped some Hershey's Kisses and one by one, dunked them into the cocoa before popping them into my mouth, a trick I soon taught Annie. Tommy singlehandedly put away most of a pie, because Mom kept asking if he'd like another slice, and he kept saying yes. Maddy finally jabbed him with her elbow.

"You're not supposed to eat it all-even if the hostess keeps offering," she whispered. Tommy shrugged and grinned a bit sheepishly.

"Aw, let the man eat. He just shoveled about two tons of snow!" Dad was relaxed and jovial again.

"Please, eat!" Mom said. "There's plenty-I don't know what I'll do with it all."

"See!" Tommy said, glowering at Maddy in mock indignation. She stuck her tongue out at him. Then I knew everything was alright between them.

"Ooh! Oh-oh...not now! Jeez! For the luva Mike!" There was a chorus of exclamations as the power flickered twice, and then everything went dark.

I got up to look out the living room window and saw a whole block full of dark houses-there was no light coming from the projects either. All the twinkling Christmas lights in the neighbor's windows had suddenly vanished, and our own tree stood forlornly in darkness. "Maybe it won't last too long," I said hopefully.

There was an advent wreath on the table with one purple and three white candles. Tommy pulled out his cigarette lighter and started lighting all four candles. You were supposed to light them with special prayers on Christmas Day, but I don't think he knew that. I looked over at Mom and she just shrugged, like she wasn't too concerned. I guess the Lord would just have to make an allowance on account of the black-out. We finished eating by candlelight, and had two less pies and almost no cookies to worry about.

"Well, we'd best get back to Ma and Tom," Uncle Danny said.

"Have they been alone all this time?" Mom was concerned.

"No, Joanie's with them; she's a big help to Ma-looks after her father too," he said proudly.

"Wait a sec!" Dad said. He went into the living room and groped around under the tree. "Ah ha!" he exclaimed, and pulled out a little bottle in a red foil bag. "Merry Christmas! I was gonna give ya this tomorrow, but I think you'll need it tonight-to keep warm," he said with a wink as he handed it to Uncle Danny.

"Gosh, thanks Joe, and Merry Christmas...but I didn't bring anything."

"Are you kiddin'?! You saved my ass out there-you and Tommy," he said in appreciation.

"And we don't want you goin' out by yourself tomorrow if it snows more tonight," Uncle Danny insisted. "We'll be back, won't we Tommy?" Tommy nodded yes.

"I'm worried about Flopsy!" Annie interrupted loudly. "What if he gets snowed in again?"

"Don't worry; I think it's almost over," I said.

"We'll send Tommy round to check on 'im tomorrow morning," Uncle Danny assured her. "He'll make sure you can get in to feed Flopsy."

"But it's so cold," Annie whined.

"Flopsy loves the cold! Did you see the meat on 'im?" Dad asked. "And that thick fur coat too! That old rabbit's as fat 'n furry as a polar bear!" Everybody laughed except Annie. She didn't seem convinced.

Mom made sure that her coat was all buttoned up and I tied the strings on her knit hat. Maddy told her to put on her gloves and took her hand firmly. The four Malones tried to shuffle through the door without opening it too wide, but the wind whipped into the kitchen and blew at the candles on the advent wreath. The flames bent low and flickered. Before I got the door shut behind them, one went out.

"Brrr," I said, shivering as I watched out the window. Then the starless night swallowed them up like a great black whale. I pressed my face up against the glass, trying to find them in the darkness. Suddenly I felt as if I had a team of wild horses inside me; I fought a terrible urge to run out like a fool without stopping for a coat, and snatch Annie back.

I turned away from the window, trying to figure out what made me feel that way. Tommy was all tuckered out and full of pie-I wasn't worried about another fight. Uncle Tom hadn't been a threat for a long time, not since the stroke took all the meanness out of him. Uncle Danny was head of the family now, and he was doing an admirable job. Even Joanie seemed to be improving under his influence; she was turning out to be a decent, caring girl, now that Uncle Danny had got rid of Jack Mack.

The lights never came back on that Christmas Eve. The battery powered wall clock said nine-thirty when Dad apologized for being a party-pooper and went to bed exhausted. The phone lines were down, so we couldn't even call anyone. For lack of anything better to do, Mom and I sat up waiting for the electricity, but gave up at eleven and called it a night. We'd already gone into the back closet with a flashlight and dug out all the extra blankets in case we had to sleep without heat. It was 60 degrees and dropping in the house. Upstairs was colder, so I decided to bunk on the living room couch, wearing a thick sweatshirt over my flannel pajamas. Mom said they'd be fine upstairs; Dad was heavy, and generated a lot of heat. We slept for a brief time in heavenly peace, while the wind whistled and the snow fell.

***

It took a long time to figure out exactly what happened that night, with the Malones and the three us over the back hill. It turned out I'd been looking at things all wrong. I always thought our two families were like scattered pieces of a jigsaw puzzle. I thought that somewhere in the back of a mysterious closet, there lay a box cover that provided a definitive picture of our lives, a neat and complete explanation for everything. When that long Christmas Day was finally over, I began to see that it wasn't so much a picture-puzzle as a never ending story, a story that would become different over time, and change according to who was doing the telling. Each of us had our own chapters, and the book couldn't even be read until we wove all the pages together.

52

"Yeah...I'm sure. I heard 'em talkin' about a lot of money." Joanie spoke quietly into the crackling radio left abandoned in a small back room. Her sick father and grandmother were still napping. They didn't even know the power was out yet.

"How much we talkin' about?" Jack's voice shot back.

"I don't know how much."

"Well, I can't set us up if it ain't enough." The buzzing static made it difficult to understand.

"It's at least a hundred thousand...I...heard 'im say that," Joanie lied. From the bottom of the staircase, she'd only heard her sister remark that it was a lot, and her uncle seemed to agree. Her heart burned with anger at being left out. Even her stupid cousin was included in their little powwow-and she wasn't even blood! Well, they'd all live to regret it.

"Where's it at now?" Buzz...crackle...buzz.

"Still up there."

"Can you get at it?"

"I think so."

"Damn it Joanie! I don't need you to think..."

"Yeah, Jack, I can get it."

"Great, baby! First thing we're gonna buy is a nice big diamond ring for ya!"

"Thanks Jack...uh...now might be a good time; Danny's gone-they're all at my aunt's house."

"Naw, that ain't no good-they could come back any minute...bzzt...we'll take care of it later tonight, just like I told ya yesterday."

"OK...that'll be good. Danny's goin' out later tonight...bzzt."

"Alone? Where's he goin'?"

"Over by you, to Middlefield. Said he was goin' to the rectory...he's gonna pay a call on some priest he's got a gripe with...old Father Mahood."

"Who? Bzzt..."

"Jack? You there?"

"Yeah...did you say Mahood?"

"Yeah...buzz...zzzt...Mahood. Why? You know the guy?"

"Ah…no…never heard of 'im…why don't you tell me about him…bzzt…how do ya know this…bzzt…priest?"

"Ah…it's no big deal…he was our family priest…since back when Danny and Dad was kids."

"That old, eh?"

"Yeah, I guess."

"Why's Danny goin' to see 'im now all of a sudden?"

"There was some big shit-storm here last night…Uncle Danny and Tommy had a fistfight over somethin'."

"Whad they fight about?"

"How the hell should I know? Listen Jack, I'm sick of it. I'm sick of all my family's crazy shit!"

"You're sure ole Danny boy's goin' out there tonight? On Christmas Eve?"

"Yeah-I heard 'im tell Tommy he was gonna pay Father Mahood a Christmas visit…do somethin' he shoulda done a long time ago. That's all I heard…Jack…you still there?"

"Yeah, I'm here." Bzzt. "Listen to me Joanie: you contact me as soon as Danny leaves, got that?"

"OK Jack…but what about the money?"

"It'll be real early in the morning…you just get it in your hands…then listen for the horn and sneak out…got that?"

"OK. But…you ain't gonna hurt Uncle Danny, right?"

"'Course I ain't. I ain't gonna hurt no one baby, got that?"

"Yeah, Jack, I got it."

"Over and out!" The radio crackled and buzzed and went silent.

53

Tommy and Uncle Danny walked in front of the girls as they trudged home early Christmas Eve. Even the short walk around the corner drove sugar-sized crystals of snow into their faces and down their necks. As they approached the old Victorian home, Maddy stopped and stared incredulously. "Look at that!" She pointed. The vast yard that was usually nothing more than dirt and patches of weeds was buried beneath a virgin blanket of white. Gusting winds had blown deep drifts up against the north wall. Snow camouflaged the sagging roof, stuck to the weathered clapboard and covered the rotten gutters. "The place looks almost decent," she exclaimed.

"It sure does! And as soon as winter's over, we're gonna fix 'er up real good," Uncle Danny said.

They went inside, cold and exhausted but in good cheer from time spent helping family, and from being happily stuffed with pie. Then the Malones began to bed down in the black-out for what they expected to be a long winter's night, with no heat and no light. It was warmer downstairs, so they bundled the invalid patriarch on the overstuffed horsehair couch in the front parlor. The pilot light on the stove was out, but Gramma had lit the gas burners with a match and had the five gallon pot for boiled dinners simmering, filling the kitchen with warm steam. Uncle Danny hauled the wooden chairs out and lined them up in the hall, then dragged a mattress from the girls' bedroom to put down for Annie and his mother. Maddy gathered the blankets and tucked them in early-there was nothing to do anyway, and besides, they'd be warmer in bed. In the soothing warmth of the steam, with her little granddaughter snuggled by her side, Hannah Malone fell into a deep sleep at last. There were lit votive candles on top of the kitchen table; to be safe they were placed on a metal cookie tray. The tiny flames illuminated the large crucifix that had hung on the wall since she was a child, the same Dear Christ who'd suffered with them through sickness and sorrow, births and deaths, all these many long years.

Uncle Danny brought a basin of hot water and set it on the floor by Tom's head so he'd keep warm and breathe better. Then he stretched out on the living room chair with his stocking feet on the hassock, determined not to sleep. He had to stay awake to tend the steaming pot and make sure it was filled with water that night. He had to stay awake because there was something important he still needed to do.

Maddy ladled some hot water into a two quart sauce pan. She replenished what she'd taken with another saucepan from the kitchen sink, before carrying the small source of heat upstairs to her room. On the floor by the bed, it'd be better than nothing. She went to use the bathroom, but Tommy was in there. It wouldn't be habitable for a while now, she thought, not unless she could manage to get the widow open. It'd probably be frozen shut.

"Hey Tommy," she called from outside the bathroom door.

"What?"

"You want some hot water for your room? There's a big pot on the stove."

"Huh? Water for what?"

"It makes a little heat, for a while anyway. Once you're asleep you don't notice how cold it is."

"Nah, 's OK."

"Hey Tommy, wake me up when you go out to shovel tomorrow."

"OK...ah...Merry Christmas."

"Merry Christmas Tommy," she said, smiling to herself in bemused surprise.

Maddy walked carefully through the dark hallway so as not to spill the water. She was heading towards her room, the one where Eddie Murphy used to stay, but paused at the double bedroom she'd shared with Annie. She decided to sleep there instead. It was nearer the top of the stairs if she needed to find her way down in the dark. She still had clothes in one of the dressers, in case she had to sleep there because of Annie's night terrors. As she thought about it, Maddy realized with satisfaction that Annie hadn't had a bad night all week.

Before going off to sleep she unbound her breasts, and put on a clean t-shirt. The cotton felt like ice on her bare skin. Then she layered on a flannel with a sweat-shirt over it. She put on a dry pair of dungarees and lay down. The black leather jacket was downstairs, thrown over the back of one of the kitchen chairs to dry, along with the three other coats of the snow shoveling crew. She lay back on the pillow, then realized that she hadn't wished Joanie a Merry Christmas. She thought of getting up and going for a smoke with her, but was too tired to move. She didn't even have a bedtime cigarette before falling fast asleep.

54

It was late Christmas Eve. The power lines hadn't come down in West Middlefield, so the streetlamps were on. The spotlight on the entry-hall of the rectory shone on the Christmas wreath that was nailed to the front door. When Daniel Malone rang the bell, it was answered by a stout middle-aged woman who kept house, dressed in her robe with her hair in big plastic rollers. "Who is it?" she demanded indignantly.

"My name's Malone, Daniel Malone. I'm here to see Father Mahood."

"It's past eleven o'clock-Father is in bed. Surely he's not expecting you?"

"No ma'am, don't suppose he is, but I'll see 'im all the same," he said as he walked past her into the entryway and straight into the reception parlor. "I'd appreciate it if you'd send 'im down."

The woman was accustomed to the role of gate-keeper. This was not the first distraught parishioner to come knocking in the night, and she usually managed to send off all but the true emergencies with the force of a tavern bouncer. But this man was different. It wasn't just his size that intimidated her; there was a steadfast determination in his eyes, as if he could stop a locomotive just by staring it down. She went immediately upstairs. Daniel heard their urgent whispers. She returned a bit more polite. "Father will be down in a moment. Please have a seat in the parlor," she said, gesturing towards the front room.

Daniel Malone sat. At last he heard the slow steps of an old man descend the staircase. The wrinkled, gray-haired priest appeared in his blacks with his collar askew, looking sleepy and rumpled. There was fear in his eyes. He hadn't had time to put on his shoes, and was wearing slippers.

Daniel snapped to attention out of habit like a child, and almost lost his nerve. This man didn't look like a monster. It would have been easier to face a gun-wielding gangster. Nonetheless he faced him, secretly trembling inside, although he could break the old man in half if he desired.

"Evening Father," he said calmly.

"Ah, good evening...Danny, isn't it? Hannah Malone's child?"

"After all these years, you remember me?" he asked in quiet astonishment, then resolved to go on. "Yes Father, I was Hannah Malone's child, but I haven't been a child for a long time now. You'd best sit down."

The withered old man sat. "Won't you take off your coat?" he asked.

"No. I won't be stayin' long enough to take it off," Daniel said as he sat down again. "I think you know why I'm here," he began.

The priest sighed, and wiped his rheumy eyes with the back of his hand. "What is it you want, Danny?" he asked after a moment.

"You ask me what I want? Well, what I want, I can't have. I want our lives back; I want them back unscarred by your evil." His ice blue eyes bore down on the priest and demanded a response. None was forthcoming. "Dear God, Father: why did you do it?"

The priest remained silent and impassive.

Daniel found his apparent lack of emotion utterly maddening. His voice became urgent. "Wasn't it bad enough that you ruined me and Tom? Why'd you have to come back and hurt our Tommy? How many other families have you harmed?"

When Father Mahood didn't answer, Daniel suddenly sprang from the settee cushion and stood towering over him. The toes of his boots nearly touched Father's velvet slippers. The old priest didn't even flinch when Daniel stretched out his arms and enormous hands in a gesture that was at once supplicant and threatening. He wanted to wring the old man's skinny neck like a chicken. "I just want to know...why?" he asked again. He didn't shout, and his steady hands were unwavering.

Father Mahood seemed to look off under Daniel's right arm, as if the answer might be found written on the wall behind him. "Hmm...ah...I don't know, really," he finally answered. "I guess...I just don't know."

Daniel looked over the priest's head to the omnipresent wall crucifix, and seriously considered the possibility of just-not-knowing. Could this man be so sick that he knew not what he had done? Would that excuse him? Did he, Daniel Maddox Malone, have a right to judge anyone? Father Mahood had also done the work of the church. Yet this priest had ministered unto his own mother and sister-in-law as he'd silently raped their children. And his mother must never know of it; it would be the death of her. As he struggled to find an answer he only knew one thing for certain: he'd been in prison a very long time, much longer than sixteen years. If he didn't take care of this right here and now, he'd be locked away forever.

"You say you don't know?" he asked, to be certain he'd heard him rightly. "You sodomized children," he qualified, "and you just...don't know?"

"It just...I don't know why I did it Danny...I'm sorry. It's a long time ago now...it's best left in the hands of the Lord."

Daniel slowly lowered his hands and collected himself. "I'll not be leavin' this in God's hands, Father. I'm goin' to make you pay here on earth for what you've done, for every last sin," he said with dead certainty. "I'm goin' to make sure you don't ever hurt another child...not ever again."

Having finished his mission, he walked out into the night. He got into the shiny black cab that was parked under the streetlight in front of the rectory, and drove home to his family. Daniel had hoped to feel some relief, but it wasn't forthcoming. He certainly hadn't made everything right, but at least it was a start.

55

During a blackout, people tend to walk into darkened rooms and flip on the light switch out of habit. Then there's a split second when you stand there befuddled, even though you knew darned well just a moment ago that the electricity was out. Multiply that by every member of your family trying at least once to put the lights on, and add that to the lights you never shut off when the power went out in the first place. You get the picture. At four-twenty a.m. on Christmas Day, the suburban streets of East Mapleton lit up like New York City.

I awoke with a start when the twinkling tree lights popped on in our living room, sending a cacophony of color into my sleepy eyes. The heater kicked on and I sighed with relief. I was stiff with cold. I got up to shut off all the extraneous lights-in the kitchen, the hallway, the bathroom and the den. I looked out the front window and saw that the neighbors' houses were similarly illuminated, upstairs and down, inside and out. I went into the bathroom and thought I'd take a nice hot bath, then felt rather foolish. It would take about an hour before the water heater could comply. At least I could make a cup of hot tea now-we had an electric stove. Then I could go up to my own comfortable bed and fall back to sleep.

56

When the lights snapped on in the bedroom where Maddy slept, she awoke with a groan and laid a pillow over her face. It was so damned cold, she hated to get out of bed and walk across the room to switch it off. Just then she heard something go bump overhead. "Jeez...I can't believe Gramma's at it again, and in the freezing cold too," she mumbled aloud to no one, and decided to get up and make sure her grandmother was alright. She had no idea what time it was and looked outside to see if it was light. It was still dark as night, no sign of the dawn. By the streetlamps she could see that a couple more inches of snow had fallen. "Crap," she whispered, and scuffed silently from the room in her thick wooly socks. The light was on in the upstairs hallway, and she could see it coming from under the door in Tommy's room-apparently it hadn't waked him. Then she heard another footfall from the third half-story. She padded down the hall and looked from the bottom of the short staircase that led up to the former maid's quarters and the tower beyond. The door was open, and a light was on. She tiptoed up the stairs.

"Jesus Christ!" Joanie was so startled she almost dropped the cloth sack that took both hands to hold. She was bundled up in her coat, with her purple suede shoulder bag slung over her back. Maddy had given it to her just the other night as an early Christmas gift. "You scared the shit out of me!" Joanie hissed. "What are you doin' up here?" There was a faint light coming from the open door behind her, the door that led up to the tower from whence she had obviously descended.

Maddy shrugged. "I heard somethin'. I thought maybe Santa Clause was comin' down the fuckin' chimney." She pointed at the cloth sack, and screwed up one corner of her mouth ironically. "But you look more like the Grinch that stole Christmas."

"Just shut-up and get out of my way, and you won't get hurt," Joanie kept her voice low.

"What? Listen Joanie, I ain't gonna let you walk off with poor old Gramma's money. I don't know how in hell you found out, but...just go put it back."

"What if I don't want to?" Joanie's eyes narrowed to razor thin slits. "I've been slavin' for her all my life! Washin 'n ironing her stupid aprons...peelin' a shit-load of potatoes...and what'd I ever get? What do I got to show for it? Nothin', that's what. It's payback time!"

"Dad paid you pretty good if I remember. But OK-you feel you got gypped. I'm still not gonna let you do it. Not gonna let you hurt Gramma. Jesus...if you'd asked, she probably woulda give you some."

"You can't stop me," Joanie said. She was trembling.

"Aw, com' on! Even if I couldn't-which ain't the case, Tommy's downstairs, and Uncle Danny too. You're not that stupid Joanie. I don't think you're this rotten either. He put you up to it, didn't he?" Joanie didn't answer. "That son-of-a-bitch Jack is behind this...but you had to tell him about the money in the first place, didn't you? I guess that makes you just as rotten. What a shitty thing to do."

"Just shut the fuck up!" Joanie managed to keep the decibels low but the sentiment was deafening. "You've got no right to judge me...to tell me what to do...you're nothin'! Nothin' but a...you're a disgusting queer. God, I hate you! I hate this whole messed up family! You...my dumb-shit brother...we even got a kid who's a retard-don't know what happened to him...Dad's gone soft in the head...and now we got an ex-con uncle takin' care of business. I hate it! I don't want to be part of this family no more. I hate all the Malones!"

Maddy cocked her head to one side and gave the sentiment a respectful moment of consideration. "Yeah, we are kinda screwed up...though I think you got a helluva nerve callin' Tommy a dumb-shit. But you're right; I'm a dyke. I love women, and if that makes me disgustin' to you-OK. You got lots of company. But there's worse things you can do," she looked pointedly at the sack in Joanie's hands, then went on. "Yeah, Dad's toasted squash," Maddy tapped her head with one finger. "And Uncle Danny just got out of jail; but if you think Jack Mack is an improvement over the Malones...then you really are one thick mick."

Joanie's lips worked as she searched for an appropriate retort, but she couldn't think straight; she was losing her nerve.

Maddy elaborated. "For starters, your boyfriend screws around with other girls...the ones he pimps out. They ain't even regular prostitutes...I mean...he goes after poor girls when they're down. He comes on real sweet, nice and helpful, like he's gonna help 'em out of a financial jam-it's just temporary. Then he gets mean and threatens the poor girls. He even got their hours cut back and pays off some son-of-a-bitch to do it! Then they get stuck. And he don't give 'em the money if they don't put-out. Linda ran off because he tried to...first he got her fired, then...I could just kill him when I think about it...he tried to make her..." Maddy choked up with rage.

"How do you know?" Joanie asked skeptically.

"Lots of people know Joanie...everybody seems to know but you. Linda called me from Florida. She'd been done with Jack a long time ago, practically since I first met her. After Uncle Danny ran him off the place, he went at her, went at her to get to me. Linda had to run away because Jack said he'd hurt me if she went with me anymore-hurt me and her too. She was so afraid for her kid...and me. I'm glad she's safe now, but that Jack is real bad news, more than you seem to know. Joanie...he's way too hot for you to handle."

A car horn honked in the distance. Even though it was a block away, sound travels farther in winter. There're no leaves on the trees to muffle it. Joanie picked up her head to listen, then seemed to dismiss it as not important. But Maddy took notice. "OK," Joanie said. "I'll go put it back." She turned to go up the winding staircase. Maddy followed. In the tower, the kerosene lamp was still lit on the wooden table, and the faces of the two little girls stared from their picture frames.

Maddy saw the metal box open on the floor; it was empty. "Shit! I can't believe you was gonna do it, gonna waltz off with Gramma's whole life savings and leave this old lamp burning up here too! Even if you hate all the rest of us...how could you put Annie in danger?"

"You're not gonna tell, are you?"

"Jeezes Joanie...I'm sorry, but this ain't like sellin' pot or somethin'! I can't trust you; none of us can, now you got back with Jack. I ain't no snitch, but this is bad, bad and dangerous. Listen-I'll give you a chance to leave so you don't have to face Gramma and Uncle Danny. I know Jack's out there waitin' for ya...I heard the car horn. So why don't ya put that down and get the hell out of here. Wait...on second thought, why don't ya take a couple hundred bucks for your trouble! Buy yourselves a pair of one-way tickets somewhere." Maddy was seething with disgust. "Just take it and go to 'im! You deserve each other."

But Joanie had no place to go, not without the money. Jack wouldn't take her-she shuddered to think what he'd do if she turned up with only enough for Greyhound bus tickets. She also knew that everything Maddy said about Jack was true, and she hated her for saying it. Joanie bent down and laid the bag on the floor and opened it, as if to extract a few bills and put the rest back. She reached inside and instead of cash, she pulled out a gun. She stood up and leveled it at her sister-or at least she tried. Her hand shook violently.

Maddy watched in disbelief, more disgusted than afraid. "So now you're gonna shoot me? You gotta be kiddin' me!"

"Get outa my way," she hissed, "or…" Joanie didn't get a chance to say or what.

Below them the sound of shattering glass followed by something like a small explosion could be heard all the way up to the tower. Maddy's heart felt as if it dropped all the way to the basement. She knew it was Jack Mack. She turned her back on the gun in her sister's hand and barreled downwards, around the spiral stairs, through the two small rooms packed with junk and down the short flight to the upstairs hallway.

It must have been gasoline. The foot of the stairs was engulfed in flames, along with the front entryway. It was already roaring up the carpet runner towards them, licking the spokes of the mahogany banister worn smooth from generations of Malone hands, and the seats of children's pants as they took the forbidden slide.

"Jesus God no!" Maddy cried. "Uncle Danny!" She cupped her hands and shouted with all her might.

Uncle Danny appeared in his stocking feet down in the hallway between the kitchen and the front parlor. The fire was already racing towards him, devouring the chairs lined up to make room for the mattress in the kitchen. "Go round to the back stairway! Make sure Tommy and Joanie get down-I'll get the others out!" he shouted.

Maddy nodded. As she turned to go get Tommy the sirens screamed. They were already coming? Jack must have called. Who else would be up before dawn? The last thing she saw down the front staircase was her black leather jacket hanging on a chair. It was going up in flames; the leather curled and shriveled like burnt skin. She went to Tommy's door and before pounding simply tried the doorknob. It was unlocked. She ran in and shook him hard. His eyes snapped open.

"Tommy it's a fire! The whole damned place is goin' up-com' on!" She yanked on his arm and he sprang from the bed. The house was filling with smoke. The fire had almost reached the top of the stairs. "Back way!" Maddy shouted. Tommy grabbed her hand and they ran together like two children at play, choking as they went through the upstairs hall and towards the small back staircase that led down by the kitchen, the one meant for servants.

57

Hannah Malone awoke in the darkness of early Christmas morning, from the most restful sleep she'd had in ages. She sat up in the strange bed and took a moment to recall where she was-ah yes...the kitchen floor. The votive candles had burned out, and someone had the good sense to shut the kitchen light off last night. The stove was turned off too, but the room still felt nice and warm. She reached carefully across the bed and swept the air gently with her hand, searching for Annie. Finding nothing, she patted the mattress. It was faintly warm, but empty.

Suddenly there was a mighty crash in the front hall. She smelled the gas immediately, and struggled to rise from the bed on the floor. At eighty-three years old, she had to pull herself up with the help of the sturdy metal kitchen table. When she poked her head around the doorframe into the hall and saw her home in flames, her heart nearly stopped. On impulse she lifted the crucifix from the kitchen wall, and then stumbled into the hall towards the parlor. "Daniel," she called, but her voice had no power any longer. She ran one hand along the wall so as not to trip over the chairs. She must wake her sons-maybe the child was there, she thought, perhaps looking under the tree to see if Santa had come.

Daniel came charging from the parlor and nearly ran his old mother down. "Go on outside Ma!" he cried, "I'll get Tom and then come back for the others!"

"Is Annie with you?" she gasped breathlessly. "She's gone from the kitchen!"

He shook his head no and his face was a look of pure horror. "I'll find her Ma! Go out!" He almost pushed her in the direction of the back doorway as he returned to the parlor.

Danny lifted his invalid brother like a babe in arms. He ran out the back door, almost slipped and fell, then practically tossed Tom in a snow bank, out of harm's way before bolting back into the house. His mother hadn't gone out, but instead turned back and tried to make it down the fiery hallway. She would have burned to death if he hadn't run up from behind and held her back.

Maddy and Tommy made it down the back staircase to the landing, and practically ran into Uncle Danny and Gramma. He had both arms around his mother, held her from behind as she thrashed him with the two-foot cross in her hands, fighting him like a madwoman as she screamed, "Annie!"

"I got your dad outside, but we can't find Annie!" her uncle shouted over the crackling flames. "Ma woke up and she was gone from the kitchen, God help us...did she go up to bed last night? She's nowhere down here."

Maddy felt Tommy's hand slip from her grasp. She thought she saw him smile before he disappeared back up into the smoke. She tried to go after him but couldn't breathe. The smoke blinded her, but she felt her uncle's great paw of a hand wrap round her arm like a vise as he pulled her outside, half-dragging, half-carrying his poor old mother in his strong right arm.

58

Joanie had no idea what made the terrible noise downstairs, but couldn't believe her luck as she stuffed cash hand over fist into her fringed shoulder bag, into her coat pockets and the pockets of her jeans-even into her bra, as much as would fit. The rest she left on the floor with the gun. Her sister had run off; maybe now she had a chance, maybe now she could get away at last. Maddy was right about one thing: going with Jack Mack would be like jumping from the proverbial frying pan into the fire...and she'd given her an idea. A one way ticket! Why hadn't she thought of that? Maddy always was the smart one-she'd give her that. But who was smart now, she thought as she blew out the kerosene lamp and tripped lightly down the spiral staircase.

From the first little room in the third half-story, Joanie heard the commotion below, and it frightened her. They sounded pretty upset. She hesitated almost four seconds before going to the window and opening it wide. She straddled the sill. She almost went back inside for fear of the height, and the snow covered roof. Joanie thought hard, thought of herself sitting gloriously alone on a bus heading west, maybe even California. Then she got the other leg out the window, leaned inward and hung over the sill on her stomach with both legs hanging out. She lowered her feet to the roof and tested the surface. The snow went crunch as one foot sank in. It was sticky snow! Her feet had a good purchase. Then it was an easy matter to crawl around the dormer and over to the side porch. Another gable shielded her from view on the street side. Dawn hadn't broken, but the streetlights were on. Joanie looked down and saw a high snow bank piled against the side of the house, where someone had shoveled the walkway; how nice of them. She sat on the edge of the roof and felt that section of gutter start to give under her weight. Without a moment to lose, she shoved herself off and over, plunging down feet first and landing in packed snow up to her waist. Pain shot up her leg and into her right hip as one foot sank through and struck the ground; the snow was deep, but it was still quite a drop. She sucked in her breath and bit her thin lip. For one horrible moment she thought she was stuck.

Joanie used her bare hands to dig herself out. She clawed feverishly at the snow and pushed it aside, as if she were digging herself alive out of her own grave. She couldn't feel her fingers, and only knew they were torn because of the blood on the snow. Suddenly she paused and sniffed the air like a dog. Smoke! Her heart went as cold as ice, but there was nothing she could do now. Maddy was right! Jack Mack was way too hot for her to handle. She really had no idea he could do such a thing. She threw all her weight forward, then back, then side to side. She was able to pull one knee up, get the left leg loose and extract it from the snow bank. She winced in pain as she drew her right leg out, then stood a moment to check her pockets and the zippered purse. It was all there. She was free!

Joanie knew Jack was waiting for her over on Mulligan Street, a ways down from her aunt and uncle's house-and that weird cousin, she thought with contempt. Jack had instructed her to cut across the back and duck through the fence, sneak down the hill and run through the yard like a naughty child, to bring him the bag of money. Well, fuck Jack, she thought smugly. Instead of running and hiding, Joanie walked off with her head held high. No one saw her leave. She was just crossing the street that divided her block from the next when the sirens roared past behind her. She didn't turn to look, but fixed her eyes ahead-she could see the traffic on Broadway. As her invalid father sat in the snow, she turned up Broadway and kept walking towards Cambridge. Joanie walked on as her grandmother gave up and dropped the cross, walked on as her brother struggled to breathe, determined to find his little sister or die trying. The busses would run soon. She would catch one and ride all the way into Grand Central Station. She'd buy a one-way ticket to California. Joanie couldn't have been happier if were a ticket to heaven.

59

Four fire engines, two ambulances and six police cars raced up to the Malone's house. The front of it was completely engulfed in flames, all the way up to the second story and heading fast towards the tower. Thank God the wind had died down; it gave them precious seconds.

Daniel walked with difficulty through the deep snow, holding fast to his mother and young niece. He knew if he let go, they'd turn around and run back inside, though he doubted his mother would get very far. The snow was too deep and the fight was nearly gone out of her. Maddy was still twisting in his grasp, trying to reason with her uncle. "I can get 'em! Lemme go! I know I can get 'em!" At a safe distance he just stopped, unable to drag his mother any farther. He looked back to where his brother sat in the snow. Tom didn't look particularly distraught-more like an oversized child in pajamas playing in a snow bank. If it weren't for the fire, it would've been comical.

The firemen were at the curb, shouting at one another, trying to find the fire hydrant buried in the snow. Two big men carrying fire-blankets charged over and through the drifts, towards the man who was obviously struggling with two people who wanted to run back inside. They saw it all the time. "Everybody out?!" one shouted.

"There're three inside!" Daniel shouted back. "A big boy, a teenaged girl, and one little girl missing! Please take my muther," he implored. "My old brother's there." He pointed to the man sitting complacently in a snow bank. "He's very ill," he explained.

One of the men made his way towards the sick man, while the other took charge of the old woman. He wrapped her in a blanket and hoisted her gently over his shoulder-only a few yards to the ambulance anyway...be faster than bringing over a stretcher.

She let go the crucifix. Jesus dropped into the snow feet-first and stuck up at an angle, as if He were looking straight at her, Gramma said later. She cried softly as the man carried her to the ambulance. Two others went with a stretcher to fetch Tom. Uncle Daniel looked back to the house, but could see there was no going back. There was nothing left to do but lead Maddy to safety.

"Wait," Maddy told her uncle firmly. She pointed towards the head of Christ peeking above the snow. "Gramma'll be wantin' that."

Uncle Danny nodded and let go her arm. Maddy plunged her hands into the drift to get a firm grasp round his middle, and hauled Jesus out. Then she trudged through the snow with her uncle towards the rescue vehicles, awkwardly shouldering the cumbersome cross, like a ragged pilgrim from the dark-ages.

60

I stood at the sink, rinsing the tea mug-Mom got annoyed if I let the tea stain set in. When the sirens roared past the end of Mulligan Street, I ran to the back door in time to see several fire engines go up the hilly road. My breath stopped. I ran back to the sink and looked out the kitchen window that faced our backyard, looked up past the little hill we'd climbed so many times, looked past the lilac bushes sleeping under a blanket of snow, and over the fence that ran along the border between the Malone's property and ours. Outside it was still black as night. The tall pointed tower that always reminded me of a witch's hat now looked like a flaming rocket about to launch to the moon.

I screamed. Then I ran from the kitchen, past the merry twinkling lights to the foot of the staircase and looked up to where my parents slept peacefully only a moment before, oblivious to the horror just over the hill. My mother was already out of bed, stumbling towards me with worry on her face. It was just before five am. Dawn wasn't even breaking. "Mummy! Daddy-come quick! Maddy's house is burning down!" I yelled as loud as I could.

"Are you sure?" Mom was astonished.

For a split second I considered whether I was imagining things. I had a glimmer of hope. But we could hear the sirens. She started down the stairs and Dad came behind her in his flannel pajamas. I raced back to the window hoping that this time I'd see something different. Perhaps it wasn't that bad. Perhaps I'd seen the flashing red lights of the fire engine reflecting on the stained glass.

My fantasy was short-lived. The tower was engulfed in flames. Mom had just put her hand on my shoulder and leaned in close behind me to look out the window. "Dear God! Joseph, it's true, it's all burned up! The children! Oh Dear God please let the children be out of there!" I'd never seen my mother so frightened in my life.

Dad had taken one glance out the window and dashed back upstairs without a word. He came down wearing pants over his pajamas, trying to do up the zipper with the flannel getting in the way. He ran to the doormat and was stuffing his feet into his boots. "Get my coat!" he hollered to either or both of us. I got it quick. As he threw it on, Dad checked the driveway to see which car was behind the other. It was the Buick.

"Joe..." Mom began in a worried tone.

"Listen!" My father interrupted. "No matter what happens, no matter what, I want you two to stay right here-understand?"

We nodded obediently. "Be careful Joe." Mom gave Dad a quick kiss and he beat it out the back door. We heard the sturdy car door close. Then the engine turned over the first time and purred like a lioness. Thanks to Tommy the driveway was clear, and he backed out with ease and drove around the corner.

61

When Joseph Orillio rounded the corner and caught sight of the blaze he was filled with an awesome dread, and a call to action that mastered all emotion. It was like just before a battle, an odd sensation he'd left back on some Pacific island, so long ago he'd all but forgotten what it felt like. He parked by the side of the road about twenty yards off, out of the way of rescue vehicles. Joe crossed himself and asked God to be with them as he jogged up the street, which was plowed but slippery. He saw two big engines hosing the front side of the house as the flames raced towards the backside, and couldn't help but wonder how the fire started, even while agonizing over the bigger question of life and death. There were already people pouring out of the projects-the police were ordering them to stay on the other side of the road. Joe made his way over to where Danny and Maddy stood with some police by a cruiser and an ambulance. When he saw Danny Malone in hand-cuffs, he feared the worst.

"Uncle Joe!" Maddy shouted as he came up, huffing and puffing from the exertion of running. "Uncle Danny didn't do nothin'! It was Jack set the fire...he threw a jug of gas-smashed right into the front entry! We can't find Annie...help us Uncle Joe, please do something!" she pleaded like her heart would break.

"You're under arrest for the murder of Father John Bernard Mahood. You have the right to remain silent..."

"Maddy! Hey Maddy!" A voice rang out from on high. They all stopped and looked up; even the policeman who was reading the Miranda Rights stopped and looked towards the voice that seemed to call out from heaven above.

"Tommy! It's Tommy," Maddy cried with joy. "Hold this for Gramma," she told her Uncle Joe as she thrust the large crucifix into his hands. Maddy bolted so fast into the snowy yard that no one had time to grab her. She fell twice before reaching the edge of the snowline, where the heat from the blaze had melted the snow down to the bare mud.

The people on the street started cheering to see someone still alive, but the jubilance was short lived. There was a truck with a tower ladder and a bucket, but there was no clear way to get back there. The snow was piled over three feet high by the curb and packed hard from the snowplows. A fireman spoke into his radio and called for a truck with a plow; the nearest one was coming, but it was still miles away. Several men went at it with hand shovels. If they could just get the truck over the hump, maybe they could drive close enough to get the kid off the roof. The hoses had been blasting the side where the little girl's bedroom was; they didn't expect to find her alive. This one might have a chance.

Up close, the crackling flames were the most sickening thing Maddy had ever heard. Her brother was perched out on the ledge between his bedroom window and the third half-story, the one he used to climb through to hide his stash in the maid's quarters. Fire poured from the window behind him, and rose up wickedly along the roofline in front, like a picket fence made of flames. It had been slowed some by all the snow on the roof, but that melted quickly as the inside burned hot. Maddy glanced back to the fire trucks and saw that help wasn't coming fast enough; then she saw a way out. Tommy might be able to crawl along the roof towards the back. It was still intact, but the blaze was spreading like some demonic creature from hell, devouring the old house with perverse gusto. It was going for Tommy. Behind her the big engine roared, as the truck backed up and rammed the snow, trying to get close enough.

"Tommy! Go that way!" Maddy cupped her hands like a megaphone and her voice rang out over the flames and the revving engine. She waved her arm towards the back of the house, trying to point out where he might drop to a lower level over the backdoor entry. "Over there!" It was over the doorway by the kitchen where they'd hung all the jackets on pegs; where they'd kicked off dirty shoes and snowy boots; the place where Maddy used to check the pockets of her dad's plaid work jacket to see if he'd forgotten a pack of cigarettes, so she could nip one.

Tommy shrugged and shook his head no; the flames were pretty high. Maddy jumped and waved her arms so wildly she could feel her breasts bobbing up and down, a sensation she always detested but had forgotten, since they were usually bound and subdued. She didn't care.

"I couldn't find Annie!" Tommy hollered. "It's OK!" He announced happily.

Maddy thought the heat must've got to him. "It's OK," she shouted back. "The ladder's comin'…just hang on!"

Two things happened in a brief space of time that would play itself over and over in Maddy's brain until the day she died. Tommy stood up as straight as he could, shielded his eyes from the searing heat and looked intently towards the back fence. He pointed and shouted, "'S over there!"

"What?! What is it Tommy?!

"'He's there," he pointed. "Go git 'im Maddy!"

She paused to make sure she heard him right, then turned to look to where Tommy pointed. She blinked trying to focus; the smoke stung her eyes, and the sun wasn't even up. The light from the streetlamps shone across the snowy yard. For a second she thought something dark moved along the fence.

Suddenly a loud crack rang out like a cannon shot, over the sounds of water and engines and men shouting. Maddy whipped her head around in time to catch sight of her brother as the roof gave way beneath him. What was left of the tower pitched over into the void. The house ate him alive.

Maddy dropped to her knees in the mud. There was no cry, no human utterance worthy of her pain. A piece of her soul was ripped out, and the jagged burning hole in the roof where she'd last glimpsed Tommy might have been her very heart. Life would never be the same. Then she thought of Jack Mack. He had done this. Maddy thought of him until her eyes flowed like molten lava and burned away all tears. She thought of him hard and let rage do its work, let it fill her and devour her insides like a fire 'til there could be no grief. Not now. There would be a lifetime to grieve. Now was the time to act. "So help me God..." Maddy quietly vowed to find the bastard and make him pay. Then she rose and walked on frozen feet, still clad only in wet socks. A rescue worker came toward her with a blanket. She waved him off and kept walking steadily through the snow to where her Uncle Joe stood by, still holding the crucifix.

When he saw her face, the old sailor broke down and wept. This wasn't a war, damn-it; this was his family.

Uncle Danny was in the back of the cruiser. "Joe! Maddy! Tell Ma I'll be back soon," he yelled to be heard through the glass. "I swear on my muther's life, on my sister's graves...I never touched a hair on the old priest's head! I swear!"

"OK Danny," Joe collected himself. "I'll get you a lawyer. Don't say nothin' else." He turned to Maddy. "I wish I could do something more, but...come home with us now."

Maddy nodded with a wooden expression. She tried to mumble thanks, but her throat was dry.

"Wait," one of the officers said. "You got ID sir? You know this...ah...girl," he asked, not entirely sure of the gender of this feisty short-haired kid with the husky voice and what looked like breasts...in all fairness he tried not to look at them.

"No officer-left it at home. I'm Joseph Orillio, her uncle. I live just over the hill, at Fifteen Mulligan Street. That's my car there...I came when I heard..."

At this he looked towards the burning smoking ruin of a house and almost started to blubber. He swallowed hard and cleared his throat in time. It was tough getting old.

"I know him officer," a man's voice called. "I live on the same street; name's Fred Michaels." He pulled out his ID and spoke to Joe as he proffered it to the policeman. "Gosh, I'm sorry. Let us know if there's anything...anything at all."

"Thanks Fred. I will."

"OK sir," the officer said to Joe. "Now can you please identify this...young lady?"

"This is Madeline Malone, age sixteen. Her father's Tom Malone-you just sent him up to Mapleton Memorial Hospital with his mother, Hannah Malone. Maddy's her granddaughter. This was her house...they're my wife's family...our family. He put his arm around Maddy and pulled her in tight. "I'd like to take her home now, but please...let us know as soon as you find..."

At the mention of who needed to be found, Maddy pressed her head into her uncle's jacket and began to sob with abandon. Her knees nearly gave way, but Uncle Joe held her up and didn't let her fall.

"We're right over the hill," Joe explained to the policeman. "But we'd like a little time to ourselves first." The policeman nodded. Joe Orillio shepherded the poor child away and helped her gently into the soft leather seat of the Buick, for the short drive back around the corner.

62

"Here comes Dad!" I hollered, when I saw the headlights and the big gold nose of the Buick as it rounded the corner. Mom had been watching out the back, looking over the hill through the kitchen sink window while I peered anxiously out the door towards the end of the street. Only minutes before she had seen the tower fall. It almost made her cry out loud, but she hid it to spare me just a little longer.

I snapped the outside lights on and flung open the back door. I saw Maddy right away, sitting beside Dad, but when I saw the look on his face I knew that whatever happened had been both terrible and irrevocable. I'd seen my father boiling mad. I'd seen him neatly conceal his anguish over my pain by cooking up a pot of anger like a stew and letting it simmer. Now the fuel was all spent and the pilot was out. Dad avoided my gaze as he got out of the car, but couldn't hide his agony.

Maddy opened the passenger side door and got out slowly. The look on her face reminded me of that day in the sixth grade, when she got her first period and bled so much she had to leave school with her underwear in a bag. Only it was much worse. Dad went to help her, but she waved him off and walked up the steps on her own. Dad clomped up the stairs behind her carrying the big kitchen crucifix. I recognized it immediately, and wondered how he came to have it.

Maddy pressed back against the rail to let him pass. "Air," she whispered. He nodded, and went inside to where his wife was waiting. I stepped around Dad and went out onto the landing, and he closed the door gently behind me. My maternal instinct was to open my arms and throw them around Maddy and hold her tight. With lightening reflexes she intercepted my embrace, grasping both of my wrists and holding them fast in mid-air, as if fending off an attack by a snake. "Don't Frances. Not now...I gotta think...I gotta do somethin,'" she said gruffly.

"What happened?" I whispered breathlessly.

"It was Jack Mack. Jack set Gramma's house on fire...that bastard killed my brother...and my sister. I gotta think, so don't love me now, Frances. I can't let love get in my way."

"Which sister?" I could barely speak.

"Only sister I ever had," she answered evenly as she let go of my wrists. "Only brother I ever had went down trying to find her."

"No...no no no God, no no, Jesus please tell me no, not Annie, no no no..." If by protesting long enough I could have undone what had happened, I would have stood forever on that cold step and denied the very possibility of her loss. Now instead of a hug I wanted to kill her-or at least beat her senseless. "How could you get out without Annie?! How could you let this happen?!" I shouted into her face and the angry words frosted in the air between us. Maddy stood silent, unfazed by my tantrum. I wanted her to shout back and make me shut-up, but she didn't seem to care what I said. If I had punched her I don't think she would have even ducked. "Where was Uncle Danny? Why couldn't he..."

"Last I saw, he was in the back of a cruiser gettin' taken down to the station..."

"What? Why? My God! *What the hell is wrong with you people?!*" I screamed louder than I ever had in my life; my hands were clenched into such tight fists that my fingernails left marks in my palms.

"Ah...I've been tryin' to figure that one out for a while now," she said quietly.

"I hate you!" I cried. "Except for Annie...I hate your whole pathetic family...I hate the Malones!"

Maddy considered it a moment and said, "Yeah...there's a lot of that goin' around today."

Mom appeared at the door with a tear-stained face. I knew she must have heard me shouting, but she only said, "Girls, come inside now-too cold to stand out here." I realized I was shaking violently, but I hadn't noticed the cold. We went inside. Maddy peeled off her wet muddy sweatshirt and collapsed onto a kitchen chair with it balled up in her lap. I didn't want to sit near her, but I didn't want to be away from her either. I stood by in numb confusion. Dad had absently laid Gramma Malone's crucifix on the kitchen table by the advent wreath, the symbol of the coming messiah. Maddy seemed to study it while Mom looked her over from her head to her feet. Her jeans and socks were caked with frozen mud and snow. Her unbound breasts were evident under the flannel shirt; she was obviously very cold.

My mother snapped into action and did what she did best. She dropped to one knee and started to peel off the socks. Maddy sighed, but didn't protest. "Fran, go get a pair of Dad's thick socks...I don't think ours will fit," Mom said.

"Dad's got some old slippers too...what size do you wear, dear?" she asked Maddy.

"Uh...dunno...woman's ten maybe...I usually wear Tommy's outgrown work boots." At the mention of her brother, Maddy's chest started to heave. I saw her grit her teeth and breathe hard through her nose to quash the tears. She couldn't let love get in her way. I obediently fetched the socks and slippers.

"Can I get you anything dear?" Mom asked. "Some tea? A hot bath...a bra?" Mom whispered the last.

Dad was standing behind her and overheard. He shook his head and gave me an 'I-don't-believe-what-Mom-just-said,' look. It was perfect timing, like a life-saver thrown to one about to drown. Maddy latched onto the unintentional humor and mastered her emotions; she almost smirked. "Ah, no thanks to the bra Aunt Evelyn, but I'm dying for a smoke."

"I'm sorry...we don't keep cigarettes here...and there's no smoking in this house," she said gently but firmly.

"No stores'll be open," Dad said. "It's Christmas day..." he trailed off and went silent. We all knew why. This would be the end of Christmas for me, I thought, for all of us.

"Yeah, and we don't even got a vending machine in town," she said. "Nearest one I know is over at *Pete's*."

"We don't have time to run over there now...gotta get up to the hospital. I'll try and swing by on the way back, but for now I got somethin' might do the trick," Dad said as he went into the den. He came back with an open pack of stogies and a matchbook. He smoked so infrequently I forgot they were in the house.

"Joe, not in the house," Mom insisted.

"Thanks Uncle Joe," Maddy stood up in the dry socks and slippers. "If I could just take one outside..."

"Sure thing...here, take the rest, but go easy on 'em. They ain't like Marlboros...don't want ya gettin' sick. Wait a sec; I'll get you a coat."

Mom went upstairs to dress. Dad rummaged in the spare closet for at least five minutes while Maddy stood and waited politely for the coat. I could see she was having a nicotine fit. She happened to look down at the prone Christ, lying nailed to His cross on the kitchen table. "Fat lotta help you turned out to be," she sniped, and gave Him a dirty look to boot. I got that squirmy feeling I get whenever someone talks back to God, or takes His name in vain; not your everyday, "Oh Jesus," or "My God," but serious hard-core blasphemy, a show of genuine doubt in His power or dissatisfaction with his will. Maybe it was just superstition, but it felt like asking for trouble. It didn't occur to me until much later that although Maddy was pissed-off at God, she was still speaking to Him. I guess He listened.

Dad returned with his old navy deck jacket, part of the uniform he'd kept wrapped in plastic and moth balls in the back of the hall closet. I hadn't seen it in years, and remembered it as much larger. Now it looked absurdly small in contrast to his portly frame. I was suddenly struck by the realization that my father was hardly older than me when he wore the jacket and went to war. He proffered it to Maddy.

"You might as well have this," he said. "It sure ain't gonna' fit me again...'s real warm."

Even after all she'd been through, Maddy was clearly moved by the gift. No other worldly goods could have offered such comfort as her uncle's old navy jacket, and a couple of stogies. "Whoa...that's cool," she said as she took it carefully in both hands. She put it on. It fit. "Thanks Uncle Joe...I like this even better than my leather jacket." She stepped outside.

"We're gonna clean up and get dressed now," Dad told me. "We gotta run up to see poor Aunt Hannah." He sighed with exhaustion and plodded off upstairs. I looked at the kitchen clock-it was almost six-thirty.

Alone in the kitchen I suddenly had a selfish thought. For a moment I wished it was just us, Mom and Dad...and me. Just me. I wished I never met the Malones. They were more trouble than they were worth. Life would have been a hell of a lot simpler without 'em, that's for sure. They were complete fuck-ups! This was all too predictable. Why had I worried about being impolite, when I should have just run out and snatched that child back? It hurt too much. It just wasn't worth it to love someone with all your heart, only to lose them. It just wasn't worth it.

Then I saw Maddy through the small windowpane on kitchen door, leaning on the railing and puffing a stogie. Her face was hard-bitten and grimy with soot, and I could only imagine what was turning round in that mind. In spite of everything, she looked rather dashing decked out in Dad's navy jacket. I didn't know what might happen next, but I knew this wasn't over yet. A man had taken away her brother, her faithful friend, and her beloved sister; the family home was gone. I sighed deeply. It didn't make any sense, but I knew it was worth it after all. No matter what happened, no matter how much it hurt, it was worth it. Love is just...worth it.

Flopsy. The thought of facing the rabbit filled me with dread. I knew I'd probably lose it completely. Thank God Maddy was here; I couldn't do it alone, at least not the first time. Might as well get it over with, go out in the cold now with the food, and bring the poor creature some hot water to drink. The water bowl would be a frozen block of ice. Then I could come in and take a hot bath, and I wouldn't have to go out in the cold again to bring it more water until late afternoon. I ran the water until it was hot and filled a plastic pitcher. I took the small bag of rabbit chow and set both on the table while I stuffed my feet into my boots. I threw a parka over my flannel PJ's-I hadn't taken the time to dress. I switched on the back spotlights; they'd been aimed especially to hit the rabbit hutch, so Annie could get back there in the winter's darkness that fell by four-twenty pm. Then I braced myself; this would be the first of many times. That stinky old bunny was precious to Annie, and although I couldn't stand the thing, I vowed to care for it for the rest of its life. I only hoped I could get through it without falling apart. Tears and emotions only made Maddy feel worse.

I didn't know what to say to her now, after my earlier outburst. I wished I could take it all back, or at least offer a suitable apology. Maddy made it easy for me. She saw the bunny paraphernalia in my hands and held the storm door open. "I'll help with that," she said simply. I knew all was forgiven.

We went down the back steps towards the yard and squeezed past the Mustang, parked in the driveway close by the house. At the edge of the yard I stopped; beyond the fence where the tower had been, I saw the thick smoke as it soared towards heaven. The smell from all that had burned was sickening. I knew it was more than timber and furnishings, twisted metal appliances and clothing; more than generations of pictures and irreplaceable possessions, much more than a family home. I looked up into the gray predawn of a winter sky, and followed the black trail with my eyes. The smoke seemed to reach out and grab me by the throat and shake me, and for a moment I couldn't breathe. I knew that rising smoke could be Annie's very bones. I wished I could walk out into the backyard without a coat and lie down in the snow...lie down and just go to sleep...go to sleep and never ever wake up.

The sound of the back door behind me roused me from my dark thoughts. Mom and Dad were bundled up and already leaving. "Gotta go feed the rabbit," I explained.

"Oh...that's right," Mom said. "Well, go eat something after you're finished...make some oatmeal. Take a hot bath Fran, before the cold sets in and you catch pneumonia. We won't be too long," she added as she got into the passenger side of the Buick.

Just before Dad got behind the wheel, he gave his final orders. "I don't want either of you going back there," he said firmly. "It's dangerous; just wait for me here. OK?"

"OK Dad," I said. But he looked intently at Maddy.

"OK?" he repeated.

"Sure Uncle Joe; I won't go near the place...I promise," Maddy said.

The car engine turned over without complaint and they drove off. We resumed our mission. "What's that thing?" Maddy asked; she was right behind me. In the spotlight I saw the tracks in the snow from where we'd all walked yesterday afternoon, and realized they were the last footprints Annie and Tommy ever made. I also noticed that the snow was trampled down the hill in two different places. One looked kind of like a small avalanche and the other as if someone slid down on a toboggan.

"What's what?" I asked, turning my head back over my shoulder to see which way she was pointing.

"That thing on top of the rabbit hut." She pointed across the yard to where the rabbit hutch stood at the foot of the snowy hill, the one place I hadn't looked, probably because I was leaving it to the last possible moment. I squinted in disbelief at the shiny object perched upright on Flopsy's humble roof. It sparkled in the light; even in the artificial light, it was all golden, and sparkled like some Christmas magic.

"It can't be..." My heart began to pound and the blood rushed back into my cold veins with a fierce desire to live.

"It looks like some sort of Christmas decoration. Did you put that there?" Maddy asked.

I turned and looked at her. "No," I barely whispered and shook my head for emphasis. "It wasn't there last night...none of us put it there."

I realized that the plastic pitcher had drooped in my hand only when the warm water started to run down my pajama clad leg. I set it down on the driveway with the bag of food. Maddy dropped what was left of the stogie and began to stride into the snow. Dad's old slippers fell off and got left behind; she paused a moment. I charged in after her and took her hand. We plodded on. It was only about a forty yard trek, but time seemed to stand still. The hard crust on top of the deep snow broke with each step, as if we were wading through quicksand.

"It's the Woolworth's angel!" I shouted breathlessly when we were less than ten feet away. I had waited until I was certain. "There's something else...the door is unlatched-it's open a bit and there's something stuffed inside.

"It's an old quilt from our bedroom. I recognize it," Maddy said flatly.

Though we stood side by side, it was as if we each inhabited a separate universe. She didn't sound happy. I was full of wonder and hope, but there were so many details I did not yet know. Maddy knew the brutality of the man who had attacked her family; she considered the possibility that this could be still one more horror.

Annie. I tried to call her name but it was buried somewhere deep inside and wouldn't come out. I hadn't expected to use it again, not to call her. Annie...it was as if her name were a living thing, swelling inside my heart, about ready to burst. But if I called and she didn't answer, it would be like losing her all over again.

Maddy let go of my hand and rushed over the last few feet of snow. She dropped to her knees to open the little plywood door. She reached inside and yanked at the quilt and began to pull it out hand over hand like a rope. Then she thrust her hand inside. "Annie!"

It was only fitting Maddy should call her name first. She told me later that Annie's legs felt so cold, she thought the child had escaped the fire only to freeze to death. She wore a flannel nightie with a jacket over it, and one boot had fallen off and got lost in the snow.

"Mad'lin?"

At the sound of her voice I believed in miracles. I believed in God and Jesus, in heaven and angels, in right and wrong and good and evil. I was in the snow beside Maddy in a heartbeat. "Annie, we're here," I called. "What...how did you get...?"

"Fran? Is that you Fran?"

"Yes darling, it's Fran and Maddy."

"I got stuck! I thought you'd never come," she whined. "I'm cold."

"You silly little goose!" Maddy said as she reached in and untwisted Annie's stiff legs from the quilt. She had to crunch her down back inside in order to get her head out the door. Then Maddy reached under one arm and gently pulled, and Annie slid out onto the snow. It was like watching a birth. She lifted her and held her close for a brief moment before starting back towards the house with her sister cradled in her arms. I hurried to keep up.

"F, F, Fran!" The poor child was shivering. Please...f...feed Flopsy-and make sure to latch the door," she directed. "You always got to latch the door...so he doesn't come out and get lost...he's all white like the snow...he might get lost."

"As soon as we get you inside," I said. "I promise I will."

Annie's childish concern reminded us that she was blissfully unaware of the fire. She didn't know that her house was gone, didn't know that Tommy was gone. Maddy and I locked eyes, thinking the same thing. "We have to be careful," I whispered.

"Straight to the bathroom! We've got to get her into warm water," I ordered as we went inside. I'd learned about hypothermia in biology class. I got a mug of warm tap water from the kitchen sink and brought it to them. Maddy already had the tub running and was stripping the frozen nightgown from her sister. "Drink this," I told Annie.

"Yuck!" She made a face after she tried it; I suppose warm water from the sink isn't very tasty.

"Just drink it, and I promise to make hot cocoa after the bath…"

"I have to go out," Maddy interrupted me. "Don't worry," she held up her hand before I could protest. "I won't go back home…back to what's left of it," she barely mumbled the words so Annie didn't hear. "Don't open the door for anyone you don't know. If you see anyone but a neighbor outside, call the police. Keep the doors locked," she directed.

"What's going on?"

"Did you see that snow up by the fence…and down the hill?" She dropped her voice to a gritty whisper. I nodded. "Annie didn't track up all that snow by herself. When we were pulling her out of the rabbit hut, I noticed there were two different paths down the hill. One path stopped at the hut; the big one kept goin' straight through the backyard and headed down the side to the front-likely out to Mulligan Street."

I saw that Annie was settled in the warm bath and stepped out into the hall, still keeping her within sight. "That creep came through our yard?" I whispered. "You've got to call the police! Someone's got to call the hospital too, and tell them…" I glanced at the child resting in the tub, almost to make sure she was really there, "…Annie's alive." As soon as I said it I started to cry softly.

"Frances-get a grip! Yeah, Annie's still with us, thank God; Tommy wasn't so lucky. I still don't know what happened with Uncle Danny…somehow I know Jack's mixed up in that too. But my big concern is that he could come back. I saw the hate in his eyes. My family won't be safe 'til Jack's gone."

"What exactly do you think you can do? You can't go after that guy! He's dangerous…it's completely crazy! What're you gonna do if you find him…kill him?! Even if you could do it…you can't take the law into your own hands. You'll end up like your uncle…or worse. Maddy, listen to me: the police…"

"We already told the police; I can't leave it to them. Frances…I need you to help me out, need you to take over from here. I know you'll take good care of Annie…call the hospital and all, but I just gotta go do somethin'," she said urgently.

"You're going to leave now?" I asked in disbelief.

"I gotta go...uh...it was nice of your dad to give me his cigars, but I'm just dying for my Marlboros. It won't take me long to run over to Pete's...be right back." She gave me a knowing look and left the bathroom.

"My dad has some old boots down at the bottom of the basement stairs...better get 'em," I called after her. I knew I couldn't talk her out of it; might as well try to stop a train by arguing with it.

I heard the door slam. I sat on the lid of the toilet seat and watched over Annie. She'd been taking baths by herself for years now, but I wasn't taking my eyes off her yet. Suddenly I heard a familiar car engine. Vroom, vroom! The Mustang was revving up in the driveway! My mouth dropped open. Maddy was taking Dad's car.

Annie looked up at me. "What is it Fran?"

"Ah...mm...nothing sweetheart. I just thought I heard something...but it's nothing."

63

Maddy drove slowly down Mulligan Street. There was fresh snow on the ground; she studied it under the headlights. One set of footprints came right out the front yard and went almost to the end of the road. Joanie couldn't have been with him; he'd traveled alone. He'd slipped and skidded a few times, even wiped out once-looked like he'd gone down on his ass just before he reached the car that must have been parked at the end of the block, where the tire marks began. That bastard must have run like a bat out of hell. Hell. That's just where Maddy hoped to send him.

It was so early no one else had even driven over the new powder. It was cold, but once the sun was up, the new snow on the road would melt. No matter; he was definitely heading in the direction of Middlefield. She drove out of the small subdevelopment, past the projects, and saw Edmunds Elementary School grow small in the rearview mirror. She narrowed her eyes and watched the road carefully; she didn't want to miss any signs.

Jack Mack lived over in the white section of Middlefield-not in the projects, but not far from them. He'd grown up in those projects, grown up without a father. He was a river-rat. Everybody knew everybody over there, and Maddy still had connections even though she'd been gone for some time. Damn! It was Christmas. None of the bars would be open until tomorrow; that would have been a good place to start asking around. No matter; she didn't plan to let the sun go down before this thing was settled. When the short winter day was through, one or the other of them wouldn't be left standing.

Maddy saw where Jack's car must've fishtailed, gone out of control as he rounded a corner. Good. He didn't know how to drive in the snow, or else he was running scared. Good. She thought about Uncle Danny. What in hell was all that about? Think! Jack is behind it somehow...but how?

She wasn't exactly sure what she'd do when she found her man. She had no weapon-nothing but her two fists. It wasn't revenge she wanted; she wanted them all to be safe...and she needed answers. Had Joanie been in on it? Had he called the police on Uncle Danny? He must've! They came straight away with a warrant for her uncle's arrest-in the middle of a fire! Somehow Jack had framed him. Uncle Danny said he hadn't touched a hair on the old priest's head; Maddy believed him. But what kind of sick bastard would kill a priest, and an old man at that? She remembered all the times Father Mahood had come to the house...how much comfort he brought to her poor mother. He was there at the funeral...

Holy shit! Maybe Jack Mack killed the priest?! If he did, he deserved to die twice over. If she could only catch up with him before he had time to clean up any evidence, he'd be put away-out of their lives for good.

She drove past houses twinkling with merry lights, as children in pajamas raced to the Christmas tree to see what Santa had left. Their parents stumbled after them, rubbing their sleepy eyes in exhaustion. They smiled indulgently, snapping photos as the children tore into their gifts, and perched on new bicycles in the living room.

64

"I was so worried about Flopsy. It was cold, and nobody listed when I said he might get frozen. He's not a polar bear...he's a bunny! I was afraid the snow would cover his house again. Nobody remembered to put my new angel on the tree either, even though I asked again and again, they always said, '*Later on*, maybe after dinner.' I couldn't sleep 'cause Gramma was snoring. I decided to bring Flopsy some carrots and a blanket too, and I thought he needed a Christmas decoration on his house. The snow was deep. I fell down the hill and lost the carrots. I was sad Flopsy didn't get his carrots...and I hope Gramma won't be mad I took 'em from the pantry. I crawled inside with the blanket to visit, but then I couldn't get back out. I saw a man fall down your back hill, and he ran right out the front yard..." Annie chatted away in the bathtub until the water got cold.

The phone rang; I nearly jumped out of my socks. "Mom! I'm so glad you called...you're never going to believe what happened..."

My father waited a bit before he called the Mapleton police. He explained that his niece had borrowed the car to go for cigarettes...the kid's already a pack a day smoker...it's a shame, but what are ya gonna do? She was heading for the machine out at Pete's, but she's been gone a while now...probably got stuck in the snow somewhere. The poor kid lost family in the fire this morning...and he was getting worried.

65

"What? She's alive? But...how?" Hannah Malone lay in the hospital bed with an oxygen mask over her face and an IV drip in her arm. She looked dreadful. Old people are so vulnerable; one minute they may be up and doing great, but it only takes a single blow to flatten them. She breathed deeply, and grasped Evelyn's hand as if it were the only thing keeping her from falling over a cliff.

"She snuck out to bring carrots to her rabbit," Joseph explained. "I guess she was worried about 'im in the cold. She's with Frances and her sister at the house. The poor kid don't even know what happened yet. Tommy's gone for sure, though. I saw it happen...I'm so sorry Aunt Hannah." He struggled not to cry. "I...I didn't know how much I loved the kid."

Hannah Malone reached out with her other hand, the one with the needle stuck in the thin fragile flesh, and patted his arm. "I...ah...I know you did Joe." Her breathing was labored. "What's more, Tommy knew. You helped him so much...more than you know. He'd really turned a corner," she comforted. Then she turned to Evelyn. "There's something important I've got to tell you. I came so close to dying before I got the chance, and I don't want to wait any longer...especially after what's happened. There're a couple of things really...not sure which I should say first but..."

"What is it?" Evelyn wondered with dread what else might be in store. Family reunification was a lot more trouble than she thought it would be.

"The good news is that the old place was insured...Danny saw to it first thing; but I know he had nothing to do with the fire...I was right there." She thought her son was suspected of arson, and that was bad enough. She had no idea that the priest had been murdered, and they saw no reason to tell her yet. "And the land is worth a lot of money now," she went on. "The developers approached me several times over the past year or so. They said they could tear down my old house and build four small ones. I always sent them off. I didn't want Tom catching wind of it. Well...the whole thing is left to you and Joseph. I made out a will. Danny wanted it that way. I'll leave it up to you how you want to provide for Mad'lin and Annie...and Joanie, if she ever turns up. You'll be the legal guardian for Annie. Mad'lin too, for a little while."

"Of course we'll look after them," Evelyn said. She was overwhelmed to the point of numbness. Only minutes ago, she thought the little girl she loved like a second daughter was gone. Now she was given to her for keeps. She'd wanted more children so badly, for so long. But now she was content with her life and her freedom. She loved her job, and had secretly planned to study for an insurance license. She sighed in resignation. Guess God has other plans for me, she thought.

"It's only right you should have her. I don't know how to say it, but...you're the eldest sister."

Evelyn stared at the poor old thing, certain she'd become very confused. "What?"

"Yes, you heard me right. I'm sorry to shock you, but there's no easy way to put it: my son Tom is your father."

"How could he possibly...Aunt Hannah, what on earth are you talking about?"

"The other part I have to tell you right away, is that your mother was...well, she wasn't my sister by blood. She was adopted. My poor mother lost the last baby she would ever have. She was heartbroken, and the family doctor advised her to adopt a child to get over her grief. He turned up barely a week later with a little black-eyed, dark-haired Italian baby. It was so easy in those days to adopt; there were dozens of babies needing homes. One letter of reference from the family priest, and you were done. It brought Mother around; she loved her! Then only two years later Mum died, and Baby Margaret was my responsibility. But the point is, Evie dear...I'm really your grandmother. And the girls are your sisters, but not your nieces by blood because your mother..."

"Cousin Tom is my..."

"He's not your true cousin."

"Madeline and Annie...and Joanie are my sisters?"

"Yes. This must be such a shock."

"Why didn't anybody tell me before?"

"I wasn't sure for a long time. All those years ago, when your mother came by and accused Tom of...ah...I can't bring myself to say it. When he was just fourteen, too!"

"My God..."

"I just couldn't believe it! Still, I confronted Tom. He denied it of course. Then he stormed out and left with his family. I guess your living just over the back fence must have been pretty uncomfortable; his past came back to haunt him. After he left in such a huff, I really began to suspect it...but who wants to believe such a thing? Then all these years later, Danny told me it was true. Your mother and Danny were great friends, you know. She confided in him, but she asked him not to tell until she was ready…or until she was dead. He kept his promise. And now that Tom is incapacitated, Danny felt it was time to reveal things he never had before…like what a terrible bully Tom was when they were young. He…did things to Margaret…little Danny too. He made them do things and threatened to hurt them, even kill them if they told. Poor Tom…I always felt there was something very wrong with that boy, but I just didn't know what-I still don't know! But Danny doesn't hold a thing against his brother. He even risked his life to save Tom this morning. Ah, Evelyn…I'm sorry to shake you up like this…but I'll soon be leavin' this world; your sisters need you."

Evelyn looked to her husband for support. He sat with his hands folded, and eyes downcast. But he didn't look surprised. "You knew?"

"Danny told me a long time ago, in case something happened…so someone would know. At least he told me what Margaret told him. You were having so much trouble with your mother as it was. And you never liked Tom. I didn't think you could stand to know about it. I didn't see how it would do anybody any good."

"No…I don't see how it would have. You're right; I don't think I could've stood to know then. It's hard enough now, but… I have sisters? I already loved the girls…but sisters? Oh…that means that…Aunt Hannah…whatever happened to little Michael? Is he alive?"

"Yes, he's alive…he never did learn to talk, but the sisters keep him up nice. A few years back I had Eddie Murphy borrow a car and drive us out to see him, just to make sure. Ah, Eddie Murphy! How I wish I knew what happened to that boy…I loved him just like one of my own…but yes…your little brother Michael is alive. He became a ward of the church, in a home run by the Sisters of Mercy…all the documents I had are gone…oh, what a mess!"

"Well, never mind the details now. You need your rest Aunt…I mean…what shall I call you?" Evelyn asked in confusion.

"I guess it depends on what we want to tell the girls."

"Oh…that's right! I'm not their aunt. Aunt Hannah, I don't think it's a good idea to let Annie in on this yet. She just couldn't understand. I think this is one of those times when the truth wouldn't be best."

"I think you're right about that. What about Mad'lin and Frances?"

"They should probably know. I don't think I could hold back such a secret from my daughter…and the girls share everything. Yes, they should know, and I'm sure they'll agree to shelter Annie until she's more grown up. As for Michael, I'll get all the information from you later. Now that I know he's my brother, I want to see for myself at least once, to make sure things are right."

66

I t took barely ten minutes to reach the Middlefield River, even going slow on the icy road. The streets were empty. Nothing was open, and anyone planning to go visiting wouldn't start out for a few hours yet. Maddy took it easy. She kept the car in third gear, and shifted down to gain control if the back wheels started to skid.

The sun finally began to rise. She looked out across the frozen river; it was white solid along the snowy riverbanks, but black down the middle where the water flowed faster. She thought of the many times she'd walked that stretch of road that ran parallel to the river. This was the way to Linda's old place. Linda. Jack had taken her away too.

The Middlefield River Bridge was up ahead in the distance. At the sight of it she started to feel nervous, even shaky. No wonder! She hadn't had a cigarette in forever, and didn't get to smoke much of that cigar before she had more important things to do. This was no time to have nicotine withdrawal. She pulled over just a bit-there wasn't anybody to pull over for-and stopped to put the car in park so she could roll down the window. Uncle Joe didn't smoke in his car, after all. Damn! She couldn't believe she took the Mustang. She hoped he'd forgive her someday. She fished in the pocket of the navy jacket and found the matchbook, and the pack with two cigars left in it. She stuck one in her face, lit up and inhaled the warm smoke without a cough. "Hmm...I could get to like these things."

Maddy started out again, calmer already. There seemed to be someone else on the road way up ahead-could barely make it out. She drove on slowly. The other car was stuck in a snow bank. That stretch along the riverside was terrible; it was even colder because the wind whipped over the frozen river. It blew more snow into the road and kept it cold longer, like a giant ice box. It was like driving in a skating rink. Most people couldn't handle it, and cars lodged in a snow bank were a common sight. Through the open window she could hear the driver gunning the engine, spinning the wheels. What an idiot. Too bad; she couldn't stop to help now...

Holy shit! Was that...? Maddy thought she recognized the small convertible. Yeah, that's him alright. It was Jack Mack! She slowed down and came to a stop. He probably hadn't recognized her-wouldn't expect her to drive up in a Mustang anyway. OK, now what? Frances had a point. What exactly had she planned to do?! She tried to think rationally, but her blood boiled up and spilled over into her brain. The Malone temper! It was a blessing and a curse. It gave them the courage to endure almost anything. It took one helluva chunk out of Uncle Danny's life. She contained her rage enough to drive on, slow and steady-no point in coming this far, only to slide off the road and get stuck. It was like holding down the lid of a pressure cooker with her forehead.

She puffed on the stubby cigar and blew the smoke out the window. The windshield was frosted and she paused to rub it with her sleeve. Jack was out of the car now, trying to push it. She came along slowly. It was definitely Jack alright, and he was alone. She was glad Joanie wasn't with him-maybe there was hope for her after all.

Jack looked towards her and stopped pushing. He walked out into the road, waving his arms to flag down the other driver. Good Samaritans always stopped to push each other out of snow banks. She shifted into second gear and slowed to a crawl. Jack Mack smiled; he smiled and waved. How in God's name did you burn down someone's home, a house with an old woman and a child inside...and smile?

About forty yards away, she stopped the car. He suddenly stopped waving with his arm still in the air, as if it froze solid and got stuck. Then Jack shielded his eyes with his hand like a visor, trying to make out the strange driver who stopped in the middle of the road without coming to help.

Mad-Dog Malone opened the car door and stepped out slowly. She stood to her full height, and breathed the frigid air deeply through her nose to bring down the temperature in her brain. She walked around to the front of the Mustang and noticed how the first rays of the sun glinted off the hood-ornament, a little silver horse that reared on his hind legs; funny how you notice certain things at the strangest moments. She felt a sharp twinge of guilt, and hoped to get through whatever would happen without damaging her uncle's car. She blew a thick cloud of smoke from the stogie and assumed the stance she'd taken so many times when facing down a bully. This time she had the offensive advantage. He was running away, and no matter how evil this man was, surely he still knew right from wrong. He must be scared; perhaps she could unhinge him a bit. Jack had been raised Catholic after all-even gone to St. Clément's. The thought must have crossed his mind that he was driving straight down the proverbial road to perdition.

"Well, if it isn't Jack Mack!" she called out sarcastically.

Jack squinted across the distance. She couldn't make out his features clearly, but suddenly his arms went rigid. Then he put both hands to his head as if to tear out his hair in exasperation. He stomped his foot and swore loudly. "Go home baby dyke! Go home now if you know what's good for you!" It was meant as a threat and the words started out strong enough, but as he finished she detected a note of supplication, as if he really didn't want to hurt her. He didn't have anything left.

"Yeah, I'd like to go home Jack…but see…you burnt Gramma's house down. There's nothin left but a pile of ash." She chose her words deliberately to gauge his response. She knew Jack watched the house burn from her cousin's backyard. Tommy had seen him too, and she could still hear his last words, "Go get 'im Maddy!"

Jack didn't move, but he seemed to shrink down a bit inside his black leather jacket. The small-time punk had delved into arson and murder, and it was just too hot for him to handle. For a moment she almost felt sorry for him, but she shook it off.

"You killed Tommy! You killed my brother! Jack Mack, you little *muthah fuckah*…I'm gonna kill you." She said it with all her heart, and if wishes were bullets he wouldn't be standing. If wishes were bullets, we'd all be in trouble.

Jack bolted over to his car and leaned inside to grab a pistol from under the seat. He stood holding it in plain sight, but didn't take aim. She resisted the impulse to run, and stared him down a moment before walking slowly around the hood and easing back into the driver's seat. The heavy door slammed shut. The window was still open. She breathed the cold air and thought hard. Jack had a gun, but only his two feet. Maddy had a car. She watched as he looked around frantically for someplace to run. It was a vast white wasteland. She gunned the powerful engine. "Run!" she said far too quietly for him to hear. "Go ahead…run you *bastahd*!"

Jack started to run. She'd seen him go for the gun-no surprise there, but if he was running, he must be scared of her. Her bluff had worked. Now all she had to do is wear him out-play with 'im a little. She drove slowly, matching his pace as he ran down the road along the side of the river. He was heading for the bridge. There was no place else to go. "That's gonna be one helluva long run, Jack." She picked up speed a bit. Jack ran faster and fell for the first time. She let off the gas and barely rolled while he sprang up, but resumed once he was running again. The rear wheels fishtailed a bit. Her concentration on the man distracted her a little from the task of driving over the slippery packed snow. She straightened it out right away, but it gave her an idea.

At the foot of the bridge Jack hung a sharp right and fell a second time. He fell hard on his elbow, and didn't get up quite as fast as before. He tucked the gun inside his jacket and stood a moment, rubbing his elbow. She pushed down on the clutch and applied the brakes slowly. He must be wondering about now: Why in hell was she going so slow?! Why didn't she just try and mow him down so he could get this over with? Maybe he should stop running?

Maddy came to a full stop and gunned the engine. With no trees or traffic to dampen the sound, it roared across the snow and blasted through the quiet blessed morn like some beast from hell coming to get him. Jack looked around anxiously, like he couldn't decide what to do. Once he was on the bridge, he'd be vulnerable, out in the open until he reached the other side. She let off the clutch too fast and lurched forward, then mashed on the brakes. The back end swung around almost perpendicular to the road. She eased back carefully against a snow bank...and spun the wheels.

Jack started over the bridge at a run, but looked back twice over his shoulder; each time she spun the wheels again and pretended to be stuck. He was almost half-way across when he stopped and turned to watch. The wheels of the Mustang were spinning impotently. Jack Mack smiled. He gloated with triumph, and paused long enough to slap his left hand over his right bicep and snap up his fist in a Dago salute. You didn't have to be Italian to understand the universal sentiment.

The wheels stopped spinning. The Mustang growled low, eased around slowly and drove steadily down the street, heading towards the bridge. There was no going back for Jack. His mouth hung open a bit, then he turned and ran faster.

Mad-dog Malone swung around the corner onto the bridge and screeched to a halt to stick her head out the window. "That's right! Run Jack! Run, ya murderin' little prick!" She pulled her head in, and the Mustang rumbled over the icy bridge. As she picked up speed, it fishtailed for real, but didn't spin out. The gap between them closed. Jack ran as fast as he could.

Thwap! His feet went out from under him and he fell for the third time, flat on the back of his head. She rolled to a stop, and waited patiently. Jack struggled to his feet and pressed his hand over the spot; when he took it away it was covered with blood. Even a small head wound bleeds like a sonovabitch. He panted for breath and stood watching in horror as the red drops fell on the hard white snow.

She bit down on the stogie and drove slowly over icy bridge. The windshield had frosted solid. She turned her wool collar up against the cold, and stuck her head out the window to see his face clearly. Jack was spent. She used her sleeve to rub the frost from the windshield. She gave it some gas and watched the speedometer climb to twenty, then thirty. Her eyes bore down on him like iron nails.

Jack couldn't run anymore. Suddenly he drew his gun and leveled it at the oncoming windshield, holding it steady with both hands. She could see him framed by the round patch cleared in the frost as she squinted into the whiteness.

Jack fired. The windshield shattered. Maddy was jolted by a sharp blow over her left eye, but managed to slip the clutch and crank the wheel in a desperate attempt to miss the man who'd just missed putting a bullet in her head. The Mustang obeyed.

Jack fired again. The driver's side rear window shattered. The car turned sideways and skated over the bridge, gaining momentum as it headed straight for him, more like a tank than a car. There was blood covering her left eye from the piece of glass that'd struck her forehead. Maddy scrunched her blind eye, cocked her head and saw the world spin round from her good right eye. She slipped the clutch and tried to drive out of the skid, drive out and around him. She didn't want to kill Jack, no matter what he'd done. There'd probably be plenty of evidence back in his car...they'd know he was guilty 'cause he ran and shot at her...her family would be safe. For a moment it looked like she was going to sail right past...it was going work! Uncle Joe had done one helluva job...

There was a sickening thud. The rear driver-side fender had swung out just a foot too far as she'd almost, almost driven past. Maddy caught a glimpse out the window as Jack's body was flung high in the air and disappeared over the cement wall. She heard the dreadful yelp that came from some primal place, like a poor old dog getting hit in the road, a sound you never forget once you hear it. The car whirled like a Zamboni and smashed sideways into the cement wall. Then everything went silent.

Maddy reached for the door handle automatically with her left hand, but her arm just wouldn't work. It was broken. The door wouldn't open anyway; it was broken. She reached across with her good right arm, opened the door and crawled out. She struggled to stand. It was as if her legs were unsure of the very ground beneath her feet. She felt no pain, felt nothing at all, almost as if she had no body. She considered briefly the possibility that she was dead. Then she licked the salty blood that ran down to her lips. Ghosts probably didn't taste anything. She staggered around the hood of the Mustang. *Ah, the little horse still stood boldly on his hind legs.* At the cement wall, she hung her head far over the edge and peered through one eye like a pirate. There was no sign of Jack, nothing but a jagged hole where his body had shattered the thin ice in the middle of the river. The river had swallowed him whole. The dirty water flowed swiftly, and swept him away beneath the black ice. Red drops of blood fell from her head into the running water, and disappeared.

The Middlefield cops arrived within minutes. Someone from the projects called right after the first gunshot. Jesus...only last night there'd been a murder in that neighborhood-an old priest at the rectory no less, clubbed to death with a blunt object. What a mess! Now some nut was out on the bridge firing a weapon. Jesus...what a night!

Maddy was still hanging over the cement wall when she heard the sirens. She stood up and looked over her shoulder, still leaning against the wall for support. She saw them coming from the Middlefield side-at least six cars. Just then her attention was drawn to the sirens from the Mapleton side. The squad cars converged from both ends and surrounded her. It didn't matter...Annie was alive, and no one was ever going to hurt her family again.

"Turn around slowly with your hands in the air!"

She turned slowly; she certainly wasn't going be moving fast any time soon. She raised her right arm, and tried to lift the other. The pain almost made her throw up. "Sorry officer, I can't. I think it's broken." Then she collapsed in a dead faint.

67

In the ER, my father stood protectively by Maddy's side as she answered the policeman's questions. She calmly confirmed his story-she'd borrowed her uncle's car to go on a cigarette run...you know how it is. She saw a stranded motorist and stopped to help. When Jack recognized her he pulled a gun, so she got back in the car. He started running, so she decided to follow him-he must've been running for some reason, after all. She drove slow and careful. When he fell on the ice, she stopped. She tried to drive around him on the bridge, to get to the Middlefield side and notify police, but she lost control of the car when he shot through the windshield-twice. She even looked for Jack over the cement wall and would've gone in after him, but he had already washed away under the bridge, beneath the dark ice.

The officer concluded his report and left us. I exhaled in relief. He hadn't seemed all that concerned about Jack, and I had to wonder: what really happened, and was it gonna come off that easy?

We didn't know it yet, but they'd already found the bloody steel baseball bat in the trunk of the Chevy convertible. Jack also fit the description of the little man who barged into the rectory just before midnight that Christmas Eve. The housekeeper was on the john when she heard the priest cry out. She kept her head, and waited until the front door of the rectory banged shut. Then she watched the man leave from an upstairs window; he made the mistake of turning to look back, and she saw his face clearly under the streetlamp. The police were pretty sure that the man at the bottom of the river was the one with the bat who killed Father Mahood; almost certainly the one who threw a gasoline bomb into the family home and killed Tommy Malone. And it wasn't negligent driving, after all, since Jack Mack shot at the kid. If the officer had any suspicions, he sure didn't show it.

Maddy's left arm was in a cast. It was a good clean break, and the doctor didn't expect it would give her any long term trouble. The gash over her left eye from the shattered windshield was deep, and required twenty-four stitches. They called in a plastic surgeon. The thin white line was hardly noticeable after a few months, and as she aged, it disappeared completely into her furrowed brow.

"Uncle Joe...I'm real sorry about the Mustang. I know you loved that car. I'll make up for it somehow...I'll work and save money 'til I can pay for it-soon as I can use my arm again."

Dad shook his head in disbelief. "Oh well...I guess ya gotta do, what ya gotta do," he said with a shrug, and if I'm not mistaken, a bit of a sly look. "Besides...it was insured; I can always get a new car. You can't be replaced."

"That's for sure," I said. "Maddy's one of kind."

"Thank God!" Mom blustered. "I mean...thank God you're alright." She went to retrieve Annie from her grandmother's bedside.

When they returned, the sight of her sister in bandages and a sling made Annie's face go white as the hospital sheets. I brought her to sit by me in a chair.

"Hi, I'm Dr. Vanderburgh," a handsome young man in a white coat stepped in. "I'm a neurologist," he explained, as he took out a little light. He shone it into Maddy's eyes. "Now watch the light...don't turn your head, just follow with your eyes. Ah-huh...mm...OK. Good." He looked at my mother to tell her something, but suddenly paused to study Annie. She was sitting with me on the same chair, looking off past everything again. It seemed to get worse when she was stressed, and she knew her house was gone. She didn't know about Tommy yet.

"Well...what have we here?" the doctor asked quietly with a look of concern.

"Oh, it's nothing doctor...I mean, nothing out of the ordinary," Mom answered quietly.

Doctor Vanderburgh watched Annie as she blinked and began to look about. He went over and asked gently if he might look at her pretty eyes with his little light. He smiled at her. She shrugged and nodded yes. "Great job!" he said, then stood up and motioned my mother to follow him out of the room. I slipped out behind them and stood by her side.

"How long has that child been having seizures?"

"Seizures? You mean the daydreaming is...?" Mom trailed off.

"Daydreaming? So it happens quite a bit?"

"Yes, especially when she's at school...she has a terrible time paying attention too," I interrupted. "It happens more when there's...stuff going on around her, but it can happen any time."

"Difficulty paying attention too? How about impulsivity?"

"Yes!" my mother and I chorused.

"It's like you know her!" I added.

"Hmm, sounds like ADHD too, very common for them both to occur together..."

"Doctor, what is A-D-H-D?" I interrupted again.

"It stands for Attention Deficit Hyperactivity Disorder. It's a neurological condition. It runs in families. I specialize in pediatric neurology, and I see it a lot. I want you to make an appointment." He handed my mother a card. "I can't make a diagnosis without running some tests...I need a cat scan, an EEG, and I'll need a complete medical history, a family history too. I'm more concerned with those absence seizures. It's a form of epilepsy, and they usually outgrow it, but...what's wrong?"

I thought of Miss Blodget and it brought tears to my eyes; I'd already cried so much that day it's a wonder I had any tears left. "It's...it's just..." I sniffed, "she's been blamed for it...punished for it...not by us, but in school. And I always knew she couldn't help it!" My mother nodded in agreement.

"That's the worst part about these disorders," he affirmed. "Without a diagnosis, without help, it can take quite a psychological toll. I work closely with a colleague on these cases; she specializes in child psychology. After I finish my evaluation, we'll set you up for a consultation with Dr. Schreiber...Dr. Sarah Schreiber. Don't worry, we'll sort it all out," he spoke comfortingly to me. "We won't let anyone punish her for her illness, ever again."

"What exactly is child psychology?" Mom asked me when the doctor had left.

"I'm not entirely sure. One thing's for sure, though: Annie's got to have it! Think of the big picture...the whole family..." I couldn't figure out how to put it.

"I agree. What a relief! I don't know how I could've raised that child without help."

"Raise her?"

"Yes. Frances...there's something else I have to tell you, and I might as well do it now; it won't get any easier."

***

Before we left the hospital late that afternoon, my mother went in to face her father alone. She said she wanted to make sure she had a few words with him before it was too late. I don't know what happened in there, but she

374

returned looking calm and resolved. Then we had an impromptu powwow and told Maddy the truth right away. We all agreed it would be best to let Annie go on believing that my mother was her Aunt Evelyn, at least until she got a bit more mature. Someday she should know the truth, but not yet.

"You're my big sister? You're a Malone?! Gosh, I'm sorry," Maddy wisecracked after she digested the news. She offered her right hand to my mother. "My condolences," she said with a smirk.

"Good lord...that means you're my aunt?" I said. "Ha! I should call you Auntie Maddy!"

"No...no you really shouldn't," she said, looking a bit alarmed.

"But seriously...that means I'm the only one who's not related by blood...I feel kinda left out."

"Are you outa your mind?! Like I said before...she's not a Malone, thank God!" Maddy looked pointedly at my mother. "Us Malones are kinda screwed up."

"Thanks a lot!" Mom said with a sarcastic smile. "It certainly is going to take a bit of getting used to."

"Hey, Guido!" Dad directed at Mom.

"Huh?"

"Yousa gotta learn to speaka Italiano!"

"Oh my God, that's right! I'm half Italian!"

"Yeah, welcome to the grease-ball clan," Dad said mischievously. He'd never forgotten the time my mother referred to one of his cousins as a grease-ball.

At last we drove home. I sat in the back seat of the Buick with Maddy on one side and Annie in the middle, leaning against me. On the short trip across town, the speedometer happened to turn over: one hundred thousand miles. That's a lotta miles, but this wasn't the end of our journey.

I was the only one who knew for sure that Maddy went out after more than cigarettes that Christmas Morning. Dad and I were the only two people who truly understood her skill behind the wheel. I guess she panicked and lost control. How could anyone see to drive with one eye full of blood and a shattered windshield? I couldn't be certain, but there are some things you just don't ask. It isn't polite. Sometimes, you just gotta mind your own business. Whatever happened out on that icy bridge was between Maddy and God.

When we pulled into the driveway, it seemed strange not to see the Mustang parked by the house. I got a sad empty feeling in my stomach; it was almost like losing another person. I guess the Mustang was a casualty of war.

I got out, and Annie crawled out after me. Maddy was on the passenger side so she could open the door with her good arm. Dad gallantly went round and helped her out. "You don't wanna slip and break the other arm," he said. She wore his navy jacket with her right arm though the sleeve, and the other side draped over the sling. There were bloodstains on the jacket. With her bandaged head and broken arm, she looked like a wounded soldier.

Mom and Annie went inside quickly to get out of the cold. I was right behind them, and glanced back to see if Dad and Maddy were coming. He was standing in front of her, carefully adjusting the jacket on her left shoulder where it had slipped. Then he took a step back and stood at attention. He looked her straight in the eye, and snapped a full military salute. She returned the salute, and for a moment her face was somber. Then they were at ease. Dad looked at her knowingly and gave her a sly 'we have a secret wink.' One corner of her mouth turned up in a funny half-smirk, half-grin as if arguing with itself, but in the end, Maddy smiled.

68

The hard frost finally broke in early February. It had been one of the coldest winters on record, but that year, the merciful spring came early. What was left of the Malone Mansion was quickly cleared away, and by March the builders were able to break ground for a new foundation. Gramma Malone had the little house set towards the back of the property, closer to us. It was finished by the end of May, in time for the lilacs that bloomed most gloriously on account of all the snow. They decided to hold off selling the rest of the land. It just didn't seem decent yet, especially since the family had so recently buried the eldest son. Tom Malone died peacefully in a nursing home. My mother was with him.

We tore down the old wooden fence. My cousins still lived with their uncle and grandmother, but Annie and Maddy ran up and down the back hill so much it was beginning to look like a goat path. My father decided to set heavy slate step-stones into the earth, and made a staircase on the hill, wide and solid enough even for Gramma to tread.

***

"Hey, Frances!" she cupped her hands like a megaphone and shouted about as loud. The kitchen window was up, and I could see her standing on the side porch.

"What's up?" I hollered, even though Mom told me it was unlady-like.

"I got a letter from Eddie Murphy! Come up here!" she insisted. It wouldn't have occurred to me to say no.

"'The Rosanfelds were so kind to take me in. I don't know what would have become of me without their help. Rachael and her mother sat with me day and night, until the madness finally passed.'"

Maddy looked up from reading and said, "Just like we thought: Eddie Murphy went nuts...right off the deep end. He still don't say why he had to ditch the seminary...must 'ave been pretty bad, whatever it was. Hmm...Rosenfeld...never heard of the name...sure ain't Irish!" She chortled.

377

"No, not Italian either," I said.

"I can't believe Eddie thought the war was still going on, and they were comin' to get him for the draft. Those people found him half-frozen in a field after he snuck across the border."

"That explains Canada."

"Yeah. The whole Rosenfeld family sounds...ah...pretty special," Maddy went on. "Eddie says here that Rachael's parents survived a concentration camp. That's why they don't believe in war. They helped a lot of our boys cross over and gave 'em a place to stay. I guess I woulda thought that was a bad thing once...but I don't blame them. After what they went though, they can believe whatever they want. They're probably right, come to think of it."

"Yeah, they're probably right," I agreed.

"Ah...I'll skip the next part. It's about Tommy...he's real sad about it, and says we'll talk more when we get together." I nodded.

"'Finally, I want to share with you the joyous news: Rachael and I are getting married. The wedding will take place in August, after I have made my Bar mitzvah'." Maddy paused again. "What's that?"

"I'm not sure, it's some sort of Jewish ceremony," I said hastily, "but keep on reading! Eddie Murphy is getting married?!"

"Yeah...how 'bout that...OK. *'I have been in the process of converting to J...Ju-dasm...'* What's convertin' to Ju-dasm?"

"Well...it means he's converting over to the Jewish faith...Judaism," I explained. "I guess it's because he's marrying a Jewish girl..."

"What?! Eddie Murphy's turnin' into a Jew?"

"Basically, yeah...that's what it means."

"I didn't even know ya could do that! I thought people only got converted to Catholic. Hey Frances, did you know ya could go the other way...go Jewish?"

"I never really thought about it...believe me, it's not something they tell you at St. Anne's. But I guess you can convert to any faith you want. Are you...ah...disappointed?"

"Disappointed? Me? Hell no! Why would I be disappointed? I'm glad Eddie's happy. Sounds like he went through some pretty heavy shit."

"Like you didn't?"

"Yeah, well...me...I'm made outa different stuff. Don't get me wrong; not a day goes by I don't think about Tommy," she said more quietly. "But somehow my head stays screwed on....least as much as it's ever been screwed on," she smirked. "Eddie Murphy is...special. Like my Ma. Like Annie...speaking of Annie, I'm so glad Auntie's got her seeing that doctor...the one for special kids. What's she called again?"

"Who?" I was distracted.

"That lady doctor...Frances, what's the matter?"

"I still can't believe Eddie's getting married!" I said wistfully.

"Yeah...guess he's not gay after all," she said.

"Rachael sounds just wonderful too...the way she took him home and nursed him...it's so romantic," I said with a sigh. I secretly wished it were me. Funny thing was, Maddy knew me so well, yet never suspected. "And to answer your other question: Dr. Schreiber is a child psychologist. I've been reading all about it; it's the most interesting stuff I've ever read."

"Hey Frances...I been thinkin'... Why don't you go to college to be one of those doctors?"

"Me?"

"Yeah, you! Somehow I just can't see you traipsing through the jungles after monkeys. You never even wanted to camp out, 'cause of the mosquitos!"

"Yeah, I'm really not much of an outdoors girl..."

"And you ain't much for animals either," she said with a chuckle.

"Flopsy and me never really saw eye to eye," I said wryly. "I was glad when Dad and Uncle Danny moved that rabbit hutch over the hill; next time Annie gets sick, he's all yours."

"Thanks a lot...but like I was saying, Annie's doin' much better now, and you was always so good with her: it's like you were born to be a...like that lady doctor."

Epilogue

You never know what small thing will influence a young woman, and for better or worse, change the course of her life. It may have begun twenty-two years ago with the tiny light the doctor shone into Annie's eyes. My mother's good sense to bring her for treatment at a time when many people found such things frightening and shameful definitely had a lot to do with it. I'm sure that without my fine, Catholic school education, I never would have made it through college and graduate school; but I still don't even want to think about the reason I got packed off to St. Anne's.

I never did find Jane Goodall, but if she hadn't bushwhacked a trail through the jungle of gender-discrimination that snarled my brain, I probably wouldn't have found my way. One thing's for certain: without the friendship that began back in the alley, I never would have had the courage to look.

Over the years we've had many reunions. Some were happy occasions, and some were sad, but they all seemed too far apart. My cousins came out for my mother's wake, Maddy from Florida, and Annie and her husband all the way from California. We lost Mom to breast cancer far too soon, not that there's ever a good time to lose a beloved wife and mother. She just missed seeing me fulfill the dream of making my Ph.D., but she read my dissertation from her bed:

<u>What They Can't Tell Us: Why Children with Dyslexia and Expressive Language Disorders are at High Risk for Abuse.</u>

This visit is long overdue. It's been almost four years, but I'm finally going to see Maddy's cool place on the Santa Fe River. Our last reunion was bittersweet. Gramma Malone turned one hundred years old, and we all gathered for a big birthday bash. I baked the carrot cake-finally got the hang of it. She took the opportunity to inform us that she'd had enough funerals in her lifetime. Gramma wanted a quick cremation, and if we didn't follow her wishes she'd come back to haunt us. She died peacefully in her bed that very night. Maddy carried her ashes back to Florida and scattered them over the river, so I guess I'm going to visit her too.

It's funny how I was always the one who complained about the weather, and she turned out to be the one who ditched New England. Now she owns a canoe rental business with Linda, her partner of...I guess it's not quite four years, because I don't think she was with her the last time we met. When Maddy first mentioned her, I thought she was the Linda from Middlefield, but she said no, she's a different Linda.

I'd been standing in the Jacksonville Airport for almost an hour when a plump, middle-aged woman dressed in jeans and a t-shirt approached me tentatively. I thought she was going to ask me for money. She was black. As soon as the thought popped into my head, I felt secretly embarrassed. Old feelings die hard. But I guess it's not what we feel-we can't really help that, after all; it's how we choose to behave. I smiled. "Can I help you?"

"You mus' be Miss Frances! Ah mean *Doctor* Frances," she drawled.

"Ah...yes, but Frances is just fine. Is Madeline alright? Did she send you to pick me up?"

"Uh-huh, she wasn't feelin' too good today...I supposed to say she busy...but she sick."

I picked up my bag with a sinking feeling. I didn't know what to say. "By the way," she said, "I'm Linda." With that she turned and headed for the exit. I'm glad she didn't see my mouth drop open.

We got into a rust-bucket of a pick-up truck. "So, you rent out canoes," I said, trying to make conversation.

"Mmm-hmm."

"I haven't been down here in far too long. It's so beautiful...so warm."

"Mus' be cold up north dis time a year."

"This November isn't bad at all. It was in the fifties when I left this morning."

"Dat's too cold."

We were on I75 for what seemed like forever. Finally we left the highway. We drove past a small town and then wound down a rural back road. It took almost two hours, and Linda didn't have much to say after the conversation about the weather. When we came to the long gravel driveway that led to their place by the riverbank, I breathed a sigh of relief, and not only because the trip was over. Just as the sun was going down, I saw a lovely little cottage under a great Live Oak, draped with Spanish moss. There were several outbuildings, a picnic spot, and a row of shiny silver canoes by the gently flowing water. After the beat-up truck, I was worried that they lived in poverty.

"Here we are," she said as she got out. I followed her inside with trepidation.

Maddy got up to great me as I went into a cozy den. "Hey, Doc!" she said, and opened her arms wide.

"Auntie!" I said as we embraced. I warned her years ago that if she called me doctor, I'd call her Auntie.

"I'll leave you two alone a while," Linda said. Then she leaned in close to us and spoke in a low southern drawl, "Don' worry Miss Frances, I's a *good* nigger...I ain't like dem other *bad* niggers." She rolled her eyes, and the whites looked so big and so white. This time she saw my mouth drop open before she turned and left. Maddy busted out into raucous laughter, and then coughed so hard I thought she'd drop dead.

"You unmitigated ass!" I hissed in a hushed whisper. It took her a while to catch her breath.

"Frances...I'm just a dumbshit that dropped outa high school. Is that anything like a regular ass?"

"No, it's a great big extra special ass...and you're dumb like a fox! I can't believe you put her up to saying that...it's not funny." I tried to be serious.

"The look on your face is pretty funny." She sat on the couch and motioned me to join her.

"She must think I'm the biggest bigot alive."

"No...are you kidding? Now I was a first-class bigot. You got into trouble once 'cause you tried so hard not to be."

"Yeah, I guess...but I still don't have any Black friends, though not intentionally. It's just that back home, it's very easy to live your life and hardly cross paths with a person of color. It's not the virtual apartheid...ah, I mean, it's not like when we were kids. Still, all except a handful of my graduating class were white. None of the graduate students were black."

"Yeah, well, it's a different kind of racism down here. Some ways it's not as bad, some ways it's worse...you don't even wanna hear what her grandma says about me."

"*Oh*. But *you* can't have any prejudice?"

"Depends on what you mean by prejudice. They're different, but you learn how to get along. Linda should get a prize for putting up with me."

"Guess you learned how to get along pretty good," I said with a satirical smile.

"Yeah, guess I did. So, uh, how's your dad?"

"He's OK. He misses me when I'm gone."

"And how's Uncle Danny holdin' up?"

"Without Gramma to care for, he's...kind of lonely, to be truthful. I run up the hill to say hi whenever I can. He and my dad go out to a poker game every Saturday night...right after the seven 'o clock mass."

"That's good-they deserve a game of poker after sittin' through mass."

I smiled and added, "I think Uncle Danny has too much time alone to...to think too much. I'm trying to get him to make a trip up to Lac du Bonnet and visit Eddie and Mickey-that's what Rachael still calls him after all these years, little Mickey Malone."

"How's he doin?"

"He's one of the lucky ones. He says a few words...he's really happy, that's the main thing."

"They should make Rachael a saint for takin' him on."

"Jews don't make saints."

"Well then, they should start with her."

"They really should; sometimes their own parents don't even want children with autism."

"Hmm...autism. And it had nothin' to do with us? Nothin' to do with...my Ma?"

"Absolutely not. I always knew it too!" I said with a touch of bitterness.

"Yeah...like I told ya a long time ago-you were born to do this. Anyways, ah...how 'bout you Frances?"

"Oh, I'm fine."

"No one special yet?"

"No...not since...oh, I don't want to talk about it."

"Well then forget all about 'im! You deserve better anyway." She patted my shoulder.

During the entire conversation her breathing was raspy. "Well, enough pleasantries. Tell me...what's wrong, Maddy?" She hesitated a moment.

"I'm sick," she said with a fatalistic shrug. "I gave up smoking a few years back, but...I still got...it's lung cancer. I'm sorry Frances," she added hurriedly.

"Dear God no...why didn't you tell me?"

"I'm tellin' ya. Seriously, I held off 'cause I hate to see you upset."

"What can I do?"

"Hang out with me for a while...go canoeing...the manatee are up the Santa Fe River. I never was much of an animal person, but I love those guys. They're great for business too. And there's just one more thing..."

"Anything."

"Try not to cry...'cause you've cried enough already."

I compromised. Somehow I kept my tears in check until she'd gone to bed. Then I went outside to a place by the river and sobbed as quietly as I could, while the water flowed, and the frogs filled the night air with their song. Suddenly I wasn't alone. "There, there, shh...hush baby, it's alright." Linda sat down on the bench beside me. "I hope you're not mad at me. I only gave in and said dat because I knew it would make her laugh her pasty-white Irish ass right off, huh, huh!" She laughed gently.

"How...how bad it?" I choked out between sobs.

"'Bout as bad as it gets...I'm glad you could come. She talked about you so much, I was almost jealous."

I sniffed. "That's kind of funny. I said something like that when she got her first girlfriend...when we were just kids," I added hastily.

"Oh, I know she had lots of girlfriends over the years," she said with a warm smile. We were silent for a moment.

"I can't believe it!" I suddenly felt angry. "It's just so...unfair!" I spoke belligerently to death, as if by calling him out, I could fight him face to face and maybe win, just this once.

"I sad too, but I glad we got to spend this time together."

"No! It's not enough time!" I pouted like a sullen teenager. "Life is just too damned hard! I can't do it without Maddy!" Grief swelled inside me like some demonic spirit trying to escape my body. It stuck in my throat like a poison apple.

"Well, she not gone yet, so jus' enjoy every last minute. But ya know, she never really gonna be gone, Frances. Not da way you luvs her. She gonna live forever right here."

Linda touched the place over my heart gently with two fingers, right over the ancient scars left by Beulah May Bone. Then she pulled me to her breast and held me tight, and I wept like a child in her soft, black arms, while the river flowed, and the frogs filled the night air with their song.